D1216049

Perfect Match: Book Two

Mildred Gail Digby

Yellow Rose Books
by Regal Crest

Copyright © 2019 by Mildred Gail Digby

All rights reserved. No part of this publication may be reproduced, transmitted in any form or by any means, electronic or mechanical, including photocopy, recording, or any information storage and retrieval system, without permission in writing from the publisher. The characters, incidents and dialogue herein are fictional and any resemblance to actual events or persons, living or dead, is purely coincidental.

ISBN 978-1-61929-416-5

First Edition 2019

9 8 7 6 5 4 3 2 1

Cover design by AcornGraphics

Published by:

Regal Crest Enterprises

Find us on the World Wide Web at
http://www.regalcrest.biz

Published in the United States of America

Acknowledgments

I'd like to thank the great people at RCE for their patience and support. Cathy, for always getting the job done even when life happens, Patty who helped me hone my writing technique even though my bad habits have a way of popping up like Whack-a-Mole, and Micheala for her tireless efforts to promote RCE authors.

Dedication

This book is dedicated to my wife.

You are my inspiration and my driving force, my best friend
and my biggest fan. Thank you for always being there.

Chapter One

THE LONG, WHITE tiled hallway of the Ruth Kurtz Jewish Hospital gleamed in the early morning sunshine. Outside, the weathered buildings of Suito City seemed soft and radiant. The cherry trees were bedecked in green leaves, their snowy-blossomed glory only a memory.

The light embraced Doctor Megan Maier in her crisp white coat and shone off the stethoscope she had slung casually around her neck. Brilliance bathed her form as if she were walking through a tunnel straight from heaven instead of taking the fastest route from the entrance to her assigned examination room in the Pediatrics Department.

Happiness radiated from her. She felt that everyone she met immediately knew what had happened the previous night. Upon further consideration, Megan realized she didn't care. What started off with tears and confessions ended in the purest, most passionate love Megan had ever known.

It was wonderful to wake up in Syler's bed, held in Syler's arms with the knowledge that she was loved. After a delicious breakfast they'd made together in the newly kosher-compliant kitchen, Megan went home briefly to change for work and perform her morning prayers.

The morning passed like a shooting star. Megan breezed through her daily routine and tried not to smile too much, aware of the concerned parents and the suffering of her young patients. Megan washed her hands after examination hours finished and didn't even miss the ring on her finger. It was still in her room though, nestled carefully in a small box she dug up. She didn't feel that taking it off was disrespectful to Yasu's memory and the too-short time they were together as lovers and life partners. While Yasu's death threw Megan's life into chaos for a while, her slow journey to recovery progressed a step forward every day.

Megan would never forget the person Yasu had been, what they'd shared, and what she'd learned about herself in the time they'd been together. In fact, when Megan thought about it, leaving the ring on as she proceeded with her life was the disrespectful option.

The fact that she'd bared herself, body and soul before Syler and was accepted with such tenderness and love made Megan catch her breath. All the torment and pain she'd been through up until that moment wasn't erased, but tempered into another shape, one that didn't have the sharp edges or spikes of the one before. She was floating and everything seemed glowing and golden.

Megan drifted back to her desk and found a present waiting for her, a single red rose and a scrumptious-looking sandwich from the cafeteria—incidentally her favorite, whitefish spread with lots of sweet cucumbers and sundried tomatoes on a cinnamon raisin bagel. After slipping the rose into her breast pocket where the delicate scent wafted up as she moved, she got herself a cup of tea from the dispenser in the corner and tucked into her lunch.

While she ate, she kept a surreptitious eye on the clock. That afternoon, Megan had a meeting to discuss a surgery scheduled for of her patients. She quickly finished her bagel and hurried to gather the relevant files before she headed to the hallway.

As she passed the surgeons' office, a familiar voice reached out and stopped her in her tracks. The same voice that moaned her name in passion the previous night was sharp and taut with barely contained anger. Megan didn't mean to eavesdrop, but a nagging sense of unease prodded her to stay. She didn't know who had sparked Syler's fury, but she had a good idea. There was only one person who brought out Syler's bad temper without fail. That idea was proven as Charles Brockman, their department head and son of the hospital's new owner replied.

"If you would just let me finish," he said in his annoyingly bland way. "As I was saying, yes this drug is experimental but I think the data we get from this test would be invaluable."

"My patients are not guinea pigs," Syler spat. "Keep your fucking dirty hands off them. If I see this travesty on any of their charts, I will personally rip it up and shove it into the trash."

Megan closed her eyes. A worried furrow knit her brows. Syler clashed with their department head before and the result was only a deeper rift in their professional relationship. One thing Megan loved about Syler was her undying commitment to putting the needs of her patients first, although her way of expressing it put her job in jeopardy by challenging their boss in her direct, American-raised way that went against the grain of their foreign-owned but Japanese-run hospital.

Charles was speaking again, but Megan couldn't listen anymore. She didn't want to hear him threaten Syler's job as he'd done to Megan herself not too long ago when she dared to step out of line and red-flag the file of a young patient whose injuries she suspected weren't just the result of a rough-and-tumble child's life.

Megan hugged her files and slipped into the stairwell. She soon arrived at the third floor where the briefing rooms were.

The patient, an eight-year-old named Foster was already there with his parents and one of the nurses. Like Megan, he was American on paper even though he was born and raised in Tokyo. Due to his father's job, they'd been living in Suito City for several months. For that reason, when he was diagnosed with pyloric stenosis and needed surgery, they opted against travelling all the way back to Tokyo for the procedure, choosing instead to stay close to their home and Foster's current school. Syler was assigned to the case. Megan shivered with both pleasure and nerves as she waited for her to join them.

While the nurse helped out with the whiteboard, Megan briefly went over the hospitalization procedure with the family. Syler arrived just as Megan was passing out the pack of documents with waivers for them to sign. Megan's heart beat faster as she acknowledged Syler's entrance with a nod. She looked very professional in her lab coat and tailored outfit with her collar-length hair tied back with an elastic. Her expression was calm, she carried no trace of the argument with their department head. Megan's gaze rested on Syler's trim form longer than she knew was prudent.

"This is Doctor Syler Terada," Megan said in a voice that came out more breathless than she planned. She hid her sudden flustered state by shuffling around her own papers. "She will be the surgeon in charge of Foster's operation."

In a flurry of polite greetings Syler sat down at the table.

"How are you feeling?" Syler asked Foster.

"Okay I guess," he answered with a shrug and shifted in his seat.

"Do you know what's wrong with you?"

"Uh yeah," Foster said and wrinkled his brow in thought. "Like, the hole out of my stomach's too small so I can't eat right."

"That's exactly it," Syler said with a brilliant grin. "And I'm going to tell you how I'm going to make it better."

"You're gonna cut me open, right?"

"Not quite like that." Syler reached into her bag and took out two plastic dinosaurs and a Slinky, which to Megan's great interest and amazement, she used, along with judicious sound effects, to describe Foster's surgery. Even though the details were simplified, Syler hit every factual point. His unease disappeared as Foster got into the explanation. Even his parents nodded and sat back in their chairs with smiles on their faces by the time she'd finished and handed the floor back to Megan with a few quiet and respectful words.

As Megan and the nurse went over some more administrative details, Foster made his dinosaur fly over the table. Soon Syler joined in, using the Slinky as a make-believe launching pad. Still in professional-mode, Megan fought to keep a straight face, not helped as Foster staged a "dino-fight" with Syler at one end of the table, which culminated in Syler's velociraptor losing the battle, tangled up inside the Slinky.

The meeting continued and Megan caught herself a few times as she nearly brushed against Syler, whether she was handing over documents, or simply leaning over the table. If they were merely coworkers, Megan wouldn't think twice about those small gestures and accidental touches, but now that they were lovers, the gestures took on a deeper meaning and Megan knew she would have to be careful not to give them away.

Her caution was not only based on the fact that Suito City's location in the backwoods of Gifu Prefecture meant it was fairly conservative, but also that both of their jobs were at risk due to a non-fraternization clause in their employment contracts.

In order to divert suspicion, Megan moved her chair away on the pretense of checking something on the laptop the nurse had set up. Syler was also reserved and professional with her, but Megan didn't miss the small glances Syler sent her way. Once, when the entire family was occupied with listening to the nurse going over the list of things they'd have to prepare for Foster's short hospital stay, Megan felt a soft brush against her thigh and she dropped her hand under the table to ever-so-gently twine her fingers around Syler's. Her heart nearly burst from the brief contact and she didn't dare meet Syler's eyes for a while after that, certain her professional mask would crack.

Once the briefing was over, Syler excused herself to return to her duties, and the nurse showed Foster to his new room. Megan was busy erasing the whiteboard and didn't realize Foster's mother, Donna stayed behind until she spoke.

"That surgeon, Doctor Terada, she's yours, isn't she?"

Megan whirled to face the woman who stood with one hip leaning against the table and a calm look on her face. Mind blank, Megan gaped at her for a moment before she decided to go with the truth. Megan let the smile she was fighting bloom.

"Is it obvious?"

"Not to everyone," Donna said. "I may be boring and married now, but I've had a few girlfriends in the past and I know what to look for." She paused and continued, "Hold onto her."

"Excuse me?" Megan blinked as her heart gave a quick jolt.

"I saw the way she looked at you. The way you looked at each other. She's the one, isn't she?"

Equal parts pride and fear welled up within her. Megan cast her eyes down and fumbled with the papers in her hands. "I hope so," she said.

"Good," Donna said with an air of finality. "I just wanted to say it actually makes me feel better, knowing the two of you are in charge of making my boy better."

Megan was speechless for a moment before she said, "I'm glad it doesn't make you uncomfortable."

"Not in the least. Anyway, I have to go see where they're going to put Foster."

With that, Donna left the room and Megan drifted out to the hallway. Her heart brimmed over with feelings, happy and excited about where she'd ended up with Syler as well as the unexpected support. Megan's worry about what the future might bring and the dangers lurking in her past quieted to a whisper in the back of her mind. For the first time, she almost forgot about the box shoved deep into her closet. The one hidden behind the others that held the leftovers from her eighteen months in Thailand and contained the evidence of her mistake, the mistake that would haunt her for the rest of her life.

Her head was stuck in a golden fog. She stopped in her tracks when she saw the sandy-haired, well-built man hanging out by her desk as if he lived there. His suit was immaculate and his obviously expensive tie was knotted tightly.

"Excuse me Doctor Brockman," she said. Her good mood faded and was quickly replaced with annoyance. Megan hugged the files she was carrying. She wondered why his eyes lingered on her chest area. At once, she realized he was looking for her ring.

She held her head with a proud tilt and mentally dared him to comment on its absence. All Charles said was, "There are a number of documents you need to sign, mostly for tax purposes."

"All right," Megan said. She dropped her files onto her desk and sat down, purposefully not making eye contact with Charles. "You could have told me that in an email."

"Is it such an anomaly to wish to speak to my staff face-to-face," Charles said, "instead of hiding behind technology?"

"No, I guess not," Megan said.

Charles sounded hurt, in his starchy and bland way. Megan relaxed her stance and leaned back in her chair. She was feeling too good to be angry for long and her defensive barrier evaporated.

"These documents need to be returned as quickly as possible. I assume you don't have your *hanko* on you at the moment."

"Actually I do," Megan said. She made a move to delve into her bag to retrieve the small wooden seal bearing the phonetic characters of her family name, which served instead of a signature for official documents. "Where are the documents?"

"They still need to be printed out," Charles said.

With her bag sitting on her lap and a puzzled feeling, Megan said, "All right. Just get them to me, I'll fill them out and return them ASAP."

"That would be most productive," he said. "In addition, there are a number of things I would like to discuss with you; however, the time for that is slightly in the future."

"Whenever is convenient for you," Megan replied in an automatic way. Her mind was already on the next time she'd be in Syler's arms. She couldn't stop her expression from softening.

"I am gratified to hear that. And now I must take my leave."

After Charles left, Megan dismissed the nagging sense that

something was off about the whole interaction. She was digging around in her bag for the sesame bars she had stashed in there when she got a text from Syler.

> If you're not busy, want to join me on the roof?

Snack forgotten, Megan didn't bother to send a reply. She leaped up from her desk and dashed up the stairs. She burst out to the roof where Syler stood with her hands in her pockets. Their eyes met. Syler held out her arms, looking so gorgeous and welcoming that Megan didn't hesitate before she threw herself into them. Strong arms came around her. Megan reached up to draw Syler into a long, deep kiss that threatened to knock them both onto the concrete rooftop.

"Thanks for the show, gals. Again." The voice cut into Megan's happy-infused brain. She pulled away to see an exasperated Luka Carmichael Goto, half-Nigerian, half-Japanese and one hundred percent fabulous, glaring at them. Beside him was Doctor Jacob Hartman, who was known as Jayco in their little circle of friends. An open box of matzos was in front of them.

"Oops," Megan said.

Syler still had her arms wrapped loosely around Megan's waist. Luka huffed again. Syler just shrugged and bent her head to slowly and softly press her lips to Megan's cheek then move slowly up to her ear.

"Ignore them," Syler whispered. "Maybe they'll go away."

"I wish I could," Megan said.

Luka heaved a theatrical sigh. "We can hear you, you know," he said. "Anyway, pause the girl-on-girl extravaganza and come over here and have a sit. Who knows how long we'll have before someone gets paged."

"That's true," Syler said. She let go of Megan and slung her long body down.

"Thanks for lunch," Megan said in a quiet voice. "And this." She pulled the red rose from her pocket and playfully drew it over her lips, aware of the hungry way Syler's eyes tracked the movement of the soft petals.

"How do you know that was from me?" Syler took Megan's hand in hers and brushed a kiss across her knuckles. The courtly gesture caused Luka to roll around faking a stomachache while Jayco chuckled and poked at him. "Maybe you have a secret admirer."

"Really, now," Megan said. She tucked the rose back into her pocket. "A secret admirer who knows all my favorite things? Everyone else I've ever met thinks whitefish on cinnamon raisin is gross."

"Okay, it could be a stalker. I think Gramma Marta in the cafeteria's been giving you the eye recently."

"Uh huh. Try again, Terada." Megan crossed her arms and leveled Syler with her best misbehaving-in-shul look she'd learned from her mother.

It had the desired effect. "Okay, I give up. Yeah it was me, and you're welcome," Syler said. She brushed her thumb lightly over Megan's lower lip before drawing away.

"How about a nosh?" Jayco asked. He held up the box. "I bought a ton of matzos for Passover but people kept inviting me to their homes for meals so I hardly ate any. It's gonna take me ages to get through it all so I thought I'd just bring some in and we could share."

"Thanks," Megan said. "I actually wanted a snack right about now."

Jayco broke a piece in quarters and popped open a container of almond butter Megan recognized as from the health food store near the train station. With a flourish, he produced a butter knife with a ceramic dragon curled around the handle and quickly prepared snacks for everyone. As they crunched on the matzos, Megan let her fingers drift to hold Syler's. She didn't mean to be so clingy, but she was addicted to the way Syler's skin felt against hers. Syler didn't seem to mind either.

"Oh, stop with the touchy-feely," Luka said with a toss of his head. "What if someone comes up? We already look suspicious enough."

Syler just said, "What's suspicious about four friends hanging out on the roof?"

"It looks like a double date!"

"What's wrong with that?" Syler asked.

"Because not everyone here is out, you know," Luka said with an arch of his brow.

"It doesn't have to be gay. We've got the ingredients for two straight couples right here." Appearing to be deep in thought, Syler tapped her finger against her lower lip and said, "And I get Jayco."

Megan sat up suddenly. "And I get Luka? No way, I want Jayco."

"And what's wrong with Luka?" the young man in question asked in a huffy way.

"You're too high-maintenance," Syler said. "And you make us all look like fashion-deficient frumps in comparison."

"Well, I can't argue with the second point," Luka said, preening.

Jayco sputtered in laughter and covered his mouth as a few bits of matzo flew out. "Sorry," he mumbled. He swallowed and said, "Actually, you're all wrong." He glanced over at Luka and Megan held her breath. Something significant was about to happen. She wasn't disappointed as Jayco shyly reached out a hand and said, "Luka gets me."

As Luka went silent and placed his hand in Jayco's, Syler nudged Megan and gave her a knowing look, which Megan returned, her chest filled with a wondrous warmth.

"What do you think?" Syler asked under her breath as she leaned close to Megan. "Should we leave these two lovebirds alone?"

Megan didn't get a chance to answer because their hospital-issue personal handy-phones all went off at the same time. She drew in a sharp breath and looked up to meet Syler's gaze before she dug out her old-style mobile phone.

"Suito Elementary School's been hit with mass food poisoning," Megan said. She scrolled down through the message on the small screen of her PHS.

"Yup," Syler confirmed. She breathed a curse and said, "Asahi General's taking some, but one hundred and twenty students and eight teachers are heading this way. ETA, seventeen minutes. Okay people, break time's over."

Without another word, the four friends put on their serious faces and, as one, headed back inside. Announcements echoed through the halls, calling all full-time staff to the conference room for an emergency meeting. Megan was the first through the door and the sight of a roomful of people stripping greeted her. Various items of clothing and lab coats were thrown over the backs of chairs and a harried-looking pair of nurses handed out light blue scrubs, booties, and gloves from a cardboard box at one end of the long, dignified oak table at the front of the vast room.

Soon in possession of such a set, Megan didn't hesitate before she shrugged off her lab coat and kicked off her shoes in preparation to get changed. Syler was right beside her and she unbuttoned half of her shirt before she yanked it roughly over her head and dropped her trousers shortly after that. A wolf-whistle echoed through the room which caused Megan to pause in her preparations.

"Cool briefs, Terada-kun," someone called out from across the room.

Megan glanced over. She identified the man as an intern named Taki. She frowned at his mocking tone as well as the casual masculine suffix that was a dig at Syler's androgynous presentation. While Megan thought Syler had every right to dress and act as unfeminine as she wished, not everyone agreed. She wondered how often Syler put up with such offhand comments and jokes.

Taki called out again, "They seem lonely. Where'd you hide your sausage?"

"Same place you hide yours," Syler said as her head emerged from the scrub top. "Bedside table."

"Ha! Nice one," someone else, who Megan identified as Syler's scrub-tech Dani, said.

Megan pulled the back zipper of her dress down. Her skin prickled. In his expensive suit and lab coat, Charles stood at the front of the room and he stared directly at her. His eyes were cold and predatory, like a shark's. With a shiver, Megan moved so that Jayco was between herself and Charles. She yanked on the scrub bottoms before she removed her dress.

Instead of taking off her slip, Megan stuffed it into the scrubs and put the top on over her camisole. Finally, she put her lab coat back on and made sure her ID was around her neck. From the open box of hygienic masks on the table, Megan grabbed a handful and stuffed them into one of the pockets of her lab coat along with a bunch of spare gloves. The rose Syler had given her got slipped into Megan's bag and stashed under the table.

"Quiet please," Charles's voice boomed over the room. As the talking and rustling calmed down, Charles faced the assembled people and said, "Today we are going to receive a large number of patients and I am acting as Incident Manager. Due to the fact that most of the patients are children, the staff of the Pediatrics Department will be in charge. Please look to them for direction if in doubt."

Someone pulled down the screen at the front of the room and Charles started up the overhead projector. He stood in front of it, casting a Charles-shaped shadow in the lab report.

"As you know, we are expecting close to one hundred and thirty patients. Symptoms reported include vomiting, diarrhea, and abdominal cramps," Charles said. "The initial results indicate staph, but there is a possibility it could be norovirus or listeria, and they haven't ruled out c. perfringens yet either. Until our own lab confirms it, consider this a class one epidemic."

Class one operating conditions would be a pain, but Megan was all right with that, especially if the mass poisoning was caused by something nasty and highly contagious like norovirus. At least if they were vomiting, it wasn't botulism, which was a blessing.

"Here is how we've zoned to accommodate the large number of patients," Charles said, pitching his voice to carry over the crowd. He called up a schematic of the hospital. "The emergency operations center is in meeting room one and meeting room two has been set aside as a waiting room and meeting area for the families of the discharged children. This room will be locked to protect everyone's valuables, so please see me if you need to retrieve anything from here. As usual, if you require fresh scrubs or other supplies, the staff prep room on the first floor will be available."

He continued, pointing out the side entrance they'd cleared to use as a triage area and the section of the parking lot they'd reserved for the fleet of ambulances and later for the families of the patients. Every spare bed in the pediatric ward had been reserved for possible hospitalizations. All of the staff of the pediatrics department were given high-level positions on the duty roster. Megan was assigned to be a leader of one of the four treatment rooms where they would be responsible for taking the youngest patients. Jayco and Luka were both put in triage. As Charles ran down the list of assignments, Megan's dismay grew as Syler's name failed to come up. He seemed about to go on to the next topic when Syler's voice rang out.

"Excuse me Doctor Brockman, but what am I doing in all this?"

Charles made a show of looking over the assembled people before he focused on Syler, who stood with her arms crossed over her chest.

"Oh yes. Thank you for reminding me. You have a most special assignment." He walked over to one corner of the room where a mop and bucket stood. He wheeled the contraption over to Syler and unceremoniously dropped a pair of rubber gloves onto the floor at her feet. "In light of your recent habit of non-cooperation, you will be in charge of keeping the floors spotless. If there is anything, and I mean *one single thing* on the floor, liquid, solid, or somewhere in between, you will be on report. Is that clear?"

"What?" Syler spat. "I'm a fucking pediatric surgeon, if you think I'm—"

"If this assignment is not pleasing to you," Charles spoke over her protests, "feel free to take the day off. Go home, watch TV, or read a book."

"Fucking hell. I'm not leaving in the middle of a crisis," Syler said. With a scowl, she looped her nametag over her head and made a move as if to take her lab coat off as well.

"None of that, Miss Terada," Charles said. He tutted and waved a finger at Syler in a way that made Megan tremble with rage. She had the sudden urge to stomp over and snap his finger clean off and shove it down his throat. Her hands balled into fists as he said, "You will be in high demand for the next few hours, I believe. It wouldn't do if we couldn't identify you, now would it?"

Syler didn't reply but she pulled her lab coat straight and re-clipped her nametag to the front pocket, her head held high. Around the room, voices buzzed. Megan felt sick with anger and disgust. Most people looked indignant, especially Dani and Taka-chan, who seemed to be on the verge of running up to the front of the room and were being blocked in by Atsuko and Nobu. Megan also felt the burn of unspoken words rise up in her throat, especially when she noticed a number of staff members sneering in Syler's direction.

One of the orderlies, who had just come in with a bunch of

part-timers, looked especially triumphant. Megan made a note to see if she could pull him into her treatment room to keep an eye on him. He was stooped, thin, and pale in an unhealthy way with greasy glasses and thinning hair. The way he gloated over Syler's humiliating treatment with almost obscene glee set off a number of warning bells in Megan's head.

"Attention please," Charles said and clapped his hands. He looked quite pleased with himself as he continued. "I have called in Rabbi Kleiner to finish this meeting with a short blessing." The door to the conference room opened and the rabbi walked in. Charles walked over to help her wade through the jungle of scrub-clad people. Immediately the grumbling and whispering stopped. Respect for the rabbi effectively silenced those who would interrupt the proceedings to speak up in Syler's defense.

Rabbi Sharon took her place at the front of the room and said, "We're going into battle today, and I'd like you all to join me in reciting the physician's prayer by Maimonides."

As one, the assembled people bowed their heads as the rabbi recited the prayer. Megan and several others joined in and her heart gave a warm jump as she heard Syler speaking the words along with her. She ached to reach out and give Syler's hand a squeeze for reassurance and luck, but squashed the urge.

After the last amen had faded, Megan joined her department members and left as quickly as safe hallway-travel permitted. She got to her post in her assigned area just as the wail of ambulances filled the air. The first wave of patients hit and soon the beds in her treatment room were filled with crying, retching children.

PATIENTS KEPT COMING in great waves and at all times Megan was doing several things at once while being buffeted by people asking for her opinion on treatments. The hallways resounded with calls for cleanup. Megan winced at each and every one. The only person receiving more pages than Syler was Mr. Mori, the gentle man who volunteered to hold babies in neo-natal, who for some reason could calm a crying child in an instant.

On one rushed trip to the triage area, Megan ran into Paolo Gomes lending his help to the porters in the triage area where they unloaded patient after patient from the never-ending parade of ambulances. The big man was impossible to miss. He wasn't an employee of the hospital but he might as well have been.

Ever since his wife, Gabriela, fell into a vegetative state during a routine operation—one incidentally led by none other than Charles—he spent most of his days at her side. Even after his visa ran out, he stayed illegally in the country to keep vigil over his comatose wife. The hospital paid for her care, which Megan found both charitable and suspicious. Megan wouldn't blame him if he chose to stay hidden during the emergency, he had no obligation to help out, but there he was, right in the middle of the melee.

Paolo had a child in each arm. He carried them toward a bank of medical personnel for assessment. Even though they were both run off their feet, Megan's chest warmed. When he passed her on his way back to the entrance for more small passengers, Megan reached up to give him a pat on one massive shoulder plus a few words of heartfelt thanks. Paolo just answered with a shy but courteous bob of his head before he hurried to continue his task.

Charles demonstrated his one talent by being an undeniable force of nature as he mobilized staff and supplies, dealt with demanding and panicked parents, and kept traffic through the hallways and parking lot moving smoothly, all the while corralling the media away from sensitive areas. For the first time, Megan was grateful for his stubborn and unyielding presence, even as she seethed at his underhanded treatment of the woman who held her heart.

More than half of the patients had arrived when the word buzzed through the hallways that the culprit was indeed staph. As she heard the news, Megan didn't look up from her task of ripping open a new box of gloves, but she breathed a sigh of relief. If something highly contagious like norovirus got loose in the hospital, it could be deadly to immune-compromised patients like Sakura Yamane. The four-year-old was under Syler's care and had been since the day she was born. She was one of the most important people in Syler's life, although she would never admit it.

"Doctor, we need an IV here right now," one of the nurses called over from a bed where a very small girl lay on her side with a kidney-shaped bucket next to her. From the look of uncertainty on the nurse's face, the tiny veins flummoxed her.

"I'm on it," Megan said. She ducked under the arm of another nurse, who dashed through the room with several bags of saline solution in her hands. With what she hoped was a reassuring smile, Megan grabbed the chart in the clear folder at the girl's feet before she asked her name and birthday. She was only five. Behind her mask, Megan bit her lip.

"Would you hold your arm out for me?" Megan asked and the girl sniffled and hugged her arms to her chest. Megan wished Syler was there to work her magic on the little girl.

"I want my mommy," the girl said and started crying in earnest, which set off a spate of coughing that ended up with Megan holding the bucket for her as she retched into it.

"Your mommy is coming soon," Megan said. She reached out a gloved hand and patted the girl's sweat-damp hair, very much aware of the other patients waiting for her and the clamor of people dashing around her. Five more arrivals were hustled into the treatment room and Megan bit back a curse. Reports flew over her head. There were at least seven other places she had to be at that particular moment. Her PHS buzzed in her pocket but she ignored it.

Megan focused on her small patient. She said in the gentlest voice she could, "I need to give you some medicine so you feel better and can go home soon. You have to be a big girl. It'll only be a *chiku*." The word indicated the smallness of the sting.

To her wonder and relief, the girl obediently held out her arm and Megan, with the seamless ease that earned her a place in the pediatrics department, inserted the needle and had the IV hooked up in seconds. She paused to give a few words of praise and a couple more pats before she rushed off with her PHS at her ear.

After she answered a number of dosage questions in quick succession, Megan rushed over to attend to a group of boys who only needed to have her check their vitals and confirm they could be sent to the non-urgent treatment area down the hall. Megan opted to take them herself and kept her eyes out for the creepy orderly. Her efforts paid off on her way back as she spotted the man. He was heading toward her and Megan scanned his nametag.

"Masato-kun," Megan purposely called him by his first name and she spoke with all the authority she could muster. "Come with me, we need you in treatment room two."

She noted that while he didn't protest, he also didn't give a verbal answer, which was a blatant show of disrespect. Unimpressed, Megan herded the new recruit into the room where she assigned him to hand out buckets. As she dashed from one place to another, Megan made a quick call to the leader of his original treatment room to explain the reassignment. It could have been her imagination, but she thought there was a note of relief in the doctor's voice.

More patients streamed through and she had almost forgotten about Masato when a page for Syler caught her attention.

"*Terada Saira oyobidashi desu.*" The voice was thin and the querulous, almost unnaturally high tone sent a shiver of disgust through Megan. The announcement called Syler to Megan's treatment room.

Her suspicions on high alert, Megan did a quick survey of the crowded and bustling room. She pushed aside a privacy curtain to find Masato standing over a generous puddle with a pristine bucket clutched in one hand and his PHS in the other. Beside him, a young boy was doubled over on the stretcher, crying. The orderly's expression was one of such anticipation that Megan knew at once he'd done it on purpose.

A white-hot shaft of anger stabbed Megan in the gut and she didn't even think before she shoved past a group of nurses to face down the orderly.

Even as he avoided looking at her, Megan accused him of orchestrating the incident on purpose in a terse, "*Wazato desho?*"

He took a step back and denied Megan's sharp accusation. The startled look on his face vanished when Syler pounded into the room. It was replaced with an expression of such gloating pleasure that Megan wished she had a machete so she could remove it. Accompanied by her wheeled bucket, Syler had both sleeves rolled up to the elbow and wore thick rubber gloves.

"I'm here! Where's the target area?" Even as she was being used as menial labor, Syler's voice and posture gave away nothing. In fact, she radiated an air of pride and purpose.

"You don't have to—" Megan began only to be stopped by Syler's dark eyes meeting hers. There was a sparkling warmth in them that resonated all the way to Megan's soul.

Syler placed her mop firmly on the floor and struck a pose. She announced, "Cleanup Team *go!*" She swirled it around a bit and made sound effects.

Several children in the room turned to look at her, a few of them even smiled. Tears of rage and absolute, crushing love welled up in her eyes as Megan watched Syler first use her mop, then get down on the floor with a roll of paper towels and a handful of alcohol wipes. The boy who had made the mess apologized and looked humiliated, but Syler just sat back on her heels and said, "Don't worry about it. Look, everything's fine. Cleanup Team *away!*"

She stood and struck another pose, which elicited even more smiles, before she swept out of the room, heralded by the squeaking wheels of her bucket.

Megan brimmed with annoyance. She glared at Masato and he scurried off. Breathing a stream of Thai curses in a singsong chant under her breath, Megan attempted to school her face into a smile behind her mask, so her scowl wouldn't show in her eyes and upset her small patients even more. A nurse came over with a chart for Megan. It was for one of the teachers.

"He's refusing treatment," the nurse said. "He says until all of the students are taken care of, he's not going to sit down. Watanabe-sensei's tried to talk to him, but he won't listen. We thought, maybe he'd listen to a woman."

"Why? Isn't there any next of kin to talk to him?" Megan asked.

The nurse hesitated.

Megan pressed, "Isn't there anyone coming in for him?" She glanced at the clock on the wall. They'd been treating patients for over three hours, ample time for word of the incident to get out to everyone. Thanks to the combination of the PTA phone-relay system plus the media, it had probably taken an hour or less to get the word out—to both parents and the media. She was willing to bet if she stepped out of the restricted areas, she'd be inundated with reporters and cameras.

"Just his roommate. He's in the waiting room, but we can't let him in. He's not family."

Something clicked in Megan's mind.

"Yes, he is," she said. Without another word, Megan barreled off down the hall, the chart clutched in her hands. She burst through the doors and scanned the room. Several small groups of parents huddled around, talking worriedly with each other. Most of them looked up in alarm at Megan's hurried entrance.

Megan kept her movements deliberate and casual as she went over to the one single man in the room. He was hunched over, as if trying to blend in with the background, but raised his head as Megan came over to his side. He got the typical look of terror Megan was used to that told her he was frantically trying to recall his high-school English lessons.

She headed off the inevitable murder of her first language by introducing herself in Japanese. His posture relaxed a fraction as he gave his name as Akihiro Hayashi.

"Inagaki Shuichiro-sama no tsukisoi kata desu ka?" Megan asked if the man was there for Shuichiro Inagaki in a quiet but business-like voice.

"Yes, I'm here for Sh—Inagaki-san." He sat up with a worried look. "Is something wrong?"

"Come with me," Megan said. As he got up, Megan passed him a hygienic mask from her pocket and didn't even wait for him to finish putting it on before she started walking. She didn't mean to be so abrupt, but she was taking a risk by leaving her treatment room for so long. Her PHS buzzed and she took two quick calls as they walked down the hallway. She didn't bother putting it away and she called Doctor Watanabe, the leader of the treatment room the teacher was in.

"I'm bringing in a visitor," she said. "Have Inagaki-sensei meet us."

"Understood," came the harried reply.

In the instant before Doctor Watanabe cut the connection, Megan heard him hollering into the background.

"Hayashi-san," Megan said with a glance at the man hurrying along beside her. "I'm going to arrange for a private place for Inagaki-sensei to sit down and I need you to make sure he stays put. Talk to him, hold his hand, anything you need to do to keep him in one place. We can take care of the children."

"Shu-san's always thinking of his students," Akihiro said. Even though Megan couldn't see his expression behind the mask, she heard the note of tenderness in his voice.

"In here," Megan said. She shouldered into the bustling treatment room and located Doctor Watanabe. "Do you have a free bed we could use?" she asked without preamble.

"There should be a few over there." He nodded over to the

far wall where a number of empty beds had their privacy curtains drawn back. "Most of the fifth and sixth graders are in here and they want to be with their friends so we've got extras. Sorry, but Inagaki-sensei's off again. He wouldn't even let me speak to him."

"Got it," Megan said. She sidestepped an orderly with a full cart of fresh plastic-lined buckets and motioned for Akihiro to follow her through the chaotic room. She located the teacher standing with a group of students. As a nurse checked their vitals and adjusted IVs, he spoke encouraging words to them and as Megan came close, he let loose with a few corny jokes that had a bunch of the kids groaning and pretend shivering in response.

"Inagaki-sensei's jokes are so cold!" a few of them said in delight.

He turned and saw Megan, who placed herself firmly in his path. "You need to sit down and let me examine you."

"I'm all right," he said.

"No you're not," Megan told him. "You're dehydrated and in pain. I can tell."

"Shu-san, please," Akihiro piped up from behind Megan.

Shuichiro took a step toward them. His head swiveled from Megan to Akihiro.

"Come on," Megan said. She stepped back and let out a breath of relief as both men followed her. She led them over to one of the unoccupied beds and pulled the curtain around it. She tuned out the soft conversation as she gave Shuichiro a quick examination and internally marveled at his stamina in the face of his debilitating condition. She ducked out of the enclosure to grab a bag of rehydrating solution and when she returned to the enclosure Akihiro pulled his hand back with a guilty look on his face.

"Don't let him go," Megan said. She turned her attention to the sharp needle she was holding in her hand and continued in a casual tone, "I'm going to give your Shu-san an IV and I don't want him running off again. Okay?"

"Okay," Akihiro said. He reached out once more and shyly took Shuichiro's hand in his.

"If anyone says you can't be here, have them call me, all right?"

"Thank you, Maier-sensei."

"I should be apologizing to both of you, for the way the

hospital treated you," Megan said.

She bent low over the teacher's arm and, with a word of warning, slipped the needle into his vein. Once the IV was properly in place, Megan backed out of the enclosure. She raced back to her treatment room and got there just in time to see a small boy vomit all over the front of his shirt and pants. While her mind said bad words, Megan hurried him into one of their long washrooms where she briskly got him cleaned up and into a set of the hospital-issue pajamas.

"You're going to be all right," Megan reassured him. He wiped at his eyes and sniffled. Her heart went out to him and Megan held her arms out. "Can I give you a hug?"

The boy's face brightened and he snuggled into Megan's arms. She had only just patted him on the back once when his body gave a heave and Megan felt something hot spill down her back. She closed her eyes and froze as her face contorted into a grimace.

"*Gomen nasai!*"

"It's all right, you don't need to apologize," Megan said. She winced and carefully moved her patient back a step. She tried not to squirm too much as she walked him back to the treatment room. The sticky warmth reached her waistband and soaked into the back of her slip by the time she got him settled on a bed. Megan called over a nurse to find his chart while she gave the boy a quick examination.

She scowled when she read his chart and determined he needed an IV as he'd just returned the electrolyte drink someone had given him. After setting up the drip and giving the boy a few encouraging pats on the head, Megan ducked into the bustling hallway. She dug out her PHS on her way to the staff prep room and called the intern who had given the drink to the boy to inform him not to give anything to the young patients by mouth.

"But he said he was thirsty," the intern said in a defensive voice.

"It's different with children," Megan said. She edged past a nurse who hurried by with an armful of towels. "They can't always understand what's happening and don't think about the consequences."

After she ended the call, Megan tried not to run as she travelled down the hallway, but the slow leakage down her back

spurred her to move with haste. She made it to the staff prep
room just in time to catch three orderlies leaving. A quick peek
inside revealed the room was empty and Megan gratefully
slipped inside.

Wincing with every movement, Megan grabbed a fresh set of
light blue scrubs and found a plastic bag to dispose of her soiled
personal garments. She was glad she hadn't been wearing her
front-opening bra that day as she had good memories of it and
wanted to make more of them in the near future. She struck gold
when she found a pack of alcohol wipes under the sink. She
quickly piled the contents of her pockets on the counter.

Megan shrugged off her lab coat and tried not to move
around too much. She was steeling herself to peel off her scrub
top when she heard a voice behind her.

"You know you've got *gero* all down your back?"

She turned quickly. A man in crumpled blue scrubs stood in
the doorway. It was Taki, the one who heckled Syler in the conference room.

"Yes, I know, but thanks for pointing it out," Megan said.
Her skin was already burning and she didn't care about modesty
as she gingerly squirmed out of her soaked scrub top off. Taki
showed a modicum of decency as he turned away and buried
himself in the supply closet. By the time he emerged with a number of plastic-wrapped packs of pajamas in his arms, Megan was
decent once more. She went commando under her scrubs, but it
was a vast improvement from the damp mess that had been down
her back until a few moments ago.

Megan was re-tying her hair when Syler and Atsuko walked
in. Syler was without her mop and bucket. Both of them looked
tired and drained.

Taki called out, "Hey Terada-kun, what's with you and Doctor Brockman? You steal his girlfriend?"

"Maybe." Syler stripped off her gloves and mask and tossed
them into the waste receptacle. She sank down onto the bench
that ran the length of the room and said, "But that's assuming he
could actually get a girlfriend. With that man's personality, I'm
sure women naturally run away screaming the instant he opens
his mouth."

Taki snorted and left.

"It's so good to see you, Meg," Syler said and reached out to take Megan's hand in hers. In the background, Atsuko busily scrubbed up at the sink and pointedly didn't pay attention. "How are you holding up?"

"I feel disgusting," Megan said. She trailed her thumb over the back of Syler's hand. "But other than that, I'm all right." She paused and said in a low voice, "I wanted to strangle Charles for making you do such a demeaning, dirty job. I could just kill him. You were so wonderful about it, though. He doesn't know what a blessing you are to this hospital."

"Hey, if I'm the designated puke-sweeper then I'm gonna own it," Syler said with a grin that lit a flame to Megan's desire. "Management's assholery has nothing to do with our patients. Besides, growing up with three brothers has made me pretty much immune to being grossed out by anything."

Megan had to laugh at that, but soon sobered. "I'm not happy with that orderly, Masato either."

"He's a creepy little thing, isn't he," Syler said. "Don't turn your back on him. I don't think he'd ever hurt a child, but the way he looks at some of the female patients makes my skin crawl. Particularly the ones who can't defend themselves."

Megan shivered. "I'll make sure to keep an eye on him."

Atsuko slipped out of the room and left just the two of them in the room. Megan gave into the urge and pulled Syler to her. Without any resistance, Syler wrapped her arms around Megan's waist and buried her head against Megan's chest.

"I'm sorry if I stink. I received a secondhand electrolyte drink from one of my patients earlier," Megan said. She wanted to press a kiss to Syler's temple but refrained as she wasn't sure what either of them had spackled over them. "I just changed, but I'm still a complete biohazard."

"Me too," Syler said. "But I still love being in your arms." She nestled against Megan with a happy sigh.

Syler ran a hand up and down Megan's back, smoothing the well-washed material of her scrubs. Even sweaty and gross as she was, Megan's body grew warm and responsive under Syler's touch. She shivered as her nipples hardened and a heavy, sultry heat thickened between her thighs. Megan swayed as Syler let go of her. She wished for the contact to continue but at the same time she knew how dangerous it was for them to be in that position for long.

Syler leaned back on her hands and said, "I'm staying here tonight to help deal with the extra inpatients we got today. At least that way I can actually do what I'm trained to do."

"Good plan. I think I'll offer to stay as well," Megan said. She was very aware of the fact that only a thin layer of cotton separated her bare skin from view and it wasn't doing anything to hide the twin symptoms of her arousal. It seemed Syler had noticed her predicament as well, because her gaze lingered on Megan's chest.

"God, you're so sexy," Syler breathed.

"That's your fault," Megan said. "You make me so hot."

"Really? How about I check that out for you."

In a single, quick motion, Syler slipped her hand under Megan's scrub top. Megan's skin flushed with heat as Syler's fingers found her and teased her fully erect with a single deft touch. Megan bit down on the gasp of need as Syler dropped her hand and moved away. Megan stifled a groan at the loss of skin contact. Her body hummed with tension and she felt an exquisite slickness between her legs.

"My diagnosis," Syler said in a serious voice, "is to agree that you are seriously hot for me. I'm afraid this is going to require specialized treatment. Quite intensive *hands-on* treatment, in fact, that must continue until the symptoms have been thoroughly relieved and your attending physician is satisfied."

"Did I mention how you are a complete *hentai*?"

"You don't have to," Syler said in her low, husky voice. "I fully accept the fact that I am a complete and total pervert. Admit it, you like that about me, right Meg?"

Megan clapped a hand to her mouth. After a beat, she answered, "Guilty as charged."

Syler just answered with a half-grin and a raised eyebrow that did not help Megan's bodily issues calm down at all. Megan couldn't walk around in such a state, so she got a fresh lab coat from the supply cabinet.

As Megan buttoned the front of her lab coat, Syler gave her a cocky grin and said, "Good idea to cover those before you take someone's eye out. You're hard as little bullets."

"Syler!" Megan stomped over and grabbed Syler from behind in a headlock. She ground herself against Syler's back and growled, "How about I shoot you with my little bullets right here, huh?"

"Oh please yes," Syler said, her teasing tone deepened. "Shoot me, baby."

"Maybe later if you behave," Megan said. She released Syler and plopped down on the bench beside her. Megan's entire body was alive and on fire, only heightened by the stress of the past few hours and ignited by the feeling of Syler in her arms. She was shaken by how good it had felt to grab Syler and take control of her.

Syler leaned close to Megan and said, "I've reserved shower stall 3B on the fourth floor. If you happen to be passing by there in an hour, you can use my Keshet body soap. I always keep a bottle stashed here for special use only."

"Really?" Megan asked. She was lightheaded and breathless and not nearly as scandalized as she should be. In fact, she was very much looking forward to the rendezvous. She stood and glanced at the doorway. They'd been lucky so far, but anyone could come in at any time. Megan had to give her answer soon and return to her duties. "All right," she answered, "But only because you've got Keshet."

"I knew it," Syler said. She got to her feet as well and joined Megan in gloving up again. After she refilled her pockets with the items she liberated from her previous lab coat, Megan pulled out her antiseptic spray and gave a mint-scented squirt into two masks, one of which she handed to Syler.

On their way out of the prep room, Syler said, "Seriously, that soap's the best. I discovered it when I took gross anatomy. It's the only thing that got the smell of coffin-wax out of my hair. Without it, I might have quit, especially that first summer."

Megan fell into step with Syler as they breezed down the hallway. At Syler's words, Megan's face broke into a joyful smile behind her hygienic mask.

She spoke without thinking, "I'll have to tell my zayde that. He'll be so pleased that soap kept at least one surgeon in the game." Megan stopped in her tracks, heart pounding. Syler stopped as well and fixed Megan with a long look.

"Why?"

"He invented it," Megan said with deliberate lightness. It was time for Syler to know the truth. She raised her head to meet Syler's eyes with her own. "My mother's Stefania Teitel and she's the daughter of Abram Teitel."

"As in Teitel Pharmaceutical Supplies and Medical Equipment?" Syler shook her head with a note of awe in her voice. "My God Meg, they make half of the stuff we've got in this hospital. More actually if you count their cooperative ventures, not to mention the people who went to med school on their scholarship programs. My assistant Nobu was a Teitel student, actually. It's one of the really humanitarian companies out there. You must be so proud to be part of it."

"It's just the family business," Megan said and resumed walking. "My zayde always says it's his way of giving back to the country that granted so many visas to Jews fleeing Europe during the war, including his family."

"Wow, you're a Teitel," Syler said. "Is that why you went into medicine?"

"Maybe," Megan said. "Growing up, everyone around me was a doctor, dentist, or at least some kind of researcher. But I really do want to help people and I'm good at it. I hope you don't think I was hiding this for any reason. My parents don't have much to do with the business and it's not really something I flaunt. Half the time I forget about it, but I've had so many crappy off-brand speculums snap on me I always check for the Teitel mark when I get one."

"I do too. And don't worry Meg," Syler said. "It doesn't change how I feel about you one bit."

"I'm glad," Megan said. She glanced at the clock on the wall and said, "Anyway, let's finish up here and I'll see you in fifty-five minutes."

Syler gave her a quick salute and charged off, PHS in her hand.

HER HEART SANG and her blood thrummed through her body. Megan could barely concentrate enough to deal with the last of the cases. Most of the patients were released after rehydration with only a few having to be relocated upstairs to the pediatric ward. There were no more messy incidents, but Megan longed for the feeling of hot water and soap on her skin, almost as much as she hungered for Syler's hands on her.

The hour dragged until Megan was finally able to take a break from her duties. She got yet another new set of scrubs from the hospital's seemingly endless supply of them, glancing at the double T logo on the tag. She made a brief stop by the scheduler's desk to see if there was an opening for her to stay on duty that evening. The scheduler was only too glad for Megan's offer and promptly assigned her an overnight shift.

With a pounding heart and sweaty palms Megan breezed through her office and grabbed her bag with her change of underwear and toothbrush in it before she raced up the stairs to the fourth floor. In contrast to the bustling chaos of the first floor, the area was quiet and the hallways deserted.

The row of shower rooms met her. Megan glanced up and down the hallway before she let herself into 3B and locked the door behind her. The tiny prefab changing area had a small pile of clothing on the plastic bench in a silent offer for Megan to use the single basket. The sound of running water filled the room. A shadowy shape moved languidly behind the folding frosted glass door. The unmistakable scent of the body soap wafted out on the hot, damp air, a heady blend of citrus and spice. It filled Megan with the feeling of being welcomed home.

"Syler, it's me," Megan said softly.

The door creaked open. Megan drew in a breath as she was greeted by indeed a most welcoming sight. Syler's long body was barely covered in streams of fragrant bubbles. Her hair was slicked back away from her face and Syler looked singularly striking. She had her toothbrush in her mouth and grinned around it.

"You're overdressed," she said.

"Give me three seconds to fix that," Megan said.

The electric sizzle of arousal that had been simmering within herself grew stronger. Megan didn't fight it. She couldn't. Syler held the door open. Megan's breath came harder as the soap gently trailed down Syler's body, leaving a luscious expanse of bare skin that glistened under the spray. Megan didn't turn away as she pulled off her scrubs and dropped them to the floor.

Syler had put away her toothbrush by the time Megan stepped through the narrow doorway. The first dash of warm water on her sticky skin felt wonderful. Megan didn't complain as Syler came up behind her with the frothy sponge in her hands. The cramped confines of the stall meant they had to stand pressed together, but Megan had a suspicion they'd be like that anyway, no matter how much room they had.

"How about I return the favor from last night," Syler asked in a low voice, "and wash your back?"

"Yes please," Megan answered. She waved her toothbrush and asked, "Do you have any toothpaste I could borrow?"

"Just use the soap," Syler said. She reached over to the small ledge where the bottle was standing and offered it. "Another awesome thing about Teitel is everything they make to put on you is also safe to put in you." She smiled as Megan hesitantly held her toothbrush out for a dollop.

"Huh," Megan said with her mouth full of bubbles. "Doesn't taste too bad. Do I want to know how you discovered this?"

Syler paused in working up lather with her sponge to say, "In that same anatomy class. Let's just say there was an incident with some splashback and I was desperate to get the taste of formalde-hyde-pickled cadaver out of my mouth. Worked like a charm."

"Glad to hear that." Megan rinsed her mouth and leaned over to spit. The movement caused her backside to press up against Syler's front, which she didn't mind at all.

"I never thought bathing with someone could be so fun," Syler said as she scrubbed the crawly feeling from Megan's back. "But I have to say, I really like it."

"It all depends who it's with," Megan said. She closed her eyes against the falling water and lifted her chin in pure enjoy-ment as Syler continued to wash her body. The touch was gentle and respectful, not opportunistic. Syler paid attention to all of Megan, from under her arms, over her shoulders and down her back, even over and into her backside and down her legs to her feet. Slowly the touch changed from clinical to sensual as the last suds fell.

Megan drew in a quick breath. Syler's careful fingers stroked down over her belly and traced wet designs over her skin until she reached the thatch of hair between Megan's legs.

"Is this okay?" Syler murmured in her ear then pressed a kiss to the back of her neck.

"Oh yes. Don't stop," Megan said. Her body hummed with need. Syler's movements against her became more intimate, urgent, and hungry.

"We don't have a lot of time," Syler said. She drew a slick hand up Megan's body until she cupped one breast. "Turn around baby girl and let me make you my lady."

Megan's eyes popped open. A rush of desire flamed through her. Syler wanted to top her, and Megan was only too willing to let her. She did as Syler asked. Megan turned to face her and found both of her hands seized. The raw need in Syler's eyes sent a shock straight to her core. Megan let Syler guide her hands to grip the safety handles on either side of herself.

"Don't let go," Syler told her in a low growl.

"I won't, Syler. Do anything you want," Megan said. Her voice was husky in the steamy air. Her body trembled with need. "I'm yours."

Syler answered by taking Megan's face in her hands and claiming her mouth in a devouring kiss. Their bodies came together, slippery and wet. Megan opened her mouth and accepted Syler's insistent entrance. She fought the whimpers of need that threatened to give away their secret tryst.

The kiss ended with Syler moving to hungrily nip at her neck. A thigh pushed between hers. Megan shifted and spread her feet a bit more. She basked in the feeling of Syler's softness against her own. She bit back a groan of frustration as Syler released her and stepped back, but that groan soon turned to a harsh gasp when Syler sank down to her knees before her. A jolt of arousal shook her. Megan's knuckles turned white from the grip she had on the handles.

Deep, trembling need spiraled up her legs as Syler reverently came forward and took Megan into her mouth. It was the first time anyone had done that to her. Megan had to bite down on her lower lip in order to keep from crying out at the pounding waves of pleasure that Syler's lips and tongue called forth. Even in sub-mission, Megan felt worshipped.

"You taste so fucking good," Syler murmured.

Syler looked up and held Megan's eyes with hers as she gave a slow, lascivious smile. She nudged Megan's thighs farther apart until she was spread wide with her feet braced against the walls of the small shower stall. Megan couldn't tear her eyes from the erotic sight of Syler as she went to work once more. Her spread-wide stance meant Megan could see exactly what was going on. Syler ran her tongue over the swollen, velvet folds between Megan's legs. She traced up and down her slick length without hurry. Under the deft ministrations, Megan was filled with pounding desire and her breath came in short gasps. She was unable to make a coherent thought as Syler gripped her hips and Syler's mouth came down on her, suckling at the hard nub of her clit without mercy. While Megan panted into the steamy air, Syler moaned in obvious enjoyment. Her eyes drifted closed as she gave herself to the task.

It took everything Megan had within her to keep her hands in place as she surrendered to Syler. Her only previous lover, Yasu had been a pure dominant, and while Megan had been comfortable as a pillow princess for a while, after she'd gained some experience with physical intimacy, Megan had felt frustrated at being confined to what she saw as the passive role. However there was nothing passive in the position she was in at the moment. Syler's entire body and consciousness was focused on her, ready to react to the slightest cue from Megan. It was Megan who was in charge, and the knowledge took her breath away.

The tremors of release were almost on Megan when Syler placed one last, slow kiss to her most intimate area and stood. Megan nearly sobbed with need when Syler's arms came around her and held her body tightly.

"I want to see your face when you come for me," Syler rasped in Megan's ear.

It was the one thing she could do for Syler. Megan opened her eyes to meet Syler's heated gaze.

"Do you want me inside you?"

"Yes," Megan gasped. Her body shivered with desire. She moved against Syler in a silent plea.

Mouth open, Megan was powerless to do anything else but move to accept Syler as she pushed two fingers into her. It wasn't enough, Megan knew even as the flashes of climax sparked into life deep within herself.

"Please, Syler. I need more of you. Could you give me another one?"

"God yes, Meg." Syler said. "I'll give you as much as you want. Just tell me if it's too much."

Megan fought to hold herself up as Syler withdrew, only to fill her once more, burying herself deep. The tight fit was almost overwhelming in its intensity, but Megan welcomed it. Syler's body moved with every thrust, delving in and then sliding out of her with agonizing slowness. Whimpers of pleasure echoed through the tiny stall even as Megan bit down on them. Her body was on edge, her release only a breath away. Megan shook with need for Syler to take her over.

"Yes Meg, you are so beautiful. Give yourself to me," Syler said. She shifted but kept one arm wrapped protectively around Megan.

The penetrating fingers filled Megan. A deft thumb stroked her throbbing clit in tight, hard circles. That pushed Megan over the edge. A shockwave of release exploded behind Megan's eyes. Her knees buckled. She was grateful Syler was strong enough to hold her up. Megan's body arched with shuddering spasms. She didn't care where Syler's mouth had just been. Megan took Syler's lips in a demanding kiss as waves of release crashed over her and shook Megan to her core. Her breath came faster as she tasted herself on Syler's tongue. Riding Megan's climax, Syler pumped in and out of her, hard and fast. Between thrusts, a sudden hot gush from between her legs shocked Megan. Her eyes flew open and she gasped with the realization of what she'd just done to Syler.

"Oh my God, I'm so sorry," Megan said. "I think I just had an accident on you. I can't believe I did that!"

"You didn't, baby girl." Tender fingers cupped and held Megan's throbbing sex. While she stared in awe into Megan's face, Syler said, "What happened is a natural response. It doesn't happen every time, but when it does it's very intense. And also a huge compliment. Thank you, Meg."

"You're welcome," Megan replied. She blinked a few times and tried to get her brain functioning once more. While she knew Syler prided herself on being flexible, she was a fucking good *tachi*. Megan's heaving breaths calmed down and, with a soft word of permission from Syler, she let go of the death-grip she'd had on the safety handles. She shook out her numb hands while Syler turned off the water and passed her a towel.

They stood side by side in the tiny changing room and hurriedly dressed. The shower room reservations were only in thirty minute increments and they were pushing the limit. She didn't know if anyone had made reservations for the next time slot, but Megan didn't want to be there to meet them. After her most thorough loving, Megan glowed and her legs felt like jelly. Unable to help herself, she pulled Syler close for one last, lingering kiss.

"I love you so much Syler," Megan whispered and was

rewarded by Syler's arms tightening around her. "And I loved being your lady and giving myself to you."

"I know you did," Syler said. "And I loved taking you."

"But I want you to remember this," Megan said with a wicked note in her voice, "I'm not the only lady around here. Prepare for payback. And I mean it. I'm going to have you at my mercy and I'll take care of you as well as you did to me just now."

"God Meg, you don't know how hot you are when you say stuff like that." Syler closed her eyes and gave a soft moan.

Megan gathered up her discarded scrubs and rolled them up in her towel. Syler cracked open the door and peeked out to the hallway.

"Is anyone out there?" Megan asked.

"Coast is clear," Syler said. She threw the door open. Both of them burst into the hallway just in time to come face-to-face with Luka.

Megan froze. There was no innocent explanation for the two of them to be coming out of the same shower stall, both with wet hair and, especially in Megan's case, a giant case of afterglow.

"I thought you said the coast was clear," Megan said. She floated on billows of happiness and couldn't summon up the necessary angry tone to back up her words.

"Yeah, it's only Lukie," Syler said. "And he's not going to tell, is he?"

"What am I not going to tell?" Luka looked from one to the other and clapped both hands over his mouth. "Oh my God, you didn't!"

"What?" Syler said and gave a lithe stretch that Megan appreciated very much. "We were just saving time and water."

"Uh huh," Luka said. He shook his head and flapped his hands at them. "Just go. Go!"

"Whatever you say, dear. I'm going," Syler called back over her shoulder as she sashayed down the hallway, idly swinging her towel-wrapped bundle in one hand.

Wordlessly, Luka stared at Megan with a mixture of awe and envy. She just shrugged and followed Syler's retreating back, careful to keep a judicious distance between them.

The rest of the night passed much less eventfully than the day. Megan spent most of the shift in the on-call room where she played cards with the other physicians on duty and occasionally answered calls between sporadic rounds. It was difficult to keep the smile from her face. In addition, Luka made a big deal of huffing at her whenever he passed by.

The next morning saw most of the children who had suffered from food poisoning released. The culprit was found to be improperly cleaned pots that the lunch staff had used to make curry, and the school was launching an investigation. Megan hoped there never would be a repeat of the incident.

Chapter Two

THE THURSDAY EVENING following the food-poisoning incident, Megan relaxed on her sofa after her bath, not really paying attention to the variety show on the TV in front of her, when there was a knock at her door. Megan glanced at the clock with a happy jolt. Syler's shift in after-hours admissions wasn't scheduled to end for another half-hour, but it could be earlier if things were slow. Besides Luka and his snide references to what he called *the shower incident*, things at the hospital were back to their usual smooth operation.

Megan bounded up and threw the door open only to freeze in horror. Charles was on her doorstep, as bland and immobile as ever.

"Oh, uh, hi," Megan choked. She felt incredibly underdressed in her tank top and loose cotton skirt that just brushed her ankles. At least her knees were covered so she wouldn't have to listen to another lecture on proper attire from Mr. Conservative.

"Good evening," he said and took a step forward, forcing Megan back.

"What brings you here?" Megan asked in what she hoped was a polite way when she really wanted to slam the door in his face. She didn't dare. He was her boss and his father owned the hospital. She'd crossed him once already when she'd red-flagged Nikky Okamoto's file for suspected child abuse, and considered herself lucky all she got was a veiled but real threat to her continued employment. While she didn't want to risk angering him again, Megan resolved to be as quick and brusque as manners would allow.

"I have two items for your attention," he said and held out a long paper bag, which Megan's hands closed over in an automatic way. "The first, a fine vintage I believe might appeal to your palate and second, on a more mundane note, some forms for your signature."

"Thanks," Megan said. The clear file he passed her took up Megan's free hand. She was forced to let go of her hold on the doorknob only to have Charles reach out and grab the door and hold it open. Megan held her breath, waiting for Charles to leave. When he didn't, she nervously wet her bottom lip and asked, "Is that all?"

"I would hope that you are not planning to accept my gift and simply show me the door." His presence was a solid wall that blocked the entire doorway. "I must be mistaken about your complete lack of manners. In addition, those documents need to be signed immediately. Our financial department needs them first thing tomorrow morning or I'm afraid your taxes are going to fall into chaos and put several members of our staff in very difficult positions."

"I'm sorry, I, um, wasn't expecting company," Megan said. At least, she hadn't been expecting male company. She covered her stab of worry with a fake laugh. She stepped back and said, "Please come in." She turned her back and, with a pounding heart, showed Charles into her room.

The last thing Megan wanted was Charles's tightly-clenched ass on her sofa but she had no choice. Once again she was backed into a corner. After the accident that stole her previous partner Yasu from her, Megan spent a year in recovery, trying to reassemble some kind of order to her life. The year-long absence from practicing medicine meant her job prospects were extremely limited. Charles had already made it clear he had no qualms about firing or reassigning her.

Megan's heart gave a quick thump. Now she had so much more to lose than just her job.

Desperate to put some distance between them. Megan went over to the kitchen cubby while Charles settled onto her sofa with a look of disdain at the piles of cushions.

"How about a glass of wine?" Megan asked.

"Yes, I believe that would be pleasant."

Her hands were sweaty and she fumbled the corkscrew of the gifted wine. Of course one of those bottles with twist off caps would be beneath him. Megan's mind whirled as she struggled with the cork and got out two glasses. A quick search of her fridge resulted in some cheese, which Megan put out on a plate with a few crackers. She had a bad feeling in her gut. She wanted Charles out as soon as possible.

She brought the tray over and set it down while mentally

measuring the distance between herself and her phone, which was charging on the table—or it had been. Megan looked up from the bare end of the charging cord. Her phone was in Charles's pocket, just like that night when he'd taken her out for dinner. He seemed to relish having control over her.

"Just in case," he said with an air Megan found insufferable. "It wouldn't do to have distractions while you are filling out these important forms, now would it?" He reached over and turned off the TV as well with an aside about "the idiot box."

The fact he had taken away her lifeline to the outside world worried Megan, but she just dug out her family seal from her bag and accepted the expensive-looking gold pen Charles offered her from his pocket. It was still warm from his body. Revulsion stained from her fingertips. As Charles leaned forward to pour the wine, Megan glanced at the window. She was hit with an idea. Of course!

"How about a bit more light?" Megan asked.

She didn't wait for the reply before she skidded across the room and threw herself down to plug in the string of lights. They blinked into life, showering the room with their gentle glow. While she was loathe to create anything resembling a romantic environment, she prayed that Syler would see the signal on her way home. It was the only thing she could think of.

Meanwhile, Charles settled quite firmly into her sofa and didn't look like he would leave anytime soon. Something in his eyes as he studied her set off more than a few warning bells. It was that same look he got just before he grabbed her by the shoulders and tried to kiss her at Passover. In her life, Megan had never attempted to associate with men on an intimate basis. She could only hope she was reading the signals wrong.

"First a toast," Charles said.

"Uh, okay." With a sigh of regret, Megan put down the handful of forms and picked up her wine glass.

"To the future, prosperity, health, cooperation," Charles intoned. Megan nodded and took a large swig. "And love."

"PHFF!" Megan sprayed her mouthful back into her glass at the last words, spoken in a flat monotone but nevertheless disturbing. She sputtered and grabbed at a tissue to attack the red droplets she sprayed onto the table.

"Does the beverage not agree with you? I assure you it is of the finest quality, straight from my family's wine cellar."

"No, no, sorry," Megan said. "I just, um, think I should fill out those forms now."

She clutched the package of paperwork and scooted back as far as she could get without having to vault over the armrest. She felt a sick sense of foreboding and an angry fear that her sanctuary and safety were compromised. While she was reasonably sure Charles wouldn't full-on attack her, she was not mentally prepared to ward off his advances, should he decide to make any.

Once more, Megan silently pleaded for her instincts to be mistaken. Her hands shook as she scribbled over the forms, pausing only to press her hanko to the red ink pad and leave a number of stamps in various places.

"You do not dream of love?"

The question caused Megan's hand to spasm and nearly rip a hole through the form she was filling out.

"Charles, I don't think we should be having this discussion."

"Why not? It is merely a case of two colleagues sharing opinions on life's philosophy." Charles swirled the deep red liquid in his glass and crossed one leg over the other. He moved as if he had a backache. "Or are you devoid of any feeling, only going through the motions of caring as if in a stage-play? It is indeed a pity for a physician especially to be one of such shallow conscience."

He downed his glass of wine in one go and poured himself another. His eyes didn't leave Megan as she worked.

"Okay, that's the last of them," Megan said with a fake laugh. She gathered up the papers and shoved them messily back into the clear file. She held the file out for Charles to take, glad to be rid of it. She hoped to be rid of him as well. He reached out. Megan tried to jerk back, only to have his large hand close over her wrist.

"I believe you are a woman of deep passion," he said. Megan gaped at where he held her. The clammy warmth of his skin revolted her and she got the urge to kick him. "And you are in need of someone who can appreciate that passion, as well as your beauty."

Without releasing his hold on her, Charles put the clear file down on the table. He kept his hand wrapped around Megan's wrist. He didn't let go even after she gave a couple experimental tugs. His thumb jerked around. It rubbed at her skin and sent worms of disgust crawling up Megan's arm.

"Let go of me," Megan said. Her throat was tight. He didn't move.

"You are indeed a beautiful woman," Charles said. He didn't meet her eyes. Instead he stared at the mess of papers spilling from the file folder on the table. His grip tightened to a painful level. Megan was too shocked and panicked to speak. The doorbell broke the spell.

"Whoever could that be?" Megan said in an overly-loud voice.

As if Megan had suddenly caught on fire, Charles yanked his hand back. Freed from the unwanted grip, Megan jumped to her feet and was in the entrance hall in an instant. Her heart gave a huge leap, tears of gratitude and relief welled up in her eyes when she saw Syler on the other side of the door, still in her smart work clothes. With her back to Charles, Megan mouthed, "I love you." Syler answered with a grin and kicked off her shoes. She held a plastic bag that gave off a mouthwatering aroma and the pockets of her jacket bulged. Megan quickly ushered her to the living room.

"Hey, it's a party," Syler said as she trotted over to the sofa.

Megan followed. Her heart felt like it was going to explode with love. Syler plopped herself down right in the middle of the sofa and kicked her long legs out in front of herself with a sigh and a stretch.

"Thanks for dropping by," Megan said as she settled down on the other side of Syler. "As you can see, Charles was just here with some paperwork for me."

Syler bobbed her head in his direction, but Charles didn't respond. Syler said, "Hope you don't mind me gate crashing, but I got chicken. They were having a two-for-one sale and I kinda went overboard so there's plenty for everyone." Syler shook off the bag and put the plastic takeout pack of *yakitori* down on the table. She dug two cans of Chu-Hi from her pockets and handed one can of the fruity alcoholic beverage to Megan. Charles fixed Syler with a look of absolute disgust. She seemed immune to it as she cracked open her can and chugged from it.

"Sorry I only got two," she said. "I didn't know you were going to be here, Chuck. We're all off-duty here, I figure it's okay if I call you Chuck, right?"

"No, you may not," Charles said. His lips thinned and his hands clenched into white-knuckled fists, incidentally the first sign of actual emotion Megan had ever seen from the man.

"Okay." With a shrug, Syler slurped at her drink, then let go with a belch. "Whoops! But you gotta get the air out before it goes past the point of no return, because there's only one other way out and that's the back door." Syler chuckled heartily to herself. She nudged Charles with her elbow. He recoiled and looked most offended as Syler made fart-noises with her mouth, complete with lifting up one side of her backside from the sofa cushions.

Megan was in the middle of taking a sip from her can. Syler's actions made her drink nearly go up her nose. In order to hide her laughter, she got up and darted into her kitchen cubby. She came back with a bowl of chocolate takenoko snacks just in time to see Syler waving a half-eaten skewer of chicken in the air as she finished off what appeared to be a long-winded joke.

"And then she asked: Aren't your ears cold?" Syler said. She let loose with a cackle. Still chuckling, Syler lifted a finger from the hand holding her beverage and poked Charles in the shoulder. "Get it? Not his hands, his ears!"

Charles moved out of poking range. His face creased into an expression of repugnance. "I am afraid I have no appreciation for such lowbrow humor."

"Aw come on, loosen up a bit Chuck," Syler said. She looked up at Megan's offering and said, "Nice! Bring somma that over here, Meg."

Syler fed herself a handful of the chocolate snack. Megan fought with all of her strength to avoid throwing herself bodily into Syler's lap and smothering her with kisses. Charles stood.

"I believe I have worn out my welcome," he snarled, then quickly smoothed his tie. His face went back to its usual bland expression once more. "Megan, if you would see me to the door?"

"Of course," Megan said.

Syler got up as well and made a big show of wiping her hand on her trousers before she stuck it out. "Put 'er there, Chuck." He stared at the extended hand as if Syler was holding a live snake out to him. "What? Just to show you there are no hard feelings about how you royally fucked me over in front of the entire staff with that barf-bucket move. That was really good. It sure put me in my place!"

Charles sneered and ignored her hand. "Out of respect to our hostess, I refuse to be drawn into the sort of petty one-upmanship you are attempting to engage in. And I would like to remind you of our hospital's dress code. It would not kill you to wear a skirt from time to time."

"I'll show up in a skirt the day you do, big boy," Syler said.

Charles's face twisted as he snapped, "Goodnight, Miss Terada."

"Hmm," Syler replied with the can of Chu-Hi at her mouth. She stuck her hand in her pocket and turned her attention to the poster on the wall of a tuxedo-clad member of the Takarazuka all-female theater troupe.

Charles went into the entrance hall where Megan waited with the clear file.

"I hope that woman doesn't impose on you much longer tonight," Charles said over his shoulder as he bent down to lace himself into his Italian shoes. He lowered his voice and said, "It would be for the best if you did not allow yourself to be left alone with that person for long. She has a reputation for getting, er, rather *handsy* with young ladies — eligible or not."

"That's all right," Megan replied with a touch of venom. "I can take care of myself."

With a frown, Charles tapped his toes against the tiled floor once each and, almost as an afterthought, handed Megan her phone. "Thank you for what could have been a lovely evening."

"Don't forget this," Megan said. She thrust the file at Charles and stepped back as he opened the door for himself.

The door eased shut behind Charles. Megan quickly locked the deadbolt and drew the chain. She turned around and sagged against the door. The tension evaporated from her body. She was left drained and shaking. She took a few steps into the room and was met by Syler, who scooped her up in a tight hug and rained down kisses on her cheeks and hairline.

"Thank you for coming," Megan said. She sank into Syler's arms.

"Something's not right about this," Syler said in a quiet voice. One hand stroked up and down Megan's back. She drew away and took Megan's chin in one hand. Their eyes met. Megan was startled to see the pain in Syler's expression. "Why was he really here?"

"Oh God, I don't know," Megan said. The fear and uncertainty returned. "I'm sorry, I couldn't get him out and he was being so weird, accusing me of not having feelings and then he was saying something about me being a passionate woman and it all seemed so fake. I didn't know what to do and then he grabbed me—"

"He *what*?" Syler barked. Megan recoiled from the barely-contained rage in her voice. "Don't worry, I'm not angry with you baby girl," Syler said. She led Megan over to the sofa and put an arm around her. Megan settled down next to Syler, who said softly, "Tell me what happened."

In a halting way, Megan did. She tried to keep to the facts, but her voice started to shake halfway through. The comfort of Syler's presence gave her the strength to continue. By the time Megan finished her story, she was more annoyed than anything else.

"It was almost as if..." Megan paused and gathered her thoughts before she said, "As if he was trying to, I don't know, be romantic or something."

"Do you think that's what he was doing?"

"I don't know," Megan said with a deep sigh. "Why would he do that? I mean, we have zero chemistry, he's always putting me down and disagreeing with me, and just being around Charles makes me sick to my stomach. He's not even the right gender!" Megan took Syler's hand and twined their fingers together. "More than anything else, I already have someone."

Syler was quiet for a while after that. A frisson of tension sprang up between them. To break the dark mood, Megan ducked out of Syler's loose hold and got to her knees on the soft cushion. She draped herself over Syler's lap and made a happy sound as Syler's arms came around her once more.

"Sorry, Meg," Syler said. She brushed back a strand of hair from Megan's forehead. "I was just thinking about something." She paused and spoke in a hesitant voice, "I can understand why Charles would set his sights on you. Your family, his position, age, religion, everything. On paper, you are a perfect match for each other."

Megan recoiled at the words. "Maybe on paper," she said, unable to hide the disdain in her voice. "But in real-life, it would be hell. Everything else aside, our personalities are complete opposites, we don't get along at all."

"Baby girl, I think you have been chosen for something and personality is not going to make any difference."

"What do you mean?" Megan breathed.

With an expression of pain on her face, Syler was silent for a long time before she said, "Meg, I don't want to ruin your evening. Maybe I should go too."

Megan's heart gave an unpleasant lurch. "If you're sure," Megan said. She made a move as if to draw away, but Syler seized her and held her almost too tightly.

"No, I'm not," Syler whispered into her hair. The arms around Megan trembled. She held her breath, waiting for Syler to speak again. When she did, her voice was small and Megan's heart broke at the sadness in it. "I hate this," Syler whispered. "I hate feeling like this — like I'm on the verge of losing you."

"You're not going to lose me," Megan said. "I promise."

The wry, humorless laugh Syler gave cut Megan's soul. "I'm sorry, but I've heard that before."

"Syler, look at me," Megan said. She drew back and took both of Syler's hands in hers. The fingers that had given her such comfort and pleasure were cold, unresponsive. "We both have demons from our pasts that we have to face. You remember when I had that dream about the accident? It happens a lot and I've had to make a tough decision." Megan pressed her lips together for a moment, steeling herself to continue. "And that was to believe, absolutely one hundred percent, and have faith that every time you walk out that door, the next time I see you, you won't be broken, lying on a stretcher. I believe that I won't have to crack your chest and hold your heart in my hand as you die. It happened once before, but I have to believe it will never happen again. Otherwise I'd go insane." Megan's voice gave out and she was silent for a moment, unable to meet Syler's eyes. She trembled with the effort it took to keep her emotions in check.

Megan drew in a breath and said, "I've beaten my demon, but you haven't. Let me fight it with you. I love you and I want to be with you." She paused as a thorn of pain hit her in the chest. "I know Yukina hurt you when she left you for that guy. I'm not her, okay? I don't care what Charles or any other man or woman or person of any kind is offering me. It's you I want. Only you.

Believe me, Syler. Trust me."

Megan was startled as Syler tugged her hands free and buried her face in them.

"You don't know how much I want to," she said. Her voice was muffled as she spoke again, "You said your parents were okay with you being gay, but there are a lot of privileges only married people get—legally and socially. A lot of people see it as a rite of passage into adulthood." She dropped her hands and stared off into the distance, away from Megan. Syler gave a derisive snort. "Try being a single woman in this country and making a purchase of anything bigger than a designer handbag. Being married, especially to a rich guy, can pave an easy future for you. Your parents might see this as an opportunity for you to have a future you'd never get otherwise."

"What?" Shocked, Megan gaped. She wished Syler would look at her. "I don't care about all that. That's not enough to take me away from you."

"Not even for the business?"

"No way, my parents would never think about that. Teitel got the way it did not through subterfuge or making underhanded connections or even guilting any of us to join the company. They employ good people and support talent. Everyone in the family is free to do whatever they want. It wasn't a big *tsimmes* when my mother decided to go into dentistry. I've got an uncle in California who's a dog trimmer and nobody cares who marries who as long as everyone's happy."

Syler was still silent and Megan wondered what she was struggling with.

"Is there anything I can do to convince you I'm not going to do what Yukina did to you? I want a way to show you there's no man alive that can make me turn in my lesbian card." Megan persevered. "How about I join a softball team? I could get a mullet and wear nothing but flannel and overalls. I'll listen twenty-four-seven to that band with all the lesbians in it. Tell me and I'll do it." She reached out and put a hand on Syler's shoulder. The muscle beneath her palm felt like knotted steel.

At last, Syler turned her head and met Megan's gaze. A spark of humor returned to her eyes and Megan breathed again. She reached out and smoothed back Megan's hair. "No softball. I wouldn't want you to risk injuring your hands, flannel and overalls are so last century, and I'm sure half of Kitty in the Corner are only pretending to be into girls to be more edgy. But I think you would look absolutely adorable with business-in-the-front and party-in-the-back hair." She let out a long breath and gave Megan a smile. "Meg, sweetheart, you don't need to convince me. This is my issue."

"It's mine too. We're in this together," Megan said in a rush.

Syler gave her hand a squeeze. "You don't know how much that means to me. I'm sorry for bringing up my baggage and making it your problem. You're right, Meg. I have to believe you're not going to leave me for some putz. I don't trust Charles any further than I can punt him, but I trust you with all of my heart."

"Good," Megan said. She took Syler's face in her hands and asked, "Stay with me tonight?"

Syler's answer was to meet Megan's kiss and fall back into the sofa cushions with her. Eventually they made it back into the bedroom where they welcomed the night's peace.

THE NEXT MORNING, Megan opened her eyes to find Syler already awake, head propped up on one hand. Her other hand absently trailed up and down Megan's bare arm.

"Good morning, beautiful," Megan said. She scooted over and snuggled her face into Syler's warm chest. Her words were muffled as she asked, "What time is it?"

"A little after five," Syler said. She kissed Megan softly on the temple, then moved down to her neck. Megan purred under the caresses. "The alarm's set for six. You have a choice, sleep for another hour, or..." Syler trailed off, but a slender thigh pushing between Megan's hinted at what the second choice was.

"I'll take the 'or'," Megan said and let out a gasp as Syler pulled her close. They hadn't made love the night before. After Megan had unceremoniously dumped the bottle of wine down the sink, she'd offered her shoulder and held Syler in the comforting cocoon of her futon. With Syler in her arms, they talked about everything and nothing until both of them drifted off. Megan enjoyed the closeness, but her hunger was only delayed, not satisfied.

A hand slipped under Megan's tank top. She welcomed the burn of desire that Syler's deft fingers brought as they found the fullness of her breast. Perhaps because of the odd hours of their profession, neither of them were grumpy morning people. In fact, Megan found Syler usually playful and sweet when she woke up, no matter what hour of day or night.

A sudden twinge in her lower belly reminded Megan there was someplace she needed to go, and a mint-scented kiss on the side of her neck told Megan that Syler already went. Megan held up a hand.

"Hold that thought. Morning duty calls."

Syler laughed deep in her throat and withdrew her hand. Megan launched herself off the futon and made a beeline for the bathroom. Morning duties were carried out in record time. Megan rushed happily back and burrowed under the covers that Syler held open for her.

"Where were we?" Megan asked.

Syler's arms came around her once more.

"About here," Syler said. She reached down and Megan felt her panties slipping down her legs. Megan twitched her hips to help Syler free her from the small garment where it promptly disappeared into the drifts of the comforter.

Syler let out a low sound of approval as Megan slipped her leg over Syler's body and slowly moved to straddle her. Gentle hands stroked up her legs and settled on her hips. Syler's T-shirt rode up over her belly, exposing a line of skin. With the thin material of Syler's boxer briefs as the only thing between them, Megan got a kick of arousal deep in her belly.

Megan lay down and pressed herself against Syler. She dropped a soft kiss to Syler's long, slender neck. Syler responded by stroking her hands very slowly over the swells of Megan's hips before they drifted to cup Megan's backside and kneaded her lightly. It seemed like Syler was in the mood for a bit of morning fun, which Megan was only too happy to participate in. While she was aware of the limited time, Megan was determined to make the most of it.

"Is this all right?" Megan asked between kisses.

Syler moved beneath her, and took in a deep breath before she said, "Oh yes."

Megan added a few light nips to her kisses. Syler's body reacted to her. Syler's muscles tensed under Megan's lips and between her spread legs. The hands on her urged Megan to slowly rock against the resilient plane of Syler's stomach. The warm wetness building deep in her belly was dizzying, but Megan focused more on Syler than herself. She drew back and pulled her tank top over her head. Megan enjoyed the appreciative look in Syler's eyes. Her nipples were already hard, her skin buzzed with excitement in anticipation of Syler's touch.

"You are so beautiful," Syler said in a harsh whisper. Her hands came up to catch Megan's fullness and cradle her. Her gaze met Megan's.

"Come here so I can taste you."

Hungry for Syler's lips, Megan pulled herself forward until her breasts were positioned over Syler's face. Her breath was hot on Megan's skin. Syler's thumbs stroked her into taut excitement. Megan's breath came faster. She arched her back and gave herself to Syler. Her hips bucked and she ground herself against Syler.

"Down a bit," Syler said,

"You'll suffocate," Megan teased.

"Maybe," Syler said. Her fingers quickened along with Megan's breaths. "But at least I'll die happy."

There was only one way to respond to that and Megan lowered herself to Syler's waiting lips. She gave a quick gasp when Syler pulled one nipple into her mouth. Megan's body trembled with need. In response, Syler's tongue teased her, first one side, then the other, never stopping but never hurrying. Megan's breaths heaved in her chest. Each one seemed to reach all the way down to her toes.

"You're so good at that," Megan said. Syler didn't reply but Megan felt the soft lips against her curve into a smile before a gentle nip startled a cry from her.

"Sorry baby," Syler pulled away enough to say. "Did I hurt you?"

"Not at all," Megan said. She spread her knees a bit wider and pressed herself against Syler. The feeling of teeth closing on her ignited something within Megan. She wondered for an uneasy moment if Syler could feel the wetness between her legs. Her body's hunger drove her to continue. Megan lowered her head and whispered in Syler's ear, "Do it again. Harder."

With a happy growl, Syler seized Megan around the waist and rolled her over onto her back. One hand reached down to urge Megan's legs to wrap around Syler's lean hips while the other held her breast captive. Megan crossed her ankles, locking Syler's body in place. A second bite came, this one more intense than the previous one and caused Megan to throw her head back into the pillow. The new position had Megan spread open against the tight muscles of Syler's belly. Each movement of Syler between her legs sent dizzying spears of pleasure straight through her.

Megan soared on the feelings blazing into life within herself. Harsh breaths warred with moans of desire. She wanted Syler to hear how much she was enjoying the attention. Her thighs ached. Her muscles bunched. Megan was electrified with desire. She was desperate for Syler to do something, and soon, or she was going to lose her mind.

"Syler, please, I need you," Megan begged. "I can't stand it anymore."

The taunting lips came off her breast and Syler caught her mouth in a deep kiss. Megan bucked against Syler as talented fingers trailed down her side. The crushing pressure between her legs lifted for an instant before Syler slipped down her belly and came home for the most welcome touch, right where she craved it most. Syler's fingers parted her and slid between her slippery folds.

The kiss ended abruptly and Megan was left panting. Gripped by a roaring hunger, Megan forced herself to open her eyes and gaze up into Syler's face as Syler worked her thickening clit with a thorough and demanding touch.

"Beautiful girl," Syler said in a tight voice. "Is this good?"

"Yes," Megan said. "It's so good. Don't stop."

She couldn't help herself as she cupped her own breasts while Syler watched her with ravenous eyes. With a twist of her fingers, Megan pinched her nipples, hard. The combination of Syler's unrelenting attention to the slick bud within her wet, swollen lips and the twinge of pain sent a shockwave of white release through Megan. She gave up the fight as her back arched and her body shuddered.

The fingers on her didn't let up. Megan cried out as she fell over the edge once, then again, and again as the waves rolled over her. When she finally came to the end of the rises and drops, Megan ended up in a happy, quivering pile in Syler's arms. She floated on a cloud of sweet release, comforted and caressed by knowing hands on her back. Gentle words of love were whispered into her ear, followed by a kiss on her sweat-damp temple.

Megan sprawled herself out in a long, feline stretch. She met Syler's gaze and said, "How about I take care of you now?"

Just then the beeping of the alarm cut into the morning stillness. Megan breathed a curse.

"Don't worry, I planned on this morning being all about you," Syler said. "Just making you feel good was enough. I can't tell you how unbelievably hot it is when you come and I know it's all for me."

"If you're sure," Megan said. She flushed as she imagined the show she gave Syler. "You always take such good care of me. I feel like I'm being selfish."

"Of course not sweetheart. You don't need to do anything." Syler waggled her eyebrows suggestively. "At least not until tonight. Come over to my place after you finish work. We can have a barbecue on the roof and then I'll take you downstairs where you can light me on fire and then put me out."

"I like that idea," Megan said. She cast around in an attempt to locate her discarded tank top and panties for a moment before she gave up on getting dressed and rolled over onto the tumble of her futon. She propped her chin up on her hands. "There isn't time to run a bath, but you're welcome to join me in the shower."

"Sounds good," Syler said. She stood up and shucked her T-shirt, followed by her boxer briefs. Without an ounce of self-consciousness, Syler held out a hand to Megan who took it without a moment's hesitation. Naked as the day she was born, beside the woman she loved with all of her heart, Megan reflected that she could very easily get used to waking up like that every day.

Chapter Three

WITH HER HEAD still fuzzy from the lovely wakeup that morning, Megan sat at her desk with her lunch bagel. She sighed dreamily around a big bite of whitefish spread. That morning, she had asked Syler to join her in reciting the daily prayer. They stood side by side in the narrow kitchen cubby, shoulders barely brushing, voices twining together. It was nice. She wanted to get used to that.

Her PHS rang. Startled, Megan jumped hard enough to drop the last bit of her bagel. The screen lit up with a message to report to Charles's office immediately. Megan groaned and closed her eyes as a heavy feeling of dread came over her. What if he was in the mood to continue what he'd started the night before? In a way, Megan hoped he would come straight out and ask her so she could tell him to get lost. She didn't care about sabotaging their working relationship. Charles had done that all by himself when he'd grabbed her wrist.

"Come in," Charles's bored-sounding voice answered Megan's knock.

"What did you want to see me about?" Megan asked. She didn't take a seat or approach the desk. Charles sat in his chair with his fingers steepled in front of himself.

"Sit down, please."

With a sigh, Megan did as she was instructed. She folded her hands in her lap and waited. She didn't attempt to make the conversation any easier.

"I see you have removed your shackle to a dead man," Charles began. The blunt words felt like Charles had slapped her across the face. His eyes lingered on her. With a jolt of disgust, Megan stifled the urge to tell him exactly why she'd taken it off and who she had been "shackled" to. He continued in a monotone, like he was reading from a script. "It seems to be indicative of your willingness to move on with your life. As such, I have a proposal for you."

"I'm not interested," Megan shot back.

"You haven't even heard what it is. Are you always this defensive or have I done something to personally offend you?"

She declined to answer. Instead, Megan took a deep breath to calm herself. All she had to do was let him get the words out and the whole matter would be settled. She bit her lip and tried to keep her knee from jiggling.

"My proposal is the following: would you do me the honor of accepting my application to upgrade our relationship from professional to personal?"

There it was. It was almost a relief to finally hear Charles say the words, even in his odd, unnatural way.

"Nope," Megan said. She got to her feet, more than ready to leave. "Is that all? I have work to do."

Face set and bland as ever, Charles blinked twice. "Would you care to tell me the reason for your refusal?"

"I don't think I need to justify my answer to you. No is no, Charles."

"Very well," Charles said. His eyes hardened. "If I cannot appeal to your heart, which seems to be as tender as a dried-up piece of rawhide, I shall take a different approach. Think about what I'm offering you, Megan." He paused and gave her a significant look. "I'm certain your family would be most pleased to know that you will one day be the co-director of this hospital."

"What?" Megan barked out. She shook her head in disbelief. Her heart, far from being a leathery lump, pounded as anger warred for dominance over the instinct to flee.

"All this will be yours if you ally yourself with me."

Megan tensed. Her hands curled into fists.

He held up a hand. "Don't worry, I will not force you to fake emotional attachment to me, all I require is your loyalty, or at least the appearance of it. I ask only for your presence at my side for official functions as well as your support of this hospital's business as Abram Teitel's granddaughter. Of course, you will be required to give up your rented room and take up residence in my family's home, which you will certainly find much more hospitable than where you are presently."

Outraged, Megan started to speak but was overruled by Charles's voice talking loudly over hers.

"I wish to inform you that I do not even require your sexual services," he said with a sneer, as if the mere thought of touching

Megan was anathema. "I am not an animal and I assure you, I have no intention of taking part in loveless copulation. Once you give me two healthy children of either sex, your body is your own. I will even concede to allow you to continue your medical career as long as it doesn't interfere with your familial duties."

Megan choked.

"As for your personal needs, what you do to whom on your own time is your own business," he said with as little emotion as if he was discussing the operation of a particularly complicated piece of machinery. "However, as I do not wish to be ridiculed as a cuckold, I require your discretion when you indulge in your base dalliances."

For an instant, Megan's gut clenched and she wondered if he knew about Syler. She dismissed the thought at the calm way Charles spoke. There was only one person who could elicit an emotional response in Charles and that was Syler.

"I also demand your word that you will practice safety. I will not allow my household to be polluted with any diseases you may acquire from rolling around in the gutter with whomever as well as prevent the inconvenience of unplanned bastard additions to our family."

Unable to find words, Megan just gaped at him, highly offended. A thin breath of relief came after that. Charles still thought she fucked men. Syler was safe.

Charles continued in his annoying monotone, "If you fulfill these conditions, you will be richly rewarded with a stable life of utmost consequence. That is all." Charles folded his hands on the desktop. "I believe I have been most forthcoming and am awaiting your answer, which I hope you will think about carefully before you throw away the best opportunity of your lifetime."

Silence fell. Megan took a step back and her heel hit the leg of the chair behind her. She collapsed into it and tried to dredge up a semblance of dignity. She held onto the arms of the chair so tightly her fingers dug into the upholstery.

"My answer is still no," Megan said in as calm a voice as she could muster. She steeled herself and glared into Charles's face. "I won't 'ally' myself with you. I won't carry out some domestic farce for this hospital or my family's business or any other reason." Megan stood filled with strength. She held her head high and said, "You will not bring this matter up ever again. If you do, then let's just say once he finds out management has been pestering his granddaughter with unwanted propositions, I'm sure Abram Teitel will not want to deal with this hospital anymore. As well as that, I won't hesitate to report you to HR for harassment. You may be the boss's son, but I can still take your conniving ass to town if you don't leave me the hell alone." Megan crossed her arms over her chest. "That is my final answer." She lowered her voice to a growl and asked, "Do you understand?"

There was a moment of silence.

Megan snapped, "I will not ask you again, Charles. Do you understand?"

"Yes, I believe I do," he answered in a bland voice. "As I hope do you."

"Only too well," Megan said.

With that, Megan whirled and stomped out of the office. Her veins sang with rage but she was fiercely glad that she'd said her piece. Charles would never bother her again.

She didn't want to think about the look of cold calculation that settled on Charles's face as she issued her final ultimatum.

MEGAN SEETHED FOR the rest of the day, only coming out of her mood that evening when she joined Syler for a rooftop barbecue. Megan came straight from the hospital after she finished her paperwork and evening rounds. She didn't even bother to change out of the skirt and blouse she'd had on that day. While Syler tended the grill, Megan told her about her run-in with Charles.

"Finally I told him to leave me the hell alone, and that's how the tale of Charles Brockman and the Nasty Proposal ended," Megan finished by swinging her can of Chu-Hi in a wide arc.

Beside her, Syler paused in arranging the sizzling bits of meat and vegetables on the compact gas grill that sat on the low table between them. At the beginning, Syler looked upset, but as Megan's story progressed, she relaxed and by the end, she was snickering.

"You really told him all that?" Syler asked. She shook her head and put a piece of grilled beef on Megan's plate. "Not that I blame you. What a proposal! Did he actually say loveless copulation? And base dalliances? Good God that man has *chutzpa*."

"You're telling me," Megan said with her mouth full of the juicy morsel.

"So he just let you walk out? It doesn't seem like Charles to give up so easily."

Syler's words sent a thrill of unease down Megan's spine, but she simply shrugged and said, "Maybe he knows when he's beaten."

"Maybe," Syler echoed softly. She paused, head down and hands still. Megan was sure she was about to say something more but Syler just gave her a knee-melting grin and turned her attention back to the grill.

Megan watched as Syler turned over a row of cut green peppers, their skins glistening in the heat. "This is the best barbeque I've ever been to," she said as she happily accepted a few rounds of onion from the grill. "Everything really does taste better outside."

"I'm glad you like it," Syler said. "Until now, I've only had my team up here, but it's more fun with the two of us."

Megan put down her chopsticks. "I hope I'm not monopolizing your schedule and keeping you from spending time with your team. I always used to hate it whenever a friend of mine would suddenly ditch me the second she got a new boyfriend and now I'm making you do that."

"No way," Syler said with easy grace. "I think my team's only too happy I finally have someone to occupy me so I'm not always calling them and bothering them by being lonely and making them hang out with me. Besides, they love doing stuff with you too so it's not like an either-or situation. I just like having you to myself."

"That's good to know," Megan said with a pleased glow. She tended to a row of pumpkin pieces as Syler put more meat on the grill plus a bunch of sausages.

The scent of cooking food filled the air, carried on the warm breeze that swept over the rooftop. Sunset came and went an hour ago. Clusters of candles and twinkling lights illuminated the cozy scene. The talk drifted to other things and ended in a comfortable silence. As the stars revolved over them, Megan relaxed with a cup of homemade peach *kanten* jelly Syler brought up from her kitchen. Syler's phone alarm beeped and broke the stillness of the evening. She picked it up with an apologetic look.

"I've got to go downstairs for a bit. I'm Skyping with my dad and he said my bros are coming over too."

"Okay, you go ahead and I'll clean up here," Megan said. She got to her feet and started gathering up the scattered cushions. Syler stilled Megan's industrious tidying with a gentle hand on her wrist.

"Why don't you come down with me?" Syler asked. A shy flush that Megan thought was the cutest thing she'd ever seen pinked her cheeks. "I'd love to introduce you to my family. I mean, if you're okay with that. They already know I'm seeing the most amazing, beautiful woman in the world, but it's kind of a big step to actually meet face-to-face. Not that it means, you know, what meeting the family usually means in Japan. It's not nearly that serious. My dad's pretty American that way. I mean, just say hello and show them you're not a figment of my imagination." She faltered to a halt. Megan drew in a breath of wonder.

"Really?" Megan ran her hands through her hair, unconsciously smoothing the ruffled strands. "That would be great. I've been wondering what your brothers and dad are like."

"They're all right," Syler said with a nonchalant shrug that didn't do anything to offset her delighted grin. "Kinda like bigger, scruffier, and ruder versions of me."

"Then just my type," Megan said. "I think I like them already."

Megan rolled up the rug and put away the cushions while Syler snuffed the candles and took care of the now-empty dishes and Tupperware containers. The grill was still hot so it was left for later. Together, they headed down the short flight of stairs to Syler's room.

Megan washed the dishes at the designated meat side of the sink while Syler went into the bedroom to begin the call. After she put the last dish away, Megan ducked into the bathroom to brush her teeth and check to make sure her hair wasn't too wind-blown. She peeked into the bedroom.

It was only the second time Megan had been in Syler's room, but the scene felt familiar already. Syler owned the entire building, and had lived on another floor with her now ex-girlfriend.

In contrast to the rest of the apartment, which Syler left bare and unfurnished, the bedroom was comfortable and lived-in with Syler's weights and small collection of books, including two slim volumes Megan was almost certain were Jewish prayer books. She didn't ask about them even though she was curious. If Syler wanted to tell her then Megan would let her speak when she chose.

Syler didn't have either a bed or a futon, a mattress sat directly on the carpet. Having spent a very eventful night there, Megan knew it was good quality and very comfortable.

Instead of the blue sheets that Syler fashioned into a kingly cape when she dressed up as Mordechai for Purim, the ones currently on the mattress and comforter were a crisp white with tiny green stripes running through. Like most things Syler owned, they were classy and understated.

Syler was perched on the somewhat crumpled comforter with a laptop on a pile of books in front of her. She held a can of grapefruit Chu-Hi in one hand and waved it about as she talked animatedly with whoever was on the other side of the call.

"Hey, Meg, come over here," Syler turned from the screen to say. She reached out a hand and Megan shyly stepped over to sit beside Syler. An older man with a stringy, grey ponytail was on the screen. While he didn't physically resemble Syler very much, the way he was sprawled out over the worn brown sofa was so familiar Megan couldn't help but smile.

"*Oton*," Syler addressed her father, "this is Megan Maier, my girlfriend. And Megan, this old fart's my dad, Junpei."

"*Beppin-san da ne!*" Junpei announced by way of greeting. Megan felt her cheeks get a warm glow at the frank words calling her a beauty.

"Oton!"

"Sorry, but I call it like I see it," Junpei said without remorse and took a swig of his beer. "Sai-chan, you always had an eye for a good-looking lady."

"I had an eye for *her*, actually," Megan piped up with pride.

While Syler was busy looking adorably embarrassed, Junpei hooted and said, "I like you, Megan! It looks like you've got a better personality than that light-bottomed Yu—"

"*Sunda hanashi.*" Syler told her father the matter was in the past with those two clipped words.

Megan couldn't stop the jolt of surprise at Syler's abrupt words. Yukina cheated on Syler and broke her heart. Syler had every right to join in on insulting her, but she didn't. Megan's gaze softened. She wouldn't expect anything less of Syler.

"Are you drinking already?" Syler continued in a loud voice. "What time is over there?"

"You're drinking too," Junpei pointed out without missing a beat. "Maybe I'm operating on Japan time, eh?"

"Uh huh, sure. So are the barnyard animals around?"

"Yup," Junpei said. He turned from the screen and hollered, "Boys! Your sister's on the line and she's got somebody she wants you to meet."

Thundering footsteps preceded the screen filling with three curious male faces. Megan gulped. They were indeed big, scruffy versions of Syler, although Megan wasn't sure about the rude part yet. While Syler wore her androgynous beauty effortlessly, her three brothers were unapologetically masculine — sculpted, tanned, and muscled like soccer players. Megan was glad she wasn't straight, because she'd have a terrible time deciding which of the three to fall for.

After a short flurry of introductions, Megan listened to a few well-chosen family legends from the four men of the Terada family while Syler lounged back on the bed. She nursed her beverage with an amused look on her face and occasionally interjected a comment or two.

After a particularly amusing anecdote, Syler sat up and scooted over to sit next to Megan. "Okay guys, you've talked Meg's ear off long enough. How about saying goodnight, then?"

"Sure," the youngest brother, Gene, said. He fixed his sister with a knowing look. "We don't want to keep you from spending some quality time with your special lady."

"That's right," Syler said. She made a gun with her fingers and pointed it at him.

"It was very nice meeting you all," Megan piped up to hide her sudden flush of embarrassment. She was glad Syler's family was so open, but it was going to take a bit of getting used to.

Junpei poked his head into visual pickup range. "Take good care of Sai-chan for us, now."

"I will," Megan said.

"Come and visit sometime soon, eh?"

Syler said, "Oton, you know things are really busy at the hospital. You guys should come here." She turned and gave Megan a nudge with her shoulder. Syler lowered her voice and said,

"Unless you want to journey to the land of giant hamburgers and hang out with a bunch of zoo escapees?"

"Sure," Megan said. A warm feeling filled her. "I've only been to the States a couple times to visit my grandparents when I was younger. It might be fun."

"The lady has spoken," Syler said. "Bye guys!" Several good-byes came from the screen and Megan could hardly wait for Syler to tap on the keyboard before she threw herself into Syler's arms and pressed her back into the mounds of pillows.

"It was great talking to your family, but now I believe," Megan said in a throaty purr, "I owe you some payback for your good work this morning."

"Mmm, yes you do."

Strong arms surrounded Megan and she bent her head to claim Syler's neck with hungry lips. Syler's breath quickened as Megan kissed a line down to the dip at the base of her throat. She stroked her hands over Syler's trim body and found her hands gently guided to cup firm breasts. Megan was just getting into a good position where she could unbutton Syler's shirt when a chorus of male voices froze her in place.

"*Gochiso sama!*" They called out, thanking Megan and their sister for the show.

Syler spat out a curse and launched herself toward the laptop where the screen showed her brothers' grinning faces.

"Oh God, Meg, I'm so sorry!" Syler slammed the laptop closed and shoved it into the corner. She finished off by throwing a bunch of towels over it. She flopped back down next to Megan and raked her hands through her hair. Syler gave Megan an apologetic look. "I can't believe I was such an airhead. I hope you're not too embarrassed."

"It's all right," Megan said. She rubbed her hands over her face and found her cheeks hot, but soon she was laughing with Syler. "At least now they know we're not just making it up to get attention."

"I don't think we need to convince anyone how much we mean to each other," Syler said in a voice that turned Megan's thoughts to a sultry, tempting place.

"No, we don't." Megan leveled Syler with a heated gaze, letting her eyes roam freely. Under her scrutiny, Syler's cheeks flushed. A wonderful heat breathed into life within Megan.

"So you were about to give me some payback? What exactly did you have in mind?"

Megan paused and pursed her lips for a moment. She had an idea that would be quite fun to try and she hoped Syler would be willing to let her.

"Get undressed and get under the covers," Megan said in a low, but commanding voice.

In accordance with Megan's order, Syler quickly stripped off her clothes and slipped into the bed.

"Hands where I can see them," Megan told her.

"All right," Syler said. Obediently, she rolled over with both arms outside the cocoon of her quilts. Under the green and white patterned cover, her long body was curled slightly in repose.

Just looking at Syler, knowing she was ready and waiting for her sent a thrill through Megan. Her breath came faster and her body trembled with desire.

Megan forced herself to keep a level tone as she said, "These are the rules. I can't touch you and you can't touch me until I say so. Now, what are you going to do?"

"I can't touch you?" Syler asked with a puzzled tilt of her head.

"That's right," Megan said. She paused before saying in a coy voice, "But you can use your oral skills on me."

Syler got a sudden, sly look on her face. "So I can tell you what to do."

Megan just nodded and pulled herself into a ladylike sitting position with her hands clasped in her lap.

"Command me," she purred.

"God, that's so hot," Syler murmured. She gave Megan a long look and said, "If there's anything you don't want to do, just say *pass* and I'll think of something else. Is that all right?"

"Very," Megan said. Her heart thumped. Every nerve ending in her body came alive with anticipation.

"Good." Syler shifted under the covers and propped her head up on one hand. "First, take off your blouse. Slowly." She drew out the word with dark enjoyment. Megan swallowed hard at the tone, coupled with the lingering look Syler graced her with.

Taking her time, Megan unbuttoned her blouse and slipped it off. With a word from Syler, Megan rose up onto her knees and soon her skirt was on the floor next to her discarded blouse. A low, "Keep going," encouraged Megan to strip off her slip and camisole as well. With every motion, she was very aware of the hot throb of arousal building between her legs. Her nipples were tingling and hard, her electrified state was not helped at all by Syler's forthright appreciation. That day, Megan had decided to wear sexy lace-trimmed thigh-high stockings instead of her usual plain ones and by the hungry look in Syler's eyes, it had been a good decision. The weight of Syler's gaze was almost tangible and Megan shivered under it.

"Are you cold, baby girl?"

"Not at all," Megan answered. She tilted one shoulder in a sultry pose. She let one strap of her bra come down, enjoying the catch in Syler's breath as she did so. "Now what do you want me to do?"

"Show me your tits." The words were low, dirty, and urgent.

Megan's body flooded with desire. She reached for the clasp between her breasts. With a twist of her fingers, Megan freed herself to the air and Syler's eyes.

"Get them in your hands," Syler told her in a tight, breathless voice. "Play with yourself, tease me."

A flush sprang to her cheeks, but Megan did as she was told. She cupped herself and stroked her own nipples into taut peaks. Taking a bit of liberty, Megan leaned forward and supported herself on one hand. She let her breasts swing free for a moment. She arched her back and brought her hand up once more to cup her breast. Megan dragged her thumb over her nipple as the thickening bud came alive.

Under the covers, Syler's long legs moved against each other.

"Does that feel good?" Syler asked.

"Yes, it does."

"Are you getting turned on?"

"God, yes I am."

"Tell me how hard you are."

"They're like little bullets," Megan said. The burgeoning feeling of wetness between her legs increased as a twinge of arousal ignited Megan's insides. She bit back a soft moan and breathed, "Please Syler, I need more."

"You're so sweet Meg," Syler said. She was bent almost double. The quilt fell away from her. Megan was treated to a nice view of Syler's firm breasts and slender body.

Syler didn't move to cover herself. Her voice was strained as she said, "Turn around. I want you on your knees, ass in the air and spread."

Too aroused to be shy anymore, Megan turned her back to Syler. She rested on her folded arms and pressed her breasts to the soft quilt under her knees. Her hair spilled over her shoulders. It pooled around her face in a wavy, golden-brown cloud. She spread her knees and arched her back to raise her hips higher. Her thighs were slick, her panties soaked through with the essence of her arousal. Megan closed her eyes. Syler would be able to tell how much their play affected her.

With her head down, Megan couldn't see Syler, but she could hear Syler's harsh breaths and appreciative murmurs. Megan had a hard time keeping her own breaths even. She wriggled her hips, silently begging for permission to do something, anything to ease the tension that gripped her.

"Get your hand in your panties and show me your pussy. I want you to touch yourself for me."

The words hit her right in the belly and Megan gasped. She was hungry to be touched. Hungry enough to do it herself. The muscles of her thighs clenched and trembled. She had to fight to keep her hips from bucking as she slid one hand up the inside of her leg. With a low moan, Megan pulled aside the crotch of her panties and bared herself. The air hitting her slick skin was cold, but Megan soon heated up again as she slipped a finger into her slippery folds, then one more. The touch brought a wave of arousal, only inflaming Megan's body as she slowly rocked herself back and forth, riding her hand in a wanton display of self-pleasure.

"Fuck that's hot, Meg," Syler purred. "Good girl, get yourself wet."

"Syler, I need you," Megan whimpered. She raised her head and said, "I'm almost there, Syler. I want you to take me over. I want you on me and in me. I need you to touch me. Please."

"Come here then, baby girl," Syler said. She held the covers open and Megan threw herself into Syler's arms. She still had her stockings on, but she didn't care. Megan's body was on fire for Syler's touch. She was desperate for release. Megan impatiently kicked herself free of her panties and welcomed the urgent hands on her hips that guided Megan to straddle Syler's long body.

"My God Meg, you on your knees for me was the hottest thing I have ever seen in my entire life," Syler growled into her ear. "Are you ready for me, baby girl?"

"Yes," Megan said. "Take me Syler. Right now."

With a quick, fluid motion, Syler rolled them over so Megan was underneath her. Megan tensed her legs around Syler's body and let out a quick moan of pleasure as Syler slipped into her.

"You're soaking wet," Syler breathed.

"Don't stop," Megan panted into Syler's shoulder. She canted her hips as Syler started to move, thrusting in and out of her. She was flying, only able to ride on the waves of pleasure as her body welcomed the touch. Megan moved with Syler, hungry for more. Syler's breasts pressed against hers. Megan greedily reveled in the long expanse of bare skin on her own.

"Hang on to me Meg," Syler said in a tight voice. "I want to come with you."

A rush of desire filled her. Megan trembled with suppressed tension. She let Syler guide her so her thigh was pressed hard against Syler's wet sex. The feeling of Syler spread against her as well as within her ignited the first sparks of release. Megan couldn't hold back the strangled moans as their lips met in a plundering kiss. Their hips moved in counterpoint against each other until Syler broke the kiss with a quick gasp.

"I'm almost there, Meg. Tell me you are too."

"Yes I am, Syler, please!" Megan let out a short cry and threw her head back as the first wave of release whipped through her. Syler followed her an instant later and the shockwave of Syler's climax coursed through Megan as if they were one. Megan's world narrowed to a pinpoint of bright light. She could only focus on the explosion of pleasure Syler's fingers stroked into life between her thighs. The waves came like a rollercoaster. Megan let them take her until she melted into Syler's arms and lay there, unable to do anything other than take in deep, shuddering breaths.

After the last tremors of her own climax faded, Syler collapsed on top of her and Megan stroked back the sweat-damp hair from Syler's forehead and kissed her softly, first on the temple. She moved down to her ear and finally captured her mouth. Syler's breathing still came fast and her lips were eager and hungry. In response, Megan's body hummed with energy. Even as she shifted under Syler, shocks of pleasure zinged through her.

"Fuck Meg," Syler said between gasps, "I'm not done yet."

"I don't think I am either," Megan said. Her body was awake and charged. She grabbed onto Syler's shoulders as their lips came together with urgent, breathless hunger. The kiss broke.

"I want your mouth," Megan panted.

"You have it," Syler said and moved to kiss her again but Megan stopped her with a soft touch.

"Not here," she said.

With a look of understanding, Syler kissed the fingers on her lips before removing them. She sat back on her heels and leaned over to quickly grab the two pillows from where they had fallen off to one side.

"How about sitting up for a second?" Syler asked gently.

Confused, Megan did and Syler tucked the pillows behind Megan's head, which raised her enough so Megan could see down the length of her own body. Syler was giving her the means to watch everything Syler was going to do to her.

Megan threw her head back as Syler slowly moved to kiss her neck, then trailed down lower over her breasts and belly. Soon Megan arched back against the firm mattress as Syler bowed down between her legs.

"I want you to spread wide for me," Syler murmured as she nuzzled Megan's sex. She paused to drop a kiss onto her proud clit, already standing hard within her generous inner lips. "Is that okay?"

"Yes. Syler, I want you to have all of me," Megan answered. She let out a gasp of desire as Syler bent her knees and lifted Megan's feet from the crumpled bedcover. Syler held her legs open and Megan felt nothing but air caressing her. Lying back, legs open as wide as she could get them, Megan had never been so exposed. Syler could see everything from her wet, gaping pussy lips to the puckered ring between her buttocks. Just knowing that gave Megan a rush and she jerked her hips, begging silently for Syler to take her.

"God you're so beautiful," Syler said. "I need you so bad, Meg." She lowered her head and gently sucked Megan's inner lips into her mouth, slowly teasing her with soft kisses and rough tonguing. Megan forgot her momentary shyness and rocked back and forth, loving every inch of Syler's mouth on her. She heard her own voice making little mewling sounds of pleasure and she brought her hands up to cup her breasts, rolling her hard nipples between her fingers as she watched Syler making love to her.

"Can I put one in you?" Syler asked between deep kisses that left Megan shivering and breathless.

"Yes, please," Megan said. The idea alone gave her a kick of arousal. "Yes Syler, I want you in me."

"Meg, I'm going to let you go now, can you take over here?" Syler asked as she carefully took her hands from where she'd been pressing Megan's thighs open. With a tight grunt of understanding, Megan took her hands from her chafed nipples and hooked them under her bent knees. She missed playing with her nipples, but forgot all about that as Syler slid a finger into her. Syler paused, holding still as Megan looked down to where Syler entered her.

"I want you to do something," Megan said, her voice tight. "I want to hear you call me by the name closest to my heart. My true name."

"Of course, my sweet Meirav," Syler said.

The sound of her Hebrew name on Syler's lips was like an electric shock to her spine. Megan arched and let out a soft cry of delight. "More, Syler, I need more of you."

"Like this?" Syler asked. She slipped free from Megan, then pushed two fingers into her with a wet sound.

"Yes, thank you, oh yes," Megan babbled. She was in heaven.

In the wake of Megan's garbled pleas, Syler thrust gently in and out of her. The movement pulled Megan's lips tight between her spread legs. Each time Syler buried herself deep, Megan let out a moan of pleasure and arched her back.

Syler said, "God that's so hot, Meg."

Megan couldn't find the words to answer. She drank in the sight of Syler sliding into her. She had never felt as worshipped as she did that moment. Every move was slow, savoring her. It was nice, but it wasn't enough. Not by a long shot. Megan didn't want gentleness or procedure just then. She wanted action. She wanted to be fucked hard and eaten until she screamed Syler's name.

"Do me harder," Megan said.

Syler picked up the pace. Megan's breasts jumped along with the force of Syler's thrusts.

"Like that?"

"God, yes," she hissed.

Megan bucked her hips as Syler went to work. She fastened her lips on Megan's clit, batting her into a frenzy of arousal with her tongue while pumping in and out of her, sometimes licking down to Megan's stretched opening. Megan couldn't take her eyes from the glorious sight of Syler between her legs. Her belly fluttered as the first jolts of her climax thundered through her.

"I'm coming!" Megan gasped out. Her thighs shuddered from holding herself back and when Syler looked up, locking eyes with her, Megan lost the little control she had. She bucked hard as her climax broke. She spasmed, head thrown back, cresting the waves that shook her entire body while Syler continued pumping her.

"It's so good," Megan cried out as a rushing fullness started to build up between her legs. "Oh God, Syler, I'm coming too hard."

"Give it to me," Syler growled against Megan's rigid clit. "I want all of your sweet juice."

Megan let go with a hot gush that spilled down between her spread cheeks. She shook with the need to empty herself, to give everything she had to the woman she loved.

"Yes do it," Syler said before she brought her mouth down over Megan and sucked hard. The fingers inside Megan stilled as the last jolts of her climax faded. They left her with a slick whisper and Megan twitched as a final spurt of hot liquid came out with them. The wet pressure over her clit eased and Megan let go of her knees. Her legs flopped limply to the messy comforter. Her chest heaved. She was in shock at what she'd just done.

"My God," Syler said. She gathered Megan up in her arms and held her tightly. "I have no idea where that came from, but I have never been so turned on in my life. God you are fucking amazing."

"That's good," Megan said. She looked down between her legs a little sheepishly, expecting to see a huge wet stain. "Um, did I make a mess?"

"No sweetheart," Syler said. She kissed Megan on the temple and said, "I bet it felt like Niagara Falls down there, but really it was just a trickle. Thank you for sharing that with me. Just so you know, I fucking loved it."

"Okay," Megan said. In the wake of her explosion she was somewhat at a loss. "As long as it wasn't gross."

"No way. Try extremely hot."

Limp and happy, Megan snuggled up to Syler. Supple and strong arms wrapped around her. Megan dropped a quick kiss to the soft skin of Syler's chest, then looked up into her face and said, "It was hot for me too." Megan froze as a thought occurred to her. "Did you swallow me?" she asked in a small voice.

Syler's low chuckle answered her. "I might have. Does that bother you?"

"No, not if it doesn't bother you."

"Good, because I was honored to take what you gave me."

Reassured but admittedly still a bit self-conscious, Megan snuggled into Syler's hold.

They lay like that for a while, just talking and sharing the intimate moment until Megan was almost asleep. Syler prodded her into a leisurely bath time together and finally Megan surrendered herself to the lure of the soft depths of the bed, held in Syler's arms.

Chapter Four

"CAN YOU DO me a favor?" Megan asked when she met Syler in the hospital the next morning.

"Sure," Syler answered. She shifted her armful of files so they were balanced on one hip. She dropped her voice to a low purr and said, "Name it Meg, and I'll do it."

Megan flushed at the innuendo in Syler's voice. She glanced around. The corridor they were in led off the main lobby. It was empty at that hour of the morning. Megan swallowed a nervous giggle and said in a rush, "I want you to check and see if I'm walking funny."

"No problem," Syler said. She looked at Megan with concern and pain in her eyes. "Are you okay? Did I overdo it last night?"

"Not at all." Megan flushed with pleasure. She loved being spread wide for Syler. "I'm actually feeling much too satisfied for my own good but I don't want to broadcast it. Luka's finally stopped mentioning the 'shower incident' as he likes to call it."

Relief loosened Syler's posture. "Glad to hear that. And it's not like I wouldn't be checking out your butt anyway. Go ahead, sweetheart. Strut your stuff."

Megan rolled her eyes theatrically. She took a few steps down the hallway before she turned and trotted back. The elevator at the end of the hall pinged and the doors opened. Megan steeled herself as a bunch of nurses piled out. She didn't stop walking in an attempt to appear as normal as possible. Syler didn't speak either, just gave her a nod and a thumbs up before she fell into step with Megan.

"I'm staying here with Sakura-chan tonight," Syler said. They reached the wide concrete stairway and started climbing up side-by-side.

"Date night?"

"That's right."

"So where is Toshi taking Chiho this month?" Megan enjoyed hearing about the monthly outings Sakura's parents went on. As if it was the most natural thing in the world, Syler gave up a night of her time once a month to spend with Sakura, allowing her parents a night off from their exhausting vigil.

Syler grinned. "It's Chiho's turn to decide so they're probably going to karaoke where Toshi can show off his power moves. Tomorrow I'm gonna have to sit through like an hour of videos she took on her phone."

"Sounds fun."

"I'm sure it is, but I think I'll be having a better time playing Zoo Cards with Sakura-chan here."

"That does sound like a good time. It is okay if I gatecrash your party?" Megan asked. "I don't have anything on my schedule for tonight and I'm pretty good at Zoo Cards if I do say so myself."

Syler's face broke into a brilliant grin. "You're always welcome. I'm warning you, Sakura-chan's a bit of a card shark. You may just have to slink home in defeat."

"We'll see about that," Megan said.

They reached the floor where the Pediatrics Department lived. Syler stopped with her hand on the door lever before she opened it. She glanced around the deserted stairway before she swooped in and planted a firm but swift kiss on Megan's mouth.

"Syler!" Megan whispered.

"Sorry." Syler didn't look repentant in the least. "It's just you're so—"

Her words cut off as Megan pressed her up against the door with a kiss of her own. It was considerably longer and hotter than the previous one. Megan drew back and took a breath. She ran her tongue over her lip and tried not to smile at Syler's stunned expression.

"Mmm, very nice," Megan said.

"Yeah, it was. Wow, Meg."

Megan smirked to herself. She put her hand over Syler's and eased the door open. They stepped into the hallway.

"See you tonight," Megan said. She waved as she went on her way to morning rounds. Her lips tingled from the brief kisses. Her body burned for more. The extra energy manifested itself in Megan floating though her rounds and examination hours.

At noon, Megan was on her way to the cafeteria when she ran into a slender, elegant woman in an expensive dress. She was fixing her perfect updo in a small gold mirror when she caught sight of Megan. She stuffed her mirror into her handbag and quickly walked away. Her stilettos clacked against the tiled floor.

Megan broke into a trot and caught up to the fleeing woman as if people normally bolted when they saw her. She prayed Charles didn't see her talking to Nikky Okamoto's mother after he'd warned her to stay away from them. Megan seethed inwardly at the memory of Charles heavy-handedly telling her that her suspicions of abuse in the household came second to the Okamoto family's reputation as a wealthy supporter of the hospital.

"Fabia, how nice to run into you today," Megan said, a little breathless from her run. "Are you here with Nikky?"

"No, he's at school." Her words were clipped. She didn't slow down.

Megan winced internally at the pronoun. While Nikky was completely certain she was a girl, Fabia refused to believe it.

"Is everything all right at home?" Megan asked quietly.

"Fine," Fabia said.

"Has your husband come back from his business trip?" Megan asked. Fabia shook her head and Megan breathed again. "You still have my card, right? Remember you have a safe place if you need to get out."

Fabia didn't meet Megan's eyes. Her posture was defensive. "How did your husband like the cufflinks?"

"Pardon me?" The question caught her off-guard. An instant later, Megan remembered the tiger-eye and platinum cufflinks she'd bought at Fabia's boutique with Syler in mind. While Megan hadn't said *husband* explicitly, she said just enough for Fabia to assume. The old habit came only too naturally. Megan's gut clenched with guilt. She hated to lie about Syler the way she'd lied about Yasu.

Fabia turned sharp eyes to Megan, who manufactured a laugh. Her mind worked frantically. The thought of just coming out crossed Megan's mind, but she shut it down. Fabia couldn't accept the fact her own child was transgender. Blurting out that her assumed husband was actually her girlfriend would only lose the tiny amount of trust Megan managed to build.

"I didn't give them yet," Megan said in a flippant way.

"You didn't?" Fabia's deep red lips curled as she spoke. As she had in the boutique, her eyes went to Megan's hand — looking for the ring that was no longer there. Megan twitched in alarm.

Megan blurted out, "Not that I don't like them, they're gorgeous. I'm just waiting for, uh, a special day. To give, um, well. Yes." Megan cringed. Her words sounded blatantly false to her own ears. At the boutique, they'd spoken Japanese. Pronouns were much more difficult to avoid in English. Megan gritted her teeth and smiled through her discomfort.

Fabia's lips thinned but she didn't reply. Instead, she reached into her bag and thrust something at Megan. Automatically her fingers closed over it. Something sharp poked into her palm. Megan looked down in surprise at the purple-jeweled butterfly barrette she gave to Nikky. It was the twin of the one she wore in her hair.

"You can keep that," Fabia said. "I don't need you encouraging my son in his delusion."

Without another word, Fabia swept away and burst through the doors to the parking lot. Left behind, Megan stared sadly at the returned barrette. She slipped it into her pocket and went back to her desk with a heavy heart. Worry for Nikky stole her appetite completely.

A FEW HOURS later, Megan packed up the last of her reports and stretched both hands over her head. The setting sun slipped in through the blinds and cast golden pink bars of light over the landscape of desks. Several other doctors sat at their desks, a few tapped away at their computers and others scribbled handwritten reports like the ones Megan just finished. She glanced at the PHS where it lay on the desk. No new messages. She picked it up and fired off a quick, "What are you doing?" text to Syler. The answer came back right away.

        Hanging with Sakura. Breaking out Zoo Cards
        soon. Come on up if you're finished your reports
        and not afraid to get your butt kicked.

A happy warmth filled her. Megan stood and stashed her PHS in her pocket. She pulled her hair back into a ponytail as she raced up the stairs. Outside Sakura's room, she put on a fresh hygienic mask and rubbed alcohol on her hands. She knocked and slid the door open at Syler's cheerful greeting.

The scene that met Megan's eyes was welcoming and cute. Syler was in scrubs, capped and masked, sitting cross-legged at the foot of the bed, while Sakura was propped up on a number of pillows across from her. Sakura was hooked up to several machines and had tubes and wires tethered all over her small form. Megan's heart lurched as she recalled Syler's heartbroken admission that there was nothing more she could do for Sakura. They could only wait and let nature take its course.

Sakura looked up and waved. She had a large violently-blue dragon-looking thing in her arms.

"*Kon'chiyaa* Megan-sensei," Sakura chirped in greeting.

"*Konnichi wa*," Megan replied properly. She pulled over a chair and plopped down next to the bed. She reached out and patted the dragon. "That's a fine-looking fellow you have there."

"This is Slyly," Sakura said. She held him out with both hands. Megan tried not to notice how fragile her thin arms were in her pink pajamas. "You can pet him but you can't hug him. He doesn't like that 'cause he has to do flips when the Carp get a home run. He's their mascot and my best friend. Because I love the Carp."

"Really?" Megan said. Obligingly, she patted the mascot's head. She glanced over to Syler, who was also masked, but Megan knew by her eyes she was smiling. "I wonder what the mascot of Syler's favorite team is?" she asked innocently.

Sakura opened her mouth to answer, but Syler silenced her with a hooded look.

"Don't even think about spilling my secret," Syler said. She scooted across the crumpled blanket and lightly tickled the small girl's sides. Sakura screeched in glee and launched herself into Syler's lap. Both Megan and Syler jumped at her sudden move. Syler managed to catch her before she dislodged anything. Slyly got squashed between them.

Once her heart started beating again, Megan faked annoyance. She puffed out her cheeks for a moment before she said, "It's no use to hide from me, *Saira-sensei*. I'll find out what team you support eventually."

"Maybe. But not today," Syler said. She folded Sakura into her arms, careful of the tubes and wires. Her eyes were challenging. "Okay Meg, get up here and let's break out the Zoo Cards.

There's tissues over there for when you lose and cry."

"We'll see who cries," Megan said. She kicked off her shoes and clambered up onto the bed while Sakura squirmed in excitement and giggled. Her skirt prevented her from sitting the way Syler was, so she primly folded her legs underneath herself. She leveled a long look across the bed and intoned, "Let's get this party started. Deal the cards."

Syler grabbed the deck. She handed it to Sakura. The child stopped giggling. She cut the deck and shuffled with the lightning-fast skill of a professional dealer. Megan met Syler's eyes over Sakura's head. For the first time, Megan regretted her boastful approach. The cards hit the table and the battle began.

In short time, Megan lost three games to the combined forces of Syler and Sakura.

As Sakura shuffled for a new game, Syler said, "This one's the last. I'm getting tired."

"I'm not," Sakura said in a stubborn voice.

"Actually, I'm a bit tired myself," Megan said. During the games, Sakura's energy level slowly dropped even though she struggled to stay alert. Her skin was bluish and pale. "I should go after this."

"Okay, but I'm still gonna beat you," Sakura said.

"Do your best," Megan replied.

The game commenced. They played in silence. Even though her little head drooped, Sakura let nothing get by her. She swiped a pile of trump cards, penguins, from a three-turn trick Megan built and tried to protect with all her might. As Megan put on a show of sulking, Sakura fixed Megan with a long look.

"Do you have a boyfriend?" she asked.

"No, I don't."

"Oh," Sakura said. She picked up a card from the pile and integrated it into her hand with a perfect poker face. "Do you have a girlfriend?"

Megan squeaked. Behind her mask, her cheeks got hot. She didn't know how to answer that. She shuffled her cards together to stall for time.

"It's okay Meg," Syler said. She brushed back Sakura's hair in a tender gesture. "She's cool."

"In that case," Megan said. She straightened her back and tilted her head with pride. "Yes, I do."

"Is she pretty?"

"I wouldn't say pretty," Megan said. She tapped her finger on her hygienic mask and studied Syler carefully. Syler's attention was on the fan of cards in Sakura's hand, but Megan knew she was smiling. "She's more than pretty. My girlfriend is the most beautiful person I have ever met."

Sakura nodded thoughtfully before she threw out a blue lion, that was absolutely no use to Megan. After she stared at the card like it was a suddenly appearing cockroach, Megan huffed and drew a card from the pile in the middle. Another blue lion. With a grimace, Megan shoved the card into her hand.

"Does she like ice cream?" Sakura asked.

"Not really," Megan answered with a smirk. "She prefers salty things like chips and peanuts but she eats all my chocolate snacks if I have them."

"Hm. Does she let you choose the TV channel?"

"Every time except when Crime Scene Woman is on."

"What's her favorite color?"

"I'm not sure, but I think it should be purple."

"Why?"

"Because I always remember the time she wore it. She looked like a hero, showing up just at the right moment," Megan answered with more frankness than she planned. The image of Syler striding into the scrub room of the Angel Hand Clinic, resplendent in purple scrubs was forever burned into her mind. The injured young man on the operating table wasn't the only person Syler saved that day.

"She sounds funny."

"I agree. She's pretty funny. And smart, and cool." Her eyes met Syler's. "And the center of my universe."

Sakura pursed her lips and hummed in the way Japanese people did when they didn't really understand what someone was talking about. She picked up a card and discarded it.

Syler bent her head and asked Sakura in a low voice, "Do you want to know who she is?"

"Yeah!"

Syler paused. Her eyes locked with Megan's for an instant before she said, "She's me."

Sakura's eyes and mouth went perfectly round. She twisted to look from Syler to Megan.

"Do you have sleepovers?" Sakura asked.

Syler turned her head and let out a cough, which sounded a lot like a laugh.

"Yes, we do," Megan said.

"Lucky! You can play Zoo Cards anytime you want."

"Oh yeah," Syler replied. "We play tons of fun games."

As Sakura pouted, Megan thought her entire face was going to burst into flames. She bit her lip and put down a pair of green turtles.

A few more hands in and Sakura's little head nodded in exhaustion. She cuddled up to Syler and her eyes drifted closed. Syler very gently took the cards from her hands and gathered up the rest. It didn't matter who won or who lost. The end of the game was coming and nobody could stop it.

Megan stood. Syler cradled Sakura to her chest with a mother's gentleness. She bent her head to press a kiss to the sleeping child's forehead through her mask. Megan felt as if she were interrupting a private moment. She eased herself off the bed and stepped into her shoes. She stood up but couldn't bring herself to leave.

"If she was mine," Syler whispered in a broken voice. She trailed off with a shake of her head. The pain in Syler's voice froze Megan on the spot.

Syler's eyes squeezed shut. A tear slipped down her cheek. Syler angrily swiped at it with the back of one hand.

"Fuck," she spat in English. Syler stopped, swallowed, and continued in the same language, "Meg, if she was mine, I would take her to the States. I'd get her on the list for the transplants that could save her life. Fuck this country and their age limits. I discussed this with her parents and I get why they chose this route, but if she was mine, I'd take the entire earth on my shoulders to give her a fighting chance. Fuck everything else. If she was mine, I would give her the chance to live."

Megan froze. A fist of tension grabbed her chest. She could barely get the words out. "But she isn't yours."

"I know," Syler said. She swiped at her eyes again. Her words were sharp. "Do you think I don't know that?" She grabbed onto the cotton of her scrub pants and hissed out another curse. Over Sakura's sleeping body, Syler was bent almost double. Megan ached for her, but she had nothing to say.

Syler spoke first.

"This is why I'm never having one," she said, more to herself than Megan. Syler ground the palm of one hand into her eyes. When she spoke, the words were halting and muffled. "I can't do it. I can't accept the fact that I might have to say goodbye some-day. Illness, accident, it doesn't care how old you are or who's waiting for you. I can't do it, Meg. I swore I wouldn't. I've seen it too many times and I swore it would never be me. Fuck me, I tried to escape it but it still caught up with me."

Megan couldn't stand still any more. She put her arms around Syler and held her. Syler trembled in her embrace. She turned her head and buried it against Megan's shoulder. Her breaths were labored and shaky. Megan freed an arm briefly to take a tissue from the box on the bedside table.

"Ironic," Syler said with a crooked grin as she took the tissue and blew her nose into it. Megan wasn't sure if she meant who ended up needing a tissue or something else.

They stayed that way, like the three of them were a human matryoshka doll, sheltering in each other. Megan wished she could shield Syler from all the pain in the world, but she couldn't. The only thing Megan could do was exist. She brushed her hand over Syler's shoulder and rested her palm on Syler's chest. Syler's heartbeat thrummed against her skin. Megan pressed a kiss to her temple.

"I'm here," Megan said.

"I know," Syler said for the second time that night. She lay a hand over Megan's. "I'm sorry for being such a downer."

"Don't be sorry," Megan said "You can't help the way you feel. Remember I'm here for you. Believe that."

Syler nodded. She cradled Sakura to her breast as if she would never let go.

Chapter Five

THE NEXT TWO weeks passed in a blur of work and prayer. Syler spent more time at the hospital than out of it. In addition to her usual busy schedule, Syler often sat with Sakura or took her on very short walks around the hospital. Megan couldn't shake the feeling Syler was afraid to leave her alone for too long. After the operation Syler said was the last one her body could take, Sakura rallied. She had more good days than bad and even gained a tiny bit of weight. But the end was coming for her. Megan had seen it many times before and she knew this was Sakura's last peak. How long until the eventual decline was up to no earthly person.

With Syler's time taken up with Sakura, Megan spent a lot of time in solitude, which she didn't mind because it gave her the chance to play her newest *Zenith of the Dead* video game. Oddly enough, she was left alone on another front as well. Perhaps in response to Megan's refusal, Charles kept an exceptionally low profile in the hospital. In fact, Megan hadn't seen him much at all since his ill-fated proposal. Maybe he was avoiding her. That was fine with Megan. She didn't particularly wish to see his face either.

After a long and tiring day, Megan walked back to her apartment alone. When she reached her door, her body relaxed. She instinctively craved the soft comfort of her futon and the peace of her sanctuary. She was happy. Perfectly and completely happy for the first time in as long as she could remember.

The first thing Megan noticed when she opened the front door was the gust of wind that whipped through her apartment. She shivered and looked around in confusion. Had she left a window open? The door eased shut behind her. Megan flipped on the overhead light. Her bag fell to the floor with a thump. She stared in shock at the cracked glass of the doors leading from her balcony.

A sick chill raced down her spine. Megan threw herself toward her bedroom in a blind panic. The sight that met her knocked the breath from her lungs.

Her herd of boxes sat on the floor, all of them ripped open. The contents were rifled, but nothing appeared to be missing, not even her passport or any of her jewelry. Whoever was there wasn't interested in valuables. They came for something else. Megan's chest seized up. She grabbed the front of her blouse and sank to her knees. Even as her vision narrowed to a pinpoint and her entire body shook, she crawled over to her closet.

She had to believe it was untouched. The one box that she hadn't looked at since she packed up her clinic, the one she purposely shoved to the farthest reaches of the closet as if she could eradicate its existence by shutting it away from her eyes. Her clawing hands grabbed at the box. It was far too light and tumbled end over end into her lap. The contents were gone. Only a few remaining papers listed against each other.

Megan's strength gave out and she collapsed onto the floor, just short of her folded-up futon. Her mind was blank and her hands were useless with shaking. The reality of what she had done came crashing back as if it were all new again.

For an instant, Megan considered running away. She could leave everything behind her and remove herself from Syler's life. Someone like Megan didn't deserve to be happy. She didn't have any right to allow others to share her sham of a life.

Just as quickly as the thought came, Megan's common sense banished it. What good would that do, other than to callously injure the one person Megan had come to love more than anyone else, and who loved her in return? Until Syler decided otherwise, Megan would not leave her.

She hadn't realized she'd dialed Syler's number until she heard the voice in her ear. Guilt and fear stole her breath and Megan sat on the cold floor, numb and silent until the note of concern filtered through.

"Meg, answer me, are you okay? Please, baby girl, talk to me."

"Syler I—" Megan's voice gave out. She wished she had never called. *I need you.* She ached to say the words, but couldn't.

"Are you at home?"

"...yes."

"Stay right there."

Megan sat and stared at nothing until strong arms came

around her from behind. Syler's panting breaths were warm against her skin. Even as her heart cried out in gratitude, Megan shrank away from the comforting embrace.

"Sweetheart, what happened?" Syler asked. She was out of breath as if she came from wherever she'd been at a dead sprint.

"Someone was here," Megan choked. She closed her eyes and gave into the urge to nestle back against Syler. "Someone broke into my apartment while I was out."

"What did they take?"

"Some...some documents."

"Anything valuable?"

"No. At least not to anyone else."

"I'm calling the police."

"No!" Megan jerked out of Syler's arms and whirled on her. "No, please don't!" Her heart felt like it would explode. A buzzing sound filled her ears and Megan clutched at her head. "Please no. They won't do anything and I'll just be filling out forms all night. Please." Megan quailed at the note of desperation in her voice, but she could not let the police become involved.

"It's all right, everything's going to be all right. Just talk to me, please Meg. Why don't you want me to call the police?"

"I don't want them to know."

"You're shaking. Come on, let's get out of here." Syler let go of Megan and stood. "I'll patch up the window and you can come over to my place. You can stay as long as you want. I don't like the idea of you staying here with no lock on the balcony."

Megan bit her lip and nodded. She couldn't feel anything. Her panic receded and left nothing in its wake.

"Will you be okay here for a moment?"

Megan nodded again. Her mind whirled. A sick sense of dread grabbed her through the numbness. The inevitable truth was barreling down on her. She owed Syler the knowledge of what she'd done. She owed it to them both. Megan made up her mind to accept whatever came from her confession. She shakily got to her feet. If it was the end, at least Megan would have the memories. Nothing could take them from her.

Belying Megan's bleak thoughts, a cheerful and supportive Syler came back with a roll of duct tape and the remnants of a cardboard box.

"Okay, I cleaned up and fixed the hole in the glass as best I could. The lock's still good but you might want to take anything valuable with you, just in case."

"Thanks," Megan said. She raised her eyes to Syler, who stood before her with careless grace. For the first time, Megan saw she was in scrubs.

"Were you working? Oh goodness, are you on shift now? I'm so sorry —"

"No, no. I was just getting off my shift in after-hours admissions when you called," Syler said. "Now I have forty-eight hours off. So do you."

"That's right," Megan answered with a rush of happiness she didn't deserve to feel. No doubt Syler had adjusted her schedule to mesh with Megan's so they had their days off together. She felt lighter as she collected the items she needed to take with her. A lifetime of living in a disaster-prone country meant Megan had all her documents put together in a slim pouch that she grabbed up and stuck in her bag, along with a few things she'd need to spend the night away. "Okay, I'm ready to go."

They didn't speak much on the way to Syler's apartment, but Megan was very aware of the comforting warmth of Syler's hand resting ever-so-gently on the small of her back. Even the bareness of the living room and the stark kitchen felt safe and welcoming. Megan changed out of her day clothes and soon she curled up against the pillows of Syler's bed with a cup of tea warming her chilled fingers.

"Do you want to talk about it?" Syler asked as she eased down next to Megan with her own cup. "What's upsetting you so much about this break in? What exactly did they take?"

"Can we go up to the roof?" Megan asked in a small voice. When she told Syler about Yasu, who Megan had tacitly allowed Syler to think was her late husband instead of girlfriend, she did it on the roof. If their relationship ended that night, she wanted to be able to make a clean exit.

Syler reached out and gave Megan's knee a quick squeeze, "Sweetheart, anything you can say up there you can say here, I promise. Besides, you're going to make me dread going up to the roof if you keep doing that."

"All right." Megan almost smiled. She gazed into the depths of her cup. She took a deep breath and let it out again.

"If it's too personal, I don't need to hear it."

"No, I want to talk about it."

Syler said. "Are you all right? Not scared or anything because of what happened tonight?"

"I'm still kind of in shock," Megan said. The events of the evening buffeted her. Her sanctuary had been invaded, her privacy destroyed. Her secrets stolen from her. Her hands shook and she clasped the cup tighter.

The deception would end. Megan didn't think she had the strength to tell Syler everything, but she couldn't hide the truth from her anymore. More than that, she didn't want Syler to hear it from anyone else first. Megan nervously licked her bottom lip and said, "I need you to listen and promise you won't interrupt until I'm finished."

"All right," Syler said. She reached out and put a hand over Megan's. "Meg, sweetie, you're shivering. Take your time. Look, if you're not ready — "

"No interruptions, okay?"

Syler nodded. Her fingers around Megan's tightened.

Megan's voice sounded hollow and strange, as if someone else was speaking from a distance. "What was taken — a bunch of the documents from my clinic in Thailand, plus some h-hospital stuff, but there were others about the trust fund." Here she pulled away from Syler and buried her face in the pillow, afraid to even look at her. "For the three children I fostered with Yasu."

Megan stopped and she feared the silence that met her words wasn't only because of the promise not to interrupt. However, a gentle hand on her shoulder led Megan to look up. Syler was looking at her with a calm expression, waiting and patient. There was no anger or accusation and Megan found the strength to continue.

"I didn't want children. I never have," Megan said in a cracked voice. "It was the one thing we didn't agree on. Yasu expected me to get pregnant, but I absolutely would not. I told her that from the start. It was in my online profile and I mentioned it a couple times during our initial interview. Later on, once we'd been together for about a year, I realized she'd assumed I would change my mind, but I didn't. Things hadn't been going well between us for a while, and this just made them worse. There was so much I couldn't give Yasu. I couldn't legally marry her and give her a visa, so she was employed as a clerk at the clinic—on paper anyway. I couldn't let people know we were partners and that Yasu had every right to be there. She had to put up with everyone whispering that she was some kind of no-career parasite and not my equal and that really hit her in the ego.

"She sacrificed so much for me and I wanted to repay that. The only way was for me to provide the whole family experience. I stressed about it for a while, but finally I agreed to foster one child on a trial basis, a two-year-old girl, Sunnee, whose mother was from the village we were in. She had three children actually, but left them with their grandmother while she was working in a motorcycle parts factory in Bangkok after she lost her husband—traffic accident. Seems the god of safe roads doesn't really smile on that corner of the world," Megan said with bleak humor. She paused, found her cup, and took a sip of her tea. She savored the warmth, however temporary.

Megan knit her fingers together around her cup as she tried to stop shivering. She hadn't allowed herself to go back to those days, to revisit the decision that derailed her entire life. The pain waiting there for her was still fresh and raw. "I didn't want more than one, but it seemed cruel to separate them, so we took in the other two as well: a five-month-old infant and a boy who was six. Pichai," Megan whispered his name.

Syler's arm came around Megan's shoulders and she leaned against the slender strength. With a growing blackness in her soul, Megan wondered if what she was about to reveal would make that night their last one together.

"Things were all right when there were two of us to look after the little ones. I didn't love having a house full of kids, but it was tolerable. Mostly I was happy that Yasu was happy. We were only together as a family for a few weeks. The accident took her from us and then I had to deal with everything on my own." Megan took a sharp breath. The truth tumbled out.

"I couldn't cope. I was seeing a therapist whose answer to everything was to put me on anti-depression meds. I'm not on them now, I haven't been since I started here. They messed me up pretty badly and I was barely functioning." Her empty cup hit the floor with a clank and rolled away. Megan grabbed at her chest. Her breath came faster. She struggled to get the words out. "Syler, I failed. I gave up. I handed over my clinic and dissolved the foster agreement. Their mother quit her job and came back to take care of them. The guilt was killing me, so I set up a trust fund for them, for the entire family.

"After the accident, I spent half a year there, just trying to at least leave things in a somewhat decent state. I'd like to think they are better off now, that something good came from the horrible mess I made of all their lives. The family built a new house and the mother even got married later on that year to her childhood sweetheart. But nothing can change the damage I did to those kids — the whole village actually. I made so many promises and gave everyone so much hope only to drop everything and run. So there it is." Megan drew in a breath, held it and slowly let it out. She said, "Sorry it turned into such a *megillah*."

Once the words were out, the pressure eased. The matter was out of her hands. Syler would either accept her or not.

"Okay, you can talk now," Megan said. She bit her lip and waited.

There was a pause where Megan died a hundred times before Syler asked, "Why would anyone want those documents?"

"Pardon?" Megan blinked, startled at the calm question. "Um, well, I don't really know. But I want you to know I was going to tell you. I just didn't know when, but I really was. You must think I'm a horrible person."

"No, not at all," Syler said. She lifted Megan's chin with gentle fingers and said, "Why would I? You were under incredible stress, overmedicated, and all of a sudden stuck in a situation you didn't want and weren't ready for. Honestly, I think you did pretty well, considering. It took a lot of courage to tell me what you just did."

Megan wanted to deny it, but Syler's gentle words of forgiveness were too tempting and Megan allowed herself to believe them. She relaxed into Syler's arms, her eyes damp with unshed tears.

"Thank you," she whispered.

"It's all right," Syler said and pressed a kiss into her hair. One hand drifted up and down Megan's back. Syler's voice hummed through Megan's chest as she said, "I don't want or expect you to share every deep, dark secret right away. Or ever, if that's your decision. But know I'm here and I'm willing to listen without judging you, all right?"

Megan nodded. Her breath caught in her throat.

"But I really want to know who did this," Syler said, her voice hard. "And why. It wasn't a usual burglary. Meg, is there anyone who would want to hurt you or your family? Maybe blackmail you? Can you think of anyone who wants to have some kind of leverage over you?"

The last words sent a sick chill through Megan. "I don't think this has anything to do with my family, not specifically anyway. But you're right. It's about me. Having leverage over me, oh my God Syler, this is not good."

"What? Talk to me sweetie, please."

"What if it's Charles?" Megan said, her voice tight and breathless. Her heart started pounding and Megan's chest got tight. "What if this is his way of getting back at me for turning him down? Joke's on that *zhlub*. I don't care what he's got on me, I'm never *ever* going to give him the time of day."

"If it is Charles, then we'll just have to deal with him," Syler said. She sat back and crossed her arms with a deep, thoughtful look on her face. Megan liked the way she said, "we." She fixed Megan with a steely gaze. "Remember, no matter what happens, no matter what he threatens you with, you always have options and you *don't* have to do what he says. Never forget that."

"I won't," Megan said. She shivered and hugged her arms to her chest.

Suddenly Megan felt incredibly tired and she stifled a yawn with the back of her hand.

"Sweetheart, you must be exhausted," Syler said. She got up onto her knees and gestured vaguely around the room. "I know I'm running on fumes right now too. Anyway, I'm probably going to be dead to the world for a good long while. If you wake up before me, just help yourself to anything you'd like. I have a bunch of food in the fridge and if you want a shower, go right ahead. Basically, make yourself at home. Is there anything I forgot?"

"Yes," Megan said. Her voice gained strength as she said, "Come over here and I'll let you know what it is."

"Okay," Syler said and shifted so she and Megan were separated by only the smallest distance.

Megan reached out and held Syler's face in her hands before she very slowly took possession of Syler's lips with her own. A soft groan of appreciation met her kiss and gentle hands drifted to hold Megan around the waist. Together they fell down into the valley of quilts. Megan was half-asleep and she drifted on the pleasant wave evoked by Syler's body against hers. She moved unconsciously against the lingering press of hands and brush of fingertips over her T-shirt and skin underneath.

"This is so nice," Syler murmured in her ear, "But I'm half-dead already." The wondrous softness against Megan didn't let up, but the fingers on her stilled.

"I am too," Megan said. She reached out and tugged the covers over their entwined bodies. "How about a rain check?"

"Sounds good," Syler said. She lay back and held her arms open for Megan to snuggle down into her warm hug. The last thing Megan's conscious mind registered was a kiss on one temple and Syler breathing, "I love you, Meg. Now and forever."

"Me too."

THEY PASSED THE next few hours in slumber and Megan woke to a brilliant golden sun. In full daylight, the nightmares of the previous night faded and only a nagging unease remained in the back of her mind. Syler was still curled up in a cocoon of blankets so Megan got herself up and was putting the finishing touches on a big stack of pancakes when Syler wandered into the room. She was tousled and lovely in only boxer shorts and a worn tank top that clung to the planes and curves of her body in a way that made Megan pour orange juice into her coffee before she snapped out of her reverie.

"Good morning," Megan said. She gave a happy sigh as Syler came over for a hug and long, sweet kiss.

"You taste wonderful," Syler said. She drew away and suggestively licked her lips while she lounged back against the island.

"That's because I was testing the pancakes," Megan said. She quickly gulped at her orange-infused coffee before she set a steaming mug down in front of Syler. "I must have a bit of syrup on my mouth."

"Yeah, okay, that too," Syler said and gave a long stretch. She didn't hide the fact she was appreciative of Megan's simple white T-shirt that barely covered her bellybutton over the waistband of her long cotton skirt. Syler said, "God Meg, you make me so hungry."

Megan blushed. She picked up a bowl in one hand and a plastic jug in the other. "Fruit or syrup?" she asked.

"Ooh, decisions. Can I have both?"

"Of course," Megan said. She pushed aside the bowl she used to crack the eggs into and liberally decorated the top pancake in the pile with a handful of frozen berries she found in her quick rummage through the freezer. "I hope it's okay I'm using these."

"Sure, Luka's mom gave me a bunch of frozen things a while back and I have no definite plans for them," Syler said. She hopped up onto the tall chair and propped her chin up on her hands. "I'm really going to have to get another chair."

"I'm okay with standing," Megan said. She put down the plate in front of Syler who sang out, "*Itadakimasu!*" before she took up her fork and knife and attacked her breakfast. "This is so good. So sweet and so soft and melts in my mouth." Syler moaned in pleasure. The sound hit Megan squarely below the belt. Syler speared Megan with a look of unholy glee. "Just like you."

Megan's mouth flapped open. She felt her face flaring red before she gave Syler a good-natured poke on one shoulder and was rewarded by the offer of a syrup-sticky kiss, which Megan could not refuse.

"I was thinking," Syler said after she'd demolished a second helping of pancakes, "I guess you don't want to tell your landlord about the break-in so why don't we fix the door ourselves?"

"That would be great," Megan said. "Do you know how? Because I honestly don't have a clue."

"Nope, I don't either," Syler said. She got up and gathered the dishes. "No, sweetie, you cooked so I wash. Sit."

With a grateful nod, Megan did as she was told. She took over the chair as Syler offered it with a flourish.

While Syler efficiently washed and stacked the dishes in the dairy side dish rack, she said, "Gene does a lot of home-improvement stuff for Oton's company so I thought we could Skype and he could coach us through it." She aimed a mischievous look over her shoulder. "Besides, I've heard all that DIY stuff ramps up your dyke street-cred. So, what do you think?"

"That's a great idea," Megan said. She leaned her chin on her hands the way Syler often did and said, "How about we invite Luka and Jayco over? It's too hot for *nabe*, so maybe we could have takoyaki-without-the-tako or gyoza and make it into a party."

"I like that. The women will do home-improvement and the guys can make themselves useful in the kitchen. I'll network with my bro and get back to you with the details."

Megan glowed. She was eager to reclaim her space, make it her own sanctuary and safe place again. She wanted to banish the violation of whoever had broken into her room and pawed so rudely through her stuff, who had stolen evidence of the biggest mistake of Megan's life.

She joined Syler in the warm nest of her bed while Syler sat with the laptop and composed a long-winded email to her brother. Megan rested her head on Syler's shoulder and felt happy and full. She considered dozing off when Syler's arm came around her and roused her.

"How about getting out of Suito City for a little change of scenery?" Syler asked. "Like, go here?"

Megan sat up to look at the screen of the laptop. It showed a rustic-looking inn surrounded by trees and steamy outdoor grottoes.

"Where's that?" Megan wanted to know.

"Shimo-izumi. It's a hot-spring resort town," Syler said. She shifted so Megan could have a better angle to see the screen. "This is only one hotel, but the entire town is full of them. It's only a forty-minute drive from here. Have you ever been there?"

"Not there," Megan said, intrigued. "My parents have a cottage in Atami, but this looks less touristy."

"It's kind of a local secret. I've actually never been there either, but it looks really nice," Syler said. "I'm a week behind you in my cycle and I just got finished, so I figure it's good timing for both of us."

"You track my periods?" Megan asked.

"Sure," Syler said with a grin and casual shrug. "It's kind of my ultimate relationship goal to sync up." She paused and glanced at Megan. "I hope you don't think it's weird or anything."

"Not really." Megan mulled the information. "It's actually kind of cute."

"Good to hear that. Anyway, take a look at this." She scrolled down a bit and said, "In this *ryokan*, they've got a 'ladies plan' for women guests only. We get to reserve forty-five minutes in one of their private outdoor baths and they provide a welcome drink plus free bath stuff. The dinner looks good too, lots of tofu and no shellfish. If we decide to stay there, I'll call ahead and make sure they don't have anything with pork in it either."

"You just want to get me into the bath with you again," Megan said. "Not that I mind."

"Busted," Syler said. Her arm tightened around Megan and she pressed a kiss into her hair. She murmured, "I've recently discovered that bathing with you is my favorite thing ever."

"Let's do it," Megan said. Her heart filled with warmth. The rest of the afternoon was spent planning and finally they reserved a room in the small but well-appointed inn with the private baths for the following Tuesday. That day, Syler was just on call and not scheduled to work, but Megan was. Megan dug out her Smartphone and logged into the hospital's scheduling system to arrange her own 48-hours off. She glowed with pleasure as she typed in the emergency contact details of the hotel.

They also made plans to go to the nearest hardware store to find a new door for Megan's room. Since she already had her phone out, Megan set up a group chat with Luka and Jayco and a flurry of text messages went back and forth as the non-takoyaki party was organized. They agreed on the following Friday as all of them were off in the afternoon.

In addition to lending his family's takoyaki grill, Luka gleefully offered to bring something he wanted to use for "Russian Roulette." Syler read the messages over her shoulder and gave her opinion at random intervals. Laughter filled the room. The messages from their group chat streamed over the screen of her phone and Megan felt nothing other than joy.

Instead of wallowing in the past, Megan could only see the future.

Chapter Six

"MORE TO THE left," the voice from the laptop in Jayco's hands said. "No, my left, not your left."

"How's this?" Syler grunted. She had her shoulder pressed up against the aluminum frame of the door, holding it in place as Megan hovered with a concerned expression on her face.

"Okay, you feel the groove there? Just lift the whole thing up and slide it in."

"Said the sailor to the girl," Syler said with a snicker. The door shifted in her grasp and she lunged to right it. "Oof! This thing is heavy. Give me a hand here, Meg?"

Megan lent her strength to the task. She bent down and took most the weight of the door across her shoulders.

Luka's voice rang out from across the room, "Oh my, how butch! I'm taking a piccie of this!"

With a satisfying *thunk* the door frame dropped into place. Once the weight was off her, Megan stepped away. Syler glowed with pride as she opened and closed the door a few times. Since Megan didn't want to go into the details of the break-in, she and Syler agreed the official story was the glass was broken by some kids playing baseball in the parking lot and Megan didn't want to stir up trouble with the neighbors so she hadn't pursued the culprits.

"Looks like we got it on the first try," Syler said with a quick look back over her shoulder. "Good work, people. Thanks Gene."

"No prob," Gene said. "Anything else you need from me?"

"Nope," Syler said. She stood with her hands loosely tucked under her arms. "I owe you one, bro."

Everyone else joined in on the chorus of thanks and good-byes. Jayco turned the laptop around and cut the connection.

Luka came out of the kitchen nook. His long body was wrapped in a pink apron that looked several sizes too big for him. He'd tied a brightly patterned kerchief around his head and held a bowl in his hands.

He sang out, "I'm almost done with cutting up the sausages,

so go sit down, kids. The party's about to begin."

"Great, I'm starving," Megan declared. She went to the table where the borrowed takoyaki grill sat. Earlier, she immersed the plate in boiling water and it was ready and waiting for them to begin. Instead of octopus, Megan prepared a number of different fillings, including the kosher sausages Luka had cut up as well as kimchee, asparagus, and spiced beef brisket. For dessert, Syler donated the remainder of the frozen berries to use with the soy-milk pancake batter Megan whipped up.

After he greased the rows of circular impressions, Luka poured the first round of batter and everyone got busy trying to form the typical spherical dumplings with their wooden skewers. Syler and Jayco ended up being the best and had a fierce and silent competition about who could turn over the most while Megan and Luka cheered on their favorite from the sidelines. The first batch was consumed with happy huffs around the super-hot morsels. Luka nursed a batch of takoyaki with an air of gloating secrecy, hovering over them with a dangerous-looking red sauce that had Megan intrigued.

"Russian Roulette time!" Luka said and put a generous plate on the table. "There are a bunch of 'special' ones hidden in here and the rest are normal. All right, first round, everybody choose one and on the count of three!"

"Wait!" Jayco jumped to his feet and headed over to the fridge. "Does everyone have drinks?"

"I'll have another Zero," Syler said. She tilted her head back to drain the last drops from her can.

"Me too," Luka called out. "Just in case."

"Meirav?"

"Thanks Yaakov, but I'm okay," Megan said. Her own can of non-alcohol beer was still more than half-full. They had fallen into the friendly habit of using each others' Hebrew names. Megan liked the familiarity of it.

Jayco came over with drinks for everyone and they all hunkered down around the low table, chopsticks in hand, poised over the pile. They counted down and everyone chose one takoyaki each. Megan popped hers in her mouth and chewed carefully, keeping an eye on the rest of the people at the table.

At the same time as she realized the takoyaki she had chosen was deliciously flavored with a zinging fiery tang that ignited her taste buds in a happy way, Jayco's eyes bugged out and he keeled over backward. He landed in a pile on the floor and flailed around until he got his drink in both hands.

"HHHHHHH!" he said. His legs jigged as he frantically guzzled from the can. His glasses fogged up completely.

"Ooh, I guess we know who got lucky this time," Syler said. She poked Jayco in the shoulder and asked, "You okay there, Jay?"

"Fhhhhh," Jayco wheezed, "Fhhhhine."

"I got one too." Megan raised her hand as she said, "Death Sauce, right?"

"No way, honey," Luka said. He looked at her with frank disbelief. Meanwhile, Jayco made burbling sounds from the kitchen sink where he doused himself under the faucet.

"Meg's tough when it comes to spice," Syler said.

"What can I say, I like things hot," Megan said.

While Luka sputtered in laughter, she picked up the bottle and studied it before she twisted the cap off. She held out one hand, palm up, and shook a few drops onto the inside of her wrist. The sauce was a bright red. It almost glowed with spice. Megan glanced up to catch Syler's eye before she lowered her head and slowly licked the drops off. Syler looked on in awe and Luka gaped at her.

Megan swallowed and said, "That's really good! Where did you get this, Luka?" The burning spices hit her throat. Megan gave a slight cough.

"The import store in the mall," Luka said. He looked over at Jayco who accepted a glass of heavily-sweetened soymilk from Syler. He chugged it as if his life depended on it. Luka asked, "Better now, honey?"

"Yeah," Jayco said. He came back and sat down at the table with his yarmulke in one hand. He pinned it back into place on his damp curls. "Okay, I'm ready for the next round."

Impressed, Megan raised her eyebrows as Luka picked up the plate and waved it around.

Luka said, "This time, whoever gets the lucky one has to do the dishes! Megu-chan, it's your house, so you're excused from this round."

"But they're so yummy," Megan said and pretended to pout. She helped herself to a few leftover takoyaki from the grill and took them and the bottle of Death Sauce over to the sofa where she could watch the proceedings. Megan asked, "Yakkov, are you sure you want to try for round two?"

"I'm all right," Jayco said. "What are the odds of getting a spicy one twice in a row?"

"Not telling," Luka sang. "Okay people, ready? On three! One! Two! Three!" With that, they dove in with their chopsticks.

Megan studied everyone's faces as they chewed.

She jumped up and cried out, "Syler's got the lucky one! I know that expression! I saw it just last night!"

"Oh my God," Luka said with the air of a person who had received entirely too much information. "I did not want to know what Syler's come-face looks like."

"That's not her come-face," Megan said in indignation as Syler clapped both hands over her mouth and flapped around. "That's her trying-not-to-come-face."

Syler swallowed her mouthful with a mighty gulp. She tried to speak but ended up in a coughing fit. She held up a hand and downed her entire can of beer before she staggered into the kitchen nook. She grabbed a handful of ice, which she shoved into her mouth. Slowly, she came back to the gathering. Syler patted herself on the chest and rubbed a hand across her brow while crunching on the last of her ice.

"Excuse me," she said. "Can we change the subject? I think I have to do the dishes, right?"

"Yup," Luka said. "Anyway, we've got two more takoyakis left. It's you and me Jayco and this one's miiiine!" He scooped up one of the remaining dumplings and popped it into his mouth at the same time as Jayco.

They looked at each other in expectant silence. Only half a second elapsed before Jayco keeled over once more. He batted his feet against the floor and made *MMMM!* sounds.

"Thanks for taking one for the team Jay," Syler said in a watery voice as she wiped at her eyes with a tissue.

"Hhhh," Jayco replied shortly before he dashed into the kitchen for his own helping of ice. The party suffered a brief hiatus as Syler and Jayco nursed themselves back to health using a combination of ice, water, and sweet soymilk, plus a few candies Megan found in her pocket.

"Ith not eelly thpithy ahymo," Jayco announced as he

resumed his position on the floor in front of where Luka was enthroned on the sofa. He chugged some more soymilk and said, "I can't feel anything under my eyebrows."

"Just wait until tomorrow morning in the can," Syler told him. "Burns going in, burns going out."

As Jayco's face went white. Syler stabbed a kimchee dumpling with her chopstick and fed it to Megan.

"Thanks," Megan said. She chewed happily. She thought about returning the favor, but with her mouth, then decided against it as she'd already incurred Luka's ire enough that day.

"Twice lucky! What are the odds," Jayco moaned.

"Don't worry, sweetie," Luka said. He draped a towel over Jayco's red and sweating face. "Two times lucky cancels each other out. I'll take dish duty with Syler."

"Thanks," Jayco said.

They finished off the party by making little spherical cakes from the pancake batter, filled with various frozen berries. Megan looked around with satisfaction as everyone chatted and joked with each other.

When her body and mind were busy, the nagging worry was pushed to the back of her thoughts. In the quiet moments, Megan couldn't help but wonder about the outcome of the loss of her documents with a horrible, sick feeling in her belly. She felt as if a clock was ticking over her head, one that was counting down to the end of everything she held dear. It was all she could do in those moments to keep a smile plastered on her face before she hurried off to find something for herself to do like hand out paper napkins or ferry dishes to and from the kitchen.

Luka and Syler washed up in the kitchen with a lot more splashing than necessary. Megan felt restless and wandered out to the balcony. Worry caught up to her. She chewed on her bottom lip as she gazed out to the park across the street. A guy was walking three toy poodles. Megan watched him try to control the scampering dogs, all of which seemed to want to go in completely different directions. The scene was both cute and amusing. Megan wished for her own troubles to be so simple.

She heard the door close behind her and turned around. Jayco stepped onto the balcony and stood beside her.

"Thanks for inviting us over," he said. "It was a lot of fun."

"No problem," Megan said. "We should do this more often."

"Without the hot sauce," Jayco said with a wince.

"Okay, I'll confiscate the bottle so it can no longer be used for evil."

"I appreciate that." Jayco leaned his elbows on the railing. He was silent for a long moment.

Megan wondered if he wanted to be alone, but the way he knitted his fingers together lead her to nudge his shoulder with hers and ask, "Is there something you wanted to talk about?"

"Actually, kinda yeah," Jayco said. Behind his glasses, his eyes were fixed on the road in front of the apartment, but he didn't seem to be seeing anything other than what was going on in his head. He paused. Megan didn't breathe as she waited for him to continue. Suddenly he blurted out, "How did you know you wanted to change teams mid-game?"

Megan hoped he didn't notice her worried grimace. She'd only just come out to her own girlfriend and already she was being called on to give advice and pep-talks. Before Jayco could take her silence for rejection, Megan took a deep breath and said, "I was always gay."

"Okay, yeah I get that," Jayco said in a way that convinced Megan he didn't. "But you at least tried the other way, right?"

"No, I didn't," Megan said. She turned to regard the earnest young man. She wondered how much she needed to tell him and how much she should ask him. Megan said, "I just let people think I was with a guy before, but really I wasn't. The person I lost in Thailand was a woman—she was my partner. Now, I wish I had been honest from the start. It would have saved me a bunch of trouble. But that's not important right now. Yaakov, are you, um, questioning?"

Megan clenched her hands together as she frantically thought about what she should say. A quick glance behind them showed Megan that Syler was keeping Luka busy by introducing him to the game system. It looked as if they were absorbed in having a two-player game of something, most likely *Zenith of the Undead* by the way Luka was shrieking and Syler was cackling gleefully.

"In a way," Jayco said.

"Have you ever been interested a guy before?" Megan asked. "Like, even just had a crush on an actor or something?"

"See that's just the thing," Jayco said. "I don't really think of Luka as a guy or a girl, you know? Luka is just...Luka. I've never actually had experience with either, so I don't know for sure which I prefer, you know."

"Do you have to choose one?" Megan asked. The setting sun cast long shadows over the road. The guy and his poodles were gone and the cars purring by pushed cones of light in front of them. "Maybe it's more a mental thing, like some people we just click with."

"Yeah, but there's also the physical part of it."

"There is that."

For an instant she wondered if Jayco felt like she was an older sister the way she had come to consider him something of a younger brother. She cleared her throat.

"So you haven't..."

Jayco's face went pink, but he spoke frankly, "Nothing below the belt." He shuffled his feet and said, "But, um, we've done plenty above. It's been pretty good so far. Really good, actually."

"Yeah, it is, isn't it. Go with what feels natural. At least you're familiar with the plumbing." She paused and said in a con-spiratorial voice, "And we can have a huge double gay Jewish wedding one day if everything works out."

"Okay," he said and gave a laugh. "Thanks Meirav. I feel a lot better."

"I'm glad to hear it, and you're welcome," Megan said.

Jayco turned to go back into the room but stopped with his hand on the doorframe. He twisted his body to look back at Megan, who raised her eyebrows at the questioning look on his face.

"So that means, there is actually an online service that matches up women with women? In Japan?"

"Yes, there is," Megan replied. She covered her blushing cheeks with her hands. "It's kind of a side-business of a major online matchmaker for straight people wanting to get married. Obviously, they don't really advertise it. They also have a service for men only."

"Wow," Jayco said quietly. He shook himself and said, "Good to know, but I don't think I'll be needing that service."

"No, I don't think you will," Megan said to Jayco's back as he opened the door and bounded back into the room. For a moment, Megan watched the scene with amusement. Jayco fell into the middle of the sofa and received a lapful of Luka. Syler didn't look away from the game on the screen, but her lips twitched up at the corners.

Not to be outdone, Megan burst into the living room and sprawled over Syler, who accepted her full weight with grace and wrapped her long arms around Megan's waist.

"What were the two of you gossiping about out there?" Luka asked.

"Nothing special," Megan answered. She nestled back against Syler as she said, "Just how lucky we both are."

Luka responded with a snort and grabbed Jayco in a head-lock.

"Actually, Luka, there's something I'd like to ask you," Megan said. She shifted slightly so she could see the young man better. "You've spent some time with Nikky Okamoto, right? What do you think about her?"

"Nikky's the cutest little thing," Luka said. "Smart too. As far as I can tell, she's perfectly bilingual."

Megan said. "I've talked to her mother a couple of times. I don't think Nikky's family is willing to accept her as a girl."

"That's a shame. Maybe they just need more time?" Luka crossed his arms and looked thoughtful. Jayco groaned and Luka hopped off his lap to settle down beside him.

"Maybe. At least the family should really talk to someone who can give them some advice." Megan didn't speak the words, but she hoped counseling would expose and stop what was going on in the Okamoto household before it escalated and someone got permanently damaged.

"Good idea," Luka said. "The sooner the better."

"Next time I see them," Megan said, "I'll try to mention it."

"Oh, yes. Speaking about time, I have an early shift tomor-row," Luka declared. "Thanks for the fun party, Megu-chan, but I should go." He looked down at Jayco and asked, "Can you walk me to the station?"

"Sure, I'd be glad to," Jayco said in an easy way. Megan was pleased to note he seemed relaxed and held himself with a bit more pride and confidence than before their discussion.

Syler let out a peal of laughter and clapped Luka on the back. "Early shift tomorrow, sure we believe that's the real reason why you're scampering off so soon. We know you're just angling for the chance to get some one-on-one time with your honey."

Luka brushed off Syler's hand in a haughty way. He said, "I am not fishing for an invitation to Jayco's place, and I am definitely not trying to get a kiss for my troubles."

"Uh huh," Syler said with a knowing look. "Nice misdirection there, Lukie. We all know you deny something twice and the negatives cancel each other out."

"Oh you!" Luka said. He went over to Jayco and looped one arm through his. "Let's go Jayco, before Syler makes any more baseless accusations."

"All right," Jayco said with an indulgent smile at Luka. He looked over at Megan and said, "I guess I'll see you tomorrow in shul?"

"Yup," she said.

The two young men gathered up their things including the giant paper bag that held the electric grill they used for the takoyaki.

"Syler would you stay and help me clean up?" Megan asked

Before Syler could reply, Luka poked his head up over the back of the sofa like a fuzzy prairie dog and said, "But we finished all that already. The kitchen's spotless."

"There are other rooms in the apartment," Megan said with a lofty air. "For example the bedroom."

Before Luka could say more than a scandalized *oooh* he was shooed gently but firmly toward the door. A volley of mutual thanks preceded the door shutting and once more the apartment fell into silence.

"That was a pretty successful non-tako takoyaki party," Syler said with a grin.

"It was," Megan agreed. She looked up just as Syler opened her arms and happily leapt into them for a hug. She snuggled into Syler's embrace and closed her eyes. A hand stroked over her hair and Megan settled her body more firmly against Syler's.

Megan said, "I liked having the guys here, but I like being alone with you better."

A low chuckle thrummed through her.

"I do too," Syler answered. She pulled away and took Megan's face in her hands. Her eyes were dancing. "Wanna go over to your sofa and make out like teenagers?"

Megan swallowed a dizzying burst of desire. She just nodded. No more words were needed.

Chapter Seven

SYLER PARKED HER Jimny in one of several small coin parking lots that dotted the area. As soon as the car was stopped, Megan leaped out. She couldn't wait to explore. She drank in the clear air and the rich green mountains that shrouded the hot spring resort town of Shimo-izumi. The main road was split down the middle by a shallow ravine holding a fast-moving brook. The lively brook ran through the entire town and drained into a larger river that separated the highway from the small cluster of hotels, traditional inns, unobtrusive gift shops, and two tiny, ancient shrines that were older than anything else in the entire pocket of civilization and looked it.

"I love it here already. This place has such great atmosphere," Megan said. She scampered over to where Syler leaned against the driver's side door. Without a second thought, she reached out and took Syler's hand in hers. "Can we go exploring? I want to see everything."

"Sure," Syler said. With her free hand, she tucked a strand of Megan's hair behind her ear with unconcerned affection. "They've got free hot spring foot-baths scattered around the town and a bunch of shops and places to go that look interesting. Do you want to look around a bit before we check in?"

"Let's get that over with first," Megan said. She hoisted her overnight bag over one shoulder. "I want to see our room and make sure we can reserve a good time for the open-air bath."

"Good idea," Syler said. Together they entered the lobby and exchanged their shoes for slippers. The kimono-wearing *Okamisan* who was in charge of the inn greeted them with a deep bow. She motioned for one of the staff behind the front desk to come over with the two packs of complimentary bath goods and a selection of canned beverages for the promised welcome drink.

As Syler filled out the check-in form, Megan went over to the rack where hundreds of neatly folded cotton *yukatas* of every color and pattern imaginable were on display. The pretty cotton robes were reserved for women, while the men's selection was limited to a geometric pattern of indigo on white.

While Megan debated between a light green yukata printed with leaves and a blue one with big, lush chrysanthemums, the Okamisan, without blinking an eye, handed Syler a bundle consisting of a men's yukata and close-woven belt.

"That blue one would look gorgeous with your eyes," Syler said to Megan.

"Okay, I'll go with this one," Megan said. She put the green one back and picked up a belt from the basket beside the shelf.

While she wasn't a huge fan of the way they'd been tacitly squeezed into the mold of a straight couple, at least they were acknowledged as a couple with the typical modest hospitality the country was known for. It worked out, in a way. Megan couldn't imagine Syler wanting to prance around the town in a flowery robe. The simple design and traditional deep blue and white suited her perfectly.

Their room was on the third floor. Megan jumped out of her slippers and left them messily in the tiny entrance hall in her eagerness to look around. The main room had fragrant *tatami* flooring and at one end was a narrow glassed-in sitting area with a mini fridge and two ancient armchairs facing each other over a low, square table. The futons were stashed in the closet, along with the dark blue *haori* jackets they could wear over their yukatas. Megan wasted no time and darted into the sitting area to pull the curtains closed. She came back into the main room and immediately dropped her pants and started unbuttoning her blouse.

"Whoa there Meg," Syler said. She settled onto a thick floor cushion with a teasing light in her eyes. She rested her elbows on the heavy wooden table and gazed appreciatively at Megan's undressed form. "A bit early for that, don't you think? You have to at least buy me a beer first."

"Funny joke," Megan said in a dry tone. She brought her heel down on the toe of one sock in order to yank it off, then repeated the motion with the other. Megan stood in nothing more than her underwear while she gathered her hair up in a clip. "I'm getting into the whole hot spring mentality, not trying to seduce you." She paused and said, "Yet."

Syler just replied with a knowing look. The look was quickly replaced by an *oof!* as Megan tossed the yukata at her.

"Come on, I don't want to be the only one properly attired."

"All right," Syler said. She got to her feet. She stripped and pulled the yukata on. She tied the sash with unaffected ease. Megan paused in her own preparations to appreciate the way the long, simple lines flattered Syler's lean form. Keeping in line with the way men wore the traditional garment, the sash sat low on her hips and she looked relaxed and elegant.

Syler tucked her hands into her sleeves for a moment, but she pulled them out and strode across the room to where Megan was struggling with her own sash and trying not to swear. At least the hotel trimmed the long garment and there was no need to tuck up the waist area as was usual for women's yukatas. She froze as Syler came up behind her. Strong hands came over her own.

"Let me get that for you."

"Thanks," Megan said. The sash settled around her waist like a hug.

"Is that too tight?" Syler asked.

"It's perfect," Megan replied. She twisted and glanced behind herself, surprised at the elegant knot Syler had tied. The sash wasn't as wide as the ones usually worn with a yukata, but Syler tied it beautifully anyway. "That's gorgeous! Where did you learn how to tie an *obi* like that?"

"I have many skills," Syler purred in Megan's ear.

"Yes, you do," Megan said.

"And two nieces who like to wear yukatas in the summer."

"Well, it's very convenient for me. Thank you." Megan reached down, took Syler's hands in hers, and wrapped them around her waist. She enjoyed the feeling of Syler against her back. Megan bowed her head in invitation. Obligingly, Syler kissed the nape of her neck that was revealed by her pulled-back collar. The hands at her waist started to creep upward. Megan bit back a gasp of pleasure. She arched back against Syler's long body as one deft hand found its way into the front of her *yukata*.

"We're never going to get out of here," Syler whispered against Megan's skin between kisses. "God, you're so beautiful. I can't believe how much I love having you in my arms."

"Just as much as I love being in your arms," Megan said in a breathless voice. A wild electric feeling hummed into life between her thighs. Megan was calculating how long it would take for her to get out of the yukata she'd just put on when the maddening touches stopped. Syler stepped back to leave Megan standing alone.

"How about taking a walk around the town before dinner?" Syler asked. She shrugged into the dark blue *haori* jacket which fit perfectly over the yukata. Her long fingers knotted the tie at the front with unconscious grace. "Maybe see if we can find some souvenirs for the guys. Oh, and you might want to straighten up your front."

"What?" Megan glanced down to find the front of her robe gaping open. She raised her head with a half-joking glare at Syler, who only smirked in reply. Quickly, Megan tugged everything back into place before she put on her own jacket.

In the lobby, they swapped their slippers for traditional wooden clogs provided by the hotel. Syler ducked under the half-curtain that separated the entrance hall from the street when Megan called out, "Syler, we forgot to reserve a bath for tonight."

At Megan's words, Syler stopped and looked back over her shoulder.

"That's right. Let's do it now."

"Just wait here, I've got this," Megan said. She slipped off her clogs and stepped barefoot into the lobby. A minute later, she darted into the street with her clogs making merry clacking noises against the cobblestones. Syler waited for her on the bridge over the river. She leaned on the railing and looked like the dashing heroine of a samurai drama. The stone pillars of the bridge and the cobbled street made the perfect backdrop. Megan caught her breath at the beauty of the scene. The silent, still tableau was broken as Syler turned to her with a smile and an appreciative look of her own.

Suddenly filled with giddy energy, Megan grabbed Syler's hand and pulled her into a noisy trot. Together they headed toward a group of bushes that made a shimmering arch over a footpath. The path led to a number of small shops Megan was eager to visit.

"Slow down Meg," Syler said. "They're not going to run out of souvenirs before we get there."

"I know," Megan said. She swung their clasped hands, drunk with the freedom of being in a town where nobody knew them. "But I'm just having the greatest time. It's so nice being here with you. Thank you for everything."

"Anything for you, Meg," Syler said in a soft voice. "By the way, what time did you get for the bath?"

"Eight thirty," Megan said. A shy, happy feeling blossomed in her belly. She pointed back at their hotel. "The baths are on the roof, you can see them there. I got one overlooking the river. The front desk guy said it doesn't have a shower so we have to wash in the main bath first."

She studied the bamboo blinds that shielded the rooftop baths from view. Megan couldn't help but imagine sinking into the steaming depths with Syler. Her heart sped up and a warm, tense feeling started up south of her *obi*.

"Hopefully no one can see in," Megan said.

"If it's dark we should be okay," Syler said. She tucked her hands into her sleeves and stared thoughtfully at the enclosures. Their *ryokan* was about the same height as the surrounding inns and in the daylight, the walls around the roof didn't provide much cover.

"Good, because I can't wait to get wet and naked with you," Megan said. She took Syler's hand in hers. She spun to continue on her way but nearly tripped over a large man who was crouched beside the footpath.

"Paolo!" Megan gasped. She yanked her hand out of Syler's. Her heart pounded in alarm.

Syler strode over and greeted the big man, who looked up with a startled expression.

"I am here alone," he blurted out. "Just to relax."

"That's fine, we're here to relax as well," Syler said. "I'm glad you're spending some time away from the hospital. Gabriela wouldn't want you to be cooped up there every day."

"No, she wouldn't," Paolo said. His voice was very small and pinched, as if he had to force the words out. Paolo scrambled to his feet. He had an expensive-looking, brand-new camera in his hands.

"Very nice," Syler said. "I didn't know your were a photographer."

"It was a gift," Paolo said. "I am practicing."

His face shone with sweat even though the day was cool. His hands worried at the strap of the camera. Megan guessed he was flustered at catching them in a situation that looked quite compromising. She forced herself to calm down. Maybe he wouldn't figure it out. Friends went to hot spring resorts together all the time, she reasoned. After all, they were on a plan that was for women only. Moreover, the idea of co-bathing was traditional and most natural, nothing suspicious going on at all. She tried not to think about what she said just before she discovered him. Not to mention the fact they'd been holding hands.

Not seeming concerned about being discovered, Syler bent her head to look at something Paolo showed her on the camera's screen. Her posture was open and easy as she complimented the delicate photos, which seemed to be mostly of flowers and plants with a few shots of the traditional-style buildings in the town.

"You've really got an eye for detail," Syler said. She straightened up and added, "And I can't think of anywhere more photoworthy than here. Have you been to the old Shimo-izumi shrine yet?"

As the conversation meandered, Megan tried to school her worried expression into a smile. How much he heard of their conversation worried her.

Megan couldn't imaging Paolo having any reason to spread rumors about them. Syler wasn't being particularly cagey around him, which reassured Megan greatly. Syler trusted him. Megan decided to take a risk. After all, Paolo had his own secrets he'd trusted Syler with. Anyone who overstayed risked deportation at any moment. It only took one call to Immigration and his life in Japan would be over. Megan took a deep breath and slipped her arm through Syler's. Without any hesitation at all, Syler leaned into the caress, holding Megan with calm strength.

"I guess you caught us," Megan said. Her face went hot. She wondered if she was making a mistake. The gentle pressure of Syler's body against her side told her she wasn't. "I'm sure you've already figured out we're not here as friends, but I just wanted to get it out in the open."

Instead of looking shocked or surprised, Palo just gave them a smile and seemed a bit nervous. Not the best reaction, but not the worst. Megan would probably act that way too in the same situation.

"You are a beautiful couple," Paolo said. He hoisted the camera in one hand. "I will take your photo, with your permission?"

"Thanks for the generous offer," Syler said. She shared a long glance with Megan, who held her breath. The thought of capturing the magic of their day out was tempting, but she didn't know if it was a good idea to have something like that floating around out of their control. Syler cleared her throat and said, "But I don't think we should. This isn't exactly common knowledge."

"How about no face?" Paolo asked. He waved his hands and said, "You and your lady standing over there." He indicated the end of the arch, which was filled with golden afternoon sunlight. "I will take a photo from behind."

Another long look at each other ended with Megan giving a tiny nod of assent. This time it was Megan who spoke. She turned back to Paolo and said, "All right. That sounds nice."

They walked slowly away, back down the path. A spark raced up Megan's arm straight to her heart as Syler's fingers slipped around hers. They paused at the edge of the arch, just as the sun streamed down over them. Megan closed her eyes against the light and felt like the entire universe was revolving around them.

Soon Paolo hurried up to them and showed the shots he'd taken. One in particular caught Megan's eye and she studied it for a long time. True to Paolo's word, their faces weren't in any of the photos but given their stance and coloring, it was impossible to hide who they were. Still, Megan didn't mind. The photo that caught her attention was a simple one of them standing framed against the arch of dark leaves. They were looking out over the little town and the bridge they'd crossed was visible beyond them. Their hands were linked, and Paolo had caught an instant when Syler bowed her head down the slightest bit and it looked like they were lost in their own world, aware of nothing other than each other.

"This one is lovely," Megan said.

"I will print this one for you," Paolo said. "I will leave it at the front desk of your hotel. You are staying at the Wakabayashi Inn?"

"What?" Megan choked. "How did you know that?"

He pointed and Megan glanced down at the jacket where the logo and name of the inn were embroidered over her left breast. Her knees buckled in relief.

"That's very kind of you," Megan said.

"It is nothing. Please enjoy your day," Paolo said.

Before either Megan or Syler could reply, he turned and hurried away. His head was down, his shoulders hunched, and he looked unhappy. Guilty, almost. Megan wondered if that was because of his family situation or perhaps he felt bad about being seen with an expensive camera when his wife was receiving free care at their hospital. Megan didn't begrudge him in the slightest. Everyone deserved to have something nice from time to time.

All her thoughts returned to Syler as a gentle pressure on the small of her back ushered Megan toward the shops she'd been so intent on visiting. They entered a small, souvenir-cluttered shop. Megan clattered around and looked at everything before she finally decided to get Jayco and Luka matching key chains featuring the town's mascot, a somewhat neurotic-looking soft-boiled egg named Ontama-kun, plus a few boxes of the ubiquitous souvenir cookies to share with the other members of their department.

While Megan was looking at a number of postcards and wondering if she should buy one to send to her parents, Syler invested in several bottles of locally-brewed beer that she had wrapped for transport. Her interest piqued, Megan investigated and ended up with a selection ranging from pale ale to a hearty stout with a picture of Ontama-kun on the label.

On the way back to the hotel, Megan tugged on Syler's sleeve as they passed one of the ancient shrines. The red *torii* gate soared proudly over their heads.

"Can we stop here for a second?" Megan asked.

"Sure," Syler said. She switched the bag her purchases were in to her other hand so she could trail her hand down to clasp Megan's. "You don't think it's kind of like cheating? I mean, you're an observant Jew after all."

"It's not cheating at all," Megan said. She curled her fingers around Syler's. "Shinto isn't a formal religion for me. I think of it more as the spirit of the area, a special place and time, than a set of beliefs. I've hauled *mikoshi* around in our neighborhood festivals when I was a kid and my parents got me amulets when I took my exams and stuff like that, so I've always had an awareness of it in the back of my mind," Megan said as they walked slowly toward the main shrine. Syler was quiet, but Megan knew she was listening by the way she held herself with the slightest bit of tension in her stance, the almost imperceptible incline of her head.

The area was shrouded in shadows from the thick old trees growing around them and the sounds of the town were muted. It was like every step sent them back in time until the world outside was nothing more than a faded illusion. Megan paused to breathe in the cool air, very aware of Syler's presence beside her. While nobody else was around that Megan could see, she felt that they weren't alone. A presence was with them. Not a malevolent one, just something there, watching them. For a moment, Megan allowed herself the flight of fancy that it was protecting them and blessing them.

"In all the time I was abroad," Megan said, "I never felt the spirit of Shinto. I feel it here, with you." She stopped walking and Syler paused beside her. The hand in hers gave her the smallest squeeze.

"How does that balance with your Jewish faith?" Syler asked in a soft voice, as if she was also afraid to break the spell.

"If Shinto is present in a place, then Judaism is in my head and heart and bones," Megan said. She hoped she didn't sound silly, but she'd been mulling the ideas for a while and it was a good time to get them out. "I carry it with me like I carry my DNA." She faced Syler and said, "And my love for you."

"Meirav," Syler breathed. She reached out and cupped Megan's face. Her expression was slightly nervous and Megan wondered why. Syler took a deep breath before she said, "You said before your parents were still hoping you'd find a nice Jewish girl, right? I think I can help you with that."

"How?" Megan blinked. She was about to protest that it wasn't important but her words died as Syler continued.

"I'm going to convert," Syler said. She let go of Megan and stepped back. With one hand, she worried at the front tie of her jacket.

Megan's mouth fell slightly open in wonder. Several things made sense, like why Syler had the prayer books in her room, and how she was so knowledgeable about things like kosher.

"It's not easy," Megan said.

"I know that." Syler chuckled and said, "It was in the back of my mind for ages, but when I suddenly ended up single and could do stuff like organize my kitchen the way I wanted it, I formally decided to convert. Rabbi Sharon tossed me out of her office four times before she agreed to consider me. She told me to stop wasting her time and they don't need any more Jews but I didn't give up. My *beit din* is coming up in a couple months and I feel confident the judges will accept me. Rabbi Sharon's been   giving me lessons and I'm studying on my own too. Plus I've pretty much memorized all the prayers from hanging outside the shul on lunch duty."

"Syler, that's wonderful," Megan murmured in awe. "I'm sure you don't need any help, but I'll be there for you whenever you need someone to quiz you or talk about deep, philosophical stuff. You already know how to make blintzes, so you're well on your way."

"Thanks," Syler said. She reached out and took both of Megan's hands in hers. Her thumbs stroked over the backs of Megan's hands as she said, "Once I avoided the question about what I see when I look in your eyes. I'm ready to answer it if that's all right with you."

"Of course," Megan said. She could barely breathe.

"I see forever," Syler told her. "I see my future. Our future. Meg, I can't take your name and I can't give you mine, not in this country, but I can stand at your side under the same God. I respect the teachings and traditions of the Jewish faith and I want to be a part of something bigger than myself." Syler paused and said, "I want this with everything in me, just like I want to be with you. Megan, would you consider committing to something long-term with me? It doesn't have to be anything huge but I just want to know," Syler started to falter, "where I stand with you."

Her throat was tight and Megan couldn't speak. She was breathless with wonder and love for Syler. The weight of the words, the implications of what Syler told her stole Megan's voice. Megan's body came alive with the need to fling herself into Syler's arms, to hold her close and melt her with kisses. Forever. Megan welcomed the word as if it was the sunlight in her world.

The words of acceptance were almost in her mouth but Megan stopped. She didn't want to accept a promise from Syler that she would not be able to keep.

Silence fell. Megan felt as if she was poised at the top of a roller coaster, waiting only for something to trigger her fall into flight. A bus rumbled by outside and broke the mood. Syler stepped back. She still held Megan in her gaze but let some distance get between them.

"I'm sorry," Megan blurted out. "I should say something. But I can't—not yet. Please understand this isn't 'yes' but it's not 'no' either."

"That's fine, sweetheart." Pain flashed in Syler's eyes, but she recovered quickly and said, "You don't have to say anything. I dropped this load on you without warning. This isn't a game of ping-pong where you have to return every shot right away. Take your time, think about it, and we'll talk about this again when you're ready." Syler tucked her hands into her sleeves. "And speaking of ping-pong, I saw they've got a table in the *ryokan* and I challenge you to a match. Loser pays for beers at dinner."

"You're on," Megan said. The strained air from Megan's non-answer lifted. The sizzling, electrified mood of barely-contained desire was gone as well, but that was probably for the best. As private as it was, Megan didn't think it was prudent to start an erotic tussle with her girlfriend in the middle of a place of worship. And what she felt at that moment was far deeper than just skin-lust. Megan returned Syler's carefree grin with her own and said, "Get your change ready for pay-up time."

"That's my line, Meg."

"We'll see. How about we pay our respects and move on?" Megan asked. She glanced over at the main shrine, which was a small wooden building flanked by stone lanterns. The offering box was located up a short flight of stone steps.

"Good idea," Syler said.

Megan reached into her sleeve and dug out a five yen coin. She stepped up to the offering box and shook the thick cord that clanked the bells together over her head. The cheerful cacophony stilled, Megan clapped and bowed her head respectfully as Syler did the same. She raised her head at the exact same time as Syler did.

"Think your wish will come true?" Syler asked.

"I know it will," Megan said. She gave a stretch and started walking back toward the street with a slight sway of her hips. She glanced back over her shoulder and said, "As long as you don't sprain both of your wrists between now and tonight."

"Megan Maier! Why I never!" Syler said in mock indignation.

Megan, not repentant in the least, just raised an eyebrow and continued walking. Syler raced after her with her yukata flapping merrily.

"I'll have you know," Syler said in a low, intense tone as she drew up alongside Megan, "I have a number of weapons in my arsenal of pleasure and I'm positive I won't leave you unsatisfied, even without the use of my hands."

"You don't say," Megan answered in a low voice. A thrill

raced down her spine and a lovely warmth started up deep within herself even as she tried not to blush.

DINNER WAS SCHEDULED to be served at half past six in their room and in the time it took for the inn's serving staff to set up their meal, Megan joined Syler in a no-holds-barred game of ping-pong that attracted a bunch of other guests. It ended up being the major attraction of the day to the point where two cheering squads formed and a number of bets took place on the sidelines. While Megan held her own in the first few rounds, Syler had stamina and strength on her side, not to mention a longer reach and Megan was forced to admit defeat. Syler proved herself a gracious winner and treated Megan to an ice-cold post-game bottle of CC Lemon.

They returned to find the big table in their room laden with a gorgeous feast. True to Syler's word, there was no shellfish or pork. Megan had a great time with her individual hotpot that bubbled over a little blue flame. As Syler was on call, she ordered a non-alcoholic beer from the inn while Megan got a bottle of regular beer. Syler held back her sleeve to pour for Megan with elegant grace, which made her feel like a princess. They toasted each other and looked out over the darkening town as they enjoyed the rich feast.

After the dishes were cleared away, Megan fell into a soft and pensive mood. She got to her knees and picked up her bag.

"Syler, would you come with me? There's something I want to do."

"Sure Meg, what is it?" Syler asked. She was sprawled out over the floor cushions, watching something on her phone. At Megan's soft request, she sat up.

"I want to say goodbye to the past," Megan said in a small voice. She had planned on doing it alone, but she realized she wanted Syler there with her for that moment. "Come down to the river with me."

"Of course," Syler said. She sat up and quickly grabbed their jackets. The day was quite warm, but the evening carried a chill from the mountain air. A single layer wasn't going to be enough protection.

Megan was silent until they stood at the edge of the river. She reached into her bag and pulled out the ring Yasu had given her, the last concrete reminder she had.

"It's been over a year," Megan said with a catch in her voice. She paused and rubbed a hand across her face. "Yasu will always be a part of me. I will carry her in my heart until the day I die. At one point in my life, she was everything to me and I loved her. I still do." She glanced at Syler. "But it's not going to overshadow what I feel for you, Syler. I hope you understand that."

"Of course I do," Syler told her. She reached out and laid a gentle hand on Megan's shoulder. "It's okay, Meg."

"The person I was with her isn't the person I am now," Megan said. "But being with her helped me realize who I am and what I need to do. Now I have to move forward."

Megan rummaged around in her bag once more and took out a tiny paper lantern and a candle. The candle was slender, unadorned and simple, different from the Yahrzeit candles usually used for mourning. Not trusting her voice, Megan simply lit the candle and slipped the ring down over it before she nestled the whole thing into the lantern.

The walls glowed with a soft, flickering light. Megan got down on her knees at the side of the river and placed the lantern on the water. She held onto it for a moment, debating if she could really let go. The paper whispered against her fingers as the lantern was tugged from Megan's grasp by the current. It bobbed and twirled as it drifted down the river. Megan stayed that way for a moment longer before she stood and wiped her tears with the edge of her sleeve.

They stood in silence for a moment. The only sound was the rushing water of the river beside them.

Megan couldn't take her eyes from the lantern as it slowly made its way down the river. She said softly, "It's strange standing here with you, knowing that if the accident had never happened I wouldn't here. I'd still be in Thailand, watching my family grow up without ever knowing what I could have with you." She closed her eyes and bowed her head.

"And if Yukina hadn't cheated on me and dumped my ass," Syler said, "I wouldn't be here either. But you know what? I think somehow things would have worked out anyway." She glanced at Megan and asked, "Want to hear something silly?"

"Sure," Megan answered, curious.

Syler stepped back from the river. She tucked her hands into her sleeves before she said, "I have this fantasy that we all met up, the four of us, before any of that bullshit happened. Sometimes depending on my mood it's a dark, angsty drama and other times it's a shenanigan-filled romantic comedy, but the bottom line is after a bit of soul-searching and/or getting caught in compromising situations, we realize who is better off with who, swap partners, and live happily ever after."

Syler's words hit her in the heart and stole her breath for a moment. Even though Yukina had fallen prey to the perks and privileges that came with a straight union, from what Syler told her, it seemed like Yasu would be exactly her type, and Yukina in turn seemed like she would be just what Yasu had wanted in a partner. Megan hadn't been. She tried so hard to live up to the match, which looked ideal on that flat computer screen, that she nearly missed out on the random miracle that brought Syler into her life.

"That's not silly," Megan said. She shook her hair back and raised her eyes to the starry sky. "It's actually very correct. Maybe in some alternate universe, things actually happened like that."

"It's a cool idea," Syler said. "But I'm all right with the way things are in this universe." She paused and asked, "Do you want to stay out here for a bit more or go back inside? It's almost eight thirty."

"Let's head back," Megan said. She took one last glance at the nearly-invisible lantern before she reached out for Syler's hand. The weight on her heart was lighter now, although she was a bit sad the door to a part of her life had closed. Still, Megan didn't regret saying that final goodbye. While she hated to agree with anything Charles said, maybe he was right about mourning for too long. She had to move forward and meet her future, good or bad.

After they stopped by their room to get towels and bath stuff, Megan ducked under the red half-curtain at the entrance to the ladies' common bath. The changing room was small and empty save for a couple of elderly ladies who chatted tunelessly on their way out.

Glad they were alone, Megan found a wicker basket for her clothing and towel. She quickly stripped and grabbed a small towel to take with her.

Syler was already at one of the shower stations when Megan came into the steamy room. As she picked her way across the tiles, Megan held her towel to her chest in a gesture of modesty that was more out of habit than anything else. She pulled over one of the wooden stools and met Syler's excited gaze with her own. Megan entire skin flushed with heat and the idea of having the big bathroom to themselves as she ducked her head under the shower's spray.

"Want me to wash your back?" Syler asked. She held up the sudsy puff in one hand.

"Yes please," Megan answered. She glanced at the doorway to the changing room to reassure herself nobody was coming in before she twisted her hair up and pinned it with a clip. She turned around and welcomed the soft touch of Syler's puff. While she was both gentle and thorough, Syler's hands didn't stray from G-rated areas. She let Megan take care of those herself, which only made Megan hungry for more.

Syler doused her with generous bucketfuls of hot water from the tap to end the back-scrubbing. They tidied the washing up corner and placed their buckets upside down over the stools.

Across from the line of shower stations was a large bath and a smaller, circular one filled with cool water. Syler folded her towel and put it on top of her head. She bent down to splash hot water from the bigger bathing area onto the ledge and over her feet and legs. With a sigh of pleasure, she slipped into the hot water. Syler sat on the floor of the bath and the water came up to her shoulders.

"This is so nice," she said over her shoulder to Megan. Syler leaned back on her hands and stretched her long body out, incidentally giving Megan a sumptuous view that had her gulping down a rush of inappropriate feelings. Syler looked up with a quirky grin and a knowing expression. She held out a hand and said, "Come on in, the water's gorgeous."

"That's not the only gorgeous thing here," Megan said as she lowered herself into the bath.

Syler tossed her towel aside and sprawled out with her arms hanging loosely over the side. The water was indeed lovely. It wasn't too hot and the minerals from the natural hot spring left Megan's skin soft. Megan dumped handfuls of water over her shoulders and back and got thoroughly distracted by Syler as she efficiently moved herself through the water on her hands. She took a slow, circular path around where Megan sat.

The fact that she could only look without touching inflamed Megan's desire even more. Syler came around behind her and Megan could almost feel the brush of Syler's skin over her own.

"How about we move to the private bath?" Syler asked in a low voice. She stood and sheets of water streamed down the planes of her body. Megan blinked up at the sudden vision and was glad her face was already red from the steamy air and hot water.

"Good idea," Megan said in a raspy voice as she followed Syler into the changing room.

Roughly attired in their yukatas and clutching their towels and various bath things, they went over to the door of the private bath. Megan knocked twice out of habit before she opened the door to a tiny changing area with only two baskets. She slid the ancient bolt lock closed behind them and checked the clock above the door.

The chilly night breeze cooled her skin. Megan shivered as she untied her belt and slipped her damp yukata off her shoulders. She tossed her clothing into one of the baskets.

The wooden floor was cold and sleek under her bare feet. In the middle of the room, the bath was made of a circular wooden barrel that looked like it would be at maximum capacity with the two of them in it. At one side, a spout kept a steady stream of hot water flowing into the bath. The only lit area was the small changing cubby and the light from the single electric bulb that barely filtered into the bathing area. The gaps in the bamboo blinds surrounding their little grotto seemed larger than when she'd seen them from the ground and Megan was glad of the darkness. Lights from the rooms of other hotels cast sparkles over the rippling surface of the water in the tub.

Megan braced one hand on the smooth wood rim to ease herself into the bucket-like tub. Her entrance sent a tidal wave cascading over the side. Once she was in the bath, Megan stretched out her arms. She promptly forgot all of her hesitation when Syler settled down next to her. The bath was small enough that Megan had to sit pressed up against Syler's body. Of course, she didn't mind that a bit.

She leaned back into Syler's arms with the soft pressure of Syler's breasts against her skin. The hard nubs gave away Syler's aroused state. Megan closed her eyes in pleasure as Syler placed a soft kiss on the side of her neck. She had been waiting and aching for just that and wanted more. Aware they might be overheard if anyone was using the baths on either side of them, Megan bit back the moan that Syler's lips on her evoked.

"Is this all right?" Syler whispered as her lips moved over Megan's skin.

"Almost," Megan said. She shifted and turned around. She got up onto her knees briefly before she settled down, straddling Syler's lap. Under the water, Megan felt the soft brush of hair between her thighs where they met. Syler's hands traced down her body to rest on her hips. Megan licked her lips and glanced down to where Syler's breasts were cradled and buoyant by the hot water. Megan put both hands out and grasped the side of the bath on either side of Syler's body. She leaned closer to Syler and murmured, "Now this is all right."

She felt Syler draw in a quick breath as their lips met. Eagerly, Megan opened her mouth. Syler claimed her with a fierce hunger that belied the gentle restraint she'd shown earlier. The hands on Megan's hips skimmed over her thighs and dipped between her legs. Syler's fingertips just barely brushed the place where a thrumming arousal swelled.

Without breaking the deep kiss, Megan reached down and caught Syler's hands in her own. She brought them up to cup her breasts. Megan rose up on her knees. She threw her head back in ecstasy as Syler's mouth found her nipples and sucked her hard. Megan renewed her grip on the side of the tub and she rocked her hips, rubbing up against Syler's smooth body in the heated embrace of the hot water.

She spread her legs and pressed herself fully against Syler. Her breaths came faster. Megan wasn't sure how much more she could take, but she was determined to make the most of their privacy. She moved so Syler's lips left her aching hard nipple. Megan bent her head to kiss her on the mouth before moving to her neck, her shoulders, anywhere Megan could reach and claim with her lips and tongue. The mineral-rich water left a slight soapy taste in her mouth. Syler gave a soft moan of pleasure. Megan loved hearing her. They were both heating up. Megan was too aroused to think anything of it when Syler suddenly tensed against her. She did notice when Syler pulled away and held Megan still.

"Don't stop, Syler," Megan panted. She thrust her hips, begging for Syler's hands on her. She breathed heavily. Her body trembled with need. Megan said in a frantic whisper, "Don't you dare stop. I want you to fuck me right here and make me come hard."

"Sweetheart, I think we should probably move downstairs before this goes any further," Syler said. Her hands drifted down and held Megan's hips still. With a gentle push, Syler guided Megan to sink down into the deep water.

"I can't wait, I'm so hot for you," Megan said in a voice that was heavy with need. "Please, Syler." She groaned in frustration, but Syler only moved Megan away from her before she rose to step from the tub. While Megan blinked in confusion, Syler made a beeline for the changing cubby. She whirled her yukata over her shoulders and charged back with one of their towels in her hands.

"Take this towel, and come into the changing area right now." Syler snapped off the order in a tone that Megan had never heard her use outside of the hospital. She considered and rejected the option of pouting. Megan accepted the towel and ducked into the narrow space. Syler met her by wrapping Megan's yukata roughly around her still-wet body.

"Dry off quickly and don't take this off."

Holding her yukata closed with one hand, Megan briefly rubbed herself down as best she could and tied her sash into a simple knot. Even though Megan was a bit uneasy by Syler's sudden mood change, the fire in her belly smoldered and would not die.

Her body quivered with arousal, which made logical thinking difficult. Her thighs were already slick a second after she'd dried herself but there was nothing Megan could do about that. Syler stuffed their things into a towel and ushered Megan out with a gentle but firm hand on the small of her back.

They were in the elevator when Syler said, "I didn't want to scare you, but I saw someone in the window of the hotel across from us."

Megan froze with a sick feeling in her gut.

The elevator arrived at their floor. Syler held the door open as Megan shuffled down the hall to their room. The table had been pushed against the wall and two futons were already set out, side by side on the tatami. Syler locked the door behind them and stood with her back to it.

"The room was dark and at first I thought it was empty," Syler said. She took a breath and continued, "But after a while, I saw there was something in the window, just a dark shape against more darkness. It was just sitting there, not moving and I thought it was furniture or something like that. Then I saw a red light. Like a laser pointer."

Or a camera.

Neither of them said the words, but they still hovered in the air. Syler pressed her lips together before she said, "That's when I knew I had to get us out of there."

Someone was watching them. Megan's knees gave out and she collapsed onto the futon nearest her. She hugged her arms to her chest and shivered. She felt violated, the wonder and pleasure she found in Syler's arms cheapened.

"Maybe it was just my mind playing tricks," Syler said. She sank down next to Megan and put a hand on her knee. "But I don't think so. I also don't think it's just some random pervert who gets off on peeping at women in the bath. Who knew you were here?"

"Just the scheduler," Megan said. She clutched at her yukata in alarm. "I thought those records were confidential under the Privacy Act. Charles wouldn't have access to them, would he?"

"I wouldn't put it past him," Syler said. "That man thinks he owns everything and everyone in the hospital." Syler swept to her feet and had her hand on the doorknob before Megan realized what was happening. Her face was set. Syler said, "I'm going over there to see who's behind this once and for all."

"No!" Megan reached out in alarm. "Syler, don't."

"Why not? Meg, if you've been targeted, I damn well want to know who it is and put a stop to it."

"I understand," Megan said. "But they might be armed or something. I don't think it's safe to just go over there. Besides, we still have the advantage that they don't know we know."

"All right," Syler said. She looked angry but she stepped away from the door. "I don't like it, but you do have a point about it being dangerous. Whoever is behind this, I bet they've got someone doing the dirty work for them. Possibly a pro."

"Thank you for trusting me." Megan let out a long breath and threw herself backward onto the futon. The puffy down comforter billowed around her. She turned to meet Syler's worried gaze and was at once overwhelmed with the urge to put the ugly incident from both of their minds.

Megan kept her eyes on Syler. Casually, almost unconsciously, Megan drew her legs together and slid down onto her side in a sensual pose. The bare skin of her thighs slipping against each other breathed a warm glow into life within her, tinged with the electric tingle of thwarted arousal. Megan let the front of her yukata gap slightly as she purred, "But until the interruption, it was a very nice bath."

"Mmm. I thought so too."

As she resolutely put the lingering unease from her mind, Megan looked over to the sitting area and got an idea. Her breathing quickened and her skin tingled with the renewed kick of desire that coursed through her. She rubbed suddenly sweaty palms against her yukata.

"Syler, how about a drink? I'm a bit thirsty."

"Good idea, so am I," Syler said. "There's tea in the fridge. How about I get it for you?"

"Let's both go," Megan said. She sat up with a slow, sensual full-body stretch. She lowered her gaze to Syler. "I want you in the sitting room."

"You do?" Syler said with a quirk of her lips. She stood and tugged her belt into place before she followed Megan into the sitting room. On her way to the fridge, Megan made sure the drapes were pulled fully closed.

Aware Syler was watching her, Megan deliberately bent over more than necessary as she peered into the fridge. She selected a bottle of cold tea and made a show of straightening up before she crossed the small space and handed it to Syler, who sat in one of the chairs. Syler opened the bottle and took a long drink before she silently offered it to Megan, who took it and swallowed a quick gulp before she capped the bottle and set it aside.

"That's all? Aren't you thirsty?" Syler asked in a low voice.

"Yes I am," Megan said. "Hungry too." She stepped around the low table and surreptitiously nudged it away before she sank to her knees in front of Syler. She reached out and ran her fingers down the soft cotton covering Syler's lap. The action elicited a gasp. Syler's cheeks flushed.

"Do you remember that I promised to take care of you like you always do so well for me?"

"Yes," Syler breathed.

"I want you to give yourself to me tonight," Megan said. She shifted as a twinge of sultry heat speared through her and settled between her aching thighs. Megan licked her bottom lip as a frisson of nerves hit her. "If that's all right with you."

"It is completely and absolutely all right with me," Syler said. Her chest rose and fell with her breaths as she leaned back in the chair. "I'm all yours, Meg. What are you going to do with me, then?"

Megan didn't reply in words, but she cast her eyes down and at the same time shrugged out of her yukata until it hung down from the sash at her waist. Megan spread her knees and parted the soft cotton there as well. The action left her open and exposed. She heard Syler's breath catch in her throat and basked in the heat of Syler's gaze on her. She raised her head to face Syler squarely.

"Hands on the armrests," Megan said. Syler complied. Her fingers clutched at the worn upholstery. Still on her knees, Megan gently teased the skirt of Syler's yukata open and peeled the edges back to expose her thighs, all the way up to the patch of dark hair. Syler sucked in a hard breath as Megan leaned forward and kissed a trail up the inside of her thigh, heading slowly and inexorably for the juncture between her legs.

"Sweetheart," Syler said in a half-groan, "are you okay with this?"

"If you are," Megan whispered against the tense muscles of Syler's thigh. Megan slid one hand under Syler's knee and Syler jumped. Megan stopped immediately.

"Sorry," Syler said. She cleared her throat and worked her fingers on the armrests. "I want you to keep doing what you are doing, it's just, um, nobody's done this to me before."

"Really?" Megan paused in her soft exploration. "I've never gone down on a woman before, so that makes two of us." She let her eyes drift half-shut and looked up at Syler's flushed face. "Although I have to say I have been paying attention and I've learned from the best. Still if you feel uncomfortable I don't have to do this."

"No, it's okay. I've always wondered if getting was as nice as giving," Syler said. She shifted slightly, opening her legs a bit as she did so. The movement revealed a flash of silken folds. Megan drew in a reverent breath. Hunger sparked into life within herself. She bit back the moan of desire.

Syler took a deep breath and gave Megan her characteristic rakish grin. "Go on then, you have me at your mercy."

Megan was honored and blessed with the gift Syler had just given her. A gush of wetness blossomed between her own thighs. She urged Syler's leg up and draped it over her shoulder, opening Syler fully to her. A soft groan and a thrust of Syler's hips ignited Megan's thirst. She ached to taste the inviting petals spread out before her.

Syler was tight and small, inner lips tucked inside the fuller outer ones, delicate as a shell. Megan scooted forward on her knees and bent her head to drop a kiss first on those sleek lips, then very lightly flicked the nub in its sheath with her tongue. Megan had tasted herself on Syler's kiss before, so she wasn't surprised at the fact that it was not exactly sweet honey, but she loved being where she was. She loved the taste that was uniquely Syler. She basked in the scent that filled her nose and mouth. Nobody had ever been where she was at that moment, and if Megan had anything to say about it, nobody else would have the honor either.

Megan pursed her lips and blew very gently, eliciting a small jerk and whimper of need from Syler. From above Megan's head, quickened breaths welcomed and guided her. She spread Syler's thighs a bit more with her hands and latched onto her tempting clit, soft and shy within the sleek folds. A thrill kicked deep in her belly as Megan felt Syler harden within her mouth and she couldn't stop the sound of pleasure that hummed in her throat.

While she listened for any word of caution or displeasure, Megan grew bolder and dipped her head to explore with her lips and tongue, sucking and tasting. She loved every moment, drunk on the soft sounds of surrender Syler exhaled with every breath. Entranced, Megan suckled at Syler's slick inner lips. She drew back so they slowly slipped from her mouth. She loved when Syler teased her like that and apparently Syler did too as she let go with a moan and a soft, breathy, "Oh *fuck*."

Under Megan's mouth, Syler's body was tense and still, as if she was straining to keep from moving too much. Megan couldn't believe the immense feeling of power she had at the way Syler responded to her. She kept her caresses light, carefully avoiding direct contact with the center of Syler's pleasure. With Syler's harsh breaths in her ears, Megan delicately trailed her tongue up Syler's entire length before she dropped a soft kiss to the swollen bud. She gave into the urge and put her mouth down fully over Syler's clit. She teased the nub ever so softly with her tongue. The action was met by a strangled cry. Megan quickly raised her head.

Syler sprawled back with a stunned look on her face. She seemed unaware that the front of her yukata had fallen open, revealing rock hard nipples jutting into the air. Her chest heaved and she fixed Megan with a gaze that was desperate with need.

"Meg, fuck that's good, but you're killing me here," Syler said. Her hands on the armrest of the chair were white-knuckled and trembling.

Megan couldn't stand to make Syler suffer any more, no matter how pleasurable it was.

"All right. Let's move over to the bed and I'll finish you," Megan said. She lowered her voice and said, "I want you on your back for me."

"Dear God," Syler breathed.

Megan's legs trembled as she stood. Her thighs were slick as she took the few steps from the sitting area over to the main room. They both sprawled down on the futon. Syler got a wicked look on her face.

"Did you like sucking me?" Syler purred. "Did you like having me in your mouth?"

"Yes I did," Megan said. Her voice was tight with need. She raised her hips, bucking against nothing. Her entire body shook with suppressed tension.

"Well come over here and get your head down to finish what you started. I want to taste your sweet pussy too." Syler looked over at Megan. "Would you be okay with that?"

"Yes," Megan said. She had never wanted anything more.

"Good." Syler lay back, yukata disheveled and legs spread. Megan swallowed a gush of desire as she drank in the deliciously erotic scene. She was very aware of her throbbing clit, the wetness between her legs as she moved to lie beside Syler.

Megan got a pleasant jolt as Syler guided her so that Megan was halfway lying on Syler's body, her lower belly firm under Megan's cheek, the wet thicket of hair right in front of her. She fought the squeak of happiness as Syler spread Megan's thighs and greeted her aching sex with a sudden, deep kiss.

There was no need for words as Megan delved down as well. Her tongue sought the slick bud of Syler's erect clit. As Syler held her, urging her legs apart and teasing her with a slow, searching tongue, Megan rocked her hips. She silently begged for more. Syler didn't let up. Megan tried to concentrate on her own task, but she found the act of eating Syler upside down while receiving it herself overwhelmed her. She pulled back.

"I'm sorry," Megan gasped. She stilled her hips and bit off a moan.

Syler whispered against her, "What is it baby girl?"

"I don't think I'm quite ready for this," Megan said. She felt a flash of frustration when Syler broke the contact, leaving Megan wet and throbbing with arousal. "I'm sorry, I just can't really get into it from here."

"Hey it's okay," Syler said. She sat up and gathered Megan into her arms. Their bodies pressed together, alternately soft and hard, slick and wet. Syler rubbed a hand softly over Megan's back and drew her close. She dropped a kiss onto Megan's bare shoulder before she said, "I was having a bit of trouble not getting distracted myself. What you did to me was fucking amazing, but I want to concentrate on you right now." Syler looked at her with smoldering love in her eyes. "Do you want that?"

"Yes," Megan said. She let out a slow breath and twitched her hips as a deep twinge ran through her. "If that's all right. I don't want to leave you hanging."

Syler shrugged with a carefree grin. "No way. Getting you off is the best thing ever. And don't worry, I've got a few good ideas that we both should like. Now come here, Meg."

Megan sank down over Syler's sprawled body, straddling her. She still had her yukata on, even though it didn't do anything more than cover her backside. Megan liked the feeling of the sash around her middle. It held her tight as her body fought to release the humming tension radiating from between her legs. Hungry for the touch, Megan reached down and guided Syler's hand to her. She didn't have to say anything before she felt Syler at her opening. With a quick thrust of her hips, she accepted Syler eagerly.

"You're so wet for me," Syler murmured. "God, Meg, you're so tight. Fuck, I need this."

Megan felt Syler shift underneath her. A glance downward told her Syler was positioned in a way that with every movement Megan made, her hand would rub against herself as well. The idea of Megan's body controlling Syler's pleasure gave Megan a great kick of heat deep in her belly.

She got used to the intrusion, and Megan settled herself on Syler. As she did, Megan let her inner muscles work, clenching and relaxing over Syler's fingers.

"I didn't know you could do that, Meg," Syler said in a groan. Her long body trembled against Megan's spread thighs.

"I have many skills too," Megan teased in a breathless voice.

Syler placed one hand on her leg and very slowly moved it under Megan's yukata until she held Megan's hip. A wave of pleasure hit her as Megan began to move. Very slowly she drew Syler in and out of her even though her body screamed to let Syler pound her hard and fast. The feeling was so good and so right. Her body fell into a smooth rhythm. Megan kept her head up, legs spread wide. She knew Syler could see all of her. Megan loved being so exposed.

"Sorry if I don't wait for you," Syler said in a breathless voice. The body between Megan's thighs was hard with tension. "I'm nearly there and you just look so fucking hot like that."

"Do it," Megan said. "Don't fight it."

The shuddering tension between her legs built with every movement as she took Syler deep. Her breaths came faster. Megan bore down and rocked her hips. She wantonly thrust against Syler. Her breasts bounced along with her movements. Megan threw her head back as the jolts of tension quickened within herself. Syler's climax broke and her body shuddered in release. Megan opened her eyes to drink in the erotic sight of her lover sprawled out underneath her.

With Syler still firmly within her, Megan pumped herself harder, desperate to come as well. Megan didn't care if Syler knew what she was doing or not and she reached between her own legs. She drew her fingers around where Syler was pushed deep into her to gather up the slick wetness that streamed from her and brought her fingers up to stroke her clit.

Syler's reverent whisper told Megan that she not only knew, but she also approved. Megan had always been hesitant to touch herself during intimacy, as if she was being critical of her partner, but Syler's enjoyment of the act gave Megan the freedom to do as she ached to.

It was so intense and raw, Megan couldn't stop herself. While Syler thrust in and out of her, Megan bucked her hips in rhythm. At the same time, her fingers were busy on her clit, stroking herself into the stratosphere. The first jolts of climax came and Megan gave herself over to them.

She paused on the brink, hips straining and muscles clenching. Then the peak hit. She gritted her teeth as the shuddering waves broke over her. The hand on her hip held her steady until Megan fell forward to collapse onto Syler's heaving chest. The fingers within her eased out and Megan drew in a breath as Syler gently cupped her super-sensitive sex, hot and tingling with the last lingering traces of climax.

"You just keep getting better at this," Syler murmured into Megan's hair.

"Practice makes perfect," Megan said. She nestled against Syler, skin on skin and wrapped in the crumpled cotton of their yukatas. Syler's hand stroked slowly up and down Megan's bare back. Megan sighed in pleasure. She was sleepy and sated, content to lie in Syler's arms and listen to her deep breaths and calm heartbeat.

"So is it?" Megan asked, halfway into a dream.

"Is what, Meg?"

"Is getting as nice as giving?"

"I'd have to say," Syler's low voice rumbled through her, "that's a difficult question. One I don't think I have enough evidence to answer yet."

"If it's evidence you want, I'm always happy to oblige," Megan purred. She sighed happily and pressed herself a bit more firmly to Syler, who answered with a soft chuckle.

"Are you going to sleep like that?" Syler asked. "It's a really hot look for you, but I'm not sure how comfortable it's going to be in a few hours."

"Maybe you have a point." Megan arched her back in a stretch that allowed her to rub up against the length of Syler's body and said, "Actually, I was wondering if you wanted to have a late-night dip with me? The inside bath is open until two."

"That's a great idea." Syler eased them both into a sitting position and gave Megan a long, appreciative look that called up a shivery flush of heat to her skin.

After she fixed her yukata, Megan scampered with Syler to the main bathroom. It was deserted again and this time they shared a few kisses and playful touches in the echoing baths. Back in the room, Megan dropped her yukata to the floor and snuggled into one of the two futons.

"Are you going to join me?" Megan asked as Syler toweled off her hair.

Syler straightened up and said, "I'd love to." She scooped up the pillow from the unoccupied futon and also shed her clothing before she slipped under the comforter that Megan held up for her. Syler put her arms around Megan, who gave a deep sigh of happiness as their bodies came together, not with the urgency of sex, but with a soft devotion that Megan was beginning to cherish above all else.

Chapter Eight

A SHARP RINGTONE shook Megan out of a lovely warm sleep. Beside her, Syler bolted upright and grabbed her phone. She answered with a terse word. Her face hardened as she listened to the voice on the other end. After a minute or so, she barked a brief affirmative and ended the call.

"What is it?" Megan asked. She sat up as Syler leapt to her feet and started rummaging for her clothes.

"I'm so sorry Meg," Syler came over and knelt on the comforter. She held her shirt in one hand and reached out to cup Megan's cheek with the other. "There's an emergency and I have to go back. It's Nikky. She was just brought in by ambulance with numerous contusions, a possible ruptured kidney and suspected splenic lac. You can stay here and come back on the train tomorrow. We've got the room until ten—"

Megan threw back the comforter. "I'm going with you." She twisted her hands together. "This is my fault. If I had tried harder to protect Nikky this wouldn't have happened."

"You don't know what happened," Syler said. She reached out and gave Megan's hand a squeeze. "No what ifs, all right?"

Even though she had a horrible, black feeling in her belly, Megan nodded. Syler turned away and yanked her sports bra over her head. Megan was right behind her. Years of practice being on-call gave them a firefighter-like efficiency as they dressed.

"Why don't you get the car," Megan said as she stuffed the last item into her overnight bag. "I'll check us out."

"Good plan," Syler said. "I'll give you the extra for my share of the drinks once we're on the road."

"No way, I lost the ping-pong fair and square, and I want to get moving as soon as possible," Megan said. She was the first out the door, already with the envelope that contained their combined funds for the room in her hand. Even at that late hour, a young employee met Megan at the front desk. After she passed over the fee and the room key, the worker dropped his fist into his palm as if he'd just remembered something.

"Maier-sama, there was a package left for you this evening."

"What?" Megan had to think for a moment before she remembered. "Oh yes, thanks." She took the slim pack, which bore the logo of the one convenience store in the area, and shoved it into her pocket. She darted out to the street where Syler's Jimny idled at the curb. Megan knocked on the driver's side window.

"Scoot over," she said. "I'll drive and you can rest."

"All right, thanks," Syler said.

The drive back was quiet. In the passenger seat, Syler crossed her arms and tucked her chin against her chest, dozing as Megan navigated the deserted highway. She pushed the speed limit with a careful eye in the rear view mirror.

When they reached the hospital, Megan let Syler out at the after-hours entrance then found a parking spot in the lot behind the hospital.

She cut the engine but didn't move to get out. Megan sat in the car, trying to muster the nerve to open the door. Her hands shook and her chest was tight. She squeezed her eyes shut and concentrated on slowing her breathing. Minutes crawled by. Megan couldn't let her own anxiety keep her from facing the scene that was waiting for her and her own guilt. Even though she didn't feel ready, Megan forced her body to move.

Guilt dogged her heels. She picked up on the signs of abuse but she let Charles intimidate her into silence. What happened to Nikky was her fault. The walk inside seemed agonizingly long but still all too short. Megan passed through the automatic doors with fear in the pit of her belly.

The after-hours waiting room was smaller than the vast ones in the main area of the hospital. Megan crossed it in only a few steps. Syler was already there. In the short time Megan had been wrestling with herself in the car, Syler had changed into her usual scrubs and Crocs combination.

Syler crouched down on the squeaky floor with concern and compassion on her face. In front of her, Fabia slouched on one of the long vinyl-covered waiting benches. Her makeup was streaked with tears. Her usually immaculate hair was frizzy and fell down around her face in lank tendrils. She was in a velour jogging suit that looked like lounge wear. Syler spoke to her in a low, calm voice.

"When the CT results come back, we'll know if surgery is necessary or not. Don't worry, Mrs. Okamoto, your child is in good hands." Syler leaned forward and said, "I've called security and you can wait in a private room if you don't feel safe out here."

Fabia sniffled and nodded. Megan could only stand, frozen. She clutched onto the back of an unoccupied chair and felt the familiar fist of tightness in her chest. Her breath didn't seem to be making it all the way into her lungs.

Shouting behind her shattered the trapped-in-amber feeling. Megan whirled to see Junichiro Okamoto barreling into the waiting room. Two plump and elderly security guards tried to get in his way, but instead of stopping him, they only succeeded in slightly hampering his forward progress.

Megan didn't even think before she leaped in front of him with her arms out.

"That's far enough," she snapped. "I'm going to have to ask to you leave or be escorted out."

"I want to see my son," he said. He shook the guards' hands off his arms. His face was drawn and worried. "I'm his father, I have a right to be here."

Anger sparked into a blazing inferno within herself. Megan took a step forward to crowd the man back a step as the guards hovered on either side of him. It was almost midnight, but Junichiro was in an immaculate business suit and he held a briefcase. Even through her anger, Megan was struck by the incongruity of his outfit with his wife's.

"Not after what you did," Megan shot back.

"What?" Junichiro stopped. His face showed nothing more than complete shock. "What's going on? Fabia, what did you tell them?"

He weaved to peer around Megan's body. A quick glance over her shoulder revealed Fabia, now on her feet and with her back to her husband. She was pressed up against Syler, who had her hands on Fabia's shoulders and a rather alarmed look on her face.

"I told them nothing," Fabia said, her voice muffled by Syler's scrubs. "It was an accident. Why are you even here?"

"Pippa-san called me," he said. "She said she saw the ambulance from her cottage. Fabia, why didn't you tell me? I was lucky to get back in time to catch the last train from Nagoya. Any later and I'd have had to hire a car to get me back from Tokyo."

The words hit home. Both Megan and Syler gaped. Syler put her hands up and backed away a step.

"That rat-bitch," Fabia whirled to face her husband and spat, "I'm gonna fire her fat ass! This is your fault!"

"Why? I wasn't even there."

"Exactly. You're never here. You don't talk to me, you don't look at me like you used to." Fabia's voice was shrill.

Megan flinched. Fabia stood right behind her, shrieking into her ear.

"I know you hate me and Nikky. It's not my fault he's a little freak. It's yours for never being around to show him how to be a real man. Yeah I took him across my knee, the way you never had the balls to do!"

Megan turned so she could look at the both of them while still keeping her position between the two, no longer certain who she was protecting. Junichiro shook his head with a look of shock on his face. His wife lurched against the long bench with a hic-cup.

"Have you been drinking?"

"So what if I have? You don't care. I got a call from his teacher today. He won't even use the boys' bathroom at school. I've had enough of all this make-believe! You were always too soft on Nikky. I just showed him who's boss. I didn't do anything wrong. All this I'm-a-girl shit is a phase. He's just a sissy little faker."

"Get out of my house," Junichiro said in a low voice. His knuckles were white as he clutched his briefcase. "Stay away from me. Stay away from my child."

"Fine. Whatever," Fabia said. She crossed her arms and tossed her head. "I was done with the both of you anyway."

As Fabia made a move toward the door, the frozen spell that held Megan in its grip shattered. She crossed the waiting room in a single bound and turned the full force of the rage that had seized her onto Fabia.

"You did this!" Megan thundered and stabbed a finger in her direction. Fabia flinched but Megan only dropped her voice and hissed, "What kind of mother beats her child and blames her hus-band? What kind of person are you?" The words felt like pure sulfuric acid but something broke within her and she couldn't stop. She didn't want to. More venom welled up. Megan prepared to unleash it, but her vision went dark and the words were choked off by a firm pressure.

The sudden immobility startled Megan silent. She twisted violently against the arms that held her in a gentle but unyielding grip until she realized it was Syler. Megan pressed her face into Syler's shoulder and squeezed her eyes shut.

"Get family services and psych in here stat!" Syler's words were directed over Megan's head. The pressure holding Megan still eased. Syler said in a low voice, "Come on, Meg. Let's go sit down."

Megan's legs shook so hard she could barely stand. She let Syler guide her from the after-hours waiting room and down a dark hallway. Something soft hit the backs of her knees and Megan fell into a chair. As her eyes adjusted to the darkness, she saw Syler had led her into the main lobby. The hulking desks that housed the information counter and cashier stations loomed in front of them. The anger left Megan. Empty, she sagged forward and caught her head in her hands.

"Talk to me," Syler said. She drew a hand over Megan's shoulder. At the kind touch, Megan tensed.

"I'm sorry I lost it back there," Megan said in a muffled voice. "You shouldn't be here. Your patient is waiting."

"I know Meg," Syler said. "Just let me know you're going to be okay. I'm sorry I grabbed you like that, but I had to stop the situation before it got out of hand and we both said things we'd have to apologize for later on. As much as I wanted to be right there with you, giving that woman a piece of my mind, that's not going to solve anything."

The hand left her shoulder.

"How can you be so calm?" Megan raised her eyes to look at Syler. She was kneeling down in front of her, hands clasped loosely on the bench next to Megan.

"It's my job to be calm."

"But she's a monster! She hurt their child bad enough for a trip to the emergency room," Megan said. A great weight dropped into her belly. "And her husband—it's over between them, isn't it?"

"Not necessarily," Syler said. "Nothing can change what

happened or what she did, and I'm honestly shocked and sickened by this whole thing but the point is, now that it's out in the open, they can start getting help. All of them, as a family. Maybe they need some time apart, but there's still a chance for reconciliation and recovery. I believe that."

Megan was silent for a beat as she processed the information.

"Sweetheart, I've never seen you like this. What happened? Something hit close to home, didn't it?"

A thick wave of sickness roared into Megan's chest. She drew in a breath to finally excise her soul when the PA system blared into life, paging Syler.

With a hissed curse, Syler got to her feet. She laid a hand on Megan's back as she said, "I hate to leave you here, but I've got to go. You should go home, Meg, okay?" She asked in a hesitant voice, "Do you want some time alone?"

Megan knew she should say yes, tell Syler to get away from her but the roaring emptiness was too frightening. "Don't leave me," Megan whispered in a cracked voice.

"You know I won't," Syler told her. "I may not be right next to you, but you know I'm always with you." She brushed a hand through Megan's hair. "How about you go back to my place? There's a spare key in my desk drawer. It may be a while, but I'm not going to be able to sleep until I see you again and know you're okay. Is that all right?"

Megan nodded. She held herself still as the echo of Syler's hurried footsteps faded away. She stayed like that for a long time, just breathing. After an eternity, Megan found the strength to stand.

A shuffling sound startled her. Paolo's package fell from her pocket and landed on the floor at her feet. She picked it up. As if in a dream, Megan unfolded the paper wrapper. The photograph glistened in the greenish glow of the emergency exit sign. The wan light illuminated that perfect instant, the one moment in time where two hearts beat as one. She would not lose that. Megan made a promise. She would do whatever she had to, but she would not lose Syler.

With a burglar-like feeling Megan slipped into the surgeons' office, relieved no other people were there who might want an explanation as to why she was rummaging around in one of the desks.

The key was where Syler had said it was. Megan slipped out the back way. She stopped by Syler's Jimny to retrieve her overnight bag and the souvenirs she'd bought. As she passed her own building, which was silent and dark, Megan was glad she had somewhere else to go. Somewhere she felt safe.

IT WAS STRANGE to be in Syler's apartment without her. An echoing surrealism took over Megan as she stood in the entrance hall. The lingering aroma of the forest bath salts Syler favored hung in the air, reminding Megan of the good times they'd shared and hopefully a promise of more to come.

Furtively, Megan got herself a drink of water from the kitchen before she stumbled into the bedroom. She changed into the oversized T-shirt she'd ignored earlier that evening in their *ryokan* where she'd fallen asleep in Syler's arms with nothing but the silken whisper of skin between them.

The bed was soft and welcoming. Megan curled up in the comforter. All sorts of thoughts and half-formed fears buffeted her. What if Syler regretted the promise of commitment she'd made earlier? They both had been through a number of firsts together. Would Syler later regret sharing them with Megan? What if she only saw Megan as a project? Something flawed that she had to fix. Megan rejected that thought. Syler wasn't like that. There was so much more Megan had seen in her eyes. She had to believe that.

Even though Megan was certain she wouldn't be able to sleep, she nodded off in the soft nest she'd made for herself.

What felt like a heartbeat later, warm arms came around Megan and she opened her eyes to a soft kiss on her temple. The curtains glowed with the first light of dawn. Syler was next to her. She looked tired. Her damp hair hung into her face.

"Sorry to wake you up."

"No, it's okay. Is everything all right?" Megan rasped.

"Nikky's going to be fine," Syler said. She settled against Megan and continued, "We managed to save the kidney but lost the spleen. She's going to be admitted for a few days until we're sure everything is back to normal."

"What about—Nikky's family?"

"While I was in surgery, the police came and took

statements," Syler said. She shrugged in a dismissive way. "I don't think it'll really go anywhere. You know how they deal with stuff like that here. Foreigners and family affairs. It's like we're still in the fucking middle ages. At any rate, it's now on her record."

Megan made a soft sound of agreement. Her blood sang for vengeance, but maybe tearing a family apart wasn't the answer.

"They both calmed down and had a long talk with psych—I think Erika Sugiura saw them. Mrs. Okamoto has agreed to stay with her sister and go to counseling. She'll be allowed visits in a neutral environment when she shows improvement. They've also arranged for Nikky to be assessed by a child psychologist who specializes in gender dysphoria. Have you heard of Doctor Aisaku Morihara?"

"Yes, I have," Megan said, impressed. "He's coming all the way from Ibaraki?"

"That's right," Syler said. She yawned and used the end of it to apologize. "Sorry, I'm dead on my ass here."

"That's all right," Megan said. She snuggled back into Syler's arms. "I just can't believe I was so wrong. I nearly accused an innocent man."

"Don't blame yourself, you had nothing more to work with than a flawed set of data originating from an unreliable source," Syler's voice was muffled and sleepy. Her breath was warm on Megan's shoulder.

"You're so sexy when you talk technical."

Instead of answering, Syler dropped one last kiss behind Megan's ear. With a whispered goodnight, she fell silent, and Megan went with her.

SINCE SHE HAD more time to rest and hadn't performed emergency surgery the night before, Megan was the first to wake up. She basked in watching Syler sleep, her expression beautiful and untroubled. Megan reached out and very softly, so as not to wake her, brushed a strand of hair from Syler's brow. The motion only elicited an unconscious movement where Syler leaned into the caress with the ghost of a smile. She really did sleep the sleep of the innocent.

As she had before, Megan got up and got busy the kitchen.

Breakfast was the meal she excelled at and she set about making a nice one for Syler. Megan rummaged around until she found some frozen salmon fillets for grilling plus the ingredients for a hearty miso soup. She was well on her way to making the soup to accompany a bunch of plump rice balls when Syler wandered into the kitchen.

"Hey beautiful." Megan turned from her task to greet Syler with a kiss and a piece of orange for her to start with.

"Thanks." Syler made orange-peel teeth. Megan laughed for the first time in what felt like forever.

"Stop playing and eat," Megan told her in a no-nonsense voice while simultaneously trying to stifle her giggles.

"Okay, okay. You know," Syler said as she watched Megan from her perch at the island, "I could get used to this. Waking up to you every morning." She glanced at the time display on the TV screen and amended, "Or afternoon. Meg, I've been thinking..."

Megan looked up from her task of stirring the soup. Her heart quickened at the tone in Syler's voice.

"Syler, don't—" Megan wanted to head her off, tell her to drop the subject before it was breached but Syler didn't stop.

"Why don't you keep the spare key? Consider this place yours. I'd love it if you moved in with me."

Megan froze. She was sure there was a look of horror on her face. "Syler," she whispered past the tightness in her throat. "Please, I—"

"Oh shit, Meg, forget I said anything." Syler was on her feet in an instant. She raked a hand through her hair. "It's just, God, I feel like there's something out there and it's trying to take you from me. I want to protect you, hold you to me and never let you go, so I blurted out something stupid and pressured you. Again. I was being selfish. I rushed things and that was a mistake. I'm sorry."

"No, don't be sorry," Megan said. She dropped the long cooking chopsticks with a clatter and tried to get her breaths to slow down. "I can't accept your offer, not right now. I've just gotten back on my feet and I need to have my own space for a while. You understand this isn't a rejection, right?" Megan reached out and took Syler's hands in hers. "I want us to take the next step because it's something we both want and not because of some outside force. How about we just enjoy what we have right now and not think about the future?"

"Deal," Syler said. For an instant Megan's heart ached at the look of sadness on Syler's face, but she shook back her hair and gave Megan a grin. "And I am really enjoying being with you, Meg."

"Me too," Megan said.

The mood lightened as they enjoyed the hearty breakfast. While Syler washed the dishes and a noontime drama played on the TV, Megan dressed in a blouse and a slim-fitting skirt that ended a few centimeters above her knees. She kept her hair loose but clipped on both butterfly barrettes before she went back into the kitchen

Syler gave her a slow once-over. "God Meg, do you know how hot you are in that skirt?"

Megan's cheeks got warm and she made a shushing motion with her hands.

"Are you going in today?" Syler asked.

"I think so. I want to see how Nikky's doing."

"Good idea. I'll go in with you." Syler paused and gave a wry chuckle. "Look at us workaholics. We can't simply spend a day away from our jobs."

"It's more than just a job," Megan said.

"You're right. Anyway, give me a minute. I would be pleased and honored to accompany you to the hospital."

MEGAN PICKED UP her lab coat from her office before she went to Nikky's room. The child was asleep, a tiny form under the sheet. Junichiro was sitting in a chair beside the bed. He was still in his business suit but he had lost his jacket and tie somewhere along the line and his shirt was crumpled. He looked as if he hadn't slept. Megan recalled her own pleasant night spent in her lover's arms with a stab of guilt.

Quietly, Megan slid the door open and entered the room. Junichiro jumped up to greet her.

"Please tell me some news, Doctor. When can we expect Nikky to wake up?"

"Don't worry, Mr. Okamoto," Megan said. She picked up the chart and studied it. Syler's precise, neat handwriting decorated the pages. Megan paused for a moment to admire the detailed script. No illegible scrawl for her. "The procedure was laparoscopic so the recovery time is shorter than an open operation. I can attest that the surgeon who carried out the procedure is highly skilled. Nikky should be waking up soon. She'll have some soreness, and I'm afraid she'll have to take antibiotics every day plus get a flu shot every year."

"How could I have missed this?" Junichiro said. He studied Megan. "Did you know about what was happening to Nikky?"

"I suspected," Megan said. She shifted her weight from one foot to the other. "I'm sorry I couldn't do anything more." She bit her lip and fought the urge to make excuses. He didn't need that from her.

"No, it's not your job to police all your patients," Junichiro said. Even though Megan secretly disagreed she kept silent. He let out a heavy sigh and said, "This is my fault. I let my work take me away from my home and family when they needed me most. It's my duty to provide for them, but I also need to be there with them. I ignored my wife and couldn't protect my child. I'm a failure as a husband and father."

"There's still time to fix that," Megan said.

"Yes, starting today," he said. "And what about what they were saying about Nikky wanting to be a girl? Do you really think it's true and not a phase?"

"You'll just have to talk it over with Nikky," Megan said. She twisted her stethoscope around her hands. "Do you think you'll have trouble accepting that? Your wife seems to have a problem with it."

"She's from a very traditional family but if she wants me to give her another chance, she's got to change her thinking." Junichiro gave a tired shrug and said, "As for me, well I was a bit shocked at first, but I guess anyone would be. It'll take some getting used to, but I just want a happy, safe, and healthy child. Boy or girl or somewhere in between, it doesn't matter to me."

The frank words brought a warm glow to Megan's chest. "That's good to hear. Is there anything I can get you? I know the one machine in this place that makes not-horrible coffee."

"No, but thank you anyway."

Megan checked the sleeping patient once more before she let herself out of the room. On her way back to her desk, a large and unwelcome presence came up beside her.

Megan cringed as Charles fell into step with her.

"I suppose you want to say, 'I told you so,'" he said in a snide tone. They passed through a cluster of nurses. Charles had to turn his wide-shouldered frame sideways to keep up with Megan.

"No I don't," Megan said. She fought down the wave of annoyance that came up whenever Charles was near her. "This very nearly ended in tragedy, and I feel I had a chance to stop it and I didn't. But at least the worst is over and the healing can begin." Megan stopped and closed her eyes for an instant as past regrets nearly overwhelmed her. There were some things that time would never heal.

Charles didn't seem to notice as he barreled on. "Let's just hope nothing else like this occurs. You are becoming quite an albatross for this hospital." His eyes flicked downward. "And I hope I don't need to remind you about our dress code, which states the hem of your skirt must touch the floor with two inches of extra material when you kneel. Do not tempt me to test that rule on you."

Megan's mouth dropped open. She closed it with a snap and glared at Charles. Anger filled her. The words fell out before she could stop them. "I would rather die than get on my knees in front of you." She stopped in horror. Charles was still her boss. Megan forced herself to relax. She said, "I'm sorry, but I have a lot of work to do and I'd like to finish it in reasonable time."

Charles didn't react other than to straighten his tie with one hand. With the briefest of nods, he took off down the hallway. Megan was not sad to see the back of him.

OVER THE NEXT few days, Nikky gained strength and curiosity. She often wandered around the hallways, exploring the hospital and chatting with various people. A few meetings with both a family counselor as well as Doctor Morihara ended up with the decision to let Nikky live as a girl for a while before they explored any invasive medical options. Overnight, Nikky changed from the sad, withdrawn shell into a lively, cheerful child who wanted to be friends with everybody.

Sakura, on the other hand, wasn't doing as well. She was still as cheerful as ever but she lost the weight she'd fought to gain and no longer left her room, even for a stroll in a wheelchair.

Megan caught Syler worrying over her bloodwork more than once. As a precautionary measure, Sakura was moved into an isolation room.

Nikky had been in the hospital for almost a week when Megan came across her in the hallway, standing in front of the window to Sakura's isolation room. Nikky held a word puzzle book and filled in the squares as the smaller child pointed. Megan peered into the room and saw that, unusually, Sakura was alone.

Megan kept her knees together as she squatted down next to Nikky. "Are the two of you getting into trouble here?" she asked.

"Hello Doctor Megan," Nikky said. "I couldn't reach the intercom so I brought over my puzzle book so we could play and chat."

"That's a great idea," Megan said. "Would you like to talk to Sakura-chan? You can't go in but how about I lift you up?"

"Really?"

"Really. Just for a minute, okay Nikky? Sakura-chan's only little and gets tired quickly."

On the other side of the glass, Sakura scrambled around happily on her crumpled bedspread in reaction to the activity outside. Megan looked down at Nikky, then over at Sakura who couldn't reach the intercom either. She needed backup. Megan dug out her PHS and sent Syler a quick text message. It was answered sooner than she expected as a moment later Syler and Sakura's father, Toshi came down the hallway, both of them had serious expressions and were deep in conversation.

"Hey Meg," Syler said. She had her PHS in her hand. "Did you just text me?"

"Yes," Megan said. "But since you're already here, just ignore it. Sakura-chan has a new friend who wanted to talk to her and I was wondering if someone could take care of things on the other side."

"Cool," Syler said. She turned to Toshi and asked, "Do you want to do the honors?"

"*Dozo*," he said. He extended one hand in a gallant gesture to offer the task to Syler.

"Okay. Give me a minute." Syler's somber expression vanished. She let loose with her megawatt smile that hit Megan right in the chest with a wallop of happiness. She paused to rub alcohol on her hands and slip on a hygienic mask. Toshi stayed in the hallway and watched with an indulgent expression.

Syler ducked into the room. She greeted Sakura with a tender touch and a few words before she scooped the small girl up into her arms and came over to the intercom. Through the glass, Syler looked at Megan and gave her a nod.

Megan wasn't sure she could heft Nikky as easily, so she got down and turned her back. "Climb on, princess."

Two arms came around her neck. Megan clasped her hands together under Nikky's backside. She tried not to groan as she stood up. Even though she was only six, Nikky was sturdy and tall. A few nurses had gathered and, along with Toshi, watched with interest. Megan knew the scene was most likely quite amusing and enjoyed herself as well.

Her arms were busy holding Nikky up so she sidled up to the intercom and said, "Can you pick up the receiver? Press the red button and we're in business."

Nikky did as instructed. Megan listened to a volley of giggles while Syler held Sakura in her arms. Sakura had to use both hands to hold the receiver on her side. The instrument looked almost comically oversized. The two girls chatted animatedly for a few minutes. With another signal from Syler, Megan gently got Nikky to end the call.

Sakura hung up on her end and freed a hand to wave at them. Nikky waved back and Megan blinked away the mist that rose to her eyes. With Nikky's weight still on her back, Megan watched as Syler carefully cradled Sakura in her arms, preparing to return her to her hospital bed. Quick as a kitten, the small child reached out and snagged Syler's hygienic mask.

Both of her hands were occupied. Syler could only turn her head to one side as Sakura tugged the mask off. Through the glass, Megan couldn't hear what Syler was saying, but her expression was startled and worried. Sakura wriggled in Syler's arms and made a cute kissy-face. The worried expression vanished as Syler laughed and Megan caught her breath at the beauty of the moment. Again, she felt as if she were invading something very personal but she couldn't look away. Her chest brimmed with emotion as Syler bent her head and very carefully gave Sakura the briefest, softest kiss on her forehead.

"We're lucky to have Terada-sensei," Toshi said from where he was standing next to Megan. She'd nearly forgotten he was there and Megan jumped. Toshi continued, "She's done so much for Sakura-chan."

"She's the best," Megan said in a quiet voice.

"Papa! I made a new friend!"

Nikky's voice rang in her ear. Megan winced. She turned to see Junichiro striding down the hallway. He came closer and Megan bent her knees to let Nikky down. She straightened up and made a show of rubbing at her back as Nikky scampered away. On the other side of the glass, Megan felt more than saw Syler laughing at her overdramatic actions, still with the tiny, fragile child cradled in her arms.

"Who's your new friend?" Junichiro scooped a giggling Nikky up.

"Her name's Sakura-chan and she's almost five. She likes the Hiroshima Carp and wants a pet horse. She's really good at word puzzles!"

The excited chatter faded as Junichiro took Nikky back to her room. Megan leaned against the glass and waited for Syler to come back out.

"So what we were talking about earlier," Toshi said the instant Syler cleared the doorway. "You'll do it for us, won't you?"

"I don't know," Syler said. She drew a hand over her face with a pensive look. Megan fought to keep from reaching out to her. "Don't you think it would be better to get someone from psych to talk to Sakura-chan?"

"No, she knows you and she trusts you," Toshi said. "She thinks the world of you, Sensei. You can tell her in a way she can understand and won't feel like she's being replaced. I think it's time she knew."

"All right," Syler said. Her expression changed to a warm one. "In the meantime, you have to think of what you're going to do for your next date night. How are you going to top Hana-no-Sato? Chiho-san is still talking about it and always makes me look at all the photos you guys took."

"I don't know, you have to help me," Toshi said dramatically.

"No way, you're on your own," Syler told him. She sobered and asked, "How is Chiho-san feeling these days? I noticed she's not coming in as often."

"Yesterday was pretty bad," Toshi said. "She's still taking it easy."

"Let me know if her condition worsens," Syler said. "It should be getting better soon, though."

"Thank you, Sensei."

Syler gave Toshi a pat on the back as he turned and headed into his daughter's isolation room. Syler leaned back against the glass with her arms crossed and turned her attention back to Megan, who had moved away so as not to intrude on the private conversation. "So Meg, if you haven't eaten yet, could I interest you in a trip to our cafeteria?"

"That would be great. I'm starving," Megan answered. Together they walked toward the stairwell. Megan was peripherally aware of several nurses watching them. Megan knew spending a lot of time with Syler in public might cause gossip, but she didn't particularly care. Speculation would fly until a new topic of interest came up to distract the busybodies. At least the rumors about her late "husband" had quieted down.

The hour was closer to dinnertime than lunch and the cafeteria was empty except for a few scattered groups and singles. Most appeared to be only there for a snack and a cup of tea or coffee.

With Syler close behind her, Megan assembled a selection of small dishes on a tray and swiped her card at the self-checkout. They settled down at a table near the big picture windows. The late afternoon sunlight streamed over them and the corner was warm and welcoming. As they ate and talked, Megan almost reached out to touch Syler a few times but caught herself before she actually moved. She also had to watch herself so she didn't call Syler "beautiful" even though she felt it with all her heart. Megan also hesitated to broach the subject of the favor Toshi had asked her to do. While she had an inkling, she didn't want to pressure Syler into giving details about something that would no doubt be hard for her as it was. If Syler wanted to share it with Megan, it was up to her.

They finished the meal and cleaned up. Megan idly wondered when she would be free to touch Syler in public, when she could speak without censoring herself, if ever. She swallowed the sting of unfairness. Megan threw away her trash with more force than necessary.

"Are you done for the day?" Syler asked.

"Yes. There's nothing more for me to do today and I'm ready to go back home," Megan said. She lowered her voice and asked, "Why don't you come with me? I've saved you a spot on my sofa."

"That's the best offer I've gotten all day," Syler answered with a quirk to her lips. "Let's get moving, then." She held out a hand. Both of them stared at it for an instant before Syler twitched and changed tacks abruptly to run it through her hair. "Sorry," she murmured.

"Don't worry about it," Megan said. She made an effort to keep her voice calm and professional. "I'm still kind of in Shimo-izumi mode as well. Speaking of which, I have a bunch of beers chilling in my fridge waiting to be opened. Since neither of us is on call tonight, I thought it might be a nice way to relax."

"You're on," Syler said. "How about you go ahead. I'll swing by the grocery for snacks and meet up at your place in a bit."

Megan agreed with just the slightest twinge of sadness, knowing part of Syler's suggestion was to keep them from being seen walking home together in broad daylight. Someday, Megan promised herself, she would be able to hold her head up and stand tall and proud beside Syler as her partner and lover.

Chapter Nine

JUNE TURNED INTO July and the summer heat was fully on them. During the hottest parts of the day, Megan sheltered in the cool hallways of the hospital. Syler's thirty-sixth birthday came in the middle of the month and was celebrated both publicly and privately. Megan resisted giving her the tiger-eye cufflinks from Fabia's shop. Instead she presented Syler with a monogrammed Teitel medical bag, similar to her own but a limited edition done in a retro late-Meiji-era style. Delighted, Syler immediately filled it with all of her emergency medical supplies and the bag became her constant companion when she trundled around the hospital or camped out in after-hours admissions.

Summer also brought seasonal festivities and Megan looked forward to Suito City's annual fireworks festival. Syler volunteered her rooftop as a venue for the barbeque/double date Megan and Jayco were in the midst of organizing, complete with yukatas and sparklers.

Nikky recovered and was able to go home, but the members of the Okamoto family were in and out of the hospital for counseling and therapy sessions and Megan had a chance to talk to all of them in turn. She learned Junichiro had taken a leave of absence from his work and was currently living the life of a single father. Finally allowed to dress and play as the girl she'd always insisted she was, Nikky was adjusting so well that it seemed she'd always been that way.

Even in the face of Nikky's life turnaround, a dark tension hovered at the edge of Megan's mind at all times. Sakura's condition took a turn for the worse and she was moved to the ICU. Infection claimed her and fever raged. She didn't responding to any treatment. Syler was rarely away from her bedside, most often spending the night there with Chiho and Toshi as they performed their grim vigil.

On a sultry, airless night punctuated with only the sullen rumbling of thunder and the broken promise of rain, Megan lingered at her desk. She was reading an outdated but still interesting article titled *Challenges and Countermeasures When Performing the Essure Procedure on Nulliparous Patients* when the pediatric code blue came. Instinctively, Megan knew who it was for. She closed her eyes, bowed her head, and prayed. It was the only thing she could do.

She stayed at her desk until she couldn't sit still any longer. Megan raced up the stairs. She arrived at Sakura's room in time to see Syler shoving the sliding door open. Behind her, the remainder of the response team slowly wheeled the crash cart out.

A tiny, still form was in the bed, almost buried under the tubes and crumpled wrappers of the single-use items, a testament to the battle that took place. The battle that was lost. Neither her prayers nor the best efforts of the lifesaving response team were enough. Like a guttering candle, the little life faded away. Sakura passed, just three days short of her fifth birthday.

In the hallway, Syler ripped her mask and gloves off and threw them roughly to the floor. The person who met Megan's eyes was someone she had never seen before.

"Get the gawkers out of here, this isn't a fucking zoo," Syler said in a voice that was devoid of all emotion. She didn't acknowledge Megan as she passed her and strode down the corridor.

Even though she hadn't been expecting a party, Megan was surprised by the abrupt dismissal. It wasn't personal but it still stung. She wished she could help Syler, or at least be there beside her. Rabbi Sharon was paged and Megan could only look on in dumb worry as the rabbi was ushered into the family counseling room. A hand on her arm brought Megan back to the present. Dani from Syler's surgical team stood beside her with a worried expression.

The other people around them meant Megan couldn't say what was whirling in her mind. Wordlessly, Dani gave her arm a squeeze and followed the retreating forms of the rest of the response team.

THE NEXT MORNING, Megan glanced out of the window overlooking the rear entrance to the hospital with a heavy feeling in her chest. President and Mrs. Brockman, along with Charles, Syler, and a few other members of the Pediatrics Department stood in a solemn semicircle behind a nondescript black van. Toshi and Chiho walked down the ramp from the hospital to the street, flanked by two middle-aged couples that Megan assumed were their parents. Finally, four black-suited men appeared. They carried a blanket by the corners that held a small, white-wrapped form. The assembled hospital staff bowed deeply as the bundle passed before them. None of them straightened until long after the doors to the van closed.

"That's how I feel." The sharp voice jolted Megan back from the scene playing out before her. Megan whirled to face Fabia. She was immaculately dressed as always. She gazed out of the window with a frown. "I feel like I lost my son."

Megan gaped. She took a step back in disbelief. "Do you want to go down there and tell that couple to their faces? As they watch their only child be taken away in a hearse, do you actually think you can tell them you feel the same loss because you have to change pronouns? Really?"

"Okay, maybe it isn't totally the same, but I still lost my little boy." Fabia's face fell. She worried at the clasp of her handbag.

Megan took that moment of indecision to say in a firm voice, "You didn't lose anything or anyone. Not yet. That little one's story is over but Nikky's is just beginning. Do you want to be around to see the adventures and triumphs of your child's life or do you want to throw it all away and be left with nothing other than your bigotry? It's up to you to make that decision, Fabia, and I hope you make the right one."

"I'm not a bigot," Fabia said. Her shoulders slumped. She traced a painted nail down the window. "It's just that life is so much easier for boys. They have so many opportunities and are encouraged to do anything they want. Even if it's stuff like being a gymnast or figure skater, especially since that guy from Sendai brought back all those gold medals." The clasp of her bag clicked as she opened and closed it. Fabia repeated the motion like a mantra, not seeming to realize what she was doing. "Girls get judged by their looks and treated like shit by guys, but they have to take it because they don't have the options. Women aren't safe in their own bodies. Why would anyone choose that? I wanted a better life for my kid."

"It's not a choice," Megan said. "And things are changing. The world Nikky grows up in will be a lot different from the one we did. Look around. Even in this hospital, there are so many positive female role models for Nikky I'm sure she'll turn out strong and all right and ready to take on the world. But she needs you, Fabia. She needs the support and acceptance of her family in order to have a chance."

"I need a smoke," Fabia snapped. She started to stomp off down the hallway then turned. "Um, if you see Nikky tell him," she paused and said, "tell *her* I'll be in the family counseling room."

"I definitely will," Megan said. She got a small thrill of triumph when Fabia finally used the correct pronoun. Megan was glad she'd been able to speak to her and maybe, hopefully, plant the seed of understanding in Fabia's mind. Another glance out of the window showed nothing more than the empty alley. Megan sighed and closed her eyes for a moment. The only one she hadn't been able to speak to was Syler.

Since the night before, Megan found every attempt to either talk to Syler or contact her in some way rebuffed. Her calls went unanswered, her text messages unread. Syler hadn't been up to the roof or the cafeteria. In fact, Syler hadn't left her post for a moment. Megan worried that she was exhausting herself.

Megan could only watch and hope Syler would return to her for support. Syler had never pushed her away like that and Megan was frozen with indecision about what to do, or if there was really anything she could do. To make matters worse, she didn't know if Syler had been able to carry out her promise to Toshi and she knew she couldn't ask.

A tug on her sleeve brought Megan back to the present. She looked down. Nikky stood next to her.

"Hi there Nikky," Megan said. She crouched down and rested her crossed arms on her knees. She manufactured a smile she hoped at least looked genuine. "How are you today?"

"Okay."

"Just okay?"

"Yeah. Where's Sakura-chan? She wasn't in her room."

"Um, well," Megan stammered. She wasn't prepared for that question so soon. She didn't want to lie, but Nikky was only six and the concept of death, especially of a friend, might be too much to take at once. Megan compromised by saying, "She went home with her family."

"Oh. Can I visit her?"

"I'm afraid she's gone far away," Megan said. "Your friend-ship was very important to her, I'm sure of it."

"But she didn't even say goodbye," Nikky said with tears in her eyes.

"Don't cry, honey." Megan cast about, flustered and unsure what to do. She was saved by a fluttering, scampering presence that burst upon them.

"I'm glad I caught you," Luka said. He was breathing hard as if he'd been running all over the place, which he probably had by the unusually disheveled look of him. He held out a scrap of folded drawing paper. "Nikky, this is for you. It's from Sakura-chan."

Nikky eagerly opened the paper, revealing a picture of two stick figures. The smaller one had black hair and the bigger one had brown hair. They were holding hands and surrounded by flowers. Against her will, Megan's eyes grew misty.

"What's this?" Nikky pointed to the writing at the bottom of the page. "Thirty nine?"

Megan cleared her throat. She had to answer because Luka suddenly came down with an acute case of needing to be some-where else and scurried away. "Say them one by one, in Japa-nese."

"San. Kyu." Nikky said, then her face lit up. "Sankyu! Thank you!" She lunged and gave Megan a hug. "I get it! That's so cool! I want to show Mama!"

"She said she'll be in the family counseling room. Can you go there by yourself?" Megan asked. The room got blurry. Megan feared an "allergy attack" was imminent.

"Yup!" Nikky said and ran off. She paused and turned half-way down the hallway. "Thirty-nine to you too, Doctor Megan!"

Megan just waved one hand while she dug around in her pockets for a tissue with the other.

Later that afternoon, she held a rooftop picnic where she con-sulted with Luka and Jayco, but other than sharing their worries, the meeting didn't yield any concrete results.

The day faded into night, and Syler didn't speak to her or call. Finally Megan gave up and went home. She felt bereft as she gazed across the river at the dark window of Syler's apartment.

The next day brought more of the same and at lunchtime,

Megan showed up at Syler's desk with a bag from the takeout corner of the cafeteria in her hands. Syler was buried in paperwork
and didn't look up as Megan approached.

"I thought you might be hungry," Megan said. She stood as
close as she dared, barely breathing.

"I'm not," came the curt answer.

"Well, I'm sure you will be when you get a look at this super-
yummy bagel," Megan said. She opened the bag and drew out a
plump bagel that was overflowing with lox. "Come on, this one's
got your name on it. I even sprang for extra pickles."

"I said I'm not hungry," Syler pushed herself away from the
desk and got to her feet. Her face was dark with anger, the first
real emotion Megan had seen her exhibit in two days. "I don't
need your nagging, okay? So just back off!"

The last two words were spat at her with such venom that
Megan flinched. Syler's head came up and their eyes met in a
startled gaze.

"Oh God, I'm sorry Meg," she whispered. She collapsed into
her chair and ran a hand though her hair. For a moment Megan
grasped the wild hope Syler would open up to her. She was
wrong. Without looking at her, Syler just yanked her white coat
straight and grabbed a bunch of files. "Look, I'm swamped here
and I don't need a bunch of interruptions. Just let me deal with
this shit on my own." The cold mask was back in place. Her entire
body was stiff with tension.

"All right," Megan said. Sadness at her inability to do anything weighted down her shoulders. She quietly put the bag
down and backed away. "Take the time you need. I'll be here anytime you want me. Remember that." Megan dropped her voice to
a whisper and said, "Now and forever." She hoped Syler understood what she couldn't say in the non-privacy of the office.
Syler's outburst already caught the attention of a few curious
onlookers.

There was no answer as Megan walked away.

With the swift finality of the Yamane family's Buddhist
beliefs, the wake for Sakura was held that evening, which happened to be a Friday. While the *otsuya* took place, Megan stayed
home and worried. Something had to break and she hoped it
wasn't Syler. She stared at a magazine without comprehension
when her phone rang. Syler's number appeared on the screen,

along with the picture Megan snapped of them on their cherry blossom picnic where Syler wore her tuxedo and officially melted Megan's panties. Megan grabbed her phone up with a mixture of joy and apprehension. She didn't care about the fact that it was Shabbos. Megan answered in a breathless rush. She was surprised to hear Atsuko's voice on the other end.

"Can you come over? We're at Syler's place up on the roof."

"I'll be right there. What's wrong?" Megan's heart thudded painfully in her chest. She was already on her way to the door.

"Syler's been in a terrible funk and we tried to get her out of it," Atsuko said in her crisp, no-nonsense way. "Looks like it backfired. Just get up here, okay?"

"On my way," Megan said.

She hurriedly closed and locked her door. She made the short journey at a dead run. Megan didn't stop until she was at the entrance to Syler's building. She nearly bowled over the door-man as she threw herself into the lobby. Megan had met him a number of times before and he greeted her cheerfully before he opened the door for her with a worried expression at her desperate haste. Megan was winded from her sprint. She dragged in a breath to thank him as she bypassed the elevator and automatically barreled into the stairwell.

Megan exploded onto the roof but stopped when Atsuko grabbed her arm. The entire team was there, spread out on the rooftop, still in their mourning clothes. Megan was only concerned with Syler. She was in a simple black dress, the first time Megan had ever seen her wear one. Dressy black flats were kicked messily onto the rooftop but it was where she was that had Megan gasping more than her run up the stairs could explain. Unmindful of the five-story drop at her back, Syler perched on the ledge, legs spread in her usual careless sprawl as if she'd forgotten she wasn't in trousers. She clutched a can of Chu-Hi in one hand and slapped at a somber black-suited Taka-chan with the other.

"I'm not fucking going to jump," she said in a growl. She weaved and Megan let out an involuntary yelp. At the sound, Syler looked over at her. There was a long pause. Megan froze in indecision. Syler said, "Nice of them to order in some guilt trips. Thanks for coming over, but you don't need to stay, Megan." Syler's cold tone turned her name into an insult.

"I'm not here to guilt anyone," Megan said. She took a step forward. For the first time, Megan could see how glassy Syler's eyes were. Her pupils were blown wide. She'd sampled more than just alcohol that night. "Come on, let's go downstairs. I think you need to lie down for a bit."

"Ooh, hear that guys?" Syler said in a rough, loud voice. She took a long swig from her can and said, "I think she's trying to get me into bed. Hope I'm good enough to stop her from running off with some penis with a wallet."

"What?" Megan gasped, certain her face was bright red. "Syler, you know you have nothing to worry about. This isn't about me or us. Please, you're scaring me. At least come off the ledge."

"Why?" Syler barked out an unpleasant laugh. She waved her can in a broad arc. "You're just going to leave me. People leave me. That's what they do. Maybe I'm not cool enough, not smart enough, or I smell or whatever. Who the fuck knows?"

"I'm not leaving you," Megan said. "I promise."

"Yeah, sure. A promise is only fucking words."

Megan felt a keen pang of guilt as Syler dropped her head into her hands, still cradling her Chu-Hi. By that time, Megan was close enough she could hold her hand out to Syler. She forced herself to shut out the others around her. She was there for Syler. It didn't matter what anyone else thought or who heard her. "Come on beautiful, take my hand. Let's go."

She didn't expected it to work, but it did. Syler put her can down with a hollow thump and let Megan pull her to her feet. Syler's knees buckled before she rose to her full height. Both Taka-chan and Dani twitched forward as if ready to catch her if she fell. Syler ignored her discarded shoes and padded over to the stairway. Megan carefully steered her with a hand on the small of Syler's back in an ironic echo of the way Syler always escorted her.

"Don't wait up for us, kids," Syler said with a broad wave to her team. Megan mouthed a *thank you* over her shoulder as they left the roof.

Back in Syler's room, Megan got Syler to sit down next to her on the mattress.

"Do you want to talk?" Megan asked in a small voice. This Syler was someone she didn't know and she wasn't sure what to do.

"Fuck talking," Syler said.

Megan let out a surprised squeak as Syler shoved her down and pinned her to the bed by holding her wrists over her head. Syler got on top of Megan and straddled Megan's body with her long legs. Her skirt rode up over her thighs. For a long moment, Megan held her breath and waited for what was to come next. She didn't know if either of them wanted what was about to happen.

Before Megan made the decision to stop the situation or go with it, Syler grabbed her hand and brought it under her skirt to press into her crotch. For an instant, Megan caught the flash of thigh-high stockings and her fingers met the satin of panties Megan hadn't known Syler owned, which under any other circumstance would be incredibly arousing, but at that point, Megan felt only distress.

"Do it," Syler growled. Megan blinked up at her, not understanding. "Two fingers. Do it fast and hard. I don't care if I bleed. Saving something nobody ever wanted has absolutely no meaning."

Megan caught her breath. Syler wanted her to do something she never allowed anyone to do before. She wanted Megan to break Syler's only rule. Apprehension flooded her mind. Megan struggled to draw back. As much as Syler's offer moved her, Megan wished she didn't have to be stoned out of her mind to make it.

"No, Syler, I'm not going to do that. Not tonight. It would hurt you."

"I want you to hurt me," Syler said. Her grip loosened. The weight came off Megan. Syler sank to her knees on the crumpled comforter. Her head went down. She said, "I want you to break this spell. I want to feel *something*."

Megan drew in a long breath. "Let's just talk, all right? I need to make sure you're okay first."

In a sudden move, Syler got to her feet and stood unsteadily for a moment. She pressed a hand to her head. "I'm so fucked up right now. I need to induce." She turned and headed for the restroom. Megan leaped up and followed her.

"I'm coming with you," she said. "I don't want you alone in case you pass out."

Megan was glad Syler accepted her help without protest. The procedure was carried out efficiently. Afterward, they both sat on the cool tiled floor while Megan carefully wiped Syler's face with a damp towel.

"Do you feel better?" she asked.

"Yeah, I do. Thanks."

Syler took a few breaths and squeezed her eyes shut. Megan couldn't hold back at the expression of pain on her face and enfolded Syler in a hug. At the first contact, Syler twitched but soon she buried her face against Megan's blouse. Relief flooded Megan. She dropped a few kisses to Syler's hair and held Syler for a long while, gently stroking her back and whispering soft reassurances to her.

"I'm sorry for the way I've treated you these past few days," Syler said at last into Megan's shoulder. Her body trembled. "And I'm so sorry for tonight. What I did was inexcusable. I didn't prepare you or ask you, I just shoved you down."

"That's all right," Megan said. She held Syler tight to her. "I would have stopped you if I really didn't want it."

"Even so, I swear I will *never* do anything like that ever again. My God Meg, I'm lucky you are still speaking to me. I nearly threw away the best thing in my entire life."

"It would take a lot more than that to chase me off," Megan said. "I'm here and I'm staying with you. Now let's get off the floor and changed into something comfortable before I tuck you into bed. You need to drink some water as well."

"I need to brush my teeth," Syler said. A fraction of her usual self came back and she said, "And you need to kick my ass."

"Maybe," Megan said. She managed a weak smile. "But not right now."

Megan got Syler propped up against the pile of pillows and pressed a large glass of water into her shaking hands.

"I don't know why this is messing me up so bad. I've lost patients before," Syler said. She shook her head and drained the glass.

"Sakura-chan wasn't just a patient and you know it."

"You're right," Syler said. She put the glass down and raised her head. Her eyes were bright with tears. Megan hoped with all her might Syler would let them fall and cleanse her soul.

"She knew she didn't have much time left," Syler said in a cracked whisper. She chewed her lip and clasped her hands. "Meg, I need to tell you how it happened. We were hanging out, all of us. Me and Chiho-san and Toshi-kun. They left to get something. That was when Sakura-chan told me she was going to become an angel and fly away. She asked if I was going to stay with her mama and papa so they wouldn't be lonely. I told her I couldn't do that, but they weren't going to be lonely. A new little angel is going to come down and join their family to make sure they're all right."

Syler stopped and squeezed her eyes shut. "I had to tell her. Sakura-chan is going to have a little brother or sister she will never meet."

So that was what Toshi had asked Syler to do, and that also explained Chiho's physical condition. Megan reached out and twined her fingers around Syler's.

"She was so happy to hear the news," Syler said. Her thumb stroked up and down over the back of Megan's hand as she spoke. Each pass brought a wave of joy and relief to Megan. Syler didn't seem to notice the tears that spilled down her cheeks. "She stopped fighting after that. Toshi and Chiho came back and she smiled at them. She grabbed their hands and that's when she coded. It was my fault. I practically killed her."

"That's not true," Megan said in a soft voice. "It was going to happen no matter what anyone said or did. But you gave her peace and reassurance in her last moments. She knew she was safe. She knew it was all right to go." Megan paused for a beat. "You loved her, didn't you?"

"Yeah, I did," Syler whispered. She grabbed the front of her T-shirt. "I don't know what happened. I'm so empty. It feels like she took a piece of my soul with her."

"She did," Megan said. "The bad news is you won't get it back. But the good news is that a piece of Sakura-chan's soul will live with you forever." Megan reached out and brushed at Syler's face. "It's okay Syler. I've been there. Getting angry or shutting down is just a way to protect yourself. You have so much bottled up inside that you think letting out even one bit will break you. It won't. It will heal you. You're safe and I'll be here no matter what."

That burst the dam. Syler collapsed into rough sobs after that. The events of the past few days caught up with her and Megan shed a few tears herself. In the end, they used up practically an entire box of tissues.

When the storm was over, Megan ran a bath for them to wash away the lingering sadness and upsets of the day with generous amounts of hot water and fragrant soap. Megan borrowed a T-shirt and got changed as a much-humbled Syler called Atsuko to reassure her team things were all right and to apologize to them as well. Megan was glad Syler was back.

While Syler was on the phone, Megan snuggled down into the bed. She held the comforter open for Syler. Instead of lying down next to her, Syler draped herself over Megan. Her arms circled Megan's waist and Syler rested her head on Megan's chest.

"Is this okay for you?" Syler asked.

"It's perfect," Megan said. She gently stroked Syler's hair back from her face. "How about you, are you okay?"

"I will be," Syler said. She closed her eyes for a moment. A tiny, sad smile flitted across her lips. "God, I miss her. Sakura-chan was a handful from the get go. She didn't sleep through the night for the first couple years of her life. She kept the whole floor up with her unholy screeching. Not that I blame her. I'd shriek too if my body was destroying itself from the inside out."

"That sounds like a nightmare," Megan said softly.

"It was," Syler said without a trace of rancor. "I remember when she was about six months old. I was doing something in the next room and the poor kid was howling away so much I could barely concentrate. I got pissed off as hell and stomped in ready to tell them to shut the fuck up."

"Really?" Megan was surprised. She couldn't imagine Syler like that.

"Really," Syler said. She shifted. Her body molded itself more firmly to Megan's. She chuckled and said, "I was a real asshole back then. Arrogant as hell, only here to do my job and then get out. I didn't give a shit about the patients. I was above them."

"That certainly changed," Megan said.

"It did. Because of her. Because of them," Syler said. "Chiho and Toshi were there, you know how people here get all worried about bothering others, *meiwaku*, they say, and when I barged in they were in agony. They were just kids themselves. Even though they were absolutely exhausted, they couldn't apologize enough and even offered to take Sakura-chan out to the car. I took one look at them and felt like the biggest putz on the planet. I just held out my arms and said, 'show me how to hold her.'" Syler smiled, a real one this time. "I'd never held an infant before. I was above that too. I'm no angel, but for whatever reason she quieted down pretty quickly."

Megan said "That's because you have a way of charming the ladies."

"We'll go with that," Syler said. She went quiet for a moment. Her words were soft and introspective when she spoke again. "So I stood in that room with this sleeping little baby in my arms and I didn't dare move in case I woke her up so I just stood there for like ten minutes in dead silence. There was nothing else to do, so we got to talking. You know them, they're good people. Then it hit me. They weren't trained for any of this. Fate dumped it all on them but they were doing their damned best with the shit hand they got dealt. I was the one who should be looking up to them. It changed the way I did my job. It changed my life, Meg. That's what I owe Sakura-chan. I can never pay her back." Syler closed her eyes and a line of pain appeared between her brows. Megan smoothed it away with her fingers.

"No, but you can take the lesson she taught you and pay it forward," Megan said.

"That's exactly right, Meg. Damn, you're good," Syler said. She caught Megan's hand in hers and drew it down to kiss her fingers. "In more ways than I can count."

Megan flushed, but she was glad Syler was recovered enough to make naughty innuendos. Megan cleared her throat and said, "I have a story for you." She recounted the incident of Sakura's last message to Nikky. Both she and Syler teared up at the end. It seemed they were headed on another trip to tissue-land, so Megan gave her sense of humor a workout and told a number of increasingly bad jokes until eventually she was rewarded by Syler's bright guffaw.

Megan joined in with the conviction Sakura would want them to laugh instead of cry over her.

THE NEXT DAY, Megan left Syler in a deep sleep. She fidgeted through shul, left early, and raced through her morning rounds, grateful the hospital didn't have examination hours on the weekend. She was on her way out when Jayco ran up to her. He pressed a full plastic container into her hands.

"Here are some leftovers from lunch to take back with you. There's plenty to share," he said. He didn't have to ask where Megan was going or who she would be sharing the lunch with. They both knew. One hand fidgeted with the fringe of his prayer shawl as he asked, "Is everything okay?"

"It will be," Megan said. "Thanks Yakkov."

"No worries," he replied.

Megan hurried off with her treasure clutched to her chest. The doorman let her back in with a smile. Megan left him with a few choice morsels from her container. She got to Syler's apartment and found her still curled up in her bed, awake but looking groggy, which wasn't unexpected.

Syler peeked out from her crumpled nest.

"Hey beautiful," Megan said. "How are you feeling?"

"Better," Syler said. She gave Megan a smile that set her heart and mind at ease and sparked a warm feeling deep within herself.

"Do you feel like getting up or would you like to rest some more?"

"How about you come in here with me?" Syler counter offered.

"You know, I think I like that option best," Megan said.

She settled onto the yielding mattress. Two arms snaked around her waist and pulled her into the warm depths of the comforter. Even though Megan's good dress got scrunched, she snuggled under the covers to put herself more firmly in Syler's arms. She lay her head on Syler's chest and closed her eyes, content and relaxed.

"You must be hungry," Megan said after a long, peaceful moment. She rolled over and propped her cheek up on one hand. "Jayco gave me a bunch of leftovers from lunch including a couple pieces of Stan Cohen's cheesecake."

"Oh shit, I missed shul," Syler said with a groan. She heaved herself into a sitting position and held her forehead. "I should have known by your lace cap, which I have always thought is really cute, by the way."

"I'm glad you like it," Megan said, flushed and glowing with the complement. She reached out to brush a strand of hair from Syler's cheek. "But don't worry about missing the service, you know how casual things are there. I went but skipped out early. I finished everything I needed to do at work too, so I can spend the whole day with you. If that's all right, I mean if you want a bit of time to yourself just say the word. There's plenty I can do to keep myself busy over at my place."

"No way," Syler said. She dropped a quick kiss into Megan's hair. "I still can't believe you actually want to be around me after the way I acted. I was so—"

Megan cut her off by placing a gentle finger on her lips. "You don't need to apologize any more. The matter is settled, okay?" Megan leaned forward and replaced her finger with a swift kiss that only lasted an instant. She pulled back. Syler looked at her with a longing expression. Megan said, "I'll give you a better kiss once you're up and moving."

Syler catapulted out of the bed, long-limbed and elegant even in boxers and a slightly ratty T-shirt. "I'm up!"

"Good," Megan said. "Get dressed and meet me in the kitchen for your reward."

Even though she wanted to stay in that warm nest with Syler for all eternity, Megan got up and headed into the kitchen. She just finished laying out the dishes on the island counter when Syler came in, looking like her usual gorgeous self in her Wonder Woman T-shirt and jeans. She opened her arms. Happily, Megan fell into them. Megan took Syler's face in her hands and pulled her into a long, deep kiss that filled Megan with a rush of love.

"Now that's a good incentive to get out of bed," Syler said in a breathless voice as they slowly separated. She sat at the island. Megan hovered with the pitcher of cold tea as they did justice to the lunch. After the meal, Syler stood at the sink and washed the dishes while Megan dried them.

Syler passed the last dish to Megan. She said, "I was thinking, the weather's perfect and we've both got the day free. How about I show you around a bit? I bet there's a bunch of places around town you haven't seen yet."

"That sounds nice," Megan said. She bumped Syler's hip with hers. "Can you show me a private place where we can steal a kiss under the sky?" The one they had just shared started up a low, smoldering hunger. Megan wasn't going to be satisfied until she had a few more like it.

Syler laughed and bumped her back. "There may be one or two places around that will fit the bill."

Once the cleanup was done, Megan twined her fingers

around Syler's as they went down the stairs together, but when they left the safety of the stairwell, Megan let go. They passed through the lobby and were greeted by the doorman who thanked Megan for the good lunch.

While Megan didn't allow herself to touch Syler as they walked, she nevertheless basked in their mental and emotional closeness. Any lingering melancholy feelings soon took a back seat as Syler led her on a long, meandering walk through the town where she pointed out various oddities and points of interest she'd discovered in the years she'd been living there.

They wandered up and down the cobbled streets and crossed over numerous bridges. Megan felt the charm of the place more than ever. The excellent guide walking next to her had a lot to do with that.

"Have you ever been to Suito Castle?" Syler asked as they strolled down a nostalgic side street lined with quirky shops of all kinds. Her face was alight. She almost glowed with excitement.

"Not yet," Megan replied.

"Come on, it's just over here," Syler said. She held out her hand and Megan joyfully took it. The burst of happiness overshadowed any uncertainty about being casually demonstrative in public. Syler took her down an alley that was squeezed between two industrial-looking buildings. At the end of the alley, they burst into a wide courtyard surrounded by a moat thickly lined with trees. Behind the row of greenery a proud castle rose like a phoenix. Its swooping white walls and green roofs towered over them. In contrast to the cramped entrance, the actual castle grounds were vast and sprawling, filled with trees and decorative rock gardens.

Megan let out a breath and stood still in wonder.

"What do you think?"

"It's amazing," Megan said. She turned slowly to take it all in. Megan still had Syler's hand in hers and Syler obligingly followed her tracks. "It's like I just stepped back several hundred years in time."

"You should come back here next spring," Syler said. "The moat is surrounded by cherry trees. They put up lanterns at night and it's magical. You'll love it."

"Just me?"

Syler fixed her with a long, lingering gaze. "Would you care for company?"

"Is that an invitation?" Megan asked.

"Sure is," Syler said. She paused and said, "If that's what you want."

Megan got a burst of nerves at the concrete statement. When Syler tried discussing long-term commitments before, Megan always wriggled out of making any kind of promise. The worry about the information her missing documents revealed kept her from giving all of herself. But Megan couldn't hold back any more. She hoped with all of her heart they would be able to keep the promise she was about to make.

Megan started to speak but lost her nerve at the last moment. She couldn't bear to look at Syler. She didn't want to see the flash of pain that was etched on her face. Finally she spoke.

"I've done things I'm not proud of," Megan said. "Bad things, things that if you knew you wouldn't want to be with me."

"Don't do that, sweetheart," Syler said. "Meg, don't push me away, it's all right. You keep telling me you're here for me. You know, I'm here for you. I love you and I don't care what you've done. Who you are right here and right now is the most beautiful, wonderful person I've ever met. I'm not going to let you go so easily." She paused and asked, "What do you want?"

Syler was giving her the choice. Megan stood with both feet planted firmly on the ground. She couldn't wreck this.

"In that case, I formally accept Syler Terada's cherry-blossom viewing invitation to take place next April." She swallowed and added, "If things are going to end between us, you'll have to do it."

"I won't, and thank you." Syler gave Megan a smile that melted her. She took a step backward. "Come on, there's somewhere I want to show you."

Megan's curiosity was piqued as Syler led her deeper into the castle grounds. The sound of the town stilled and was replaced by the rustling of the trees and a few odd bird calls. The serenity of her surroundings seeped into Megan. They walked alongside a mossy rock wall that meandered through the rough brush, away from the well-kept castle grounds. The wall was about two meters high and sported regularly-spaced depressions big enough for at least two people to hide in.

"This wall pre-dates the castle," Syler said. "When the castle was built in the sixteen hundreds, they kept it standing. The castle and pretty much everything else in this town was wrecked in World War II but this wall survived. Even when they rebuilt the place they kept it here. Maybe they left it for defense or just because it looks nice, or..." Syler trailed off. She got a wicked gleam in her eyes. She fell back into one of the depressions and pulled Megan along with her. Megan came forward most willingly. Strong arms circled her waist and nestled their bodies together. Syler bent down and breathed into Megan's hair, "Or maybe the old-timey folks appreciated a bit of privacy just as much as we do." She moved back enough to gaze into Megan's face. "Like it?"

"I love it," Megan replied. She reached up to trail her fingers through Syler's hair.

"Good," Syler said. She cupped Megan's face with one hand and buffed her lower lip with her thumb. "And I just wanted to tell you I'm glad you don't wear lipstick. I hate eating that stuff."

Megan had to smile at that. A quick look back over her shoulder reassured Megan that they were completely alone in the thickly wooded area. She rose up. Syler came forward to meet her lips, but Megan moved away at the last moment. With a playful growl, Syler followed her. She managed to get a split-second kiss before Megan once again evaded her.

"You're not making this easy," Syler said.

"Doctor Terada," Megan answered in a prim voice, "I will have you know I am anything but easy."

With that, Megan opened her mouth and drew Syler to her, only to dodge the swift attempt and duck away once more as Syler tried to head her off. Syler chuckled as she met the challenge, dogging Megan's lips with her own until Megan was also stifling her giggles. It was the first time Megan had ever truly laughed and joked around with a lover. Before, she'd tittered out of awkwardness and embarrassment. But now, the feeling that held her at that moment in Syler's arms was glorious. Megan never wanted to give that up.

"Tell me how much you love me," Megan whispered, close enough their lips brushed as she spoke.

"I could never tell you how much," Syler said in a breathless rush. "Meg, I love you from the bottom of my soul up to the top of the cosmos."

The heat in Syler's gaze and the barely concealed tension in her voice burned off the last of Megan's amusement brought by the gentle teasing. She'd had enough of playing. She leaned forward, allowing Syler to finally meet her in a kiss that shook Megan to her toes. The kiss got deep fast. Megan had to stop herself from moving against Syler's long body. Syler's hands dropped to her hips and Megan lost the will to fight. Her entire body lit up as Syler spread her legs and brought Megan's thigh to nestle between hers.

"I missed this," Syler panted against Megan's mouth.

"I did too," Megan said. The flash of skin revealed by the gapping collar of Syler's T-shirt was too tempting. Megan dropped her lips to kiss Syler's neck. She wasn't thinking clearly as she slipped her hand under the hem of the T-shirt, guided only by the force of her desire.

Nothing other than sleek skin met her fingers. In that way, Megan discovered Syler wasn't wearing a bra. The heat of Syler's heaving breaths under her hand was intoxicating. Megan's fingers curled reflexively around Syler's breast. The hard nipple chafed against her palm. Things were getting hot. Megan wasn't sure how far she should go. She froze with her hand resting on the heavenly fullness.

"Don't stop, baby girl," Syler rasped in her ear. "This is too good. I'll keep a lookout but this place is dead at this time of the day."

Megan could only gasp in desire as Syler brought up one hand to press Megan's palm to her breast. Syler whispered a string of *oh yes* as Megan gently took the firm nub between her fingers and slid it up and down their length. Syler's hands went down again to press against Megan's backside, which brought their bodies together with an urgent intimacy. Megan kept one hand on Syler's breast while she stroked the other down and slid it between them.

Emboldened by the secluded location and burning with need for Syler, Megan pushed her hand between Syler's legs. Even through the denim, Megan could feel the heat of Syler's arousal swelling in her palm.

"Is this okay?" Megan asked. Syler had her head back against the rough stone wall, her eyes half-closed in pleasure.

"Fuck yes," Syler panted. She rocked her hips, silently begging for more. "I need you so bad, Meg. Keep going."

Megan was dizzy with desire. She cupped Syler's breast and teased her nipple by tracing circles around the nub with her thumb while her other hand slowly rubbed back and forth over the crotch of Syler's jeans.

While Megan stroked and held her, Syler was still, her body tight like a bowstring. Even as she teased Syler hard under the concealing confines of her T-shirt, Megan listened carefully for any sounds of life around them. Besides their heavy breathing and the rustle of clothing, there were none.

"Is this all right?" Megan asked.

"Yes, Meg, oh fuck yes don't stop," Syler rasped. She met Megan's heated gaze with her own. She drew her tongue slowly over her lower lip. Syler spoke again, her words low and urgent, "Meg, let's do this. Under the sky. I know what you like, and I'm going to give it to you."

Megan wondered what exactly that was before she let out a gasp of understanding. One hand left Megan's hip. Syler grabbed the hem of her own T-shirt. For an instant, her gaze held Megan's.

Syler moved. A rush of pure fire thrummed through Megan as Syler hauled her T-shirt up to her armpits. The golden sunlight fell onto the skin of Syler's exposed breasts, making a dappled pattern over her heaving fullness and tight nipples.

"I need your mouth on me, Meg."

They were the only two people under that vast sky. Megan didn't think twice before she claimed the sweet prize Syler presented to her. She bent down and quickly took one nipple in her mouth while buffing the other between her fingers. Her lips and tongue worked in a rhythmic bliss. Above her, Syler moaned.

Megan switched sides. She greedily lapped at Syler's pebbled aureole and swirled her tongue around the hard nipple. She rode high on the burgeoning arousal that burned through her body. Megan's fevered sex grew thick and wet between her thighs. She couldn't help but thrust her hips against Syler. The back of Megan's hand pressed against herself, but it wasn't enough.

Megan lifted her head from her task and looked into Syler's face. This was the last chance for either of them to turn back. Megan knew what she wanted to do, but she wasn't sure if

Syler would let her.

"I want to make you come right here," Megan whispered. "I'll do it quick. Will you let me?"

"Oh fuck yeah, do it Meg," Syler answered. "I'm dying to have you get me off." She freed a hand from hanging onto Megan to open her jeans with a quick jerk.

Megan couldn't resist the invitation. She urged her hand past the band of Syler's underwear just as Syler surprised her with a sudden, fierce kiss. It lasted until Megan's fingers met the hot, wet center of her goal. With a shudder, Syler pulled away.

Her lips skimmed over Megan's mouth. Syler said, "I want to touch you too."

"Please," Megan said. Her thighs were wet. She held her own fingers still. Syler's hand delved under her skirt. Gentle fingers met the soaked cotton crotch of her panties. Megan whimpered and rocked her hips to meet Syler. She was eager and desperate to be packed full. "Syler, I need you to fuck me deep and hard."

"Get ready for me, Meg."

"I am."

The panties slipped from her hips. Megan shimmied them down until she could draw one leg out to free herself. Megan spread her legs in anticipation. Syler didn't disappoint her. Megan let out a long breath as Syler filled her with a sure push between her trembling thighs. Megan needed more. She lifted one knee. Syler caught it with her free hand, hoisting her up and opening her. Megan leaned fully against Syler, spread wide and impaled deeper than she'd ever been. Syler's strength was the only thing holding her up. The position had Megan fully entrusted to Syler and she gave herself without hesitation.

Her hand was still on Syler's breast, teasing the rigid nub under her fingers while the other was tucked deep between her legs. Megan found the taut bud of Syler's clit and circled it with her finger, pressing hard into the resilient folds. She was careful not to go too far, not to press too deep. The motion drew a ragged breath of desire from Syler, which Megan echoed.

The sensation of Syler within her at the same time as she was stroking Syler's slick hardness set off waves of searing electricity. It wouldn't be long for either of them. Megan couldn't speak, but gasped as Syler started to move, pumping in and out of her. She thrust fully within Megan and drew out, slipping all the way up to circle her throbbing clit before plunging into her once more, harder and faster each time. Urged on by Syler's harsh breaths, Megan increased her own speed and pressure.

"Fuck that's good," Syler said.

Her eyes drifted closed. Megan imagined what they looked like, locked in that erotic embrace, hands working between splayed thighs, bodies tight with tension, hips thrusting. Syler's firm breasts shook with each impact of Megan driving hard against her. Megan was desperate and greedy for Syler between her legs. Each deep thrust drew the taut skin over Megan's straining clit and sent a shock of pleasure through her. A burning, buzzing rush filled her. Megan didn't know how long she could hold out. She didn't want to. She needed to come and wanted Syler to be right there with her.

"More—Syler I need more," Megan said. Her words came in bursts along with the rough slam of Syler driving into her.

"You got it," Syler gritted. The next thrust was three fingers, entering Megan with a firm, expert push. She held still for a moment and Megan did as well to get used to taking so much. "God Meg, you're so fucking tight on me. Fuck that's good."

With a buck of her hips, Syler started to move again. They both sucked air as if they were in a race. Megan's skirt fell away from her cocked leg so the top of her stocking was visible. Her ears were full of their frantic breaths and the rhythmic, wet slap of Syler ramming deep into her. Megan was bare under her dress. She felt the air hit her opening as Syler pulled out of her. She wriggled her hips, needing to feel Syler push and pull against her inner walls. Megan was too far gone to be shocked at the force of her desire. She locked eyes with Syler before they met in a plundering kiss, hot and sloppy and desperate.

"Shit, I'm close. Come with me, baby girl."

With the images that came to her of their bodies bucking, thrusting hard against each other, coupled with Syler's urgent movements within her and against her, Megan couldn't have stopped herself even if she wanted to. Megan let go with a liquid shudder. She felt Syler's climax come as well. Syler's back arched. Her hips rose and a shudder rocked her entire body. Megan's inner muscles clenched around Syler's penetrating fingers. With gasping cries, Megan urged a few more final pumps into herself. Each one hit deep. She shivered against Syler until she was wrung dry.

The hand holding her knee up relaxed as Syler withdrew from her. Megan eased back as well and let her skirt fall back down. Syler's arms came around her and held her tightly. Megan closed her eyes, content to simply breathe with Syler's heartbeat thundering in her ears.

"Thank you," Megan said between heaving breaths that felt like she pulled them from the depths of the earth. "When you said you knew what I liked, you weren't lying."

"I never lie," Syler said. Without a hint of bashfulness, she tugged her T-shirt down over her bare breasts before she nestled Megan more firmly in her arms. "Especially about things like that. I take it you liked it?"

"Very much," Megan said. Her legs were shaky and she was certain she would wobble like a newborn fawn if she tried to walk at that moment. She didn't even have the strength to bend down to pick up the panties that were coiled damply around one ankle. "You know what, you have a standing date to take me at, I mean, take me *to* Suito Castle anytime."

The softly rustling trees and gardens rang with Syler's pure, joyful laugh.

Chapter Ten

MEGAN LEANED ONE hand on her cheek. She tapped her unresponsive phone's screen to life for the fifth time in as many minutes. Megan hated the worry that gnawed at her. After the storm of Syler's grief had passed and the lovely time they'd had at the castle the previous day, she was certain things were back to normal between herself and Syler. Better than normal, actually.

That morning, Megan texted Syler to see if she wanted to meet up for lunch and had not received a reply. That was hours ago. Even if she was busy, Syler had her fully-charged cell with her at all times. Megan didn't want to be a hovering nuisance but she couldn't shake the feeling that something was wrong. Syler didn't have anything scheduled other than her rounds and it wasn't like her to vanish or ignore her phone. Megan shuffled things around on her desk for a while before she decided to take a walk around. She wasn't consciously looking for Syler. If she happened to bump into Syler on her way, then she'd consider it a lucky coincidence.

Megan wandered through the surgeons' office without any luck happening. She went up to the roof. It was empty so Megan went back downstairs. She took the scenic route that led her through the long hallways of the hospital. Just as Megan gave up on finding Syler anywhere, a page rang out, calling none other than Doctor Syler Terada to the pediatric nurse station. Megan rushed over and was greeted by a grouchy-looking Nurse Murase.

"At least *you're* here," she groused. With a decisive thump, she handed Megan a pile of files.

"Excuse me?" Megan hopped on one foot. She used her knee to try and contain the armful of papers before they spilled all over the floor. "Where's Doctor Terada?"

"That's what I'd like to know," Nurse Murase said. "She was scheduled for rounds today, but she never showed up. Got a bunch of patients waiting to be seen by a physician. If she's not going to do it, might as well be you."

"I'm sorry, I can't stay here," Megan said. She heaved the pile back onto the counter. Her body twitched with the need to be in motion.

"At least take this back to transfusion. We ended up not needing it and I have things to do too."

Before Megan knew what was happening, she found herself in possession of a small red-filled bag. She shoved it into one of the many pockets of her lab coat, her mind elsewhere. She had no idea where Syler could be. Megan worriedly gnawed at her knuckle as she raced down the hallway, away from the nurse station. Her phone buzzed. Impatiently, Megan yanked it out of her pocket. She almost dropped it when she saw the text. It was from Syler.

> Hello. Meet me in front of the after-hours entrance.

Lightheaded with relief, Megan raced down the stairs like a white-plumed ostrich on a battle-mission. She nearly collided with the dusty dark-blue sedan that was idling at the entrance. Syler was nowhere to be seen. Megan stopped in her tracks with a sick sense of disappointment. The passenger side door popped open in front of her. Someone inside called her name. Puzzled, Megan bent down to peer inside.

"Paolo? What's going on? Why are you here?" Megan asked abruptly.

"Please come with me," he said. He shifted and looked uncomfortable. The phone lying on the dashboard in front of him caught Megan's attention. It was the same model as Syler's and even had the same cover. That was no coincidence. It *was* her phone. Fear stroked a cold finger down her back.

"Why?"

"I will take you to Doctor Terada."

"Where is she?" Megan asked in a tight, breathless voice. Her heart constricted. "Has there been an accident?" Please God, no. Megan prayed for anything but that.

"She is safe," Paolo said. "But we must hurry."

Megan could barely speak. She got into the car and buckled up. Paolo zoomed into traffic and pulled onto the raised expressway.

"I am sorry, but I need your phone," Paolo held out his hand.

"Why?" For the first time, Megan looked at Paolo with alarm.

"I cannot say, but if you want to see your friend again, then you will hand it over and not try anything. She is being held in a secure location. She is unharmed. Here is proof."

He reached into the pocket of his shirt and opened his hand. Megan gasped when she saw the two delicate silver rings and single diamond stud. Her body buzzed with adrenaline. She clearly remembered Syler putting them on as they got ready for work that morning.

Possessiveness gripped her. Megan snatched the earrings and cradled them to her chest with numb fingers. The logical part of her mind noted there was no blood on them so whoever removed the earrings had done so humanely. The stud even had its backing replaced. Megan shoved the items into her own pocket, loathe to hand anything of Syler's over to the man beside her.

"Again, your phone please."

Hands shaking, Megan did as he asked. She also gave him her hospital-issue PHS even though it was useless outside of the building. Tears of panic sprang to her eyes. The familiar pressure clenched in her chest. Megan fought to control herself. She took in one slow breath and let it out, even as a primal scream that she was suffocating ripped through her mind. One breath. One more.

Whatever had happened to Syler, Megan owed it to her to keep calm. She could not and would not give in to fear.

"What did you do to her?" Megan asked. She twisted in her seat to glare at Paolo. "Syler trusted you — she considered you a friend. You're not going to get away with this you know."

"Please," Paolo said in a shaking voice, "do not shout."

"I'll do whatever I want," Megan said. "And I have to pee. Like really bad so get off the highway."

"I cannot stop," Paolo said. "If you must, do it here."

"No. I can hold it," Megan said. What business was urgent enough that a man would allow his passenger to use his car as a toilet? She crossed her arms over her chest as her brain kicked into overdrive. In the same manner as when she made a diagnosis, Megan had to narrow down the possibilities and find the cause.

"Are you stalking me?" she asked.

"No, I am not," he replied with a startled expression. He gripped the steering wheel and hunched his shoulders. "It may seem false, but I have no personal interest in you."

"Then why are you doing this? Are you trying to get at Syler?"

"Please stop. I cannot answer any more questions," Paolo said. He sounded desperate and afraid.

Megan was quiet for a beat before she asked, "Who is making you do this?"

With his mouth clamped shut, Paolo trained his eyes on the road and turned on the radio. The silence was eaten by the jokey and raucous voice of the radio announcer who spoke half in English and half in Japanese, smooth and fluent in both. Megan tried a few more questions but Paolo's only answer was to turn up the radio until Megan had to clamp her hands over her ears to block out the harsh blaring.

The town gave way to deeply forested mountains. Paolo took an exit that led them down a narrow road. Trees lined both sides. Even though it was midday, the road was fully in shadow. Megan swallowed hard. Outside was nothing other than trees. Not even a gas station. Even if she escaped, she had nowhere to go.

As they drove, Paolo consulted a handwritten map. He made an effort to keep it out of her line of sight, but it didn't matter. Megan didn't know the area well enough for it to be of any use to her.

At a small gap in the trees, they slowed and Paolo pulled onto a private road. A gate stood open at short ways from the main road, but after they passed through, it swung closed and locked behind them. Unless the gate was automatic, that meant someone was watching them. Megan soon found out who as Paolo parked the car in front of a rustic two-story cottage. It was a fussy version of the cottage her own family owned. As they neared the front porch, the name on the toll-painted mailbox sent Megan's gut into a dead drop.

Paolo cut the engine.

"This way please."

In the sudden silence after the blasting music, Paolo's words sounded like they were being spoken into a fishbowl. He got out of the car and opened Megan's door for her. He extended a meaty hand in a gentlemanly way. Megan mentally scoffed at the irony and ignored him. She bounded up the wooden steps to the porch. She didn't bother to knock before she threw the door open and stormed into the room.

"Charles what have you done with her?" Megan spat the minute she was inside. Her shoes rang against the hardwood flooring. She didn't take them off, wanting to be able to make a quick getaway if necessary.

"It's a pleasure to see you again as well, Megan," Charles said. He was sitting on an overstuffed chair in front of a large fireplace and rose as Megan came over to him. A mostly-empty bottle of wine sat next to a glass on the table in front of him. Apparently he'd been enjoying some refreshment while he waited.

"Where is she?" Megan spat. She was peripherally aware of Paolo's bulk hovering in the doorway. Megan scanned the room and let out a cry. The strength left her legs and her knees buckled. Megan landed on the floor in a crumpled pile.

Syler was propped bonelessly in a straight-backed wooden chair pushed back against the far wall. Her eyes were closed and her head was tilted back, resting against the dark wallpaper. She was unconscious, either drugged or concussed. Her hands were behind her, possibly bound. Megan could see the unnatural bulge of a dislocated shoulder under the cotton of her shirt.

Her feet were bare, tied together at the ankles with rope. She was in her usual work clothes, but her lab coat was nowhere to be seen. Besides the shoulder, it didn't look like she had any other injuries. Megan was able to discern that she was breathing normally, her chest rising and falling in a regular rhythm. Megan forced herself to stay calm. Losing control at this point would bring only disaster. She needed to assess the situation and then act.

She had the front door at her back. Megan was in a good position to keep an eye on Syler and the rest of the room, from the antique-looking writing desk against the wall that appeared to be the source of the chair Syler was in, to the stiffly-organized bookshelves and expensive-looking umbrella stand and coat-rack. A dark wood staircase behind Syler led to the second floor. Opposite the writing desk was a set of fancy carved double doors, leading perhaps to a dining room or whatever rich people equipped their fancy weekend-getaway cottages with.

Megan couldn't stay still. She took a step toward Syler.

"That's close enough," Charles said. He scooped up his

glass and dumped the last of the wine into it. He moved to stand between Megan and Syler. His face was flushed from the drink. The look in his eyes was not his usual steely calm.

"She's hurt, can't you see that?" Megan said.

"Blame Paolo," Charles said. "He was a bit too enthusiastic when he brought her in. Works for me, though. At least she's quiet."

"*Mamzer*," Megan hurled the epithet for "bastard" at him. "At least let me treat her and give her something for the pain."

"You are in no position to make demands." He swirled the wine in his glass before he chugged it down. His face twisted with sadistic glee. "But since you're so desperate for company, let's wake your little butch bed warmer up, shall we?"

Megan's entire body went cold. He knew.

"Come in Paolo," Charles called as if to a dog. "I need you to keep an eye on our guests. Make sure they don't get uppity and start breaking the furniture or anything like that." As Paolo sidled into the room, Charles strode over to Syler. He took a small tube from his pocket and broke it open under her nose. One second passed. She remained still and unresponsive. One more. Syler's body gave a jolt. Her head snapped up and her eyes opened wide as she dragged in a sharp breath.

Syler struggled against her bonds but stopped abruptly as her injured arm jerked. She bent over nearly double in the chair, her mouth opened in a silent scream of agony that resonated through Megan in sympathy.

"Good morning, darling," Charles said in a voice thick with loathing. He set his wine glass down on the writing desk and grabbed a roll of duct tape from the drawer. "Have a nice sleep?"

"What the fuck are you doing, Charles? Lay one dirty finger on Meg and you'll be having a *nice sleep* in the morgue." Syler stopped shouting and gritted her teeth. Her face was pale and the hair at her temples was tacky with sweat. "When I get done pounding your ass into *mm!*" Syler's head went back and banged against the wall with the force of Charles slamming a length of tape over her mouth. Chest heaving, Syler lowered her head. She glared at him with nothing more than absolute hate.

Duct tape still in hand, Charles rocked back on his heels and looked extremely pleased with himself. "Now that is something

I've been wanting to do for a very long time. I must say it's a vast improvement."

From the dangerous look in Syler's eyes, Megan knew that if she could speak, the air would be violet with curses.

"Your business is with me, Charles," Megan spat, incensed. Her legs twitched as a red, killing haze gripped her. Her hands balled into fists. Her voice shook with rage as she said, "Syler has got nothing to do with this. Let her go and then we talk."

"Oh, I don't think so," Charles said. "This very much has to do with Miss Terada. After all, I would like her to understand what kind of woman she's chosen to get under." Charles paused to sneer at Megan. "We have much to discuss, you and I, and it is always good to do so in front of witnesses. Just to make sure everyone is on the same page."

The flash of fear turned into anger. Megan levered herself off the floor. At once, Paolo was at her side. He gently took her elbow and began to guide her over to sit on the sofa. Glaring, she yanked her arm away and sat down on the prissy paisley upholstery without help. She crossed her legs, purposely yanking the hem up over her knees.

Megan calmed her expression and her breathing. She had to show Charles she wasn't intimidated by him. Inside, Megan was shaking to bits but she would be damned if she'd let him know that.

"What do you want?"

"I'm glad you asked," Charles said. He came over and placed himself on the chair to Megan's left, the one he'd been sitting in when they'd arrived. With the decorated fireplace housing a merrily crackling fire and the natural stone wall behind him, he looked like the benevolent host of a socialites' weekend getaway. "Why don't we start with a bit of refreshment?" He glanced over to Paolo. The big man came forward with a heavy silver tray. It held a crystal decanter of red wine and two glasses.

"What is he, your butler?" Megan asked with a raised brow.

"Something like that," Charles answered. He looked across the room where Syler was struggling against her bonds. "Now, now, missy. We can't have that. Somebody needs to show you your place. And that is with your backside in that chair." He looked at Paolo and jerked his head. Syler was already on her feet when the big man came over. With an apologetic look, he put his hand on her uninjured shoulder and eased her back down into the chair. She rewarded him with a look of betrayal and hurt that Paolo answered by turning away with slumped shoulders.

As Paolo hovered over Syler, Charles picked up the decanter and poured a good measure into both glasses. He made a move as if to pass over one of them but stopped.

"I apologize. I will allow you to choose for yourself, just to assure you neither has been tampered with."

Without uncrossing her legs, Megan leaned forward and selected a glass. A wave of nausea rose up in her throat as Charles clinked his glass to hers. They both drank. Megan felt like she was trapped in a noontime suspense drama.

"Enough ceremony," Megan said. "I am assuming you have another proposal for me."

"You assume correctly," Charles put down his glass and steepled his fingers. His voice was loud and rough, belying his cultured appearance. "You're a conniving little thing, aren't you? I'm sure you and your lapdog-bitch had a good time laughing at my efforts to woo you as a proper gentleman should when all it took was just finding the correct price." He reached down and opened a drawer in the heavy coffee table. He withdrew an official-looking form and placed it on the table. It was a marriage registration certificate.

Megan couldn't believe the gall of the man. She gaped at him before she spat, "What the fu —"

"Language, Megan," Charles cut her off. Over her protests, he said, "I have taken the liberty of filling it out. All it needs is your hanko and the signatures of two witnesses."

"I'm not signing that," Megan said. Across the room, Syler made a move as if to get up but stopped as Paolo raised a hand with an apologetic expression.

Charles said, "We shall see if you change your mind after you hear what I have to offer. To start with, I have recently come into possession of some rather remarkable photographs that may be of interest to you."

Megan went as still as death as Charles opened the drawer again and took out a manila envelope. She started shaking as he withdrew a number of glossy prints and spread them out on the table. The images swam before her eyes. The wine in her glass splashed over the rim. She forced herself to look at the photographs.

The pictures captured her night with Syler in the outdoor bath. She saw Syler's hands full of her breasts as she threw her head back in pleasure, leaning down to capture Syler's mouth with hers, her body rising from the steaming water, her back arched as she pressed herself against Syler. A wave of bile rose in her throat. Megan slammed her glass down and frantically gathered up the photos, crumpling them in her haste.

"Keep them, I still have the original data files," Charles said in a bored voice. He drained his glass and sloshed more wine into it. Drops spattered over his cuffs, but he didn't appear to notice. "As for the content, Megan, I believe you are familiar with the hospital's policy on staff relationships. To that end, it would be a pity for one or both of you to be forced to seek employment elsewhere. However, as detailed in our previous discussion, I would allow your discretions to go unnoticed if you fulfill your end of the bargain."

Megan's breath sobbed in her throat. Across the room, Syler's brows drew together in an angry knot. Syler twisted to glare up at Paolo. He just hung his head, hand over his face.

Charles leaned back in his chair, taking his glass of wine with him. He sipped it and said, "I have also acquired a number of documents I believe you might wish to have back. The first being information about a certain trust fund. I assume the family it benefits would be greatly inconvenienced if it suddenly ceased to exist."

"You wouldn't." Megan leapt to her feet, hands clenched at her sides. The rage had returned. It filled Megan with mad strength that wouldn't die.

"I certainly would." Charles slurred his words only slightly. He swirled his wine in the glass with an affected gesture and looked every bit the villain he was playing. "However, if my *wife* asked me to spare them I believe I could find it in my heart to do so. After all, they've suffered quite enough. And that brings me to the final part of the trade. I believe you are familiar with a little place in Thailand called the Saint Ignatius Clinic? I seem to have found an admissions form that apparently went walkies from there."

"No," Megan whispered. She had to stop him before he spoke and her life ended.

"I'm sure if I went to that hospital today, there would be a different form in their files. One that—"

"Shut up!" Megan couldn't stop the words. She raised her voice and shouted over him, "You think you can buy and trade people but it's going to come back and bite you in the ass. Why can't you just leave me alone and live your own life? Why do you want me? I despise you!" Megan grabbed the front of her lab coat as she yelled, "Why me, Charles? Why does it have to be me?"

Charles held a hand to his ear and winced. "If our children have anything close to your lung capacity, I believe we can expect an opera singer or two."

"I'm not having anybody's children!" Megan screamed.

"Yes you are," Charles pursed his lips and tilted his head. "It's not every day you get a do-over. Maybe this time you won't—"

His words choked off as Megan threw herself over the table. The impact of her body landing on him bowled Charles over backward. The chair hit the side of the fireplace and crashed onto the hearth, pulling the metal screen down with it. The wineglass was knocked from Charles's hand and smashed against the floor. Charles rolled over with a grunt as Megan pummeled him, trying to smash his face with her fists.

He reached up and seized her wrists. Megan gasped with pain. Charles hauled her upright before he threw her down onto the coffee table. Megan's flailing legs swept the remaining glass and papers off the table as she struggled to regain the upper hand. Charles grabbed her by the shoulders and slammed her into the table again and again. The breath was jolted from her lungs, but Megan didn't give up. She kicked out and felt her foot connect with the decanter. It exploded into a shower of jagged shards, soaking them both in wine spray.

"That was a fine vintage you wasted," Charles gritted.

"Good. It tasted like cat piss." Megan coughed up a wad of phlegm and spat into his face. Charles reeled back in disgust and she used the moment of his distraction to kick him in the leg as hard as she could, driving him back a few steps. He stood for a moment, swaying slightly.

"You dirty little bitch," he growled and came at her again. This time his entire body landed on top of her. Megan let out a scream of disgust as he ground himself against her. He was hard.

"You felt that, didn't you?" His mouth was close enough to

her ear that Megan could smell the wine on his breath. She squirmed, desperate to get away again but Charles was too strong and too heavy.

"You're disgusting," Megan said. He just pinned her arms and came down fully over her. His weight crushed the breath from her lungs. Megan couldn't move other than to turn her face away from his. She bit her lip and whimpered in fear and revulsion. Her body had been taken from her. She had never felt so powerless.

"No, you are the disgusting one," Charles said. He grabbed a handful of Megan's hair and hauled her head back, forcing her to look at him. He drove himself against her once more. An anguished cry was wrung from her. Charles hissed, "You did this to me and you're going to take care of it."

"Not on your life," Megan said. Tears of pain and rage leaked from her eyes.

"All right then." Abruptly Charles released her and stood up, cupping the bulge in his pants. He looked over to where Syler struggled against Paolo's hold. Megan's heart stopped. "You're not the only one here, but you're the only one who can use her mouth. I normally wouldn't go for sloppy seconds, but I'll make an exception in this case. In fact, I think it would be a pleasure."

He took a step forward while slowly rubbing at his crotch, making no secret of his intentions. Syler held herself still and met Charles's gaze squarely with her own. Charles crossed the room in two steps and grabbed Syler by the collar. He yanked her forward out of the chair with a vicious jerk and threw her face down on the floor. Megan held her breath, waiting for Syler to move, to fight or try to get away. As Charles lowered himself to straddle her long body, still she didn't move. Syler wasn't going to fight him.

With slowly dawning horror, Megan watched as Charles reached down to loosen his belt buckle. The breath in Megan's lungs turned to ice when she realized the sacrifice Syler was going to make for her. Megan wasn't going to let it happen. She couldn't. In that instant, Megan knew what she had to do. She dragged her abused body into a sitting position on the coffee table.

Megan got to her feet. She forced herself to stand tall even as her knees shook and threatened to give out.

"Stop right there, Charles," Megan called out. At her words, Charles stopped and turned to her. She lowered her voice and purred, "Nobody services my husband except me."

"I thought you'd see it my way." Charles whirled and came back over to the sitting area. He righted the toppled chair and settled himself into it, legs spread so his trouser-tent stood up proudly. He rested one foot on the coffee table and barked, "Get over here and perform your marital duty then. Quickly before I change my mind."

Megan swallowed the acid wave of bile that welled up in her throat. She shook as she stepped around the table. She tried to will her knees to bend, but she couldn't. Megan felt as if the floor in front of her was a black hole that threatened to suck her into oblivion if she got too close.

"Turn around and eyes on the wall." The words were directed over Megan's head. She flinched. "Ah ah, not you Miss Terada. Here's the deal, as long as you're watching, I'll let her go at her own pace. Turn away, even for a second and I grab her hair and shove it down her throat. It's up to you."

The muffled sounds of Syler's verbal protests filled her ears, but Megan couldn't bring herself to look back. She clenched both hands and stilled her mind. Megan told herself she could do this. It was one of the few ways she was able to please Yasu. Megan had performed the act before, she could do it again. She'd just never done it with anything *alive*.

Megan couldn't move. Her gut clenched. She swallowed the bile that rose up in her throat.

Behind her, Megan heard Syler's voice. She was trying to tell her something. One syllable, one more and then two. Her mind went blank as Charles's big hands came down over her and grabbed her by the hair, forcing her head down. Her feet slipped and she hit the floor hard. In that split second, Megan took in the crumpled papers amid jagged fragments of the decanter spread around her, the wine that dripped down the legs of the chair, pooling in dark red puddles.

It came to her.

You have options.

She knew what she needed to do. Megan tensed herself to move, to break the hold Charles had on her no matter what the consequences. She clawed at the meaty hand in her hair and had almost freed herself when something huge impacted with Charles.

The abrupt release sent Megan tumbling backward. She had only an instant to reach out and seize her prize before she rolled free of Paolo's stomping feet. The big man grabbed Charles by the front of his shirt and slammed him against the wall.

"I cannot let you do this," Paolo said, his voice rough with emotion. "As God is my witness, I cannot stand by and watch you brutalize innocent women. I don't care if you throw my Gabriela out on the street. I will not let this continue."

Charles growled. He grabbed the iron poker from the fireplace and swung it at Paolo. His aim was off by a mile. With one hand still on Charles, Paulo grabbed the poker. He tried to wrestle it from Charles's grasp, but Charles hung on with mad persistence.

While the men scuffled, Syler pulled her knees to her chest and slipped her bound hands under her feet to get them in front of herself. With a ragged groan, she collapsed facedown onto the floor. Her injured arm flopped limply, the elbow pointing at the ceiling. Her eyes fluttered closed but she pulled herself up with a savage jerk. Syler's head rolled forward once before she got to her knees. Every movement was shrouded in agony.

With a sick thud, Charles's expensive leather shoe connected with Paolo's knee. The big man crumpled. On his way down, he threw the poker away. It skittered across the floor. Charles stood over Paolo's fallen body before he unleashed a swift kick to his gut.

"Everybody STOP!" Megan thundered. The entire room froze and turned to Megan. She stood in the middle of the room, proud and tall. With one hand, she held a large shard of crystal to her throat, the other was in her pocket. Megan drew in a shaking breath and said, "This is going to stop right here and right now."

With her hands still bound, Syler ripped the tape from her mouth. She retched and spat out a stream of vomit before she cried out, "Don't do this, Meg. Please."

"I have to," Megan said. She backed up until the knobby presence of the writing desk at her back stopped her. Tears came to her eyes. Megan swallowed desperately and said, "As long as I'm in the equation this isn't going to end. I'm a liability. I have too many weaknesses. So I'm taking myself out." Charles took a step in her direction and Megan stopped him with a sharp word. "Stay away from me. One more inch and I cut my jugular. I'll be dead before I hit the floor." She looked over at Syler who was struggling out of the ropes that bound her wrists and ankles. The agonized look on her face sent a shaft of pain through Megan. She hated herself for causing it.

Megan steeled herself and said, "You too, Syler. Stay back. I have to do this."

"Calm down and be rational," Charles said and held his hands out as if confronting a petulant toddler. "You can't stand there forever."

"I don't have to." Megan withdrew the hand she'd been keeping in her pocket and raised it, displaying the blood-soaked cuff. Her entire palm was red with blood and drops fell from her fingers. "We have a time limit." She locked eyes with Syler and said, "I'm not playing *Russian Roulette*. This isn't a *trick*. I'm serious. Serious as death."

Syler drew in a quick breath. Megan couldn't be sure, but she thought she saw a flash of understanding flit across Syler's face. Megan didn't dare waste more time. She focused on Charles.

She couldn't fight him physically, but she still had words and intuition in her arsenal. Megan put her hand back in her pocket and felt a fresh gush of blood between her fingers. Dark red stained the white of her lab coat. Megan didn't pay attention to the seeping wetness as she said, "Charles, you need to find someone else, someone who can love you. Everyone deserves to be loved and to love in return."

"Love? What a ridiculous delusion." Charles let out a harsh bark of laughter. "Those without souls don't deserve anything, you know that as well as I do," he said. "Admit it and stop dragging poor Miss Terada down with you. Don't forget, I have seen the files. I know what you've done."

Waves of emotions threatened to flatten her—fear, panic and guilt. With a great effort, Megan shut that part of herself down. Behind Charles, Paolo got to his feet. He braced one hand on the mantelpiece and favored one leg.

"Yes, I made a huge mistake and I tried to cover it up," Megan said. She looked up. Syler jerked her head in Paolo's direction, as if to tell her something. He was standing still with a look of sadness on his face. Several things that Megan had been mulling in the back of her mind became clear. She had one chance and she was going to take it. Megan brought her attention back to Charles. "When you hide something like that, it doesn't make it go away. It festers under your skin until it becomes a giant pit of poison, staining through everything you do. Even though it may hurt, the wound needs to be brought to the light and the infection drained before healing can begin. Keeping a secret like that slowly kills all the light in your life. It takes away your humanity. We both know what that's like."

Charles stared at her, his face rigid with distress. Megan took a step forward, the shard of crystal still at her throat. "Tell us what happened that day in the OR With Gabriela Gomes. It's all right to speak. The secret has been eating at you all this time, hasn't it? Now is your chance to tell us your side before it gets out. It's your last and only chance."

Paolo's head snapped up at the same time that Charles flung out his hand and spat, "It wasn't my fault! It was the goddamned stupid cow of an anesthesiologist! She was new. She didn't take the meds the patient was on into account and miscalculated the dose!"

So that was it. Megan got a jolt at the words. Her bluff had paid off. She forced herself to stay calm as she said, "Gabriela woke up. And you put her down."

"What else could I do?" Charles looked around at each of them in turn. The words spilled from him as if he could no longer hold them back. Drink and adrenaline seemed to have loosened his tongue. "Yes, she woke up in the middle of the procedure and started thrashing around, ripping at everything she could and screaming loud enough to wake the dead. I had no choice!" He reached out a shaking hand to Megan, as if seeking forgiveness.

"What did you do?" Megan breathed.

"I had to stop her," Charles said. "Everything was going to hell. Everyone in my team was panicking, so I did it. I pinched her air hose and covered her face so she couldn't scream any more. Her heart couldn't take it. She coded and by the time we got her back, it was too late. I didn't mean for it to go so far, but I had to stop her!"

Charles gestured around himself wildly, eyes focusing on each of the members in the room in turn. His tone grew rough and desperate. "There was nothing else I could do!" His pleading eyes found Syler and he cried out, "You know how important your team is to you, mine was once too! When I saw their fear, I knew I had to act."

There was a moment of silence when Megan could only stand and watch Charles crumble in front of them.

"And the cover-up," Charles continued in a rush, as if he couldn't hold back the words anymore, "I had to save my family's reputation and our hospital so I made sure I erased all the evidence. I split up my team and rewrote everything to hide what had happened, but it could never make the memories go away. It could never undo the horror I caused. So damn me, all of you! Hate me and despise me, it's your right. I hate myself, what I had to do and what I became. My life ended that day. I can still hear her screams. Every time I close my eyes I see my scalpel sinking into her flesh." Charles covered his face and howled into his hands. He cried out in a hoarse, broken voice, "I'm sorry, I'm so sorry. What have I done? What have I become?" He collapsed onto the floor, sobbing wildly.

For a long moment, nobody moved. Then, Paolo crouched down beside Charles and placed a hand on his shoulder.

"I forgive you," Paolo said. The gentle words were a stark contrast to his roughed-up appearance. "I do this for my Gabriela. I know she would not want this senseless accident to destroy any more lives. I also do this because my Lord and Savior preaches forgiveness above all else. We may call Him by different names, but both of us talk to God, and only He can decide our guilt and punishment. You lived with the darkness so long you forgot the light, my friend. But it is not too late. Your soul has not been lost. Not yet."

Numb, Megan let the shard slip from her fingers. She watched, frozen in place as a shaking and stumbling Charles got to his feet and picked up the marriage registration form and photos. Without a word, he dropped them into the fire. His hand went into the breast pocket of his shirt and a small data stick joined the burning papers. He went over to the wall and took down a painting to reveal a safe. With a few twists of the dial, it opened and he removed a paper bag. It was stuffed full of printed documents.

He came over to Megan and very gently set it down in front of her. Finally, Charles sank onto the overstuffed armchair. He buried his face in his hands and rocked gently back and forth, repeating the same thing...

"It's over."

Chapter Eleven

THEY LEFT A subdued Charles in the cabin, nursing a large cup of strong coffee and on the phone with his father. The ride back to civilization was silent and more than a little strained. Megan ached all over from the fight with Charles. She kept her head down in the car to avoid catching even the slightest glimpse of the darkening bruises on her face.

Megan was grateful when Paolo dropped them off in front of her apartment. Even though she must have been still in pain from Megan popping her shoulder back into place, Syler walked Megan to her door. They lingered in front of it. Syler worried at the cuff of the sling they'd dug up for her, incidentally a Teitel sample.

"I should go back to my place," Syler said. She ran her free hand through her hair in a weak shadow of her usual bravado. "It's late, you must be exhausted."

The haunted look in her eyes told Megan that was not the correct option.

"Please stay," Megan said. "I don't think either of us should be alone tonight."

Syler's taut posture relaxed a fraction. She said, "Of course."

Megan unlocked the door and Syler slung herself down on the sofa with a contented sigh. Megan nearly joined her, but she glanced down at her blood-dotted clothing and stopped. Her lab coat was tied up in a plastic bag at the bottom of the trash can in a parking area they passed on the way home. Even though she'd scrubbed her hands several times, she still felt the sticky blood drying on her skin. She wanted to get rid of any evidence of that day, stop the memories before they flooded back.

"Give me a minute to change," Megan said. She barely registered Syler's concerned look before she turned and padded into her bedroom.

Megan pulled her blouse over her head, then dropped her skirt to the floor. She stood in front of her dresser and shivered. Megan rubbed at her arms as a dirty, crawling feeling stole over her. Now that she was back in her sanctuary, she hoped the horrors of that day would die. They didn't. Megan's head went down, her chin sank to her chest. She couldn't shut out the visceral memory of Charles on her, how he used her body without her permission for his own pleasure. Megan felt sullied and worthless.

Before Megan could stop it, a sob burst from her. She clapped a hand to her mouth. She managed to contain the sound, but her body shook from the suppressed emotions. Megan choked into her palm as a wave of nausea took her. She felt a presence behind her and whirled.

"Don't touch me," Megan said. She hunched her shoulders. Syler was too good, too pure.

"Hey Meg, it's okay. You're safe," Syler said. She stepped back and gave Megan some space. "I know what happened today was really fucking scary. You're remembering it. Don't let him win. Talk to me sweetheart."

The understanding on her face helped Megan to speak.

"I just feel gross," she said. "It's stupid, I know, but I don't feel like you should touch me. I don't want to contaminate you."

"Sweetheart," Syler breathed. "Your feelings are never stupid. I love you and I don't think anything that happened made you unattractive or dirty or whatever in any way. That's his fucking problem and it has nothing to do with us. But I get it, Meg. It's okay, I won't touch you until you're completely ready. I waited for you once, I can certainly do it again."

"Thank you," Megan said. She hugged her arms to her chest. Something still felt wrong. A nagging unease in her mind wouldn't die. She turned her focus inward.

"What are you thinking about?"

"What if he hadn't stopped?" Megan said. Her voice squeaked. She rubbed at her arms once more as if she could physically erase the memory of his hands on her. "What if I couldn't—"

Megan's throat closed. She crumpled onto her futon. She wished she could bury herself in the blankets and never come out.

Slowly, Syler eased herself down in front of Megan. She held Megan's gaze with hers. "There are no what ifs. What happened happened, what didn't didn't. Nothing is going to change that. Okay, Meg?"

Syler's calm words reassured her. Megan nodded. Syler got

up briefly and came back with a T-shirt. Wordlessly, she handed it over and Megan put it on. She breathed in the scent of her laundry soap for a moment, gathering her thoughts.

Megan asked in a rush, "Would you really have let him...do...that..." Her words trailed off. She didn't know if she wanted to know the answer.

"Let me tell you something. I've met a lot of guys in my life," Syler said. "Not always the nicest ones either. I know how assholes like Charles are and how to mess with them. Believe me, he wasn't going to get what he wanted. No fucking way. It was only a matter of time before he lost everything. The closer he got to me, the harder I was going to kick his ass. Charles had exactly zero allies in that room. Remember that."

"You're right," Megan said. She shook back the hair the fell over her face and looked across at Syler. "For the record, I was bluffing too. When everyone was distracted I nicked the transfusion bag in my pocket. I'm sorry I had to waste it. And if Charles had gotten in my face, it was him who would have gotten a slashed throat, not me. I hope I managed to tell you that."

Syler laughed, a genuine, pure sound. She reached out and carefully took Megan's hand. "You did. At first I thought I was going to have a heart attack, but when you gave me the clue, I figured out what you were doing." Syler's smile wavered. She said in a carefully light voice, "Don't ever do that again, all right? I don't think my sanity could take it."

"I won't," Megan said. At once, she needed Syler's touch more than she could say.

She scooted over to bury her head against Syler's chest.

"Hold me," Megan said. "I need you to touch me like you always do, like nothing happened."

"You're going to be okay," Syler murmured. One hand stroked over Megan's hair and down her back. "You know I'm always going to be here for you, but you have someone you can talk to this about, right? Like, a professional?"

"Yes, I do," Megan said. "My therapist is really good and she's seen me through some heavy stuff already. I'll make an appointment as soon as I can."

"Good," Syler said. She was silent for a moment before she said, "Charles better not bolt. I'd hate to see him get away with everything. Again."

"Charles won't run away. He's been running long enough. I think he wants to put things right."

"I hope so," Syler said. "But if not, I'll just have to spend the rest of my days tracking his ass down so I can kick it. Every superhero needs an arch-nemesis."

Megan had to laugh at that. She snuggled closer to Syler and said, "I'm still here so you can have both a nemesis and a sidekick."

"Hey who's the sidekick?" Syler drew back and regarded Megan seriously. "We're partners."

Her control nearly gave out as she wondered how long that partnership would last. Megan dredged up the will to say, "I like the sound of that."

"I do too." Syler reached out and traced Megan's lip with a soft thumb. "It's so good to see you smiling again."

Her words rang through Megan's chest. She knew exactly how Syler felt at that moment. Then she looked down at the bag of documents leaning against the wall and a fist of guilt slammed into her chest. It was time.

"Syler," Megan said in a whisper. "I need to tell you something." She couldn't bring herself to raise her head. She didn't want to look at Syler, she couldn't bear to see the love in her eyes turn to hate. She moved away so they were no longer touching. The coldness of the room hit her.

"No you don't," Syler said. There was fear in her words.

"I do," Megan said. She needed to speak. She ached to release the poison that festered in her soul. "I need you to know what I did. What happens next is up to you."

"Meg, sweetheart, whatever it is, this is the reason, isn't it? Why you keep pushing me away, why you don't want to make promises." Syler made a move as if to take Megan's hand, but stopped. "All right. I wish we didn't have to do this but I did promise I would. Whatever you need to tell me, I'm listening."

"It was a couple weeks after the accident. I was in the kitchen," Megan blurted out. The memory came back, full and clear as if it had happened yesterday instead of over a year ago. She prayed she could make it to the end. "We all were. I was trying to get the baby's formula but my hands were so numb and I couldn't remember the measurements. Everything was lumpy and horrible, the girls were hungry and crying. God, they never stopped! I was doing my best, practically killing myself with working all hours of the day and night, never having enough time to sleep or even bathe and they just sat there and cried."

Megan's chest tightened, but she kept going. The words echoed in her mind as if someone else was narrating the moment when her life derailed. "It was a mess. I threw the bottle into the sink. Pichai came up behind me and picked it up. He started to make the formula himself and I lost it. I was so angry, so frustrated with everything I exploded."

Tears swam into her vision. Megan raised her eyes to the ceiling without seeing it. When she spoke, her voice was rough. "I backhanded him across the room. He hit the oven door. He was only trying to feed his sister and I gave him a concussion and broke two of his ribs. As his body lay there on the floor, the only thing I could think of was losing my license and getting thrown into a Thai prison. All the people I would let down, all my plans and dreams going up in smoke."

Megan stopped. She hugged her arms to her chest. "He didn't remember what happened. I told him he slipped and fell. He believed me with his innocent, trusting heart. I took him to a hospital where they owed me some favors. I bought the actual admission reports and had them write up something less incriminating. I could have had them write the fake ones from the start or have the records destroyed, but I didn't. I need to go back there and face what I did. When he's old enough to understand, I have to tell Pichai in person and let him make the decision what to do next."

With the last word, Megan felt as if a weight had come off her. She was gutted and empty after letting go of the burning baggage she'd cherished for so long. There was nothing left to hide.

"Meg. My God," Syler breathed.

"You don't have to say it. I know," Megan said in a broken whisper. "I'm no better than Charles, no better than Fabia Okamoto. I'm worse than the both of them, in fact. I took my anger out on a defenseless child and ran away from taking responsibility for it. I bribed people and lied, all for my own benefit."

It was over. Megan held herself still. The only thing she felt was a final sense of completion. The last block had fallen into place. Megan was lightheaded with relief. She understood Charles's mantra. It was over. It didn't feel good, but it did feel complete.

The worst would happen and Megan would start over again. She couldn't help but press a hand to her chest. It really did feel like she'd been stabbed through the heart with a javelin. However she herself was the one who had put it there. The stricken look on Syler's face reminded Megan that a javelin is pointed at both ends. Guilt hit her like a truck.

Through the pain, Megan took a breath and said, "Syler, I just want to say I will never forget what we had and what you meant to me. You were the best thing that ever came into my life. I can't tell you how sorry I am things had to end like this, but please remember I love you and I always will."

"Meg," Syler's voice was thick with emotion, "what are you talking about? Do you want me to leave you?"

"You should," Megan said. "Now you know who I am and what I've done."

"I didn't ask what you think I should do. I asked if you wanted me to leave you."

Megan pressed her lips together. This was her chance to set Syler free. There were two options in front of her. It would be so easy to say the words that would cut them both away from each other. But she couldn't.

"No, I don't." Megan scrubbed a hand over her face. "I don't think I could live without you."

The force of Syler grabbing her in a fierce embrace rocked Megan back. Before she could stop herself, Megan had her arms around Syler as well and was sobbing into her shirt.

"That's good because I'm staying right here," Syler whispered as she held Megan to her. "You are my life, my love, my everything, Meg. I have no right to judge you and I'm not going to. You have done so much penance already, I'm not going to add to it. Whatever anyone else thinks doesn't matter. I've got your back. I'll be with you as long as you want me."

"I do. I want to be with you, Syler," Megan said through her tears. Her entire world was reduced to one point in space and time, and that was in Syler's arms and pressed against her heart. "I'm sorry," Megan sobbed. "I'm so sorry. For all of it."

"Shh, it's all right. We'll figure something out. We'll get through this together." Syler very softly smoothed the tears from Megan's cheeks. She said in a low voice, "*Yihye beseder, Meirav.*"

Everything will be all right.

The words of reassurance were the same ones Megan's own mother used on her so many times when school-aged Megan allowed herself to show the tears of pain and loneliness she hid from her classmates. Hearing Syler say them, Megan believed at once that everything really would be all right.

"I know," Megan hiccupped. "Thank you."

"Good." One hand slowly rubbed up and down Megan's back. "Because we have a date to see the cherry blossoms at Suito Castle next spring."

"I'm looking forward to it," Megan said. The words were inadequate to express the joy Megan had found in that instant. She reached out and drew Syler to her. She fell into Syler's embrace and met her with a gentle, almost hesitant kiss. Syler's arms came around her. Megan felt complete in that moment.

A moment later, Syler yawned. "Sorry Meg. I'm just about falling asleep on my feet here and the painkiller you gave me back at the cottage is starting to wear off." She shifted against Megan with a grimace.

"That's right, your shoulder must be hurting you quite a bit by now." Megan jumped up. "How about I give you something. I've got some Loxonin in my purse. Just give me a moment to get it."

"Thanks," Syler said.

Megan came back with the pills and a glass of cold tea. She waited until Syler took one and lay back with her eyes closed. She looked tired and vulnerable and in pain. Once more, Megan felt a flash of anger at Charles and his schemes. Syler opened one eye and held out her good arm in a silent invitation. The anger faded as Megan nestled under her arm in the warm nest of blankets.

"Would you stay here with me?" Megan asked.

"Sure, I'd love to."

"How about a bath?"

"Only if you promise to wash my back," Syler said with a mischievous light in her eye. She leaned down and gave Megan a slow, sweet kiss before she whispered against her lips, "And front."

"I thought you were injured." Megan drew back with a mock-stern glare.

"Yeah, my shoulder, not my, ahem, anything else," Syler said. She backed away as Megan brandished a pillow at her.

"Okay, okay, I'll behave. Until this damn sling comes off any-way."

"That's better," Megan said. "I wouldn't want to have to pull rank and give you a 'doctor stop.'"

Syler laughed as Megan replaced the cushion. With that, Megan darted into the bathroom to start the water. While Megan's bath wasn't as big as Syler's, they both managed to fit just fine. Syler kept her word and the bath was mostly free from incident. Megan was content to just be close to Syler. Shoulder-deep in the fragrant water, she ended up in her favorite place, nestled in Syler's arms with long legs wrapped around her body.

"Do you want to know what my dream is?" Megan began. She reached down into the water and twined her fingers around Syler's, breaking their soft caresses on her belly.

"I'd love to hear about your dream. What is it, Meg?"

"I want to set up a series of clinics," Megan said. "In develop-ing countries or places where medical infrastructure is lacking because of natural disaster or war. Clinics that will provide ser-vices like HIV testing, hormone therapy and transition support, as well as birth control, even sterilization for anyone who wants it. Not only that, but educate people too. I've got a trust fund of my own that I want to use to set up my clinics and I'm pretty good at squeezing grant money out of the system. The first step was my work in Thailand." She took a deep breath and said, "And this hospital isn't the second one."

"So you're saying you're not here for good?"

"That's right," Megan said. She twisted so she could look at Syler. "I've made a two-year commitment and while I fully intend to see it through, from the start I wasn't planning on renewing my contract. But if you wanted me to, I would stay. If you asked me to, I'd do it happily."

"Meg," Syler breathed. Her arms tightened around Megan's body. "I would never ask you to give up your dream. It's a won-derful one that will bring so much good into this world." Syler freed a hand to trace over Megan's lower lip, painting it with warm water. "In fact, if you asked *me*, I would go with you."

Even as a wild flame of joy roared into life within herself, Megan said, "But your position here, and your apartment build-ing...I couldn't ask you to leave that."

"That building won't fall down if I'm not here," Syler said.

She brushed a strand of wet hair from Megan's cheek. "Even with Chucky-boy out of the picture, spending the rest of my professional life here isn't the most thrilling prospect. I already know we make a great team and my place is with you. Besides, I'm on the indefinite-term employment contract, so I can leave anytime." Syler paused with a look of uncertainty on her face, "That is, if you want me."

"I do!" Megan said. She jumped into Syler's arms, splashing water everywhere and soaking them both. Once she finished sputtering, Megan raked her sopping hair out of her face with both hands and said, "Yes I want you! You don't know how much. It would be like a dream come true to work with you, Syler." She let out a long breath and tried to calm her racing heart.

"Good," Syler said. She dropped a quick kiss to Megan's shoulder and said, "Now tell me honestly, there's no more life-shattering secrets you're still holding onto?"

"No, I've spilled everything," Megan said.

"Great," Syler said with such simple, unaffected love Megan once again wondered if she really deserved someone like that in her life. "Now that's settled, how about getting out of here before we both turn into prunes?"

"All right. I'm so ready for bed anyway." Megan rose from the bath and helped Syler get up after her. As they dried off in the changing area, Megan paused, towel in hand. She said, "Maybe there is one more thing."

"Oh God," Syler froze as well. "Don't tell me, you really are three dogs in a coat. I knew you were too loyal and cuddly to be a human."

Stifling her smile, Megan shook her head and pressed up against Syler. She said, "I am completely and totally head over heels in love with the sexiest surgeon alive."

"Do I know this person?" Syler asked in a suspicious voice. She took the fresh T-shirt Megan handed her and accepted help to pull it over her head.

"I think so," Megan said. "You see her in the mirror every day except Sabbath."

She squeaked as Syler's arms came around her and caught her up in a fierce hug.

"Good," Syler said. "Because I happen to feel the same way

about you. Ouch!" She let go and sheepishly grabbed her shoulder while Megan swooped down with the borrowed sling.

Chapter Twelve

MEGAN WOKE UP alert and refreshed at around noon. Syler lay beside her, breaths even but eyes open. Concerned, Megan sat up quickly.

"Did you sleep at all?" Megan asked. She gave Syler a quick examination to reassure herself that everything was holding together.

"Yeah, a few hours anyway," Syler said. She squirmed under Megan's prodding but didn't give any other sign of protest. "I was out until the Loxonin wore off but I was comfy enough with you so I just stayed here."

"Are you all right?"

"Yeah, pretty good considering."

Megan wasn't completely convinced but let the matter drop. She got them mugs of coffee to sip and cuddled up to Syler, determined to enjoy their semi-vacation, unplanned as it was.

Syler finished her coffee with a happy sigh and sprawled out over Megan's lap, so much like she had on their first picnic that Megan had to swallow the knot of sadness called by the wave of nostalgia. Now they were battered and scarred, but free from the secrets Megan had feared would tear them apart. They were tested through fire and came out stronger. Megan regretted so much, but she wouldn't change a single one of the events that led them to that point. She brushed a strand of hair from Syler's forehead, then continued over her cheek.

"You are so beautiful," Megan breathed, still in awe.

Syler didn't open her eyes, but the ghost of a smile kissed her lips and Megan couldn't help but lean down and do so as well. Megan drew back. She looked at Syler lying down, so strong and so vulnerable at the same time. Megan bit her lip. There was something important that she hadn't said, something she'd been putting off for fear of having to take it back after. That wasn't going to happen. Syler was not going to leave her. Megan hadn't spoken yet, but she was going to. The thought filled Megan with a wave of joy and nerves.

"Syler," Megan spoke in a rush, "I've been thinking and I haven't been fair to you. To us. I want to—" Megan began but stopped as her courage ran out.

"Tell me, love," Syler said. She looked up with such tenderness that the next words came easily.

"I want to be with you, and I want to do this all the way. Syler, I want to come out."

"What brought that on?" Syler asked. "You know I support you completely, but are you sure? Okay, it's not like in the States where you'll get people coming up to your face and saying shit like, 'I don't believe in your lifestyle choice and you're going to burn in hell' but it's going to change the way some people deal with you. And coming out isn't something you do just once. It's a process that you're going to have to repeat countless times for the rest of your life."

"I'm prepared for that," Megan said. She reached out and took Syler's hands in hers. Her eyes welled up with emotion, her throat grew tight and she had to struggle to speak. "Secrets are weapons and I am sick of having mine used against me and the people I love." Megan freed a hand to drag across her face. "I'm sick of being invisible and having to deny what you are to me. And if anyone at the hospital has a problem, then screw them. Policy or no policy, it's only a job. I'll be fine without it, but I'm nothing without you."

"Meg, you are your own person, and you are compassionate, brilliant, and badass even without me," Syler said as she gathered Megan's willing body up in her arms. Syler paused before she said, "When you say you want to come out, does that mean you're going to tell your parents about us?"

"Actually I kind of spilled it already," Megan said. She looked up at Syler and said, "My mother has a way of getting me to talk and, well, let's just say I've been in a really good mood recently."

"That's good to hear," Syler said. Her thumb brushed over the back of Megan's hand in a way that never failed to fill her with comfort. "You know, I wouldn't mind, um, forget it. Sorry."

She went quiet and Megan bit her lip at Syler's abrupt stop. She knew the end of that sentence was hovering in the air between them. The apologetic, drawn look on Syler's face stabbed her through the heart and Megan did the only thing she could think of.

She took Syler's hands in hers. "I want you to meet them. I

want to introduce you to them, not in a casual way either but not right now. After what's happened these past few days, I don't think it's a good idea to do something of that magnitude so soon."

"You're right," Syler said. She gazed at Megan with breathless wonder. "You're serious about that, aren't you, Meg?"

"Of course," Megan said. She wriggled a bit underneath the covers and aimed a smile up at Syler. "Don't think you're going to be able to get out of suffering through my dad's terrible jokes and my mama's nosy questions."

Syler gave a peal of laughter. "I'm sure they're not that bad. Anyway, how about I fix us something to eat?"

Megan said. "Oh no, I can do that. You're a guest here and injured."

"I don't mind," Syler said. "Besides, I'm at least wearing pants, and you, my sexy love, are not." She gave Megan a slow once over as she stood up. Megan laughed and threw pillows at Syler while she made her escape, leaving Megan alone on the crumpled futon.

Megan located a long cotton skirt and pulled it on before she trotted into the living room. She was greeted by a golden toasted bagel spread thickly with cream cheese on a plate in front of her accustomed place on the sofa.

"I hope you don't mind if I just went ahead and took over your kitchen," Syler said from where she was hovering in the kitchen cubby. She had a bagel in front of herself with a bite out of it.

"Please feel free to make me lunch anytime. It looks gorgeous," Megan said. She picked up her bagel and paused before adding, "The bagel is nice too."

"Yeah yeah," Syler muttered but looked pleased as she cut up some fruit one-handed. Awkwardly balancing the dishes, Syler came over with a bowl of fruit salad plus a mug of cold tea and set them down next to Megan's plate.

With a quick *itadakimasu* Megan dove into her food. Syler kept her well-supplied with cold tea and eventually brought her own bagel over as she perched on the sofa next to Megan. The eclectic playlist on Syler's phone kept them company as they chatted and enjoyed the leisurely meal.

AFTER LUNCH, MEGAN insisted on doing the cleanup and Syler sprawled on the sofa with a cup of tea in front of her. She propped her phone up on the table with a recorded local women's softball game on the screen and entertained herself by gleefully giving her Gaydar a workout on the players.

"The pitcher is totally *bian*," Syler said. "The shortstop is too, look at those highlights — yup, total woman's woman. Not sure about the batter there. A bit girly, but then again she's kind of got that look."

"What look?" Megan sat down on the arm of the sofa. "Is there a woman-loving look? Like something in her personal style, or is it an intuitive thing?"

"It's more than just hairstyle and the sunglasses. See how she stands, how she moves with that confident little swagger and doesn't have that fake smile girls get," Syler said with expert nonchalance. She tugged on Megan's hand and guided her to slip down into Syler's lap. Megan snuggled happily into the loose, one-armed embrace.

"Do I have that look?" Megan wanted to know.

"Hmm," Syler pulled back and regarded Megan. Then she changed directions and leaned in close until Megan felt her eyes crossing. Their noses touched. Megan stifled a giggle. Quick as a cat, Syler tilted her head and caught her on the mouth with a sweet, gently insistent kiss. It lasted for a heartbeat. Megan fluttered her eyes closed, ready for more when Syler broke the contact and whispered, "You are the sweetest and hottest enigma that kept me guessing for way longer than I should have. There is nothing quantifiable about you, Meg. But you definitely kiss like a lesbian."

"I hope that's good," Megan said.

"It's very good," Syler murmured. "Because the person you're kissing is me. And I think I'd like you to kiss me a bit more, you know, in order for me to collect more data to support my hypothesis."

Overjoyed, Megan hastened to comply. Only a persistent knocking on the door drew her attention away from Syler and her research.

"Just ignore it," Syler breathed between kisses. Megan tried to do that, but the knocking kept on going and it messed up Megan's rhythm, not to mention it took her concentration from the lovely feeling of being held close to Syler.

"They're not going away," Megan said with a sigh. She reluctantly picked herself off Syler's lap and crossed the room. "This better be important," Megan muttered. Having learned from experience, Megan peered out through the peephole and was surprised by Jayco and Luka standing in the hallway.

"Sorry guys, wait a minute," Megan called through the door.

With Luka's exasperated answer ringing in her ears, she peeled off into the bedroom where she grabbed a bra for herself and found something for Syler to wear as well, secretly pleased at how many of Syler's things had managed to find their way into her room. Once both of them were decent, she opened the door with a question on her lips.

Luka barreled through the entrance hall without a glance at Megan who ducked shyly behind the door. En route, he sang out, "Hello dear! Mind if we come in? We're not interrupting anything, are we?"

"Not at all, and yes you are," Megan said. She was miffed that the cozy moment she'd been having with Syler had been cut short. She closed the door and turned to Jayco as he slipped off his shoes in the increasingly cluttered entrance hall. Megan asked, "What's up? Is everything okay at work?"

"No it isn't," Jayco said. He looked up at Megan and froze. She clapped a hand to her face to cover the rapidly rainbowing bruise just as Luka's abrupt squawk rang through the little apartment.

"Girlfriend, that sling! What happened to you?"

Megan dashed into the living room to see Syler shrugging her good shoulder. "Just an old aikido injury acting up. Why the sudden visit guys? You miss us?"

"As if," Luka huffed. He whirled and gaped at Megan. "Okay, tell me what's going on. How did you get that shiner, sweetheart?"

"Bar fight," Megan blurted out. She looked over to Syler who was stifling her smile by biting her lip. Megan lifted her chin and said, "Nobody gets between me and my woman without entering a universe of pain."

"Yeah," Syler said, even though her lips twitched. "You should see the other guy."

"Oh my, *mrrowr!* Is that why the two of you are MIA from the hospital?" Luka asked. He perched his perky butt on the sofa as if he owned the place. "A bunch of the nurses are pissed at you, Syler. They said you took off without doing your rounds yesterday."

"Well they can bite—"

"More importantly," Jayco said with calm authority as he came over and picked up the remote control, "have you seen the news? It's been all over the TV since this morning."

"What's been all over the TV?" Megan asked.

Jayco turned on the screen and flipped through the channels before he settled on their local news station, which was playing an emergency broadcast.

"My God," Syler breathed.

Megan stifled a gasp and fell into the sofa, narrowly missing squashing Luka. The screen showed a flashbulb-filled press conference. A long table was decorated by a number of microphones and standing behind it was Charles and his father, along with a few other senior members of the hospital's management. All of them bowed deeply at the waist. In the middle of the line, Charles's shoulders were shaking and his hair fell limply over his face. When he straightened up, Megan was surprised once more at his haggard appearance. It looked as if he hadn't slept since the last time they'd seen him.

Charles started speaking and the instant translation spoke over him. Megan already knew the details but found herself staring blankly at the screen. Beside her, Syler did the same. Writing flashed along the bottom of the screen, echoing the long-winded formal apology and detailing the attempted cover-up of the botched operation that left a patient in a vegetative state. He finished by taking full responsibility, saying over and over the hospital itself had no part in the entire incident.

"This is the end of them. The Brockman family is leaving the hospital," Luka said. He bounced up and down on the sofa. His hands flung out wildly as he spoke. "I heard they called in Doctor Sylvia Maxwell and her husband Michael to take over. Do you know what that means? Guys!" Luka screeched, "I dated their son! I know their whole family! We're going to have the coolest management ever!"

"Really?" Megan couldn't catch her breath. She wondered if she was dreaming. It was a telling moment that Jayco didn't bat an eye at the mention of Luka's rather boy-filled past. He perched on the arm of the sofa with the remote held loosely in his hands.

"Check your email," Jayco said with slowly blooming excitement. "There's been a policy change, actually a policy erasure. Specifically of the one that puts the kibosh on inter-staff relationships. Something about private lives being private blah blah."

"Really?" Megan said again. She didn't seem to be able to get anything else out.

"You missed all the excitement," Luka told them loftily. "With your bar fights and not-made-up martial arts injuries."

"It certainly seems like it." Remembering her manners, Megan jumped to her feet. "How about some tea?"

"Sorry but we've got to get back," Jayco said. "We just wanted to make sure you heard the news ASAP."

"Thanks for that," Megan said. She saw the two young men to the door while receiving good-natured teasing from Luka about her "Warrior Princess" status, which Megan waved off with a twinge of unease.

THE FIRST DAY back after a week of holiday wasn't as jarring as Megan feared. The new president had moved in and the handover took place with a minimum of fuss. Even the rumors about herself and Syler took a backseat to the upheaval of losing their ruling family.

Megan arrived early and got back into stride quickly. She finished examination hours with no mishaps. She was in the middle of her afternoon rounds when Syler popped out of the stairwell with a big smile on her face.

"Hey Meg, I found something you might want to see."

"What is it?"

Syler didn't answer, just ducked back into the stairwell. Megan scrambled to follow her. Syler took off at a good clip with Megan following close behind. They burst into the main lobby where Syler stopped short. Megan bounced off her back.

"Sorry," Megan said as she rubbed her nose. She looked up to see what it was that had caught Syler's attention. Paolo waved at them from behind the information desk. He was wearing the immaculate white uniform of the administration department and a huge grin.

"My new job," he said. Paolo flashed his nametag as they drew near his desk. He shifted his weight from one foot to the other and said, "I was recommended by, er, our old acquaintance before he left."

"At least he's good for something. Congratulations," Syler said as Megan looked on with wonder.

He bent closer and said, "You were right, my friend, about applying for special permission to stay. My case is being reviewed and I hear it looks good."

"That's great," Syler said. "Do you need me to update that guarantor form I gave you?"

"No, it is maybe not necessary," Paolo said. His face fell and he said, "You are too kind. Again I apologize for—"

"It's okay," Syler said quickly. She glanced over at Megan. "Just forget it."

"That's great you're working here too," Megan said. She had to admit being hesitant to see Paolo again, considering he'd witnessed an incredibly personal moment between herself and Syler, plus whatever else he'd been forced to do by Charles including kidnapping Syler and probably breaking into Megan's apartment. Even after everything, Syler was unreservedly supportive of him, which helped Megan to decide to give him a second chance as well.

After Megan completed her rounds, she leaned her elbows on the nurse's station and let her gaze wander over to where Syler chatted with Fabia, looking just as breathtaking as the first day Megan had seen her. More, in fact, since Syler met her gaze with a knowing glance full of love and promises made and those yet to be spoken.

"I just wanted to thank you." At the words, Megan jumped out of her reverie. Junichiro Okamoto stood beside her. He stuck his hands in his pockets and said, "Thank you for your support through all this. We're trying to work things out, but I don't know if our relationship will ever get back to how it was in the good times."

"It will if you want it badly enough," Megan said.

"I hope so. It seems like such a waste if things end like this. Fabia actually went against her family's wishes to be with me," he said with a sad sigh. "We were so in love, the world couldn't do anything to stop us. What happened I wonder? Time, I guess. I was too busy, I wasn't there enough. I thought having a child between us would be enough, but it wasn't."

"No, it isn't. You have to go back there." Megan kept her eyes on Syler's lean form as she spoke, her voice soft and introspective. "Go back in time. Remember why you fell in love with her, how her beauty and spirit captured you. Look at the curve of her neck and imagine how lovely a kiss would feel there, how her arms around you complete your world. Think about her strength, her passion and most of all her heart, how it beats for you and yours for her." Megan's gaze didn't waver as she continued, "And how she is the sexiest thing alive in a tux and makes blintzes my bube would be jealous of."

Junichiro looked at her with a puzzled expression.

"What?" Megan said. She tilted her head and crossed her arms. "I'm not going to give you the answers. You ogle your own woman, I've got mine."

Junichiro gave a half-smothered gasp.

Megan left his side. She skipped across the hallway and ended up next to Syler. Behind her, she was vaguely aware of Junichiro and Fabia's soft conversation.

"Hey Meg," Syler said. She held out a hand and Megan took it. She drew close to Syler's side. Her heart thundered as she realized how public they were being. Megan didn't care. The faster people got used to them the better. "Are you coming over to my place tonight for the roof party?"

"Of course," Megan said. "I wouldn't miss it. What can I bring?"

"Dani and Taka-chan are taking care of the beverages, I've bought a bunch of food already, so just bring yourself unless you want something sweet to munch on."

"Ooh, good idea." Megan bit her lower lip suggestively before she said, "I have just the thing, a brand new pack of takenoko. It's limited-edition, saltwater caramel. You have to come over and pick it up in person, so we can sample them first, in private."

"You really know how to tempt me," Syler said in a low, husky voice. "I'm so there, Meg."

"My sofa is looking forward to hanging out with you, and I'm looking forward to sharing a bit of sweet munching," Megan said. She was about to drop a few more suggestive hints but was interrupted by a scampering body wedging in between them.

"Hey Doctor Megan and Doctor Syler! What are we talking about?" Nikky asked at her usual top-volume.

"Just what's for dessert tonight," Syler answered in a bland voice. She twitched away as Megan's elbow came at her ribs.

"I'm having egg tart! Papa's taking me to Ran-Ran Sushi and he said I could have whatever I want."

"Sounds good," Syler said. She reached out and ruffled Nikky's hair. "Your papa's a *mensch*. Do you know what that means?"

"Yup! It means he's a good guy and a good daddy to me." Nikky preened in a cute, unaffected way that had Megan stifling a smile. "Oh, I gotta go. See ya later taters!"

The child turned and scampered off down the hallway. Her happy footsteps echoed like stones falling into a wishing well where every wish came true. Megan gazed at Syler. Hers certainly had.

Epilogue

"STOP FUSSING, YOU'RE perfect," Megan said as Syler fixed her collar for the hundredth time since they'd gotten into the taxi from the station. The blocky grey landscape streamed by outside but Megan only had eyes for Syler.

After they arrived at Shin-Saitama Station, Syler changed from her usual jeans and Wonder Woman T-shirt to a light grey pantsuit with a white button-down shirt underneath. The jacket was lightly lined for the warm spring weather. The cut flattered her trim figure but left the slightest breath of femininity in the way it hugged her body. The suit along with Syler's new hairstyle, buzzed close to the nape with the front left long enough to hang into her eyes, knocked the breath from Megan's lungs and caused her to fall all over again. She had never seen Syler look so businesslike or so temptingly gorgeous.

"Thanks," Syler said. She raked back the hair that fell across her brow and muttered, "I shouldn't have cut it."

"No way," Megan said. "I liked your old style, but this is nice now that winter's over." Megan said with a sly grin, "Plus, I love how you've kept the front long so I can do this." She reached out and smoothed a strand of hair from Syler's brow. Her fingers brushed over Syler's cheek and trailed down to her lower lip. Syler grimaced.

"Relax, okay?" Megan said. "My parents are good people."

"I know," Syler said. She gave Megan a wan smile. "They raised you, after all. It's just I feel like I'm going to be standing there like, oh hey, nice to meet you, I give your daughter orgasms!"

Megan clapped her hand over her mouth as a laugh threatened to escape. "You don't just give me orgasms," Megan said as soon as she could get her face serious again. "You give me mind-shattering earth-rocking screaming orgasms."

Syler gasped in laughter.

It was true. After a bit of time and counseling, plus a lot of hanging out and just talking either with Syler's team, the indomitable combo of Luka and Jayco, or just the two of them, they found peace and healing. The past wounds faded to scars that barely gave any twinges any more. The healing was greatly helped by the fact that Charles was currently living in Israel on a men-only kibbutz and word had it he was doing so well there he was planning on staying there permanently.

Megan arranged her skirt over her knees in a prim way. "My dad's going to be easy to win over," she said. "He's just like me so I know he'll love you right away. It's my mother you've got to worry about. She's got the Teitel spirit and not just anybody's going to be good enough for her only daughter."

"Don't worry," Syler said with a cocky grin, "If she doesn't warm up to me, I can always break out the tux. I have it on good authority it makes women of the Teitel persuasion damp in the panties."

"I can't speak for my mama," Megan said. "But yeah, you in a tuxedo gets me a bit more than just damp." She leaned against Syler's arm, eyes dreamy.

"Yeah, I know."

While Syler preened, her usual confidence restored, Megan sat back into the soft cushions of the taxi. The windows were cracked open and the warm wind blew across her face, scented from the heavy drifts of cherry blossoms that loomed over the road on both sides. She remembered the previous spring, lying under the gentle rain of petals with Syler, so afraid to move forward and yet unable to stop herself. So much had changed since then, Megan tucked her hand under her chin and mused to herself.

Nikky's family had reconciled a few months after the incident that landed Nikky in the ER, and Fabia moved back in with them. Nikky thrived as a girl, so much that there was talk of going ahead with hormone-blockers and they were looking at other more permanent options. She had eventually been told the truth about her friend Sakura and while it had caused her a lot of sadness, Nikky was strong enough to take the loss in stride.

The previous winter, Chiho and Toshi were blessed with a healthy baby boy and they were raising him not in the shadow of the sister he'd lost, but with the knowledge he had an angel looking out for him. Syler doted on the little boy whenever they brought him around for a visit and she let them know she was available for date nights as soon as they felt ready to leave their son for the evening.

Not all the developments were completely happy. Jayco and Luka had broken up twice, the second time featuring both of them dating other people before they got back together. At the moment they were back together and doing well. If Megan had been able to wait longer, a double gay Jewish wedding might have been a possibility. But she hadn't.

A little over a week ago, Megan had dredged up the nerve to speak. After shul, she'd led Syler out to the bench in the front garden of the hospital, flanked by a number of young cherry trees that were spindly but valiantly pushing out a few popcorn-like buds here and there. One day the trees would surround the bench with frothy blossoms, but that day was still years away.

Syler looked curious but kept silent as Megan tugged her over to sit on the bench. They leaned back against the engraved plaque that read: *In Memory of Sakura Yamane.* They were in their Saturday-best—Megan with the delicately crocheted yarmulke she'd traded her lace cap for and Syler with a plain navy one. Both of them were draped in matching prayer shawls Megan found online, made by Israeli women for women. The reverent sound of Syler's voice as she'd read from the Tora still resounded in Megan's ears as she turned and took both of Syler's hands in hers.

"I was thinking about going back to Saitama to spend a couple days with my parents." Megan stopped and cleared her throat. "Why don't you come with me?"

"You want me to go back to your home?"

"My home is here with you," Megan said with all the conviction in her heart. "But yes, I'd love for you to come to my family's home. It's more than time I personally introduced them to the most important person in my life."

"Is this going to be a hanging out with the folks kind of thing," Syler began in a soft, intense voice, her eyes never leaving Megan's, "or is this the official visit?"

Megan's mouth went dry. She licked her lips before she said, "It can be either. Which one do you want?"

"I think you know," Syler said. "Is that all right with you?"

"Yes, it is," Megan said. Her heart fluttered with nerves and happiness. "As long you don't think it's rushing things. It's only been a year, and I want us both to be comfortable with the pace."

"I'm so all right with this," Syler said. "I feel like until I met you, I was just sitting on my ass. I felt stalled. Professionally and personally. Meg, you came into my life and changed it. I'm finally moving forward after being passive and out of it for so long. I want to take the next step. I'm ready if you are."

Megan caught her breath at the words. While her own life had changed for the better with Syler in it, she hadn't realized the effect her own presence had had on Syler. It was a nice feeling. More than nice.

"I'm ready too. I want a life with you, Syler," Megan said. She paused to dash away the tears that rose to her eyes before she looked back over her shoulder and shouted, "Okay everyone, she said yes!"

Syler didn't have time to get out more than a "What the—" before a crowd of hollering, laughing children converged on them, herded by a gleefully whooping Luka and Jayco and led by Nikky who looked like a radiantly happy cupcake in her new dress. All of them held buckets in their hands. As one, the buckets were dumped and the air was filled with cutout hearts of pink and white, fluttering down around them like a mass of falling cherry blossom petals.

"Oh my God, you guys," Syler said. She stood and rained papers down all over the lawn. "I'm not cleaning this up, you know." Even though her words were somewhat curmudgeonly, she was smiling. Megan saw the sparkle of tears before Syler dragged her sleeve across her face on the pretence of scrubbing off the papers that had gotten stuck in her hair. She laughed and reached out to enfold Megan into a warm hug, neither of them the least bit concerned about the children milling around them, or even the members of their congregation who came out to see what the fuss was and sprinkled them with cheerful cries of *Mazel tov!*.

The only thing Megan knew was the feeling of Syler's arms around her and the hot bursts of breath on her face as Syler whispered words that were half-prayer, half-thanks.

The taxi stopped outside the small restaurant. The front window was plastered with handwritten signs. The building looked rundown and shabby, but Megan knew from long years of eating there that the food was wonderful and the owner was like a friendly uncle to her. Megan reached over to pay the driver.

"Sorry, I should have gotten that," Syler said. The strap of her bag got tangled up in the seatbelt. She swore under her breath.

"It's all right, really," Megan said. "You'll be okay."

"Uh huh," Syler said. She finally got everything untangled. Syler unfolded her long legs and got out of the taxi. She stood still for a second. "Meg, are you sure this is the right place? It looks closed."

Megan glanced up and had to agree. The lights that illuminated the sprawling hand-painted sign were off and the doorway was dark. At once, she understood. Megan swallowed nervously.

"It's all right. It looks like Osahar closed the restaurant for us tonight."

"Oh, wow."

They stood in silence for a heartbeat. Megan felt the weight of the moment come over her. This was it. There would be no going back. She raised her head to meet Syler's gaze with her own. All her doubts vanished.

"Let's do this, Meg," Syler said.

Syler cracked a grin and tipped an invisible hat before she held the door of the restaurant open for Megan. Syler followed her inside. Their entrance was heralded by the cheerful chorus of bells. In the familiar room, Megan took a deep breath. The thick, spicy air filled her lungs and brought her back to a time before tragedy split her life into before and after. The main area boasted four mismatched tables surrounded by a herd of ancient folding chairs, overlooked by a TV broadcasting some kind of soap opera in Arabic. Osahar the proprietor was the first to greet them. He came over with both hands extended and grasped first Megan's hands then Syler's and showered them with cheerful greetings.

He directed them to a small, private room that contained a single square table set for four. Two chairs were already occupied by Megan's parents. Megan couldn't help but speed up when she saw them.

They were as different as two people could be, but they had been together for thirty years and seemed determined to stay that way for another thirty. Megan took after her father in coloring, although his short golden brown hair was slowly turning to white under his yarmulke and his forehead was getting higher with every passing year. While he was smiling broadly, Megan's mother looked Syler up and down with a stern expression before she leaned forward to return Syler's bow. Stefania was a pure Teitel, with dramatic eyes and sharp bone structure. Time had not changed her angular body. She wore the silk blouse and designer skirt with aristocratic ease.

"Mom, Dad, this is my girlfriend, Syler Terada," Megan said. She couldn't stop the happy grin that blossomed all over her face. "Syler, these are my parents, Stefania and Eli Maier."

In an instant, the nervous person in the taxi transformed into the cool professional Megan was used to seeing in the hallways of the hospital. Syler reached out and shook Eli's hand.

"It's nice to meet you both," Syler said in her perfect but slightly drawly Michigan-accented English that never failed to send a happy thrill through Megan.

"Sit, sit," Eli said. He gestured to the unoccupied chairs at the table. "We are very pleased to see our daughter has found some-one nice for herself, and it's a double honor to have the opportu-nity to meet you. Thank you for coming all this way. We've heard so much about you, and you seem to be quite remarkable, at least according to our Meirav."

"I think the source is a bit biased, but Megan deserves noth-ing but the best," Syler said. She gave Megan a smile that melted her. Still hovering in a semi-dreamlike state, Megan aimed herself at the chair opposite her mother. She jumped a little as Syler gal-lantly held the chair for her.

Syler sat down beside Megan. She folded her hands on the table and looked across at Megan's parents. Megan held her breath. However nervous she was feeling, Syler must be a hun-dred times more so. In a way, Megan was pleased Syler adhered to the Japanese style of introduction. It was old-fashioned but so was her family, especially her mother who had not only grown up a Teitel, but also a de-facto Japanese national and had deep respect for both sets of traditions.

"I'd like to formally introduce myself and let you know that my intentions with your daughter are serious." Syler cleared her throat and reached into her bag. She came back out with a num-ber of envelopes that bore the stylized water-jug symbol of Suito City. With a quick, deft motion, Syler opened them and took out several sheaves of official-looking papers. Both of Megan's parents leaned forward to study the printed documents.

"This is a copy of my *juminhyo*," Syler said. She indicated the form with all of her residential and personal information. "It probably goes without saying, but you can see I'm not currently or have ever been married, no dependents. This is where my father lives in the States and here's my current address. Also," more rustling and another document was on the table. "Here is the information for the building I own. I actually co-own it with my three brothers, but they're silent partners."

"Interesting," Eli said. He studied the documents with raised eyebrows.

Megan prickled with nerves. She knew Syler had to do this, prove herself to Megan's parents. She never pushed for more information about Syler and her property, preferring to just exist with her without the bother of financial exchange so the information was new to her as well. Megan was fascinated. It was like meeting Syler for the first time all over again. The feeling ignited a hot longing to touch Syler. Megan struggled to keep it hidden. At least until they were alone.

"I see you had the name changed from Aoyama Place to Nozomi Heights," Stefania pointed out.

"That's right," Syler said. She shifted in her seat as a faraway, somewhat melancholy look came over her face. "Nozomi was my mother's name."

Was. Megan bit back the gasp of understanding. In order to make a purchase like that, a large block of cash was necessary. Something like a life insurance settlement from the mother Syler had no memory of. Megan dropped a hand under the table. She found Syler's hand and gave her a slow, lingering squeeze. The gentle pressure of Syler's fingers came in response. After only a moment, Syler released Megan. She put a few more documents onto the table.

"Here's my most recent pay slip and health and life insurance policies," Syler said in a clipped, businesslike tone. "I've been working at Ruth Kurtz for over seven years now. I get a twice-yearly bonus and also a small bi-monthly stipend for participating in research and training activities."

"Do you have any savings?" Stefania asked.

A flash of unease crossed Syler's features. She said, "For the last two years I've been saving my bonuses and I've got some mutual funds my father manages in the States. It's not a lot, but it's a start."

Two years. Megan couldn't help the hum of understanding. Syler must have done things with Yukina the standard way for married couples in Japan, with the main breadwinner handing over their entire paycheck and control of the house finances to their partner. It seemed Yukina had not bothered to save any of the money Syler made. Megan wondered exactly what she'd used it for. For an instant, the old anger came back, but just as quickly it faded, banished by a small, intimate glance from Syler.

"I am glad to hear you are self-sufficient," Stefania said. She pressed her lips together for a moment. "I assume you do not engage in any immoral or illicit activities."

Syler leaned forward and placed her hands on the table. "I don't gamble and while I enjoy a drink from time to time, I practice moderation." Syler didn't mention the other forms of chemical relaxation she'd engaged in. She didn't need to. Since the night of Sakura's *otsuya*, Syler had not touched any mind-altering substances even though she kept the option open for her team if they chose to indulge.

"That's fine, we are not teetotalers here. So tell me, what are your plans for the future?" Stefania asked. Her tone was milder than before, but Megan knew she would not tolerate any duplicity.

Syler's eyes went over to Megan. She said simply, "I want to make Megan happy and support her in everything she does."

"That is a given, I hope," Eli said. He put on a serious face that Megan knew was only for show. Her mother was the one Syler would need to convince.

Stefania looked up from the documents and asked, "Do you have any dangerous hobbies? I'm sure you know Megan's history and we don't want a repeat of that."

Megan got a jolt of both worry and anger at that. She blurted out, "That was an accident, it wasn't Yasu's fault. Mama, you don't have any right—"

A slight pressure on her wrist stopped the flow of angry words. Syler held her gaze for an instant before she answered, "The only dangerous hobby I have is being a Yakult Swallows fan in Chunichi Dragons territory, especially since they swiped that new pitcher Ohsaki right out from under the Dragons' noses."

So that was it. Megan didn't have time to do more than suck in a shocked breath as Eli dove across the table. He grabbed Syler's hand and gave it a number of triumphant pumps. "Oh a fellow Swallows fan. I knew I liked you. With Ohsaki it's gonna be their year, mark my words they're going to win the pennant race." A stern look from his wife made Eli let go and sink back into his chair. He rubbed at his thinning hair and said sheepishly, "I mean, um, what do you think, dear?"

Stefania sat still and silent for a long moment. She gave a brisk nod and said, "It seems you are a person of merit, Doctor Terada."

"Syler, please."

Stefania acknowledged that with a regal tilt of her head. She glanced at the documents on the table once more. "I understand you've been working at a Jewish facility for several years. What are your thoughts about spending your life with one of us? I hope you are going to respect our faith."

"Of course I have no problem with Megan being a Jew," Syler said. Absently the fingers of one hand skimmed over the Star of David on the silver chain at her throat. She straightened and said with pride, "I have the utmost respect for the religion and its followers. Last October, I passed the *beit din*. I took the name Serach bat Sarah Imenu."

Megan's parents exchanged a long look of satisfaction. Finally Megan relaxed. The battle was won, and it was in their favor. Stefania extended a long hand. She solemnly shook Syler's. Her face broke into a warm smile. "Welcome to the family, dear."

"Congratulations!" Osahar shouted from just outside the entrance.

He barreled into the room with glasses and a bottle clutched in his hands. His eyes were bright with tears and he was beaming. Megan's face got warm as she realized he had listened to their exchange from the sidelines, but she wasn't offended. Osahar was an old family friend and Megan was glad to have him share this moment with them. Soon everyone had a glass and the cries of *Mazel tov!*, *Alf Mabruk!* and *Omedetou!* went up as the cheerful restaurant owner and the Maier family, plus its newest honorary member joined in a cheerful toast.

They didn't get a chance to order. Osahar bustled around, setting out platters of his good cooking and the initial formal atmosphere dissolved.

With a word from Stefania, Syler led the blessing and everyone dug in. The conversation rolled over to comfortable familiarity. The wine was Kosher, served from the stock Megan's father had Osahar keep especially for their family. Everything else was Halal, generously spiced and lovingly served. Syler did justice to the meal while being the epitome of good manners. She made sure everyone was served and complimented the chef with her usual guileless cheer that made him blush and say things like "pshaw!"

"What are you doing tomorrow?" Eli asked as he offered refills of wine.

"We'll be staying close to home," Megan said. "I want to show Syler around here. You know, revisit the places I used to hang out when I was growing up."

"That sounds lovely," Stefania said. "Why don't you go down to that little park by the river? They've redone the paths and it's a nice walk especially now the blossoms are out. There are also lots of good places for lunch around there too. Here, take this with you." She reached into her purse and pressed a card into Megan's hand. "This is our local gourmet pass for all of Sunada-cho. Most places have some kind of special for pass-holders like free coffee or a discount on their daily lunch set."

"Thanks Mama," Megan said. The park her mother had mentioned was close enough to the cluster of shops and restaurants that they could walk, and Megan remembered it fondly from her younger days. Giddy and lightheaded, Megan brandished the card and said, "My mamusia takes good care of me."

"That she does," Syler said in a low voice. She surreptitiously gave Megan's leg a nudge with her own under the table. Her thigh pressed up against Megan's for just a bit too long.

Megan forgot everything she was going to say as she hid her blush in her napkin. Seeming unaffected, Syler participated in the conversation, keeping the talk flowing with interesting topics and thoughtful questions.

As the dinner progressed, both Syler and Eli took off their suit jackets and Eli loosened his necktie. Even in semi-relaxed mode, Syler was both cool and professional; however, the little glances and almost accidental touches made Megan dizzy and dangerously warm.

After Syler used the pretence of folding her napkin on her lap to reach out and squeeze Megan's thigh, Megan was possessed by an evil urge for revenge. She slipped her shoe off and hooked her foot around Syler's ankle, sliding up and down her leg in a slow caress while they both pretended to be fascinated by Eli's monologue about the new Maglev train. Megan didn't miss the slight flush on Syler's cheeks or how she grabbed at her water glass and gulped half of it. Syler finished by slowly running her tongue over her lower lip. The glance she shared with Megan as she did so was full of mischief and desire in equal measures. After that, Megan couldn't think of anything other than how much she wanted to have that teasing tongue on her.

Her appetite elsewhere, Megan picked at her food for a while longer then abruptly stood up.

"Please excuse me for a moment, I'd like to freshen up," she said. She dug her hand towel out of her bag before she made her way out of the dining room toward the curtained-off hallway where the doors to the kitchen and the single private washroom lurked. En route, Megan dropped her towel but continued on as if she didn't notice. She let herself into the small room where she leaned back against the half-opened sliding door and waited, heart pounding.

Sure enough, a familiar form ducked under the curtain and held out her towel.

"You dropped this," Syler said. She let out a soft sound of surprise as Megan grabbed the proffered hand instead of the towel and pulled Syler into the washroom.

"Thank you for noticing." Megan slid the door shut and looped her hands behind Syler's head in one smooth motion. She took a step forward and pressed Syler back against the door. For an instant, she waited for a sign it was all right to continue. Strong hands coming up to hold her around the waist told Megan her invitation was accepted.

Megan surged against Syler, kissing her on the lips, softly at first then with growing need as their bodies came fully together. Syler's hands on her waist tightened and stroked slowly up and down her back. Megan pressed hard into the parting of Syler's legs, desperate for physical contact. The hand towel fell onto the counter next to the sink, where it was promptly ignored.

After only a moment, Megan drew away. She held the back of

Syler's neck and looked into her eyes. Megan caught her breath. She said, "You were so wonderful out there, I needed to touch you. Is this okay?"

"Yes it is," Syler said. She gathered Megan up into a hug and sank her chin to rest in the crook of Megan's neck with a happy sigh. "This is so good, Meg. But we should probably get back before your parents start getting suspicious."

"Yeah, we should," Megan said. Neither of them moved, save to settle even more closely against each other. Megan felt the heat and tension in Syler's long body. She was exquisitely aware of how each breath brought them together. Megan melted into Syler, needing her all the way down her body, from her breasts down her thighs, all the way down to her toes. On a whim, Megan repeated the motion she'd done at the table, slowly sliding one bare foot under the hem of Syler's trouser leg. Syler's body went rigid.

"Fuck it, I'll just tell them I got lost," Syler said. She leaned down and claimed Megan's mouth in a deep, hard kiss.

Megan couldn't resist any more. A shock of pure heat speared down from her belly to her knees as Syler welcomed her with hunger and confidence. Megan bit off a whimper as Syler's hand cupped her breast. Megan arched her back to press the hardening nub into Syler's palm while she gently stroked Megan's fullness. The kiss grew greedy and deep.

Megan's body was on fire. The sexual tension that started with the teasing touches primed her. Megan was ready to explode. She couldn't hold back any more.

"Syler, I want you so much," Megan whispered when they parted to draw in heaving breaths. With an impatient yank, Megan dragged her skirt out of the way. She hummed in wicked pleasure as Syler delved between her thighs.

"Naughty girl," Syler murmured in her ear. "You're already wet."

Megan could only mew in reply.

Through the material of her panties, Megan felt strong fingers part her and find the exact spot that begged to be touched. Megan rocked her hips as a liquid surge of arousal sparked from the caress. Syler's breaths against her neck grew ragged. The long body pressed against Megan's was taut and shivering. The illicit situation only made the moment more delicious.

"You're so hot, Meg. God, I can feel you right here," Syler whispered. She massaged Megan's aching clit, first in circles, then teased her with a little lateral shimmy. Syler used the motion to rub the soaked cotton over Megan's throbbing bud. Little jolts of electricity started to run up and down Megan's legs from the indirect contact. "Is this all right?"

"Yes, Syler. Touch me, I need more, please. Take me, do me right now," Megan said in a tight moan, her fingers dug into Syler's shoulders. Her hips rocked of their own volition as slender fingers pulled aside the damp and sticky crotch of her panties and zeroed in on her throbbing clit.

On some level, Megan knew having her girlfriend get her off in the washroom of the restaurant where her parents were eating dinner wasn't the most proper course of action, but Syler was willing and Megan was desperate for her touch. It only took a few hungry strokes before the deep shivers hit. Megan bucked her hips, rubbing herself against Syler's talented fingers. Her breaths ratcheted up to desperate pants.

"Give it all to me baby girl, yeah like that," Syler murmured.

That was enough to break Megan. Her body jolted with the sudden spasms as she came hard. The feeling of release was so good after the tension that had been building up all day. Megan muffled her gasps by pressing her face into the shoulder of Syler's shirt. Syler's body resonated with deep breaths in counterpoint to Megan's short ones. She eased the slick hood up and down over Megan's fully excited clit, slowly milking her climax to the end.

"Yes, oh God yes, I'm yours," Megan said. Her words came out in bursts, in time with Syler's movements on her. She put her hands on either side of Syler's face and brought them together, nose to nose, eye to eye, breaths heaving back and forth in a fierce moment of connection. She rocked her hips. Her inner muscles shuddered and clenched.

"You're so beautiful, Meg. You feel so good right here," Syler panted into Megan's mouth. She lowered her head and caught Megan with a full, deep kiss. She met Megan's eager tongue while she worked Megan's soaked and throbbing sex with ever-so-slowly lessening pressure.

The last jolts faded. Megan released Syler and took a step back. For a moment, they stood in that tiny washroom, panting and flushed. Syler grinned at Megan. She looked radiant.

"Wow, that was intense," Syler said.

"Yeah. It was. Very."

A flush of happiness filled Megan. She shifted her weight from one foot to the other, trying to get her damp panties right again. After a futile moment, Megan gave up on her panties and said, "I actually do have to pee."

"Okay, Meg. Just give me a second and I'll be out of here."

Syler turned and quickly washed her hands at the little sink. Megan let her eyes wander over Syler's trim form. She enjoyed the way Syler's tailored trousers clung to the sleek lines of her backside. It took every last ounce of willpower for Megan to stop from slipping her arms around Syler's waist and pressing her entire body up against her back.

Even though Syler appeared unaffected by the attention her butt got, she did have a twinkle in her eye when she turned around to borrow Megan's hand towel. She folded the towel before she stood with her hands in the pockets of her trousers in a casual way.

"Am I okay to go back out there?" Syler asked.

Megan glanced over her. Syler looked a bit tousled, but there wasn't anything that would give away the fact she'd just participated in a quickie.

"You're fine. More than fine, actually," Megan purred.

"Thanks," Syler replied. "I'll just go and make small talk with the in-laws so take your time, my sweet Meirav." Syler leaned close to Megan and dropped a quick kiss on her cheek, just in front of her ear. Syler lingered against her and whispered, "I think maybe they like me."

"I know they do," Megan said. The in-laws. She liked that. As much as she wanted to grab Syler and test out the little room's soundproofing, she knew that wasn't exactly an option. Instead, she started to raise her skirt and said, "Unless you want to watch, you'd better go."

"Tempting," Syler said. Megan faked affront. She flicked her hand towel at the hastily closing door as Syler made her escape.

THAT NIGHT, MEGAN lay on one of the two futons her parents had made up on the floor of her old room, redone into the guest room after Megan had left to go to university. The wallpaper was still the butterfly pattern she'd picked out what seemed to be a million years ago. It was dotted with faded marks from the tape she used to put up posters of her favorite boyishly handsome Takarazuka stars.

Megan lifted her damp hair from the pillow and allowed herself a laugh. Maybe that's why her parents hadn't been overly surprised when she told them she had a girlfriend.

"Hey Meg, are you decent?" The soft voice came from the other side of the door and Megan sat up with a happy jolt that went from her chest all the way through her.

"Sure, come on in."

Syler entered. She had already changed into her sleepwear — cutoff sweats and a tank top. She aimed for the futon opposite Megan's, but stopped and changed trajectory as Megan sat up and held out a hand.

"I'm surprised they let us stay in the same room," Syler said as she folded herself down onto the crumpled cover. Her arms came around Megan, who leaned into the embrace.

"My parents are traditional but not super-strict, plus this house only has two bedrooms. It's not like they're going to check on us or anything. Still..." Megan said. She tapped her finger against her lower lip, then dropped her fist into her opened palm with a decisive thump. "We'll have to mess up both futons so they won't suspect anything tomorrow. Or at least they can pretend they don't."

"Good plan," Syler said. She kissed Megan's bare shoulder where her oversized T-shirt slipped down. "You know, Meg, there's something I was wondering about. While Eli and I were slaving away in the kitchen making an after-dinner snack plate for you two bottomless pits, what were you and your mother whispering about in the living room?"

"Nothing," Megan said. She clapped her hands to her flushed cheeks.

"Uh huh." Syler leaned over and purred in a dangerously low voice, "Are you going to spill or am I going to have to break out my secret weapon?"

"What secret weapon?" Megan squeaked.

Syler held up both hands, her long fingers curled seductively. "If you tell me, I'll give you a foot-rub."

"Hm. And if I don't?"

"You will get tickles," Syler said in her most dead-serious physician voice. "You have five seconds to make your choice."

Megan flailed as she tried to scoot away on her butt. Syler followed her with a cackle.

Megan said, "No, no no. Not tickles, no way, that's not fighting fair."

"So?"

"Okay okay, I give up," Megan said. Her ears joined her cheeks in feeling hot and she shook her hair down to cover them. "Um, so my mother asked me, ahem, if it was true about what they say about surgeons."

"And that would be?" Syler deadpanned. She arched one eyebrow.

"You know, if you people are, um, good with your hands," Megan mumbled the last words.

Syler collapsed onto the futon in laughter.

Megan pulled herself upright and added primly, "I didn't say either way but I think she could tell. That, yeah, it's absolutely fucking true."

Still snickering, Syler sat up and wiped her eyes. "That's good to know. I was kind of worried if she was asking you why it took me so long to deliver your hand towel."

"No, they actually didn't suspect anything," Megan said. "She thinks we were just hiding out and complaining to each other about my dad's bad jokes. I didn't feel like correcting her assumption."

"That works for me. Okay Meg, come over here. Me and my talented hands owe you a foot-rub."

Megan scooted back across the futon. She lay down on the pile of pillows while Syler gently pulled her legs straight. She cradled Megan's bare feet in her lap for a moment. Syler started with slow strokes. She pressed from Megan's toes to her heels, leaning in with her entire body. Megan hadn't realized how much tension she'd been holding. As her muscles started to loosen, she pressed the back of one hand to her mouth to muffle the moan of pleasure.

"Let go baby girl," Syler said in a soft voice. "You did really good today."

"I should be saying that to you," Megan said. She let out an involuntary, "Ooh!" as Syler found a particularly sore spot.

"It's okay? I didn't hurt you?"

"Not at all, keep going. Ooh! Yes, right there."

With a knowing smirk, Syler worked over Megan's ankles and up to her calves. She cradled Megan's feet against her chest. Soon Megan arched back, riding on a lovely wave of relaxation and something a little bit hotter and more urgent than that, if she did admit it to herself. But there would be no replay of the encounter at the restaurant—that evening at any rate. Even though the bathroom separated them from her parents' room, Megan knew how thin the walls were. Besides, she was too sleepy to do much more than revel in the moment.

"How did you get so good at that?" Megan asked in a breathy whisper.

"Taka-chan's the expert," Syler said as she ran one thumb down the length of Megan's arch. "He gets to sit down for most procedures and I guess he got tired of the rest of us bitching and moaning after spending hours on our feet. I don't know how he stands us, but after a long operation he usually dishes out a round of foot-rubs. So at least I've been the recipient if not the giver. I hope I'm doing all right. I can ask him to give you one if you'd like."

"You're doing much better than all right. And I don't want anybody touching me except you," Megan said. Her eyes drifted closed. She felt as if she was floating away. Megan stifled a yawn and said, "I'm falling asleep, so come over here and get some snuggles."

Megan gently pulled her feet from Syler's grasp and rolled over. She scooted under the futon and held one side open in an inviting way. Immediately, Syler fell onto the futon and got an armful of Megan, who buried her face happily against Syler's T-shirt.

"You smell so good," Megan murmured without opening her eyes.

"I borrowed your family's Keshet in the bath," Syler said with pride.

Megan didn't say anything more, but she always loved Syler's scent, Keshet or not. In the warm silence, Syler's hand stroked over her hair and Megan drifted off on a happy wave, wrapped in nothing more than pure love.

THE NEXT MORNING at breakfast, Eli informed them he and Stefania had a prior engagement to attend an open house.

"It is mostly business," Eli said. "So don't feel obligated to go. We should be back by this evening, but if not, please feel free to have dinner without us."

"Okay," Megan said with her mouth full of her mother's homemade waffles. She was glad they weren't being asked to attend, even though in the future she would love to bring Syler with her to a similar function.

Meanwhile, Syler did a good job of distracting Megan from her breakfast as she looked dashingly fine in a dress shirt with the tiger-eye cufflinks Megan had given her after she passed her *beit din*, paired with boot-cut jeans and a tawny leather vest. Syler loved the cufflinks so much, she'd immediately invested in a dozen tailored shirts and never passed up an opportunity to wear them.

Megan didn't plan to head out until lunch, and it was the day off for the dental clinic Megan's parents ran, so everyone spent the morning relaxing at the Maier residence. The house was a compact two-story home flanked by similar dwellings on all sides. Megan had lived there from birth until university. While the walls were scarred and the sides of the driveway crumbling with the advances of adventurous weeds, she liked being there surrounded by her memories. Even though it didn't feel like home to her anymore.

Instead of the modern, uniform architecture of Saitama's Sunada-cho, Megan's heart called for Suito city and its random collection of ageing buildings, meandering roads, and eclectic shops. But more than anything, the memories of what she'd shared with Syler and the dreams of what was yet to come completed her. Wherever in the world they ended up, all Megan needed to find home was the woman beside her.

They hung out in the living room and she watched Syler interact with her parents. All of them seemed over their nerves of the previous day. Syler laughed at the jokes Megan's father told even though both Stefania and Megan assured her it wasn't necessary.

"But they're funny!" Syler protested.

"I have a good sense of humus," Eli said and chuckled to himself.

"That's true," Syler said. She stuck a finger into the air and declared, "It agrees with my sense of humerus!"

"I've eaten enough of Osahar's nice food that I've got a good sense of hummus," Megan said, not to be outdone.

Megan's mother made a pained face. Eli tried to get them to agree to drink something called a Pepsus. Nobody did until finally in the interest of family harmony, Megan took pity on him and acquiesced. Beaming, Eli jogged into the kitchen, saying over his shoulder, "Two Pepsi, coming up!"

"Not that old thing again," Megan said. She buried her face in her hands and groaned, knowing what was coming all along. Syler hooted. "Daaaad," Megan whined as he presented her with her drink. "Stop stealing jokes from Wayne & Shuster, okay?"

"I am not stealing, I am merely spreading my appreciation," Eli said. He sipped at his cola with his pinky raised.

"Uh huh," Megan said. She swallowed her Pepsus, wishing it was something a bit stronger. When she finished her drink, Megan turned to Syler. "Why don't we head out now?"

"Sounds good," Syler said. She got to her feet and held a hand out to Megan, who didn't realize the intimacy of the gesture until she caught her parents smirking at each other.

"See you tonight!" Megan called to her parents on her way out. She felt free and energized as they walked down the street to the community *junkai* bus stop.

They walked past a small sweets shop. Megan said, "Ooh, it's still there! I used to always get a snack here on my way home from school. They have these chocolate covered pickled plums that I love."

"Want to stop and get some for old time's sake?" Syler asked.

Megan pursed her lips in thought. "Better not. We'll miss the bus and I don't want to wait an hour for the next one."

"An hour?" Syler said. "I thought you Kanto people had buses every five minutes and needed uniformed attendants to shove everyone into them."

"That's the train. Buses are much more relaxed."

"Glad to hear it. I'm not a fan of being squashed together with people who aren't you. Your squashy places are located perfectly for me."

Megan flushed. She said in a quiet voice, "And I don't really feel like a Kanto person anymore. A Gifu person stole my heart and part of me will always belong there."

Syler chuckled in response and nudged Megan very gently with her hip.

They reached the bus stop. Megan gazed up at the overcast sky. "At least it's not raining. That's another thing I like about living in Gifu. The weather is exciting, not this grey, drab stuff like they get here."

"I hear you," Syler said. She slung herself down on the bench.

Megan remained on her feet to better see the bus when it came.

"I hate rain," Megan said. She glanced back at Syler. "One spring when I was in high school, we had cold, drizzly, grey weather every day for a month and a half. I felt like Margot in *All Summer in a Day*. My sneakers got moldy too."

Syler grimaced in sympathy.

The bus pulled up just then and they clambered on. The ride to the stop in front of the shopping street was fairly short. They got off along with an assortment of elderly people and young mothers who made up the bulk of the weekday bus-going crowd.

Megan linked her arm through Syler's as they wandered around and explored the many shops at their leisure. When they came to an old game arcade, Megan's steps slowed. The flashing lights of the games inside were nearly obscured by posters in various stages of tatty. Several different tunes fought with each other over numerous sound effects from the games. Her happy mood dimmed. Megan looked away.

"Something wrong, Meg?" Syler asked quietly.

"I used to come here all the time when I was young, you know, kill time when I was busy not having friends," Megan said. She forced a laugh and it came out sounding fake. She stopped laughing abruptly and studied the ground. "I watched the other girls hanging out and doing Print Clubs and wished that I had someone to do that with. I even had an imaginary girlfriend. She was so real to me I could feel her next to me sometimes. This was where we hung out the most. She was with me all the way up through school. Stupid, huh?"

"That's not stupid, Meg," Syler said. She held up a one-thousand yen bill. "As long as your imaginary girlfriend doesn't mind, your real-life girlfriend would love to photo-document our day out with a round of *purikura*. The sillier, the better."

Before Megan could think of any reason why they shouldn't, Syler led her through the main arcade, into the roped-off area that was filled with the hulking shapes of various Print Club machines.

"Wow, they updated a lot since I was here." Megan studied the array of choices available.

Suddenly she drew back. A gaggle of teenage girls in high-school uniforms sat in a group in a clear patch of floor like they lived there. They claimed the area with their schoolbags, scattered cosmetics, and other assorted junk. They did their makeup and played with their phones while chatting up a storm. Megan recognized the uniform. She had worn the same one during the loneliest period of her life.

When the two adult newcomers entered their sacred realm, the girls fell silent and stared at them. Almost immediately, they burst into giggles. Megan felt as if she'd just slipped back fifteen years in time. Darkness started to close over her soul with each whisper and nudge that passed between the girls. She heard the word *rezu* and *gaijin* hissed a few times and Megan's soul died a bit with each one.

"Um, maybe this wasn't such a great idea," Megan said. She turned away.

Mentally she kicked herself. She was a fully-licensed physician, she'd brought lives into the world and seen others out, she'd survived a tragedy that tore her life apart and even found the courage to love again; she'd been blackmailed and threatened and came out triumphant, but a group of children half her age took all of that away and rendered it meaningless.

A firm pressure on her hand brought her back. Just as soon the gentle touch was gone. Syler left her side and approached the girls, hands in her pockets and utterly confident. She squatted down until she was at eye level of the group.

"Are you laughing at my girlfriend and me?" she asked in a casual tone, her words just harsh enough to cause the girls to huddle together and glance at their leader, a bleached-blonde who tucked her uniform skirt up so high, the cutoff sweatpants she wore under it were on full display. The others looked guilty but she was defensive. Blondie sat with her legs splayed, head cocked.

"*Dattara?*" Blondie spat. She challenged Syler by asking, *What if they were?*

"Because I'd like you to stop," Syler said, her voice dropping to a tone that brooked no contradiction, growling out the words like a mobster. "Watch who you call *gaijin* and *rezu* is an insult only ignorant people use. The polite word is *bian, rezubian, dou-seiai-sha* or just shut your fucking mouth about it, understood?"

The silence stretched out. The assembled girls clutched at each other.

"Understood," Blondie said, just a little sulkily.

"Good," Syler replied. She returned to Megan and trotted past her to the main area of the arcade. "How about we play a bit before *purikura?*"

Speechless, Megan nodded.

Syler directed Megan over to a bank of glassed-in UFO catchers. With a rakish grin, Syler went to the change machine and came back with a double handful of coins. She poured the coins into Megan's hands and said, "You're the official treasurer." She cracked her knuckles and shook out her arms before she took her place in front of the biggest machine.

Over the next fifteen minutes, Megan could only stand and stare as the coins in her hands slowly vanished, replaced by a growing pile of plush animals of all sizes, crystal-decorated teddy bears, comically oversized boxes of snacks, plus a few scarily-realistic foam models of plucked chickens.

A bunch of the guys hanging out in the video game section came over and watched with obvious interest. Megan cringed as she saw a few of them with their phones out and trained on them. Syler didn't pay attention other than to return a few high-fives the more adventurous of the onlookers offered as she went from one machine to another. A couple of the guys got plastic bags the arcade provided and filled them up with Syler's prizes. When Megan's hands were empty, Syler accepted the bulging plastic bags before she headed back into the Print Club corner.

With dawning understanding, Megan followed. She couldn't stop the glow of pride as Syler presented the spoils of her UFO catcher rampage to the group of girls. They looked up with a mixture of awe and envy. There wasn't a giggle to be heard in the entire place. Megan's heart pounded and her skin tingled. Syler had just banished one of her childhood demons.

"Which machine would you recommend?" Syler asked.

Suddenly helpful, the girls pointed out one of the newer-looking machines. Syler thanked them in a casually gentile fashion before she led Megan over to it. Intrigued, Megan ducked under the curtain. She and Syler stood in the surprisingly spacious cubicle with a green background behind them and a control panel that reminded Megan of an airplane cockpit in front of them.

"I suck at these," Syler said. She fed some coins into the slot. "Meg, you have the helm."

"No problem, leave this to me," Megan said. She dialed up a menu that looked appealing and took her place next to Syler. The first few shots were more or less normal. They followed the verbal prompt to do things like make peace signs and try mid-air jump shots, until the speaker called out, *love-love!* Megan turned to Syler with an absolutely wicked idea. Obviously having the same one, Syler met her in a kiss that was both long and deep. Megan wasn't aware of anything else until the recorded voice told them to progress to the next area.

They relocated to the narrow editing booth where Megan selected a few shots for the final print. She blushed hard at the last few.

"That one's good, make that one the biggest." Syler pointed at one particularly racy shot. In it, Syler was kissing Megan's neck from behind, while holding her suggestively around the middle. Megan was glad Syler's hands hadn't strayed much lower than that, otherwise the secret Megan was saving for later would have been revealed. Syler nudged her and said, "I'm gonna keep that one for when I'm working the night shift and you're not."

"Oh God, make sure nobody sees it," Megan said.

"Don't worry, Meg. This is something special for just the two of us."

"Good."

Even though she was a bit shy, Megan had to admit it was thrilling and not a little arousing to see herself in Syler's embrace, captured in the safety and good lighting of the Print Club booth. She didn't want to remember the previous time their intimacy was caught on film. Megan studied the selected pictures before she decorated them. They made a hot couple, Megan had to admit. Her body was still warm from Syler's hands on her. She shifted on the padded bench as an undeniable wetness started up between her legs.

Syler leaned back and watched as Megan chose frames and decorated the photos. Megan hummed to herself as she dragged a bunch of heart stamps over one photo. She felt good, justified even. Being photographed this time was their choice, and Megan was healed by it.

When she'd doctored everything to her satisfaction, she hit the print button and they stood outside the machine to wait. Megan was pleasantly surprised when Blondie sent two of her underlings over with cups of tea from the machine for them. The girls handed them over with a subdued, "*Dozo.*"

Syler looked over at Blondie and raised her cup in thanks. Blondie replied with a surprisingly gentile half-bow. Megan was left with the odd feeling she had just witnessed two alphas in a turf-war truce.

Once their photos were printed, Megan used the scissors provided to cut them up. A couple girls peeked over her shoulder.

"*Hyuu hyuu!*" they commented about the hotness of the pictures with glee.

Megan squeaked and tried to shove the stickers into her bag, only to have the girls wheedle for some. After a while, Megan gave them a few of the tame ones while Syler lounged against the table. Megan left the arcade considerably lighter than when she'd entered.

Outside, the wind had picked up. Megan dug out an elastic and put her hair in a ponytail as white and pink petals whirled around them.

"What do you feel like eating?" Megan asked as they walked down the street.

"I could answer that two ways," Syler purred.

"For lunch! I meant for lunch," Megan said. She grabbed Syler's hand and pressed up against her. Megan whispered into her ear, "The second way I'm saving for when we get home. Providing my parents are still out."

Syler raised a cool brow but the slight flush on her cheeks gave her away. Syler said, "In that case, can I request fast food? Like really fast, as in sprinting?"

"No," Megan answered. "How about Indian? I know a good place near the park I used to go. Hopefully it's still there."

"Sounds good," Syler said. "Indian it is."

The little restaurant Megan remembered appeared. Megan used the gourmet card from her mother to get them the five hundred yen teatime special, which was similar to the lunch special except it came with the option of beer for the set drink in addition to chai.

After the meal, Megan decided to show Syler the park. They walked side by side with the wide river next to them. Megan slipped her fingers into Syler's palm.

"Thanks," she said in a soft voice.

"For what, Meg?"

"For being a hero back there. For standing up to those girls. You exorcised a demon for me. Again." Megan stopped walking. She studied the colored bricks of the walkway. "I wish I didn't have so many."

"Don't feel bad about that," Syler said. She lifted Megan's gaze with a gentle finger under her chin. "Do you know how amazing it is for me to know I have the power to do that? I wish I could take it all away, everything that haunts you. And I intend to do just that, even if it takes the rest of my life."

Megan couldn't speak. She just gazed at Syler who leaned back against the railing of the decorative fence that separated the walkway from the river below. Drifts of cherry blossoms swirled on the surface of the water as it rushed along. The muffled roar of traffic was filtered through rows of pruned trees and even though Megan knew they were far from alone, she didn't hesitate to fall into Syler's arms and kiss her, softly then with a little more feeling as Syler didn't seem to mind.

Megan slid her hands into the back pockets of Syler's jeans and was exploring the treasure she found there when her phone rang.

"Are you going to get that?" Syler whispered against Megan's lips.

"I don't want to," Megan said. "But I will."

She reluctantly retrieved her wandering hands to dig through her purse. Puzzled at her father's cell number, Megan answered. "Hello?"

"Meirav," her father's voice said in her ear. He sounded jolly. "Is this a good time to talk?"

"Sure," Megan said. She struggled to keep her voice calm

when Syler pulled her close once more and placed a slow, sensuous kiss on the side of her neck. "We were just taking a walk in the park. What's up?" She felt Syler's smile against her skin.

"Here's the thing. I thought your mother was going to drive back so I drank wine, and your mother thought I was driving so she drank wine. And my friend Ryo Onizuka didn't know I would ask him for a ride so he drank wine."

"Okay, you're all a bunch of winos," Megan said. Syler's hand drifted from her waist down over the curve of her hip. A sharp intake of breath told her Syler had discovered Megan's little secret. Megan raised one eyebrow and met Syler's eyes with a knowing expression. Megan wriggled her hips just enough for Syler to understand what was waiting for her under Megan's skirt. Syler clapped a hand over her mouth and groaned around it.

"Is that what I think it is?"

Megan nodded.

"Meg, you're killing me," Syler whispered.

In Megan's ear, her father continued blithely, "The thing is, everybody drank wine so we're going to walk back to Ryo's place, you remember him, don't you? He's the one with the model airplanes. He's divorced now, but he and his wife used to have those kayaks. You remember we all went out in them that one summer, with their two boys. He's got himself a not-so-little bachelor pad now and a German Shepherd. Named him Toby."

"Yes, okay," Megan said. She shifted to mold herself to Syler's body. Every place they met buzzed into life. She wanted nothing more than to throw her phone into the river. "So how long are you and Mama going to stay?"

"We drank quite a lot of wine," he said. "And we plan to drink a lot more actually, so I'm thinking we'll be gone until tomorrow morning."

"Okay, take care Dad," Megan said and ended the call. She reached up and twined her fingers together at Syler's nape. "Did you catch that? My parents are leaving us home alone tonight. Unchaperoned."

"Oh no," Syler said, not looking upset in the least. "What will we do without them?"

"Whatever we want," Megan said. She felt young, giddy, and quite ready to give Syler the full enjoyment of her surprise.

"Wanna come over?"

"Sure."

Megan didn't want to wait for the bus, so she flagged down a taxi. When they returned to Megan's place, she unlocked the front door. She paused in the doorway and looked back over her shoulder.

"This feels like the first date," she said.

"It does," Syler said. She reached over Megan's head and held the door open.

Megan tilted her head and asked, "In that case, would you like to come in for a second date?"

Syler gave a slow, languid smile and said, "I'd love to."

They settled on the couch. In keeping with the second date theme, Syler sat a bit more properly than her usual sprawl. Megan folded her hands in her lap. Her heart thundered and she was dizzy with anticipation. Syler reached out and took Megan's hand in hers. Very gently she drew Megan closer to her. With her other hand, she reached out and ran a finger over Megan's lower lip. The look in her eyes was unmistakable.

"Would it be okay if I kissed you?" she breathed.

"Yes," Megan said. She closed her eyes as she was guided to meet Syler's lips. The kiss was gentle and soft and sent a thrill through Megan's entire body. If she had ever had doubts Syler was the one for her, that moment silenced them forever. Syler cupped Megan's face in her hands, drawing out the kiss, still closed-mouth and innocent. As the heavenly softness of Syler's lips lingered on hers, Megan's body burned with need. The slow pace was exquisite torture. She was shivering and gasping already when Syler released her.

"Yakult Swallows indeed," Megan said in a low voice. "Don't worry, your secret's safe with me."

"I know," Syler replied. She tilted her head and leaned forward to go in for another kiss, but stopped when Megan spoke.

"There's wine in the kitchen," Megan said. "Want to get some to begin the third date?"

"Oh yeah," Syler said. She held out a hand to help Megan to her feet. She got a wicked gleam in her eyes and gave Megan a slow once-over from her head to her feet. Syler leaned close and murmured, "Although I don't really need any lubrication. You are so fucking sexy Meg."

Pretending to be affronted, Megan trotted into the kitchen ahead of Syler. She rummaged in the fridge and came out with the mostly-full bottle of wine they'd opened the night before. On her feet, Syler leaned back against the kitchen table while Megan poured a single glass. She came over and nestled against Syler's long body. Megan handed the glass over.

"Aren't you going to have any?" Syler asked.

"Maybe," Megan purred. She arched her body just enough to insinuate one thigh between Syler's. "If you give it to me."

Syler was sipping at her wine and froze, an interested look on her face. She swallowed and said, "Okay. Come here then."

Megan shivered with anticipation as Syler took a mouthful of wine and lowered her head to press her lips to Megan's. Encouraged by the slight pressure, Megan accepted, and a gush of wine filled her mouth. The liquid had warmed slightly and the intimate seal of their lips kept the wine from spilling. Megan felt like they were one, the trust and instinctive knowledge of each other connecting them. She swallowed and drew back. Slowly she licked the single drop of wine that trickled from her lips.

"Fuck that was hot," Syler said in a low voice. Under her leather vest, her chest heaved. "Is this still the third date?"

"Actually, I think we've moved onto the honeymoon by now." Megan moved out of Syler's embrace and put both hands down on the tabletop. Her gaze flicked to the glass in Syler's hand. Syler quickly placed it out of the way on the kitchen counter. With a little hop, Megan hoisted herself to sit on the wide, sturdy table. "And since neither of us has a kitchen table, I thought we might find a use for this one."

With that, Megan spread her thighs and gathered her skirt into her lap as she did so. She didn't need to extend another invitation before Syler pushed between her knees. She guided Megan's legs to hug her slim hips. Megan held Syler by the shoulders. Syler rested her hands on Megan's hips. The sudden movement hiked Megan's skirt up, exposing the black lace garter belt Syler brushed up against when they'd been cuddling by the river.

"You were wearing this sexy underwear all day," Syler breathed as she delved under Megan's skirt, her hands ran up and down her legs. Syler's fingers lingered on her hips then stroked down to cup her backside. Megan hadn't bothered with panties, and she didn't miss the groan that rippled through Syler when she discovered the fact. "God Meg, I thought I was gonna have a heart attack out there."

"I'm glad you didn't," Megan said. She leaned forward and nipped the skin of Syler's neck. Syler gave her an appreciative moan. "You haven't seen the top of it yet."

Megan raised her arms as Syler roughly dragged her dress over her head and dropped it to the floor.

"Wow, Meg," Syler gasped. "That's just, wow."

"Do you like what you see?"

"Oh fuck yeah."

"This is all yours."

Megan leaned back on her hands and basked in the way Syler drank her in. The garter belt laced up the front with scarlet ribbon, echoing the similarly front-lacing sheer black lace bustier. Megan lowered her chin and let her hair fall over her shoulder. The golden brown waves tickled the heaving mounds of her breasts, pushed into generous cleavage by the boned garment.

Since she'd slipped into the sexy lingerie that morning, Megan's skin tingled with anticipation and now that Syler was so close, she was wet and desperate for attention. Syler stood between her legs, spreading Megan wide so she couldn't hide how turned on she was. Revealed by her short-trimmed curls, her lower lips were parted and pouting, swollen with desire. Her clit was already thickening. Megan shifted on the tabletop. She needed Syler's touch.

"Please," she whispered, "Syler, take me."

Megan arched back as Syler gathered her up, pressing their bodies together. She moved to meet Syler's lips. Megan was hungry for her. She craved more than just the sweet, chaste kisses they had shared. Syler opened her mouth immediately, accepting Megan fully and returning the favor. They both panted hard into each other's mouths, but the kiss didn't end. Syler's strong arms held her. Megan wrapped her legs around Syler's waist, grinding herself hard against her. She didn't care about the wet patch she left on the denim.

Megan groaned with desire as Syler's hand found her breasts. Syler rubbed her rock-hard nipples through the lace. It wasn't nearly enough for Megan. She tugged at the ribbon between her breasts and the bustier fell open. She pulled away from Syler for a moment in order to shrug the straps down over her shoulders and shove the garment unceremoniously onto the floor. She didn't even have time to catch her breath before Syler pressed her to lie back on the table, pinning her with kisses.

Megan whimpered as Syler lowered her head. She kissed a trail over Megan's breasts before she sucked Megan's nipple into her mouth. Syler switched sides until both of her pink nubs were slick and fully erect. She was in heaven with Syler's weight on her. Megan loved the attention Syler was giving to her breasts, but a certain other part of herself was feeling sorely neglected. Megan pulled up one knee, rocking her hips as she did so. She knew Syler enjoyed taking her time, exploring Megan's body and reveling in her reactions, but Megan needed to speed things up.

"Syler, I'm ready for you," Megan said. She spread her legs wider, exposed and willing.

"What do you want me to do?" Syler whispered against Megan's nipple. She was flushed and tousled, her body was taut, muscles tensed.

"I want you to stop playing and fuck me," Megan growled. She threw her head back with a gasp of pleasure as Syler responded by trailing her fingers between Megan's legs, gently teasing her slick lower lips. Syler let go of her for a moment. Megan felt the jerk as Syler pulled her belt open. She dropped her jeans to the floor.

"Help me get this off, then," Syler said with a gleam in her eyes.

Megan sat up and started unbuttoning Syler's vest. She leaned back as Syler pulled the shirt and vest over her head, both half-unbuttoned. Megan let out a breath of surprise and pleasure. It appeared that Megan wasn't the only one who had stepped out of her normal underwear zone.

Syler had opted for silky black panties and a tight-fitting black tank top with no bra. Her nipples were poking up, straining against the confining material. The brief panties clung to Syler in a way her usual boxer briefs didn't. The sight of the cleaved flesh, covered as it was, sent a spear of arousal through Megan. She couldn't look away.

"Do you like what you see?" Syler said in a low, husky voice, echoing Megan's previous words.

"Mmm, oh yes," Megan said. She lay down, propped up on her elbows. She kept her eyes on Syler as she slowly opened her legs and rocked her hips, silently begging for Syler to come to her.

And she did. Syler scooped her up. Her mouth devoured Megan's. Syler trailed kisses down her neck. Her lips teased Megan lightly before she bit down. Megan accepted the small pain with a breathy moan. One hand parted her. Syler stroked up and down Megan's entire length. Her long, strong fingers swept up to circle her clit, then back down again.

"Do you want me here?" Syler asked in a tight whisper. Her fingertips paused at Megan's opening.

"Yes," Megan gritted. She tightened her hold on Syler's shoulders. She spread herself more, waiting for the thrust that would bring her home. She let out a happy mew as she felt Syler push into her, two fingers right from the start. Megan closed her eyes for an instant. She held herself still, savoring the feeling.

"Is this okay?"

"Yes, oh yes," was all Megan could think to say. She opened her eyes and threw her head back as Syler started to move against her, slowly gaining speed until she was pounding hard, the rhythmic, wet sounds of each thrust were punctuated by Megan's wordless cries of pleasure.

Syler drove into her, Megan thrust back, needing to be drilled deep. She loved the feeling of Syler over her and within her. She felt safe in the knowledge that if she gave the slightest sign of discomfort, everything would stop. Syler was giving her what she wanted, and Megan was going to return the favor.

But first, Megan was going to take what Syler dished out. Megan's body jerked as her climax neared. Syler pulled out of her and focused on rubbing her clit as she whispered words of love to Megan. Her inner muscles clenched in preparation. She couldn't stop. Megan gave herself over as Syler worked her magic.

Syler knew her, she knew what turned Megan on and how to keep her on the brink of heaven. Sometimes Megan would ask her to back off to prolong things, but right now, Megan was desperate to come. She gave no indication to stop, and Syler didn't. Megan clutched hard at Syler's shoulders.

"I'm almost there," she said.

"Beautiful girl," Syler whispered. "Yes baby, come for me."

The first peak hit Megan hard. She arched her back and cried out. Her legs jumped as the rippling spasms rolled over her. Syler didn't let up, working her until Megan shuddered in her arms. The fingers on her slowed, stroking her as she softened, tracing gentle circles on her outer lips, skimming over the slick inner ones. Megan drew in deep breaths and hung onto Syler.

For a long moment, both of them were still. The only sound was their twin, heaving breaths.

"Are you good Meg?"

"Yeah, I think so," Megan said. She took Syler with her as she collapsed onto her back. Megan lay there for a moment. She didn't care that her legs were splayed out, falling open on either side of Syler's body. After she caught her breath, Megan reached up and drew Syler to her, officially starting round two. The kiss got deep and rough, Megan felt the quickening in Syler's movements. She heard the catch in Syler's breath. She gloated inwardly, knowing Syler was getting into the swing of things. Megan pulled her lips from Syler's and said, "Get up and stand at the counter."

Syler did as Megan asked. She rested her hands on the smooth countertop and looked over to where Megan was still sitting on the table.

In a smooth motion, Megan pushed herself to her feet and came over to Syler. She guided Syler's hands to her hips and let her bare breasts press up against Syler. She rose up onto her toes and teased Syler's hard nipples with her own.

"Fuck that's good," Syler said. "You sweet, sexy thing, Meg."

Megan pressed herself between Syler's legs, grinding her own bare sex against Syler's covered one a few times before she pulled away. She knew Syler was ticklish around her hip bones, so Megan didn't reach out, but dropped her eyes instead.

"Take those off," Megan said.

The panties hit the floor. Syler kicked them away. She bit her lip and braced herself against the counter as Megan sank to her knees before her. Megan paused for a moment to give Syler the chance to choose another option if she wasn't in the mood for what Megan was suggesting.

"Right now? Are you sure about this, Meg?" Syler asked. "I mean, we've been walking around all day, I'm not exactly the freshest flower in the bouquet."

"I'm sure," Megan said. She looked up at Syler, then dropped her gaze back to the treasure between Syler's thighs, the sleek flesh was sweetly flushed and tempting. She wriggled her hips, desperate to do something as she waited in an agony of anticipation. "I want you just as you are. I need you."

"All right. Do it, Meg," Syler breathed. She shifted and spread her legs a bit, and Megan ran her tongue over her lower lip, hungry for the heady thrill of tasting and pleasuring the woman she loved.

She put her hands on Syler's hips. Megan leaned forward and nuzzled into the sparse hair, letting her questing mouth brush over Syler's velvet lips. She buffed the hardening bud that strained against the fleshy sheath. Megan's tongue traced over the thickening folds. She heard Syler's breath coming faster.

Hands came down and cupped her head with a soft hesitancy. Megan looked up into Syler's face and gave a nod, accepting her. It took Megan a while before she was comfortable being held in that position, but once the initial uneasiness was gone, Megan loved the immediacy of it.

Syler's heady, unique scent welcomed her and Megan moaned deep in her throat. She took Syler into her mouth. Megan nursed her clit fully erect before moving down to enter her very gently with her tongue. Syler stiffened at the slight contact, but soon relaxed and allowed the entry, moving along with Megan as she delved in and out.

"Fuck, you're so hot when you're on your knees for me," Syler murmured. Her hands tightened on Megan's head. In response, Megan moved her attention back to the taut bud. Syler was never very loud, but her soft moans ignited Megan in a way that nothing else did. Her quickened breathing inflamed Megan and even as she sucked Syler's clit, she reached between her own thighs. She spread her legs. Megan knew Syler saw her. She wanted Syler to know what she was doing. Megan slipped a finger inside herself. She gathered her wetness before she worked herself hard.

"Yes, make yourself feel good," Syler rasped between harsh breaths. Her hips rocked along with Megan's. "I'm close. Come with me baby girl."

Megan felt the deep tremor of Syler's release take her before she allowed herself to let go as well. Her hips bucked her spread sex against her hand. Her second orgasm was over faster than her first. She lavished attention on Syler until the hands on her head let go.

"Fuck, that was good. I'm done, Meg," Syler said. She let go of the counter and slid down to join Megan on her knees on the floor. They collapsed into each other's arms. Megan snuggled into the embrace.

"Thank you," Megan murmured.

"That's my line, Meg." Syler pressed her face to Megan's shoulder with a chuckle. She said, "I really hope your parents were serious about staying out all night because if they came home now, I think one or both of them would have a heart attack."

Megan had to agree. She glanced around at the clothing-strewn floor and their own partially undressed states. Syler was only in a tank top, freshly licked pussy out and proud. Megan's was too, flushed and pouty lips framed by the straps of her garter belt. Both of them were sweat-damp and limp with afterglow.

After a quick discussion, Megan ran the bath while Syler collected their discarded clothing and scrubbed down the sorely used kitchen table. They ended up wrapped around each other in the big bath where they rehashed the events of the previous days. Megan flew high on a wave of happiness. Nothing was going to take it away from her.

They relaxed after the bath, curled up on one futon. Megan remembered something she'd planned to do and sat up.

"Hang on a sec, there's something I want to show you," she said.

"What is it, sweetheart?"

Megan rummaged in her overnight bag for a moment. She came back with a photo album in her hands.

"I made this to keep with me wherever I go," Megan said. "It's my own personal history. I never want to forget where I came from and where I've been. Syler, would you let me show it to you?"

"I'd love that," Syler said. Her eyes shone.

Megan took a deep breath and opened the first page. "This is me," she said. She pointed at the tiny bundle held in her much-younger father's proud arms.

"Oh my God, you were such a cutie," Syler said.

Her exclamations of delight continued as Megan turned the pages. School-aged Megan appeared. Syler delighted in seeing her change through the years. Megan flushed with the lavish praise. Another turn of the page. Megan silently looked at the photo of herself and Yasu standing in front of her clinic. It was the last photo in the album.

Megan reached out and lightly touched the image of the sturdy, solemn woman standing beside her. Neither of them spoke, but Syler slipped an arm around her and slowly rubbed Megan's shoulder. Megan paused before she settled more closely against Syler. While every day took her further away from the past, she would never leave it completely behind.

Megan flipped the page, revealing only blank pockets.

"This is for our story," Megan said. "Yours and mine together."

She pulled an envelope from her bag and took out a number of photos. First she put the print of the cell phone pic she'd snapped of the two of them on their first picnic date. Next came the photo Paolo took of them in their *yukatas*. She added one of the two of them lighting the Menorah on their first Hanukkah together and finished with a photo that was taken only a few days before. It showed Syler and Megan with Luka and Jayco under the cherry blossoms of Suito Castle. Megan kept her promise to see the cherry blossoms with Syler and she planned to keep it every year from then on. Even with the new additions, the album was still less than half full.

"We're going to have a great time filling the rest of these pages," Syler said. She pressed a soft kiss into Megan's hair. "And Meg, will you promise me one thing?"

"Anything," Megan said. She looked up from the album to meet Syler's eyes, which danced with a wickedly mischievous light.

"Promise me you'll surprise me with sexy underwear from time to time," Syler said. "Even when we're both old and grey and gravity has taken its toll."

"I promise," Megan said. "And you have to take me out for classy picnics in your tux even when we're hobbling on canes or trundling around on those motorized scooters."

Syler gave her full-bodied laugh and hugged Megan tight. "You got it."

Megan fell back into Syler's arms. They snuggled together in the crumpled bedcovers. The album slipped to the floor, blank pages ready and waiting for the future.

THE END

About the Author

Mildred Gail Digby has a BSc in geology, however Takarazuka, pachinko, and no laws against drinking beer outside lured her to teach in Japan. Her favorite thing to do is add lesbians to any situation and make a novel about it. She dreams one day of working as a professional beer taster and devotes a good deal of her time honing her skills in that area which, to an uninformed outsider, appears to be simply drinking a lot of beer.

She shares her non-angst-filled life with her wife of nearly ten years where the most excitement they have is deciding where to eat and forgetting where they parked their bicycles. Mildred is a sucker for oddball characters, opposites attract, and women getting what (and who) they want. She will squeeze a happy ending out of anything and still blushes when she writes love scenes.

Other Mildred J. Digby titles to look for:

Perfect Match: Book One

After a tragedy derailed her life, Dr. Megan Maier crawls back to the land of her birth to take a job in a private Jewish hospital. There, she meets Syler Terada, a pediatric surgeon with a brash attitude and a lack of respect for authority who incidentally rocks a tuxedo. She captivates Megan with one glance. Conservative culture and rules against fraternization can't stop Megan. However the secrets she's running from can. The weight of her guilt prevents Megan from making the promise of forever, even though that's the only thing Syler wants from her.

ISBN 978-1-61929-414-1
eISBN 978-1-61929-415-8

Phoenix

What would it take to make you ditch your career, your pride, and run from everything you believe in? In private investigator Ashe Devon's case, it's the fact that her client ended up dead while under her protection. Out of the P.I. business, Ashe is just trying to survive the daily grind of her boring, vanilla life when her former boss calls her out of retirement for one last job: protect a local DJ from a violent stalker. Ashe is fully prepared to turn down the case until she meets the client.

Mystral Galbraith, aka Phoenix, is unashamedly gay, just a tad awkward and musically brilliant. Ashe is instantly captivated by her and can't ignore the fierce young woman's plea for help. Neither can Ashe ignore the stirrings of long-forgotten emotions that set both her heart and her boxer briefs on fire. While Ashe struggles to keep her relationship with Mystral professional, the tension between them simmers just beneath the surface.

More than Ashe's pride is involved — failure could cost Mystral her life. But is Ashe the right person for the job? If she doesn't get her hormones under control, the undeniable pull between them could compromise her judgment and open the door for history to repeat its tragic lesson.

ISBN 978-1-61929-394-6
eISBN 978-1-61929-395-3

MORE REGAL CREST PUBLICATIONS

Melissa Good	Terrors of the High Seas	1-932300-45-7
Melissa Good	Tropical Storm	978-1-932300-60-4
Melissa Good	Tropical Convergence	978-1-935053-18-7
Melissa Good	Winds of Change Book One	978-1-61929-194-2
Melissa Good	Winds of Change Book Two	978-1-61929-232-1
Melissa Good	Southern Stars	978-1-61929-348-9
Jeanine Hoffman	Lights & Sirens	978-1-61929-115-7
Jeanine Hoffman	Strength in Numbers	978-1-61929-109-6
Jeanine Hoffman	Back Swing	978-1-61929-137-9
K. E. Lane	And, Playing the Role of Herself	978-1-932300-72-7
Jennifer McCormick	Tears of the Sun	978-1-61929-396-0
Kate McLachlan	Christmas Crush	978-1-61929-195-9
Kate McLachlan	Hearts, Dead and Alive	978-1-61929-017-4
Kate McLachlan	Murder and the Hurdy Gurdy Girl	978-1-61929-125-6
Kate McLachlan	Rescue At Inspiration Point	978-1-61929-005-1
Kate McLachlan	Return Of An Impetuous Pilot	978-1-61929-152-2
Kate McLachlan	Rip Van Dyke	978-1-935053-29-3
Kate McLachlan	Ten Little Lesbians	978-1-61929-236-9
Kate McLachlan	Alias Mrs. Jones	978-1-61929-282-6
Lynne Norris	One Promise	978-1-932300-92-5
Lynne Norris	Sanctuary	978-1-61929-248-2
Lynne Norris	The Light of Day	978-1-61929-338-0
Nita Round	A Touch of Truth Book One: Raven, Fire and Ice	978-1-61929-372-4
Nita Round	A Touch of Truth Book Two: Raven, Sand and Sun	978-1-61929-404-2
Nita Round	Fresh Start	978-1-61929-340-3
Nita Round	Knight's Sacrifice	978-1-61929-314-4
Nita Round	The Ghost of Emily Tapper	978-1-61929-328-1
Kelly Sinclair	Getting Back	978-1-61929-242-0
Kelly Sinclair	Accidental Rebels	978-1-61929-260-4
Schramm and Dunne	Love Is In the Air	978-1-61929-362-8
Rae Theodore	Leaving Normal: Adventures in Gender	978-1-61929-320-5
Rae Theodore	My Mother Says Drums Are for Boys: True Stories for Gender Rebels	978-1-61929-378-6
Barbara Valletto	Pulse Points	978-1-61929-254-3
Barbara Valletto	Everlong	978-1-61929-266-6
Barbara Valletto	Limbo	978-1-61929-358-8
Barbara Valletto	Diver Blues	978-1-61929-384-7
Lisa Young	Out and Proud	978-1-61929-392-2

Be sure to check out our other imprints,
Blue Beacon Books, Carnelian Books, Mystic Books, Quest Books,
Silver Dragon Books, Troubadour Books, and Young Adult Books.

VISIT US ONLINE AT
www.regalcrest.biz

At the Regal Crest Website You'll Find

~ The latest news about forthcoming titles and new releases

~ Our complete backlist of titles

~ Information about your favorite authors

Regal Crest print titles are available from all progressive booksellers including numerous sources online. Our distributors are Bella Distribution and Ingram.

CPSIA information can be obtained
at www.ICGtesting.com
Printed in the USA
LVHW041833200819
628309LV00013B/747/P

9 781619 294165